THE FALL OF THE TOWERS
is Samuel R. Delany's epic trilogy, conceiv[illegible] and written on the thunderous scale [illegible] *FOUNDATION.*

OUT OF THE [illegible]
The Empir[illegible] war. But ho[illegible] civilization – [illegible] the Great Fire [illegible] barrier, behind [illegible] would they deal [illegible] Lord of the Flames – w[illegible]nce was unknown to the pe[illegible]ong whom he lived?

THE TOWERS OF TORON
'We have received warning. The Lord of the Flames is loose on Earth once more.'
Once before the Lord of the Flames had been driven halfway across the Universe. His return would mean a new era of chaos and conflict for the populace of Earth. He was a strange adversary – a force of evil devoid of physical substance. He sought warmth in unpredictable places: creeping into the soul of a worm or the stem of a flower or into the mind of a man . . .

CITY OF A THOUSAND SUNS
The war was over. The great computer which had arranged and directed the complex military operations was to be dismantled. But the computer had become expert in the science of self-defence and it resisted. Unknown to even Toromon's desperate leaders was the fact that behind the berserk computer lurked the unearthly mind of a real enemy – a foe from the most distant realm of space, intent on making Earth the first victim of galactic conquest.

The Fall of the Towers

SAMUEL R. DELANY

SPHERE BOOKS LIMITED
30/32 Gray's Inn Road, London WC1X 8JL

First published in Great Britain
(in three volumes) by Sphere Books Ltd 1968

Published as one volume January 1971

Reprinted 1974, 1977

TRADE MARK

Set in Intertype Plantin

Printed in Great Britain by
C. Nicholls & Company Ltd
The Philips Park Press, Manchester

Out of The Dead City

PROLOGUE

THE green of beetle's wings . . . the red of polished carbuncle . . . a web of silver fire. Lightning tore his eyes apart, struck deep inside his body. He felt his bones split and clutched the stomach of his coveralls, doubling around what would be pain. But it was gone. He was falling through blue smoke, cool as blown ice.

He put his hands out to catch——

Palms and knees scudded in something hot. Jon Koshar shook his head, looked up. Sand saddled away from him. His black hair fell over his eyes again; he shook it away and sat back on his heels.

The sky was turquoise. The horizon was too close. The sand was more like lime. He looked down. Two shadows fanned from his body. To his left a tooth of rock also cast a double shadow.

He staggered erect. He was too light; gravity was all wrong. The sand burned his toes. Sweat started on the back of his neck, beneath his arms. The air stung his nasal cavity. Jon squinted.

Far down the sand was a lake; rising by, or perhaps from it was a . . . city? He narrowed his eyes more, staring . . .

Jerk a man from one world; fling him into another. It will take him the same time to realize where he is as to remember where he has been. Each location defines the other.

Jon Koshar took a step forward. His left pants-leg flapped about his ankle, wet to the knee. He looked down again. Mud streaked his foot. Sometime in the past hour he had stumbled into a—mud-hole? Confused, he looked around the desert again, took another step. His hair fell forward again.

As he brushed it back, something slipped beneath his palm. His hand closed on it. Now he looked at his fist. Caught between his calloused fingers was a green fragment of fern. Sometime very recently he had been trying to move forward, brush aside the leaves, and more leaves, and more. He twisted his face against the reflected heat, looking left and right. There was no green anywhere in the dunes. He started walking again.

When he stopped, it was because his hand brushed something on his pants-leg. He shifted his hip and looked down, then looked at the underside of his sleeve. Joined corner to corner the green squares of . . . woodlice? Puzzled, he glanced up at the treeless emptiness, then back down. Yes, woodlice had caught all over the rough cloth.

By the time he had reached the lake, panting (he had panted before, but lungfuls of moist air, heavy with vegetation), he recognized the atmosphere's sharpness as ozone. He looked down at the water.

His dirty face blinked up at him. His shirt was torn across his shoulder. He reached up to touch the scratch over his collar-bone, where a branch had raked him in the dark—but the desert was blindingly bright; there were no trees.

His lips met and parted in silent struggle with the identification numerals across the front of his coveralls. That number had been part of his name for the past five years; now even that was wrong.

But it was a reflection! Of course, he was trying to read it backward. As he raised his eyes, whispered the number correctly, the creosoted walls of the penal barracks came back to him; and the chattering links on the cutter teeth he had guided for five years, gnawing at the tetron ore; and the leaves and brush that had beat his face and shoulders as he ran through the dark——

And he recognized the city.

There, across the lake, it struck his eyes with a familiarity that made him step back. What had been an abstraction, now coalesced into the towers, the looped roadways of Telphar! As the head of an arrow indicates direction, or the marquee of a theatre means entertainment, so the spires of Telphar symbolized death.

His throat dried under the next breath. His fingers clamped and slipped on wet palms. He stepped backwards while the skin over his spine crawled. His scrambling mind reached out for facts:

I am Jon Koshar and I want to be free! That was first, above the fear, first through his five-year imprisonment in the mines that had culminated when the three of them had escaped—how many hours ago?

But that was on earth. He had been on earth. So had the city. And the sight of it from the pitted edge of the jungles and lava fields meant death. But here he was looking at Telphar on an alien world, beneath a double sun. Then memory completed itself:

Exhausted, he had seen the city from the pitted rocks. At the same time he had heard something (or had he heard it): *The Lord of the Flames.*

And suddenly there had been no reason to fear further. He tried to untangle the recollection. He had entered the city, found the sending stage of the transit ribbon, the band of metal that would take him back, over the jungles, over the heads of the guards, over the sea, back to the safe, island city of Toron——

Suddenly he frowned, then the frown broke into an expression more frantic, desperate, as he searched for the silver ribbon that should have soared from the window of the far building, from pylon to pylon, gleaming across the sand.

The transit-ribbon——

No!

Gone? Broken? With the new fear, he nearly screamed. There were no pylons, there was no line of metal. The city sat isolate on the alien sand. Please, don't let it be broken! *Please . . .*

The entire scene was suddenly wiped from his eyes. There was nothing but blue smoke, cool as blown ice; he spun in blue. Lightning seered his eyeballs, and the after-image shivered, shifted, became . . . silver, red—beetles' wings.

CHAPTER I

AND above the empty stage in the laboratory tower of the dead city of Telphar, the crystal sphere dimmed. The room was silent as it had been for sixty years. From the crystal the metal ribbon soared over the balcony, above the wet ashes and puddled roadways. The sun had just cleared the ragged horizon; the dripping metal gleamed like the back of a sleeping serpent.

Miles on, darkness paled before morning. In the lava fields among the ferns sat row behind row of barracks, cheerless as roosting macaws. The light rain had stopped. Water dribbled the supporting pylon. The ribbon made a black band on the fading night.

Six people approached the barracks from the jungle. They were all over seven feet tall. They carried the bodies of two ordinary sized men. Two behind the others hung back to converse.

'What about the other one, Larta?'

'Koshar? He won't get far.' She pushed back her fur cape from her shoulder; the new sun struck the brass circlets banding her upper arm.

'If he does,' said the man, 'he'll be the first to get through us in twelve years.'

'If he tries to get back to the coast and out to Toron,' Larta said. 'If we don't get him, it means he's gone inland towards the radiation barrier.' They passed under the shadow of the transit-ribbon. The circlets, and her eyes, dimmed. 'Then we won't have to worry anyway, if he goes towards Telphar, eh, Ptorn?'

The tall man's head was shaved. 'I suppose I'm not really worried about the one escaping.' Ptorn glanced at those passing into the sun. 'But the increasing number of attempts over the last year . . .'

Larta shrugged. 'The orders for tetron have nearly doubled.' As she left the shadow, the sun lit three parallel scars down the side of her face, under her jaw, and down her neck.

Ptorn slid his right hand beneath his left arm. 'I wonder what sort of leeches make their living off these miserable . . .' He didn't finish but nodded ahead.

'The hydroponics growers, the aquarium manufacturers in Toron,' Larta said. 'They're the ones who call for the ore. Then, there's the preparation for the war.'

'They say,' mused Ptorn, 'that since the aquariums have taken over supplying fish to the Toron, the fishermen on the coast have nowhere to sell and are being starved out. And with the increased demand for tetron, the prisoners are dying like flies here at the mines. Sometimes I wonder how they supply miners.'

'They don't.' Now Larta called ahead, 'All right. We'll leave the rest to the men who guard them.' There was the gentlest contempt in the word 'men' that italics would be too strong to convey. 'We've done our part. Drop them there, in front of the cabin.' The rain had made the yard mud. 'Maybe that'll teach the rest of them some sort of lesson.'

Two dull splashes.

'Maybe,' Ptorn said.

But Larta had turned back towards the jungle, shadow from the trees brushing over her face, over the triple scar.

Streaks of sun speared the yellow clouds and pried apart the billowing rifts. Shafts of yellow sank into the lusher forests of Toromon nearer the shore. The light dropped from the wet, green fronds, or caught in the moist cracks of boulders. Then dawn snagged on the metal ribbon that lanced over the trees; webs of shadow from the supporting pylons fell over a lava bed among the trees.

A formation of airships flashed through a tear in the clouds like a handful of hurled, sliver chips. The buzz from their tetron motors descended through the trees. And Lug, who was four feet three inches tall, with a forehead high as his thumb was wide, looked up from under his boney brow.

The others around him, of the same height and rounded shoulders, grunted to one another. The word repeated most often was 'war.' Lug motioned the others; they started again, padding over the jungle floor, the palms of their feet shaping to stone and stick and root. Their semi-opposable big toes stroked absently at the textures of the ground as one might thumb the differences, running one's hands over things in the grass.

Finally Lug leaned against a tree trunk. 'Quorl?' he said. 'Quorl!' he barked.

Behind branches that had been cut down and replanted to form a shapeless shelter, something turned under leaves. The lean-to had no real form from the outside, but was limited like the outside of a bush. You could only really be sure it was a shelter when something moved within. A hand grasped one branch, and someone sat up inside.

They watched, whispered, then watched again. Quorl stood, emerging and emerging from the top of the shelter. His yellow eyes were awake, even though the muscles in his face were settling themselves into place after what must have been a huge yawn. His nostrils rounded under the scents of the morning. Then he smiled.

From their stunted heights, they blinked at his seven foot hugeness. Some only stared at the confusing wonder of his hand hanging by the thumb from his belt; others did not look above the gnarled machinery of his knee. To the neanderthals both were as expressive of marvels as his face.

'Quorl?' Lug asked.

'What is it, Lug?'

'Around the bottom of the mountain by the lake, they've come. Not the ones as big as you, but taller than us. They are like the ones at the mines, the prisoners. But these aren't prisoners, Quorl. They're building.'

Quorl nodded. 'Good. It seemed time they came. Time they built.'

'You have seen them?'

'No.'

'Someone else came and told you earlier?'

'No.' Quorl's smile was subtly humorous, more subtly regretful. 'It was time for them to come. It's simple.' For Lug it was just a smile.

They whispered among themselves, awed by the things that the tall ones knew; and smiled back.

'Come,' Quorl said. 'Take me to see.'

Lug looked at the others.

'Yes,' Quorl said, stepping from his shelter. 'Come, we will go.'

'Why?' asked Lug. 'Do you want to talk to them?'

Quorl stretched up, pulled down two kharba fruits, and handed one to a man, the other to a girl. He pulled down two more, and the leaves shook again. 'No,' he said. 'Let's just go to see.' He handed out the other two melons. 'Share these.'

Lug shrugged, and they all started through the trees. They broke the fruits among them. Two apish boys began to shoot seeds at one another, fell into a scuffle, fell into laughter. Quorl looked back, but they were already catching up.

'Why do we go?' Lug asked again. Such scuffles and laughter were so close to him he did not look, did not see. 'You know already that the men'—and there was a slight awe in the word 'men' that block letters would not quite suggest—'are there, what they are doing. What do you want to see? Will we help them build? Does what they build have anything to do with the war?'

Quorl pushed his hand into Lug's hair and arched his fingers, arched them again. 'It rained this morning,' he said. Lug bent his neck as Quorl scratched his head. 'You know how the lake looks in the morning mist after the rain?'

Lug straightened his shoulders, his muscles tensing with pleasure. 'Yes.' His lips grinned back from yellow teeth. 'Yes, I know.'

'That's why we go to see,' Quorl said. His hand dropped to Lug's shoulder.

Behind them the ribbon crossed the top of the hundred-foot pylon, just visible through the trees.

As dawn slipped across the jungle, more and more of the ribbon gleamed from beneath the receding shadows till at last it soared above the sand that marked the edge of the sea.

Fifty yards down the beach from the last supporting pylon whose base still sat on dry land, Cithon, the fisherman, emerged from his shack.

'Tel?' he called. He was a wiry man of average height. His face was cracked from sand and wind. 'Tel?' he called once more. Now he turned back into the cottage. 'And where has the boy got off to now?'

Grella had already seated herself at the loom, and her

strong hands began to work the shuttle back and forth while her feet stamped the treddle.

'Where has he gone?' Cithon demanded.

'He went out early this morning,' Grella said quietly. She did not look at her husband. She watched the shuttle moving back and forth, back and forth between the green threads.

'I can see he's gone out,' Cithon snapped. 'But where? The sun is up. He should be out with me on the boat. When will he be back?'

Grella didn't answer.

'When will he be back?' Cithon demanded.

'I don't know.'

Outside there was a sound, and Cithon turned abruptly and went to the side of the shack.

The boy was leaning over the water trough, sloshing his face.

'Tel!'

The boy looked up quickly at his father. He was perhaps fourteen, a thin child, with a shock of black hair, yet eyes as green as the sea. Fear had widened them now.

'Where were you?'

'No place,' was the boy's quiet, defensive answer. 'I wasn't doing anything.'

'Where were you?'

'No place,' Tel mumbled again. 'Just walking and picking up sea-shells——'

Suddenly Cithon's hand, which had been at his waist, jerked up and then down, and the studded strap that had been his belt slashed over the boy's wet shoulder, slashed again.

The only sound was Tel's gasps.

'Now get down to the boat.'

Inside the shack, the shuttle paused in Grella's fist the length of a drawn breath. Then it shot once more between the threads.

Down the beach, the transit-ribbon leapt across the water. Light shook on the surface of the sea like mica, and the ribbon above was dull by comparison.

Dawn reached across the water till at last the early light fell on the shore of an island. High in the air, the ribbon soared above the busy piers and the early morning traffic of the wharf. Behind the piers, the towers of the city were lanced with gold, and as the sun rose, gold light ran down the building faces.

On the sea-wall, two merchants were talking above the roar of tetron-powered winches and lorries.

'It looks like your boat's bringing in a cargo of fish,' said the stout one.

'It could be fish. It could be something else,' answered the other.

'Tell me, friend,' asked the portly one, whose coat was of cut and cloth expensive enough to suggest his guesses in business were usually right, 'why do you trouble to send your boat all the way to the mainland to buy from the little fishermen there? My aquariums can supply the city with all the food it needs.'

The other merchant looked down at a clip board of inventory slips.

'Perhaps my clientele is somewhat different from yours.'

The first merchant laughed. 'You sell to those families of the Toron who still insist on the doubtful superiority of your imported delicacies. Did you know, my friend, I am superior in every way to you? I feed more people, so what I produce is superior to what you produce. I charge them less money, and so I am financially more benevolent than you. I make more money than you do, so I am also financially superior. Also, later this morning my daughter is coming back from University Island, and this evening I will give her a party so great and so lavish that she will love me more than any daughter has ever loved a father before.'

The self-satisfied merchant laughed again, and turned down the wharf to inspect a cargo of tetron ore that was coming in from the mainland.

As the merchant of imported fish turned up another inventory slip, a third man approached him. 'What was old Koshar laughing about?' he asked.

'He was gloating over his good fortune in backing that hare-brained aquarium idea. He was also trying to make me jealous of his daughter. He's giving her a party tonight to which I am no doubt invited; but the invitation will come late this afternoon with no time for me to reply properly.'

The other shook his head. 'He's a proud man. But you can

bring him to his place. Next time he mentions his daughter, ask him about his son, and watch the shame storm into his face.'

'He may be proud,' said the other, 'but I am not cruel. Why should I move to hurt him. Time takes care of her own. This coming war will see.'

'Perhaps,' said the other merchant. 'Perhaps.'

Once over the island city of Toron, capital of Toromon, the transit-ribbon breaks from its even course and bends among the towers, weaves among the elevated highways, till finally it crosses near bare concrete, edged with block-long aircraft hangars. Several airships had just arrived. At the passenger gates the people waiting for arrivals crowded the fence.

Among them was a young man in military uniform. A brush of red hair, eyes that seemed double dark in his pale face, along with a touring power in his legs, back, and shoulders; these were what struck you in the swift glance. A close look brought you the incongruity of the major's insignia and his youth.

He watched the passengers coming through the gate eagerly.

Someone called, 'Tomar!'

A grin leaped on his face.

'Tomar,' she called again. 'I'm over here!'

Too bumptiously, he rammed through the crowd until he almost collided with her. Then he stopped, bewildered and happy.

'Hey, I'm glad you came,' she said. 'Come on. You can walk me back to father's.' Her black hair fell close to broad, nearly Oriental cheekbones. Then the smile on her strange mouth fell.

Tomar shook his head; they turned, arm in arm, through the people wandering on the field.

'No?' she asked. 'Why not?'

'I don't have time, Clea,' he answered. 'I had to sneak an hour off just to get here. I'm supposed to be back at the Military Ministry in forty minutes. Do you have any bags to carry?'

Clea held up a slide rule and notebook. 'I'm travelling light.'

'What's that?' He pointed to a picture stuck between the

rule and the book cover.

'Oh, this.' She handed him the picture.

It was a folded paper. On the cover was the picture. Tomar frowned, trying to interpret the shapes and their meaning. Inside was a poem. That made him frown more. 'I don't know much about this sort of——'

'Look at it,' she insisted. 'Read it. The poem was written by a boy at school, Vol Nonik. I didn't know him, but he printed a few poems up like this. Someone told me the picture was done by his girlfriend. Her name was——'

'Renna ... something,' Tomar read the signature at the corner. 'I can't make out the last name.' He looked at the poem again, read it slowly. Then he shrugged. 'I just don't understand it,' he said, 'stuff like this. But it's—strange. The thing about the eye in the boy's tongue, that made me feel funny.'

Clea nodded. 'Me too. That's why I like it.'

Tomar looked at the drawing again. He was looking at a strange landscape, but from behind the teeth and contorted lips of a scream. 'I don't ... understand it,' he repeated uneasily and handed it back quickly. And realized he very much wanted to look at the picture again, to re-read the words.

But Clea put the pamphlet into her notebook. 'It's funny,' she said. 'Just before I left University Island, I heard he had been expelled, for cheating on an examination. Somehow you don't know what to do with two pieces of information like that about somebody.'

'Two——?'

'One, his poem. Two, his expulsion. They fall like random parts of a puzzle, and you can't see where they fit together.'

'This is a pretty confused and random time we're living in,' Tomar said, taking her arm. 'People are starting to move and migrate all over Toromon. And there's all this preparation for the war. Well, if you don't have any bags, I better get back to the Ministry. I'm awfully busy.'

'Next time I'll be sure to bring a suitcase,' Clea said. 'I just figured I'd be back at the University for summer courses, so I didn't bring anything home.' She paused. 'Wait a minute; you're not going to be too busy for the party Dad's giving me tonight, are you?'

Tomar shrugged.

Clea began a word, but pushed her tongue hard against the

roof of her mouth. 'Tomar?' she asked after a moment.

'Yes?' He had a rough voice, which, when he was sad, took on the undertones of a bear's growl.

'There really will be a war?'

Again he shrugged. 'More soldiers, more planes, and at the Ministry there's more and more work to do. I was up before dawn this morning getting a fleet of survey planes off for a scouting trip to the mainland, to go over the radiation barrier. If they come back this afternoon, I'll be busy all evening with the reports.'

'Oh,' Clea said. 'Tomar?'

'Yes, Clea Koshar?'

'Oh, sometimes you sound so formal. You've been in the city long enough to be able to relax with me. Tomar, if the war comes, do you think they'll draft prisoners from the tetron mines into the army?'

'They talk about it.'

'Because my brother . . .'

'I know.'

'But if a prisoner from the mines distinguished himself as a soldier, would he be freed at the end of the war? They wouldn't send him back to the mines, would they?'

'The war hasn't even begun yet,' said Tomar. 'No one knows how it will end.'

'You're right,' she said, 'as usual.' They reached the gate. 'Look, Tomar, I don't want to keep you if you're busy. But you've got to promise to come see me and spend at least an afternoon before I go back to school.'

'If the war starts, you won't be going back to school.'

She stopped. 'Why not?'

'You already have your degree in theoretical physics. Now you're only doing advanced work. Not only will they conscript prisoners from the mines, but all scientists, engineers, and mathematicians will have to lend their efforts to the cause as well.'

'I was afraid of that,' Clea said. 'You believe the war will actually come, don't you, Tomar?'

'They get ready for it night and day,' Tomar said. 'What is there to stop it? When I was a boy on my father's farm on the mainland, there was too much work, and no food. I was a strong boy, with a strong boy's stomach. I came to the city and I took my strength to the army. Now I have work that I like. I'm not hungry. With the war, there will be work for a lot more people. Your father will be richer. Your brother may come back, and even the thieves and beggars in the Devil's Pot will have a chance to do some honest work.'

'Perhaps,' said Clea. 'Look, like I said, I don't want to keep you—I mean I do, but. Well, when will you have some time?'

'Probably tomorrow afternoon.'

'Fine,' said Clea. 'We'll have a picnic then. All right?'

Tomar grinned. 'Yes,' he said. 'Yes.' He took both her hands and she smiled back at him. Then he turned away, and was gone through the crowd.

Clea watched a moment, then turned towards the taxi-stand. The sun was beginning to warm the air as she pushed into the shadow of the great transit-ribbon that soared between the towers.

Buildings dropped bands of shadow across the ribbon as it wound through the city, although occasional streaks of light from an eastward street still made silver half-rings around it. At the centre of the city it raised a final two hundred feet and entered the window of the laboratory tower in the west wing of the royal palace of Toron.

The room in which the transit-ribbon ended was deserted. At the end of the metal band was a transparent crystal sphere, fifteen feet in diameter, above the receiving platform. A dozen small tetron units of varying sizes sat around the room. The viewing screens were dead grey. On a control panel by one ornate window, a bank of forty-nine scarlet-knobbed switches pointed to off. The catwalks over the receiving platform were empty.

In another room of the palace, someone was screaming:

'Tetron!'

'. . . if Your Highness would only wait a moment to hear the report,' began the aged minister. 'I believe . . .'

'Tetron!'

'. . . you would understand the necessity,' he continued calmly, 'of disturbing you at such an ungodly hour . . .'

'I never want to hear the word "Tetron" again!'

'. . . of the morning.'

'Go away, Chargill; I'm sleeping!' King Uske, who had

just turned twenty-one, though he had been the official ruler of Toromon since age nineteen, jammed his blond head beneath the over-stuffed pillows that lay about the purple silken sheets. With one too slender hand he sought feebly for the covers to hide himself.

The old minister quietly picked up the edge of the ermine coverlet and held it out of reach. After several half-hearted swipes, the pale head emerged once more and asked in a cold voice: 'Chargill, why is it that roads have been built, prisoners reprieved, and traitors disembowelled at every hour of the afternoon and evening without anyone expressing the least concern for what I thought. Now, suddenly, at——' Uske peered at the jewel–crusted chronometer by his bed in which a shimmering gold light fixed the hour. 'My God, seven o'clock in the morning! Why must I suddenly be consulted at every twist and turn of empire?'

'First!' explained Chargill, 'you are now of age. Secondly, because we are about to enter a war. In times of stress, responsibility is passed to the top, and you are in that unfortunate position.'

'Why can't we have a war and get it over with?' asked Uske, rolling over to face Chargill, a trifle more amenable. 'I'm tired of all this idiocy. You don't think I'm a very good king, do you?' The young man sat up, planting his slender feet on the three-inch-thick fur rug. 'Well, if we had a war,' he continued, scratching his stomach through his pink sateen pyjama top, 'I'd ride in the first line of fire, in the most splendid uniform imaginable, and lead my soldiers to a *sweeping* victory.' At the word sweeping, he threw himself under the covers.

'Commendable sentiment,' stated Chargill dryly. 'Seeing that there may just be a war before the afternoon, why don't you listen to the report, which merely says that another scouting flight of planes has been crippled trying to observe the enemy just beyond the tetron mines over the radiation barrier.'

'Let me continue it for you. No one knows how the planes have been crippled, but the efficacy of their methods has led the council to suggest that we consider the possibility of open war even more strongly. Isn't this more or less what the reports have been for weeks?'

'It is,' replied Chargill.

'Then why bother me. Incidentally, must we really attend

this imbecilic party for the fish-pedlar's daughter tonight? And talk about tetron as little as possible, please.'

'I need not remind you,' went on the patient Chargill, 'that this fish-pedlar has amassed a fortune nearly as large as that in the royal treasury—though I doubt if he is aware of the comparison—through the proper exploitation of the unmentionable metal. If there is a war, and we should need to "borrow" funds it should be done with as much goodwill as possible. Therefore, you will attend his party to which he has so kindly invited you.'

'Listen a minute, Chargill,' said Uske. 'And I'm being serious now. This war business is ridiculous, and if you expect me to take it seriously, then the council is going to have to take it seriously. How can we have a war with whatever is beyond the radiation barrier? We don't know anything about it. Is it a country? Is it a city? Is it an empire? We don't even know if it's got a name. We don't know how they've crippled our scouting planes. We can't monitor any radio-communication. We don't even know if it's human. One of our silly planes got its tetron (pardon me. If you can't say it, I shouldn't say it either.) device knocked out and a missile hurled at it. Bango! The council says war. Well, I refuse to take it seriously. Why do we keep on wasting planes anyway? Why not send a few people through the transit-ribbon to do some spying.'

Chargill looked amazed.

'Before we instituted the penal mines, and just after we annexed the forest people, the transit-ribbon was built, correct? Now, where does it go?'

'Into the dead city of Telphar,' answered Chargill.

'Exactly. And Telphar was not at all dead when we built it, sixty years ago. The radiation hadn't progressed that far. Well, why not send spies into Telphar and from there across the barrier and into enemy territory? Then they can come back and tell us everything.' Uske smiled.

'Of course Your Majesty is joking.' Chargill smiled. 'May I remind Your Majesty that the radiation level in Telphar today is fatal to human beings. Fatal. The enemy seems to be well beyond the barrier. Only recently, with the great amount of tetron . . . ah, excuse me . . . coming from the mines have we been able to develop planes than can perhaps go over it. And that, when and if we can do it, is the only way.'

Uske had started out smiling. It turned to a giggle. Then to a laugh. Suddenly he cried out and threw himself down on the bed. 'Nobody listens to me! Nobody takes any of my suggestions!' He moaned and stuck his head under the pillows. 'No one does anything but contradict me. Go away! Get out! Let me sleep!'

Chargill sighed and withdrew from the royal bed-chamber.

CHAPTER II

It had been silent for sixty years. Then, above the receiving stage in the laboratory tower of the royal palace in Toron, the crystal glowed.

On the stage a blue haze shimmered. Red flame shot through the mist, a net of scarlet, contracting, pulsing, outlining the recognizable patterning of veins and arteries. Among the running fires, the shadow of bones formed a human skeleton in the blue, till at once the shape was laced with sudden silver, the net of nerves that held the body imprisoned in sensation. The blue became opaque. Jon Koshar staggered forward to the rail and held on for a moment. Above, the crystal faded.

He blinked his eyes hard before he looked up. He looked around. 'Alright,' he said out loud. 'Where the hell are you?' He paused. 'Okay. I know. I'm not supposed to get dependent. I guess I'm all right now, aren't I?' Another pause. 'I feel fine.' He let go of the rail and looked at his hands, back and palms. 'Dirty as hell,' he mumbled. 'Where can I get washed up?' He looked up. 'Yeah, sure. Why not?' He ducked under the railing and vaulted to the floor. Once again he looked around. 'So I'm really inside the castle. After all these years. I never though I'd see it again. Yeah, I guess I'm really here.'

He started forward, but as he passed under the shadow of the ribbon's end, something happened.

He faded.

At least the exposed parts of his body, head, hands, and feet, faded. He stopped and looked down. Through one bare foot he could see the rivet heads in the metal floor. He made a disgusted face, and continued towards the door. Once in the sunlight, he grew opaque again.

There was no one in the hall. He walked along, ignoring the triptych of silver partitions that marked the council chamber. A stained-glass window farther on rotated by silent machinery flung colours over his face. A golden disc-chronometer fixed in the ceiling behind a carved crystal face said seven-ten.

He stopped in front of a book cabinet and opened the glass door. 'Here's the one,' he said out loud again. 'Yes, I know we haven't got time, but you're from a desert world with a double sun. This will explain it to you better than I can.' He pulled a book from the row of books. 'We used this in school,' he said. 'A long time ago.'

The book was *Catham's Revised History of Toromon.* He opened the shark-skin cover and flipped a few pages into the text.

'. . . from a few libraries and texts that survived the Great Fire (from which we will date all subsequent events). Civilization was reduced beyond barbarism. But eventually the few of us, surviving on the Island of Toron, established a settlement, a village, a city. We pushed to the mainland, and the shore became the central source of food for the island's population which now devoted itself to manufacturing. On the coast, farms and fishing villages flourished. On the island, science and industry became sudden factors in the life of Toromon, now an empire.

'Beyond the plains at the coast, explorers discovered the forest people who lived in the strip of jungle that held in its crescent the stretch of mainland. They were a mutant breed, some giant in stature, others stunted like neanderthals, both tribes peaceful. They quickly became part of Toromon's empire, with no resistance.

'Beyond the jungle were the gutted fields of lava and dead earth, and it was here that the strange metal tetron was discovered. A great empire has a great crime rate. Our penal system was used to supply miners for the tetron. Technology leapt ahead, and we developed many uses for the power that could be released from the tetron.

'Then, beyond the lava fields, we discovered what it was that had enlarged and stunted the bodies of the forest people, what it was that had killed all green things beyond the jungle. Lingering from the days of the Great Fire, an immense strip of radioactive land still burned all around the lava fields, cutting us off from further expansion.

'Going towards that field of death, the plants became gnarled, distorted caricatures of themselves. Then only rock. Death was long if a man ventured in and came back. First immense thirst; then the skin dries out; blindness, fever, madness, at last death; this is what awaited the transgressor.

'It was at the brink of the radiation barrier, in defiance of death, that Telphar was established. It was far enough away to be safe, yet near enough to see the purple glow at the horizon over the broken hills. At the same time, experiments were being conducted with elementary matter transmission. As a token to this new direction of science, the transit-ribbon was commissioned to link the two cities. It was more a gesture of the solidarity of Toromon's empire than a practical appliance. Only three or four hundred pounds of matter could be sent at once, or two or three people. The transportation was instantaneous, and portended a future of great exploration to any part of the world, with theoretical travel to the stars.

'Then, at seven thirty-two on an August evening, some sixty years ago, a sudden increase in the pale light in the radiation-saturated west was observed by the citizens of Telphar. Seven hours later the entire sky above Telphar was flickering with streaks of blue and yellow. Evacuation had begun already. But in three days, Telphar was dead. The sudden rise in radiation has been attributed to many things in theory, but for over half a century an irrefutable explanation has been wanted.

'The advancing radiation stopped well before the tetron mines, but Telphar was lost to Toron for good . . .'

Jon suddenly closed the book. 'You see?' he said. 'That's why I was afraid when I saw the dead city. That's why . . .' He stopped. 'You're not listening,' he said, and put the book back on the shelf.

Down the hallway fifty feet, two ornate staircases rose right and left. He shoved his hands into his pockets, looking absently towards another window, like a person waiting for someone else to make up his mind. But the decision was not forthcoming. Belligerently he started up the staircase to the left. Halfway up he became a little more cautious, his bare feet padding softly, his broad hand preceding him warily on the banister.

He turned down another hallway where carved busts and statues sat in niches in the walls, a light blue behind those to the left, yellow behind those to the right. A sound from around a corner sent him behind a stone mermaid playing with sea-weeds.

The old man who walked by was carrying a folder. He looked serenely preoccupied.

Jon waited without breathing, the space of three ordinary breaths. Then he ducked out and sprinted down the hall. At last he stopped before a group of doors. 'Which one?' he demanded.

This time he got an answer, because he went to one, opened it, and slipped in.

At Chargill's departure, Uske pulled the sheet over his head. Now he heard several clicks and tiny brushing noises but he heard them through the fog of sleep that had washed back over him. The first sound definite enough to wake him was water against tile. He listened to it for nearly two minutes through the veil of fatigue. It was only when it stopped that he frowned, pushed back the sheet, and sat up. The door to his private bath was opened. The light was off. But someone, or thing, was apparently finishing a shower. The windows of his room were covered with brocade drapes, but he hesitated to push the button that would reel them back from the sun.

In the bath the rings of the shower curtain slid along the rod; the rattle of the towel rack; silence; a few whistled notes. Then: dark spots formed on the fur rug sprawling the black stone. One after another—footprints! Incorporeal footprints coming towards him.

When they were about four feet away from his bed, Uske slammed the flat of his palm on the button that drew back the curtains. Sunlight filled the room like water.

And standing in the last pair of footprints was a naked man. He leapt at Uske as the king threw himself face down into the mound of pillows and tried to scream at the same time. He was caught, pulled up, and the edge of a hand was thrust into his open mouth so that when he bit down, he champed the inside of his cheeks.

'Will you keep still, stupid,' a voice whispered behind him. The king went limp.

'There, now just a second.'

A hand reached past Uske's shoulder, pressed the button on the night table by the bed, the curtains swept back across the window. The hand went out as if it had been a flame.

'Now you keep still and be quiet.'

The pressure released and the king felt the bed give as the weight lifted. He held still for a moment. Then he whirled around. There wasn't anyone there.

'Where do you keep your clothes? You are about my size.'

'Over there . . . in that closet.'

The incorporeal footprints padded over the rug, and the closet door opened. Hangers slid along the rack. A bureau drawer at the back of the closet opened. 'This'll do. I didn't think I would ever get into decent clothes again. Just a second.'

There was the sound of tearing thread.

'This will fit me, once I get these shoulder pads out of it.'

Something came out of the closet, dressed now: a human form, only without head or hands.

'Now that I'm decent, open up those curtains and throw some light around the place.' The standing suit of clothes waited. 'Come on, open the curtains.'

Slowly Uske pressed the button. A freshly shaved young man with black hair stood in the sunlight, examining his cuffs. An open brocade jacket with metal filigree covered a white silk shirt with the laces open. The tight grey trousers were belted with a broad, studded leather and fastened with a gold disc. The boots, opened at the toe and the heel, were topped with similar discs. Jon Koshar looked around. 'It's good to be back.'

'Who . . . what are you?' whispered Uske.

'Loyal subject of the crown,' said Jon, 'Clam-brain.'

Uske sputtered.

'Think back about five years to when you and I were in school together.'

A flicker of recognition in the blond face.

'You remember a boy a couple of years ahead of you; he got you out of a beating when the kids in the mechanics class were going to gang up on you because you'd smashed a high-frequency coil, on purpose. And remember you dared that same kid to break into the castle and steal the royal Herold from the throne room? In fact you gave him the fire-blade to do it, too. Only that wasn't mentioned in the trial. Did you alert the guards too that I was coming? I was never quite sure of that part.'

'Look . . .' began Uske. 'You're crazy.'

'I might have been a little crazy then. But five years in the tetron mines has brought me pretty close to my senses.'

'You're a murderer . . .'

'It was in self-defence, and you know it. Those guards that converged on me weren't kidding. I didn't kill him on purpose. I just didn't want to get my head seared off.'

'So you seared one of their heads off first. Jon Koshar, I think you're crazy. What are you doing here anyway?'

'It would take too long to explain. But believe me, the last thing I came back for was to see you again.'

'So you come in, steal my clothing . . .' Suddenly he laughed. 'Oh, of course. I'm dreaming all this. How silly of me. I must be dreaming.'

Jon frowned.

Uske went on. 'I must be feeling guilty about that whole business when we were kids. You keep on disappearing and appearing. You can't possibly be more than a figment of my imagination. Koshar! The name! Of course. That's the name of the people who are giving the party I'm going to, once I wake up. That's the reason for the whole thing!'

'What party?' Jon asked.

'Your father is giving it for your sister tonight. You had quite a pretty sister. I'm going back to sleep now. And when I wake up, you're to be gone, do you understand. What a silly dream.'

'Just a moment. Why are you going?'

Uske snuggled his head into the pillow. 'Apparently your father has managed to amass quite a fortune. Chargill says I have to treat him kindly so we can borrow money from him later on. Unless I'm dreaming that up too.'

'You're not dreaming.'

Uske opened one eye, closed it again, and rolled over on to the pillow. 'Tell that to my cousin the Duchess of Petra. She was dragged all the way from her island estate to come to this thing. The only people who are getting out of it are my mother and my kid brother. Lucky star-fish.'

'Go back to sleep,' said Jon.

'Go away,' said Uske. He opened his eyes once more to see Jon push the button that pulled the curtains to. And then the headless, handless figure went to the door and out. Uske shivered and pulled the covers up again.

Jon walked down the hall.

Behind the door to one room that he did not enter, the Duchess of Petra stood by the window of her palace apartment, gazing over the roofs of the city, over the houses of the wealthy merchants and manufacturers, over the hive-like buildings which housed the city's tradesmen, clerks, secretaries, and storekeepers, down to the reeking clapboard and stone alleys of the Devil's Pot.

The early sun lay flame in her red hair and whitened her face. She pushed the window open a bit, and breeze waved her blue robe as she absently fingered a smoky stone on a silver chain around her neck.

Jon continued down the hall.

Three doors away, the old queen lay on a heap of mattresses, nestled in the centre of an immense sea-shell bed. Her white hair was coiled in buns on either side of her head, her mouth was slightly opened and breath hissed across dry lips. On the wall above the bed hung a portrait of the late King Alsen, sceptred, official, and benevolent. On the table by the bed was a cheap, palm-sized, poorly painted picture of her son, King Uske. She reached for it in her sleep, knocked it over, then her hand fell on the edge of the bed. Her breath hissed, hissed again.

In the rooms just beside the Queen Mother's chamber, Let, Prince of the Royal Blood, Heir Apparent and Pretender to the Empire of Toromon, was sitting in his pyjama top on the edge of his bed, knuckling his eyes.

The thin limbs of the fourteen-year-old hung akimbo with natural awkwardness and sleep. Like his brother, he was blond and slight.

Still blinking, he slipped into his underwear and trousers, pausing a moment to check the clock. He fastened the snaps on his shirt, turned to the intercom, and pressed a button.

'I overslept, Petra,' Let apologized. 'I'm up now.'

'You must learn to be on time. Remember, you are heir to the throne of Toromon. You mustn't forget that.'

'I wish I could,' Let said, 'Sometimes.'

'Never say that again,' came the demand through the speaker. 'Do you hear me? Never even let yourself think that for a moment.'

'I'm sorry, Petra,' Let said. His cousin, the Duchess, had been acting strangely since her arrival two days ago. Fifteen years his senior, she was still the member of the family to whom he felt closest. Usually, with her, he could forget the crown that was always being pointed to as it dangled above his head. His brother was not very healthy, nor even (some rumoured) all in his right mind. Yet now it was Petra herself who was pointing out the gold circlet of Toromon's kingship. It seemed a betrayal. 'Anyway,' he went on. 'Here I am. What did you want?'

'To say good morning.' The smile in the voice brought a smile to Let's face too. 'Do you remember that story I told you last night, about the prisoners in the tetron mine?'

'Sure!' He had fallen asleep thinking about it. 'The ones who were planning escape.' She had sat in the garden with him for an hour after dark, regaling him with the details of three prisoners' attempt to escape the mines. She had terminated it at the height of suspense with the three men crouching by the steps in the darkness, in the drizzling rain, waiting to dash into the forest. 'You said you were going to go on with it this morning.'

'Do you really want to hear the end of the story?'

'Of course I do. I couldn't get to sleep for hours thinking about it.'

'Well,' said Petra, 'when the guards changed, and the rope tripped him up when he was coming down the steps, the rear guard ran around to see what had happened, as planned. They dashed through the searchlight beam, into the forest, and ...' She paused. 'Anyway, one of them made it. The other two were caught. And killed.'

'Huh?' said Let. 'Is that all?'

'That's about it,' said Petra.

'What do you mean?' Let demanded. Last night's version had contained detail upon detail of the prisoners' treatment, their efforts to dig a tunnel, the precautions they took, along with vivid descriptions of the prison that had made him shiver as though he himself had been in the leaky shacks. 'You can't just finish it up like that,' he exclaimed. 'How did they get caught? Which one got away? Was it the chubby one with the freckles? How did they die?'

'Unpleasantly,' Petra answered. 'No, the chubby one with the freckles didn't make it. They brought him, and the one with the limp, back that morning in the rain and dropped them in the mud outside the barracks to discourage further escape attempts.'

'Oh,' said Let. 'What about the one who did make it?' he asked after a moment.

Instead of listening, she said: 'Let, I want to give you a warning.' The prince stiffened, but she continued differently than he expected. 'In a little while you may be going on an adventure, and you may want to forget some things, because it will be easier. Like being the prince of Toromon. But don't forget it, Let. Don't.'

'What sort of adventure, Petra?'

Again she did not answer his question: 'Let, do you remember how I described the prison to you? What would you do if you were king and those prisoners were under your rule, with their rotten food, the rats, their fourteen hours of labour a day in the mines . . .'

'Well, I don't know, Petra.' He felt as if something were being asked of him he was reluctant to give. It was like when his history class expected him to know the answer on a question on government just because he had been born into it. 'I suppose I'd have to consult the council, and see what Chargill said. It would depend on the individual prisoners, and what they'd done; and of course how the people felt about it. Chargill always says you shouldn't do things too quickly——'

'I know what Chargill says,' said the Duchess quietly. 'Just remember what I've said, will you?'

'What about the third man, the one who escaped?'

'He . . . came back to Toron.'

'He must have had a lot more adventures. What happened to him, Petra. Come on, tell me.'

'Actually,' said Petra, 'he managed to bypass most of the adventures. He came very quickly. Let me see. After they dashed across the searchlit area, they ducked into the jungle. Almost immediately they got separated. The black haired one became completely turned around, and wandered in the wrong direction until he had gone past the mines, out of the forest, and across the rocky stretch of ground a good five miles. By the time it was light enough to see, he realized he had been wandering towards the radiation barrier; In the distance, like a black hand clawing the horizon, were the ruins of Telphar, the Dead City.'

'Shouldn't he have been dead from the radiation?'

'That's exactly what he thought. In fact he decided if he were close enough to see the place, he should have been dead a few miles back. He was tired. But he was alive. Finally he decided that he might as well wander towards the city. He took two steps more, when he heard something.'

There was silence over the intercom.

After he had allowed sufficient time for a dramatic pause, Let asked, 'What was it? What did he hear?'

'If you ever hear it,' Petra said, 'you'll know.'

'Come on, Petra, what was it?'

'I'm quite serious,' Petra said. 'That's all I know of the story. That's all you need to know. Maybe I'll be able to finish it when I come back from the party tonight.'

'Please, Petra . . .'

'That's it.'

He paused for a minute. 'Petra, is the adventure I'm supposed to have the war? Is that why you're reminding me not to forget?'

'I wish it were that simple, Let. Let's say that's part of it.'

'Oh,' said Let.

'Just promise to remember the story, and what I've said.'

'I will,' said Let, wondering. 'I will.'

Jon walked down a spiral staircase, nodded to the guard at the foot, passed into the castle garden, paused to squint at the sun, went out of the gate, and into the city.

CHAPTER III

THE Devil's Pot overturned its foul jelly at the city's edge. Old alleys were lined with stone houses, many of them ruined, built over, and ruined again. These were the oldest structures in the Pot. Thick with humanity and garbage, it reached from the waterfront to the border of the hive houses in which lived the clerks and professionals of Toron. Clapboard alternated with hastily constructed sheet-metal buildings with no room between. The metal rusted; the clapboard sagged. The waterfront housed the emigration offices, and the launch service that went out to the aquariums and hydroponics plants that floated on vast pontoons in the sea.

At the dock, a sooty hulk had pulled in nearly an hour ago. But the passengers were only being allowed to come ashore now, and that after passing their papers through the inspection of the officials who sat behind a wooden table. A flimsy, waist-high fence separated the passengers from the people on the wharf. The passengers milled.

A few had bundles. Many had nothing. They stood quietly, or ambled. On the waterfront street, the noise was thunderous, pedlars hawking, push-carts trundling, the roar of argument. Some passengers gazed across the fence into the thralling slum. Most did not.

As they filed past the officers and on to the dock, a woman with a box of trinkets and a brown-red birthmark splashed over the left side of her face pushed among the new arrivals. Near fifty, her dress and head-rag were a well-washed grey.

'And would you like to buy a pair of shoelaces, fine strong ones,' she accosted a young man who returned a bewildered smile.

'I . . . I don't got any money.' He was complimented by the attention.

Rara glanced down at his feet. 'Apparently you have no shoes either. Good luck here in the New World, the Island of Opportunity.' She brushed by him and aimed towards a man and woman who carried a bundle composed of a hoe, a rake, a shovel, and a baby. 'A picture,' she said, digging into her box, 'of our illustrious majesty, King Uske, with metal frame, hand painted in miniature in honour of his birthday. No cosmopolitan patriot can be without one.'

The woman with the baby leaned over to see the palm-sized portrait of a vague young man with blond hair in a crown. 'Is that really the king?'

'Of course it is,' declared the birthmarked vendress. 'He sat for it in person. Look at that noble face. It would be an inspiration to the little one there, when and if he grows up.'

'How much is it?' the woman asked.

Her husband frowned.

'For a hand-painted picture,' said Rara, 'it's very cheap. Say, half a unit?'

'It's pretty,' said the woman, then caught the frown on her husband's face. She dropped her eyes and shook her head.

Suddenly the man thrust a half-unit piece into Rara's hand. 'Here.' He took the picture and handed it to his wife. As she stared, he nodded his head. 'It is pretty,' he said. 'Yes. It is.'

'Good luck here in the New World,' commented Rara. 'Welcome to the Island of Opportunity.' Turning, she drew out the next object, glanced at it long enough to see what it was, and said to the man she now faced. 'I see you could certainly use a spool of fine thread to good purpose.' She pointed to a hole in his sleeve. 'There.' A brown shoulder showed through his shirt, farther up. 'And there.'

'I could use a needle too,' he answered. 'And I could use a new shirt, and a bucket of gold.' Suddenly he spat. 'I've as much chance of getting one as the other with what I've got in my pocket.'

'Oh, surely a spool of fine, strong thread . . .'

Suddenly someone pushed her from behind. 'All right. Move on, lady. You can't peddle here.'

'I certainly can,' exclaimed Rara, whirling. 'I've got my licence right here. Just let me find it now . . .'

'Nobody has a licence to peddle in front of the immigration building. Now move on.'

'Good luck in the New Land,' she called over her shoulder as the officer forced her away. 'Welcome to the Island of Opportunity!'

A commotion started behind the gate. Someone was having

trouble with papers. Then a barefoot boy broke from his place in line, ran to the fence, and vaulted. The structure was flimsy. As the boy landed, feet running, the fence collapsed.

The passengers hesitated like an unbroken wave. Then they ran. At the table the officials stood up, waved their hands, shouted, then stood on their benches and shouted more. The officer who had shoved Rara disappeared in the herd of bodies.

She clutched her box of trinkets and scurried to the corner, then melted with the crowd for two blocks into the slums.

'Rara!'

She stopped and looked around. 'Oh, there you are,' she said, joining a girl who stood back from the crowd, holding a box like the woman's.

'Rara, what happened?'

The birthmark wrinkled as the woman laughed. 'You are watching the beginning of the transformation. Fear, hunger, a little more fear, no work, more fear, and every last one of these poor souls will be a first-class citizen of the Devil's Pot. How much did you sell?'

'Just a couple of units worth,' the girl answered. She was perhaps sixteen, with white hair, blue eyes, and skin that had tanned richly and quickly, giving her the large-eyed look of an exotic snow-maned animal. 'Why are they running?'

'Some boy started a panic. The fence gave way and the rest followed him.' A second surge of people rounded the corner. 'Welcome to the New Land, the Island of Opportunity!' Rara shouted. Then she laughed.

'Where are they all going to go?' Alter asked.

'Into the holes in the ground, into the cracks in the street. The lucky men will get into the army. But even that won't absorb them all. The women, the children . . .' She shrugged.

Just then a boy's voice came from down the block. 'Hey!'

They turned.

'Why, that's the boy that broke the fence!' exclaimed Rara.

'What does he want?'

'I don't know. Before this afternoon I'd never seen him in my life.'

He was dark, with black hair; but as he approached, they saw his eyes were water-green. 'You're the woman who was selling things?'

Rara nodded. 'What do you want to buy?'

'I don't want to buy anything,' he said. 'I want to sell something to you.' He was barefoot; his pants frayed at mid-calf, and his sleeveless shirt had no fastenings.

'What do you want to sell?' she asked, her voice deepening with scepticism.

He reached into his pocket and brought out a green flannel and unwrapped it now in his hand.

They had been polished to milky hues, some streaked with gold, others run through with warm browns and yellows. Two had been rubbed down to pure mother of pearl, their muted silver surfaces clouded with pastels. There on green they swirled about shimmering.

'They're nothing but sea-shells!' Rara said.

But Alter reached her forefinger out to touch a periwinkle. 'They're lovely,' she told him. 'Where did you get them?' They ranged in size from the joint of her thumb to the width of her pinky nail.

'By your departed mother, my own sister, we can't afford to give him a centiunit, Alter. I hardly sold a thing before that brute officer forced me away.'

'I found them on the beach,' the boy exclaimed. 'I was hiding on the boat and I didn't have nothing to do. So I polished them.'

'What were you hiding for?' asked Rara, her voice sharp. 'You don't mean you stowed away?'

'Um-hm,' the boy nodded.

'How much do you want for them?' Alter asked.

'How much . . . how much would it cost to get a meal and a place to stay?'

'Much more than we can afford to pay,' interrupted Rara. 'Alter, come with me. This boy is going to talk you out of a unit or two yet if you keep on listening to him.'

'See,' said the boy, pointing to the shells. 'I've put holes in them already. You can string them around your neck.'

'If you want to get food and a place to sleep,' said Alter, 'you don't want money. You want friends. What's your name? And where are you from?'

The boy looked up from the handful of shells, surprised. 'My name is Tel,' he said after a moment. 'I come from the mainland coast. And I'm a fisherman's son. I thought when

I came here I could get a job in the aquariums. That's all you hear about on the coast.'

Alter smiled. 'First of all you're sort of young . . .'

'But I'm a good fisherman.'

'. . . and also, it's very different from fishing on a boat. I guess you'd say that there were a lot of jobs in the aquariums and the hydroponics gardens. But with all the immigrants, there are three people for every job.'

Tel shrugged. 'Well, I can try.'

'That's right,' said Alter. 'Come on. Walk with us.'

Rara huffed.

'We'll take him back to Geryn's place and see if we can get him some food. He can probably stay there a little while if Geryn takes a liking to him.'

'You can't just take every homeless barnacle you find back to Geryn's. You'll have it crawling with every shrimp in the Pot. And suppose he doesn't take a liking to him. Suppose he decides to kick us out in the street.' The birthmark darkened.

'Aunt Rara, please,' said Alter. 'I'll handle Geryn.'

Rara huffed once more. 'How come when we're two weeks behind on the rent, you can't find a kind word in your mouth for the old man when he threatens to throw us on to the street. Yet for a handful of shells . . .'

'*Please* . . .'

A breeze seeped through the narrow street, picked a shock of Alter's white hair and flung it back from her shoulder.

'Anyway, Geryn may be able to use him. If Tel stowed away, that means he doesn't have any papers.'

Tel looked puzzled.

Rara frowned, chastisement in her eyes. 'You are not supposed to refer to that, ever.'

'Don't be silly,' said Alter. 'It's just a fantasy of Geryn's anyway. It'll never happen. And without papers, Tel can't get a job at the aquariums, even if they wanted him. So if Geryn thinks he can fit him into his crazy plan, Tel will come out a lot better than if he had some old ten unit a week factory job. Look, Rara, how can Geryn possibly kidnap . . .'

'Be quiet,' snapped Rara.

'And even if he did, what good is it going to do? It's not as if it were the king himself.'

'I don't understand,' said Tel.

'That's good,' said Rara. 'And if you want to keep going with us, you won't try to find out.'

'We can tell you this much,' said Alter. 'The man who owns the inn where we stay wants to do something. Now, he is a little crazy. He's always talking to himself. But he needs someone who has no identification registered in the City. If he thinks he can use you, you'll get free food and a place to sleep. He used to be a gardener on the island estate of the Duchess of Petra. But he drank too much or something and I guess at last she let him go. He says she still sends him messages about his plan. But . . .'

'You don't have to go any farther,' Rara said curtly.

'You'll hear about it from him,' said Alter. 'Why did you stow away?'

'I just got fed up with life at home. We'd work all day to catch fish, and then have to leave them rotting on the beach because we could only sell a fifth, sometimes none at all. Some people gave up; some only managed to get it in their heads that they had to work harder. I guess my father was like that. He figured if he worked enough, someone would just have to buy them. But nobody did. My mother did some hand-weaving and we were living mostly on that. Finally, I figured I was eating up more than I was worth. So I left.'

'Just like that, and with no money?' asked Rara.

'Just like that,' Tel said.

'You poor boy,' said Rara, and in a sudden fit of maternal affection, she put her arm around his shoulder.

'Ow!' cried Tel, and winced.

Rara jerked her hand away. 'What's the matter?'

'I . . . I got hurt there,' the boy rubbed his shoulder gently.

'Hurt? How?'

'My father . . . beat me there.'

'Ah,' said Rara. 'Now it comes out. Well, whatever reasons you left, they're your own business. I've never known anyone yet to do something for one reason alone. Don't lag behind. We'll be back at Geryn's in time for lunch.'

'I thought if I could sneak aboard,' went on Tel, 'they'd have to let me off in the city, even if I didn't have money. I didn't know about papers. And when I was in line, I figured I'd explain to the men at the desk. Or maybe I'd give them my shells, and they would get the papers for me. But the guy ahead of me had a mistake in his. Some date was wrong, and they said they were going to send him back to the mainland and that he couldn't leave the ship. He said he'd give them real money, and even got it out of his pocket. But they started to take him away. That's when I ran out of line and jumped the fence. I didn't know everyone else would run too.'

'Probably half their papers were out of order too. Or forged. That's why they ran.'

'You're a cynic, Aunt Rara.'

'I'm a practical woman.'

As they turned another corner, the boy's green eyes jumped at the blue-hazed towers of the palace, behind the roofs of merchants' mansions, themselves behind the hive houses and the spreading tenements. He tried to memorize the street they followed. He failed.

Two contradictory impressions warred: first, the closeness of these alleys, some so small that two men could not pass without turning; second, the endlessness of the city. He tried to tell Alter what he felt, but after a few broken sentences, she smiled and shook her head. 'No, I don't understand. Try again to tell me what you mean.'

And the sea-side leapt into his head. The yellow beach lashed across his mind so that his eyes stung. He saw the salt-and-pepper rocks, shaling away and knobbed with periwinkle shells. He saw brown fingers of seaweed clutch the sand as waves went out. Tel blinked the city back into his eyes. Tears washed the broken curb, the cracked walls, the rusted window-jamb, bright and clean.

'He means he's homesick,' Rara interpreted. 'No, boy,' she said. 'It'll never go away. But it'll get less.'

The street turned sharply twice, widened.

'Well,' said Alter. 'Here we are.'

A red plaque hung over the door of the stone building. It was two stories—twice the height of the other structures. They entered.

Beams ran the low ceiling. By one wall was a counter. There was a large table in the middle, and descending into the room in a large V was a stair.

Of the men and women sitting around the room, one

caught Tel's eye. He was perhaps seven feet and a handful of inches tall, and straddled the bench before the table. He had an equine face, and a triplex of scars started on his cheek, veered down to his neck, and disappeared under his vest. As Tel watched, he turned to a plate of food he was eating, so that his scars disappeared. Tel remembered the tall forest men who had sometimes come to the fishing village; and the little ones, who came and drank too much. He'd seen the scars on the tall guards before. Then, at the stair's head, a harpoon-straight old man appeared. He hurried down, his white hair spiking in all directions. Reaching the bottom, he whirled, darted black eyes through the room. 'All right!' he cried. 'I've received the message. I've received the message. And it's time!'

Alter whispered to Tel: 'That's Geryn.'

'Are we all here?' the old man demanded. 'Are we all here now?'

A woman at the counter snickered. Geryn turned towards Tel, Alter, and Rara. 'You!' he demanded. His finger wavered so they could not tell at which of the three he pointed.

'You mean him?' asked Alter, pointing to Tel.

Geryn nodded vigorously. 'What are you doing here? Are you a spy?'

'No, sir,' said Tel.

Geryn stepped around the table and looked closely. The black eyes were two sharp spots of darkness in a face the colour of shipboards gone two winters without paint.

'Geryn,' Alter said. 'Geryn, he isn't a spy. He's from the mainland. And Geryn, he doesn't have any papers. He stowed away.'

'You're not a spy?' Geryn demanded again.

'No, sir,' Tel repeated.

'Are you a mali?'

'Huh?' Tel asked. 'What's that?'

'A malcontent. We're malis! You know what that means, don't you?'

'Huh?' Tel said again. The old man's barked questions scared him. They also fascinated him, as the magnificent confusion of the city was frightening and fascinating.

'It means you don't like where you've *been*, the place where you *are* is grim, and the only place you see yourself *going* is not an improvement on what's gone before.'

'Well, I don't like where——' He paused the time it would take a wave to break. Then he reached up and rubbed his sore shoulder. 'I don't like where I've been.'

'Then don't just stand there in the road and holler. Do something about it. You follow my plan! Come with us.'

'But I don't know——'

'—where you're going? Come anyway!' Geryn backed away. 'I like you,' he said. 'I trust you.' Slowly he turned. Then he whirled back. 'I have no choice, you see. It's too late. The message has come. So I need you.' He laughed. Then the laugh stopped, as if cut by a razor. He put his hands over his eyes, then brought his finger down slowly. 'I'm tired,' he said. 'Rara, you owe me rent. Pay up or I'll kick you all out. I'm tired.' He walked heavily towards the bar. 'Give me something to drink. In my own tavern you can give me something to drink.'

Someone laughed again. Tel looked at Alter.

'Well,' she said. 'He likes you.'

'He does?'

'Um-hm,' she nodded.

'Oh,' Tel said.

At the bar, Geryn drained a mug of green liquor, slammed the empty glass on the board, and cried: 'The war! Yes, the war!'

'Here we go,' Alter whispered.

Geryn ran his finger along the rim of the glass. 'The war,' he said again. He turned suddenly. 'It's coming! And do you know why it's coming? Do you know how it's coming? We can't stop it, not now, not any more. I've received the signal, so there's no hope left. We must go ahead, try to save something, something to start and build from again.' Geryn looked directly at Tel. 'Boy, do you know what a war is?'

'No, sir,' said Tel, which wasn't exactly true. He'd heard the word.

'Hey,' someone cried from the bar. 'Are we gonna get stories about great fires and destruction?'

Geryn ignored the cry. 'Do you know what the Great Fire was?'

Tel shook his head.

'The world was once much bigger than it is today,' Geryn

said. 'Once man flew not just between island and mainland, island and island, but skirted the entire globe of the earth. Once man flew to the moon, even to the moving lights in the sky. There were empires, like Toromon, only bigger. And there were many of them. Often they fought with one another, and that was called a war. And the end of the final war was the Great Fire. That was fifteen hundred years ago. Most of the world, from what little we know of it today, is scarred with strips of impassable land, the sea is run through with deadly currents. Toromon may be the only fragment that can hold life, for all we are sure of. And now we will have another war.'

Someone from the bar yelled, 'So what if it comes. It might bring some excitement.'

Geryn whirled. 'You don't understand!' He whipped one hand through his shocked hair. 'What are we fighting? We don't know. It's something unnamable on the other side of the radiation barrier. Why are we fighting?'

'Because——' began a bored voice at the bar.

'Because,' interrupted Geryn, now pointing at Tel's face, 'we have to fight. Toromon has got into a situation where its excesses must be channelled towards something external. Our science has outrun our economics. Our laws have become stricter, and we say it is to stop the rising lawlessness. But it is to supply workers for the mines that the laws tighten, workers who will dig more tetron, that more citizens shall be jobless, and must therefore become lawless to survive. Ten years ago, before the aquariums, fish was five times its present price. There was perhaps four per cent unemployment in Toron. Today the prices of fish are a fifth of what they were, yet unemployment has reached twenty per cent of the city's populace. A quarter of our people starve. More arrive every day. What will we do with them? We will use them to fight a war. The University turns out scientists whose science we cannot use lest it put more people out of work. What will we do with them? We will use them to fight a war. Eventually the mines will flood us with tetron, too much for even the aquariums and the hydroponic gardens. It will be used for the war.'

'Then what?' asked Tel.

'We do not know who or what we are fighting,' repeated

Geryn. 'We will be fighting ourselves, but we will not know it. According to history, it is customary in a war to keep each side in ignorance of the other. Or give them lies like those we use to frighten children instead of truth. But here the truth may be . . .' His voice trailed off.

'What's your plan?' Tel asked.

There was another laugh at the bar.

'Somehow——' His voice was lower. 'Somehow we must save something, salvage some fragment from the destruction that will come. There are only a few of us who know all this, who understand it, who know what . . . what has to be done.'

'What is that?' Tel asked again.

Suddenly Geryn whirled. 'Drinks!' he called. 'Drinks all around!' The amusement increased, and lethargy disappeared as the people moved to the bar. 'Drink up, friends, my fellows!' cried Geryn.

'Your plan?' Tel asked again, puzzled.

'I'll tell you,' answered the old man, almost in a whisper. 'I'll tell you. But not just yet. Not just . . .' He turned back again. 'Drink up!' Three men who already had their glasses cheered.

'Are you with me, friends?' Geryn demanded

'We're with you!' six more cried, clinking their glasses hard on the table top as Tel looked from Alter to Rara and back.

'My plan . . .' began Geryn. 'Have you all had a glass? All of you? Another round for everybody. Yes, a second round!'

There was a solid cheer, now. Glass bottoms turned towards the ceiling, then whammed the counter again.

'My plan is to . . . you understand it's not just my plan, but only a small part in a great plan, a plan to save us all . . . my plan is to kidnap Prince Let from the palace. That's the part that we must do. Are you with me, friends?' A yell rose. Somebody had started a fight at the end of the bar. Geryn's voice broke through the sound, in a rasping whisper that silenced them for seconds: 'Because you must be with me! The time is tonight! I have . . . I have it planned.' The voices halted, then heaved to a roar. 'Tonight,' repeated Geryn. Now hardly anyone heard him. 'I have it planned. Only you've got to be . . . be with me.'

Tel frowned and Alter shook her head. The old man had closed his eyes. Rara was beside him, her hand on his shoulder. 'You're going to get yourself sick with all this yelling. Let me get you up to your room.'

As she turned him towards the stairs, the scarred giant who had been given a drink, now rose from the table, looked straight at Geryn, then drained his drink.

Geryn nodded, drew a breath through his teeth, and allowed Rara to lead him up the stairs as Tel and Alter watched.

The noise rolled among the drinking men and women.

CHAPTER IV

SHE made a note on her pad, put down her slide rule, and picked up a pearl snap with which she fastened together the shoulder panels of her white dress. The maid said, 'Ma'am, shall I do your hair now?'

'One second,' Clea said. She turned to page 328 of her integral tables, checked the increment of sub-cosine A plus B over the *n*th root of A to the *n*th plus B to the *n*th, and transferred it to her notebook.

'Ma'am?' asked the maid. She was a thin woman, about thirty. The little finger of her left hand was gone.

'You can start now.' Clea leaned back in the beauty-hammock and lifted the dark mass of her hair from her neck. The maid caught the ebony wealth with one hand and reached for the end of the spool of silver chain strung with pearls each an inch and a half.

'Ma'am?' asked the maid again. 'What are you figuring on?'

'I'm trying to determine the inverse sub-trigonometric functions. My mathematics professor at the University discovered the regular ones, but nobody's come up with the inverses yet.'

'Oh,' said the maid. She ceased weaving the jewelled chain a moment, took a comb, and whipped it through a cascade of hair that fell back on Clea's shoulder. 'Eh . . . what are you going to do with them, once you find them?'

'Actually,' said Clea. '. . . Ouch . . .'

'Oh, pardon me, I'm sorry, please . . .'

'. . . actually,' went on Clea, 'they'll be perfectly useless. At least as far as anyone knows now. They exist, so to speak, in a world that has little to do with ours. Like the world of imaginary numbers, the square root of minus one. Eventually we may find a use for them, perhaps in the same way we use imaginary numbers to find the roots of equations of a higher order than two; if cosine theta plus *i* sine theta equals *e* to the *I* sine theta, then . . .'

'Ma'am . . .?'

'Well, they haven't been able to do anything like that with the sub-trigonometric functions as of yet. But they're fun.'

'Bend your head a little to the left, Ma'am,' was the maid's comment.

Clea bent.

'You're going to look beautiful.' Four and five fingers wove deftly in her hair. 'Just beautiful.'

'I hope that Tomar can get here. It's not going to be any fun without him.'

'But isn't the king coming?' asked the maid. 'I saw his acceptance note myself. You know it was on a very simple card. Very elegant.'

'My father will enjoy that a good deal more than I will. My brother went to school with the king before . . . before His Majesty's coronation.'

'That's amazing,' said the maid. 'Were they friends? Just think of it? Do you know whether they were friends or not?'

Clea shrugged.

'Oh, yes,' said the maid, continuing, 'have you seen the ballroom? All the *hors d'oeuvres* are imported fish. You can tell, because they're smaller than the ones your father grows.'

'I know,' smiled Clea. 'I don't think I've ever eaten any of Dad's fish in my life. That's sort of terrible, actually. They're supposed to be very good.'

'Oh, they are, Ma'am. They are. Your father is a fine man to grow such great, good fishes. But you must admit, there's something special about the ones that come from the coast. I tasted one on my way up through the pantry. So I know.'

'What exactly is it?' Clea asked, turning around.

The maid frowned. 'Oh, one can tell. Yes, one can tell the difference.'

The lock on the front door of his father's house had remembered this thumb-print.

At that moment, Jon was saying, 'So far you've been right.' He appeared to be more or less standing (the room was dim, so his head and hands were invisible) more or less alone. 'Yes, I trust you. I don't have much choice,' he added, in the pantry of his father's mansion. Suddenly his voice took a different tone. 'Look, I will trust you; with part of me, anyway. I've been caged up for nearly five years, for something stupid I did, and for something that no matter how hard I try, I can't convince myself was all my fault. I don't mean that Uske should be blamed. But random chance, and all the rest. . . . All I mean is, it makes me want out that much more. I want to be *free*. I nearly got myself killed trying to escape from the mines. And a couple of people may have died helping us. All right, you got me out of that stainless steel graveyard I wandered into back at the radiation barrier, for that, thanks. I mean it. But I'm not free yet. And I still want out, more than anything in the world. Sure, I know you want me to do something, but I don't understand it. You say you'll tell me soon. Okay. But you're riding around in my head like this, so I'm not free yet. If obey you is what I have to do, I'll do it. But I'm warning you. If I see another crack in the wall, another spot of light getting in, I'll claw my hands off trying to break through and to hell with what you want. Because while you're there, I'm still a prisoner.'

Suddenly the light in the pantry flipped on. His sudden face went from the tautness of his last speech to fear. He had been standing behind a tall, porcelain storage cabinet. He jumped back to the wall. Whoever had come in, a butler or caterer, was out of sight on the other side. A hand came around the edge of the cabinet, reaching for the handle. The hand was broad, with black hairs, and sported a brass ring set with an irregular shape of blue glass. As the door opened, the hand swung out of sight. There was a clatter of dishes on the shelves, the slide of crockery slipping over plastic racks, and a voice: 'All right there. You carry this one.' Then a grunt, and the *ker-flop* of the latch as the door slammed.

A moment later, the light, and Jon Koshar's hands and head, went out. When Jon stepped forward again, he looked at the pantry, at the doors, the cabinets. The familiarity hurt. There was a door into the main kitchen. (Once he had snagged a kharba fruit from the cook's table and ran, as behind him a wooden salad bowl crashed to the floor. The sound made him whirl, in time to catch the cook's howl and to see the pale shaling of lettuce strewn across the tile. The bowl was still spinning. He had been nine.) He started slowly for the hallway to the dining-room. In the hall was a red wood table on which sat a free form sculpture of aluminium rods and glass spheres. That was unfamiliar. Not the table, the sculpture.

(And a slight highlight along the curve of crystal brought back to him for a moment the blue ceramic vase that had been there in his memory. Its glaze was shot with myriad cracks. It was cylindrical, straight, veering to a small mouth, slightly off centre. The burnished red wood behind the turquoise was a combination that was almost too rich, too sensual. He had broken the vase. He had broken it in surprise, when his sister had come on him suddenly, the little girl with the hair black as his own, only more of it, saying, 'What are you doing, Jon?' and he had jumped, turned, and then the vase was lying in fragments on the floor, like a lot of bright, brittle leaves. He remembered his first reaction had been, oddly, surprise at finding that the glass covered only the outside ceramic. He was fourteen.) He walked to the family dining-room and stepped in. With the ballroom in use, no one would come here. Entering the room was like stepping into a cricket's den, the subtle tsk-tsk of a hundred clocks repeated and repeated, overlapping and melting, with no clear, discernible rhythm. All the shelves were filled with his father's collection of chronometers. He looked at the clocks on the shelf level with his eye. The last time he had been in this room, it had been the shelf below. The light from the doorway made crescents on the faces, some the size of his little finger nail, others bigger than his head. Their hands were invisible, their settings (in his memory they went from plain gold to ornate, carved silver. One was set in a miniature undersea bower with jewelled shells and coral branches) were dim. There must be many new clocks after five years, he thought. If he turned on the light, how many would he recognize. (When he was eighteen, he had stood in this room and examined the thin, double prong of a power-blade. The light in the room was off, and as he flicked the button on the hilt, and the sparks leapt, crescents had flared on the edges of the clock faces over the wall. Later, at the royal palace, with that same blade, there had been the same, sudden, clumsy fear of discovery, fear clotting into panic, the panic embolizing to confusion, and the confusion metastasizing into fear again. Fear had dragged him down, so that when he tried to run through the vaulted hall, his feet were too heavy; so that when he tripped against the statue in the alcove, whirled upon the pursuing guard, and swung the white needle of energy and the guards flesh hissed and fell away—a moment of blood spurting under pale flame—almost immediately he was exhausted. They took him easily.) Clumsy, he thought. Not with his fingers (he had fixed many of these clocks when his father had acquired them in various states of disrepair) but with his mind. His emotions were not fine and drawn, but great shafts of anger or fear falling about him without focus or clear source. Disgust, or even love, when he had felt it (School was great; his history teacher was very good . . . school was noisy; the kids were pushy and didn't care about anything. His blue parakeet was delicate and beautiful; he had taught it to whistle . . . there were always crumbs on the bottom of the cage; changing the paper was a nuisance) was vague, quick to metamorphasize into the other.

Then there had been five years of prison. And the first sharp feeling pierced his mind, as sharp as the uncoiled spring of a clock, as sharp as jewels in a poison ring. It was a wish, a pain, an agony for freedom. The plans for escape had been intricate, yet fine as the cracks in blue ceramic glaze. The hunger for escape was a hand against his stomach, and as the three of them had, at last, waited in the rain by the steps, it had tightened unbearably. Then——

Then with all the sharpness, what had made him get lost from the others? Why had he wandered in the wrong direction? Clumsy! And he wanted to be free of that! Now he wondered if that was what he had wanted to be free of all along while he had spluttered at the prison guards, choked on the food, and could not communicate his outrage. Later, at the horizon, was the purple glow of something paler than sunrise, deadlier than the sea, a flickering gauze behind the hills. Near him were the skeletons of ancient trees. The dirt looked as if it had been scattered black over the land in loose handfuls, bearing neither shrubs nor footprints. By one boulder a trickle of water ran beneath a fallen log, catching light on either side. He looked up.

On the horizon, against the lines of light, as though cut—no, torn from carbon paper, was the silhouette of a city. Tower behind tower rose against the pearly haze. A net of roadways wound among the spires. Telphar!

Then he had made out the thread of metal that ran from the city, in his general direction but veering to the right. It passed him half a mile away and disappeared into the edge of the jungle behind him. *Telphar!* The name had come to his mind as though on a sign attached with springs to his consciousness. The radiation! That was the second thing he thought. Once more the name of the city shivered in his brain: *Telphar!* The certain, very certain death he had wandered into caught his gut like a fist. It was almost as if the name were sounding out loud in his skull. Then he stopped. Because he realized he had heard something. A . . . a voice! *The Lord of the Flames*. Very definitely he heard it——

Music had started. He could hear it coming from the ballroom. By now the party must be under way. He looked out into the hall. A fellow in an apron, holding an empty tray with nothing but crumbs, was coming towards him.

'Excuse me, sir,' the man in the apron said. 'Guests aren't supposed to be in this part of the house.'

'I was trying to find the . . .' Jon coughed.

'Oh. Of course. Go back into the ballroom and take the hall to your left down three doors.'

'Thank you,' Jon smiled back and walked up the hallway. He entered the ballroom through a high, arched alcove in which were small white tables covered with trays of red fish roe on circlets of toast, white meat, red meat, dark meat of fish ground into patties, cut into stars, strips of filet wound to look like sea-shells, brazed shrimp, and stuffed, baby smelts.

A ten-piece orchestra—three bass radiolyn, a therimin, and six blown shells of various sizes—was making slow windy music from the dais. The few scattered guests seemed lost through the room. Jon wandered across the floor.

Here and there steel fountains spewed blue or pink liquid over mounds of crushed ice. Each fountain was rimmed with a little shelf of glasses. Jon picked up a glass, let it fill, and walked on, sipping.

The loudspeaker announced the arrival of Mr Quelor Da and party. Heads turned, and a moment later much glitter, green silk, and blue net at the top of the wide marble steps across the room resolved into four ladies and their escorts.

Jon glanced at the balcony that ran around the second storey of the room. A short gentleman in a severe blue suit was coming towards the head of the steps which expanded down towards the ballroom floor with the grace and approximate shape of a swan's wing. The gentleman hurried down the pale cascade.

Jon sipped his drink. It was sweet with the combined flavours of a dozen fruits, the whisper of alcohol bitter at the back of his tongue. The gentleman hurried across the floor, passing within yards.

Father! The impact was the same as the recognition of Telphar. The hair was thinner than it had been five years ago. He was much heavier. His . . . father . . . was at the other side of the room already, checking with the waiters. Jon pulled his shoulders in, and let his breath out. It was the familiarity, not the change, that hurt.

It took some time before the room filled. One guest Jon noted was a red-haired young man in military uniform, touring in a way usually associated with older men. There was a major's insignia on his shoulder. Jon watched him a while, empathizing with his occasional looks that told how out of place he felt. He took neither food nor drink, but prowled a ten foot area by the side of the balcony steps. Waiting, Jon thought.

By the time the floor was respectably populated, Jon had exchanged a few words with the soldier (Jon: 'A beautiful party, don't you think?' Soldier, with embarrassment: 'Yes, sir.' Jon: 'I guess the war is worrying all of us.' Soldier: 'The war? Yes.' Then he looked away, not inclined to talk more.) Now Jon stood near the door. Suddenly the loudspeaker announced: 'The Party of His Royal Majesty, the King.'

Gowns rustled, the talk rose, people turned, and fell back from the entrance. The king's party, himself and a tall, electric, redheaded woman, obviously his senior by a handful of years, appeared at the top of the six marble steps. As they came down, right and left people bowed. Jon dropped his head, but not before he realized that the king's escort had given him a very direct look. He glanced up again, but now her emerald train was sweeping the aisle the guests had left. The insignia on her cape told him she was a duchess.

Coming up the aisle in the other direction now between the bending crowds was old Koshar. He bowed. The pale young man raised him and they shook hands, Koshar spoke: 'Your Majesty,' he began warmly.

'Sir,' answered the king.

'I haven't seen you since you were a boy at school.'

The king smiled rather wanly. Koshar hurried on.

'I would like to present my daughter to you, for it's her party. Her name is Clea.' The old man turned to the balcony stairs, and the crowd's eyes turned with him.

She was standing on the top step, in a white dress made of panel over silken panel, held with pearl clasps. Her black hair cascaded across one shoulder, webbed and re-webbed with a chain of silver strung with pearls. Her hands at her side, she came down the stairs. People stepped back; she smiled, and walked forward. Jon watched while his sister reached their father's side.

'My daughter Clea,' said old Koshar.

'Charmed.'

Koshar raised his left hand, and the musicians began the introduction to the partner changing dance. Jon watched the king take Clea in his arms. He saw the soldier move towards them, then stop. A woman in a smoky grey dress suddenly blocked his view, smiled at him, and said, 'Will you dance?' He smiled back, to avoid another expression, and she was in his arms. Apparently the soldier had a similar experience, for at the first turn of the music, Jon saw the soldier was dancing too. A few couples away, Clea and the king turned round and round, white and white, brunette and blond. The steps came back to Jon like a poem remembered, the turn, the dip, separate, and join again. When a girl does the strange little outward step, and the boy bows, so that for a moment she is out of sight, her gown always swishes just so. Yes, like that! This whole day had been filled with remembrances like that, forgotten five years, re-learned with vividness that shocked him. The music signalled for partners to change. Gowns whirled into momentary flowers, and he was dancing with the brown-haired woman the soldier had been dancing with a moment before. Looking to his left, he saw that the soldier had somehow contrived to get Clea for a partner. Moving closer, he overheard:

'I didn't think you were going to get here at all. I'm so glad,' from Clea.

'I could have even come earlier,' Tomar said. 'But you'd have been busy.'

'You could have come up.'

'Once I got here, I didn't think we'd get a chance to talk.'

'Well, we've got one now. But we change partners in a moment. What happened to the scouting planes?'

'All crippled. Didn't sight a thing. They got back to base almost before I did this morning. The report was nothing. What about the picnic, Clea?'

'We can have it on . . .'

A burst of music signalled the change. Jon did not hear the day, but expected his sister to whirl into his arms. Instead (he saw her white dress flare and turn by him) an emerald iridescence caught in his eye, then rich mahogany flame. He was dancing with the Duchess. She was nearly his height, and watched him with a smile hung in the subtle area between friendship and knowing cynicism. She moved easily, and he had just remembered he ought to smile back out of politeness when the music sounded the change. The instant before she whirled away, he heard her say, very distinctly, 'Good luck, Jon Koshar.'

His name brought him to a halt, and he stared after her. When he did turn back to his new partner, surprise still on his face, his eyes were filled with whiteness. It was Clea. He should have been dancing, but he was standing still. When she looked at his face to discover why, she suddenly drew a breath. At first Jon thought his head had disappeared again. Then, as shock and surprise became as real as her wide eyes, her open mouth, he whispered, 'Clea!' And her hand went to her mouth.

Clumsy! he thought, and the word was a sudden ache in his hands and chest. Reach for her. Dance. As his hands went out the music stopped and the languid voice of the king came over the loudspeaker.

'Ladies and gentlemen, citizens of Toromon, I have just received a message from the Council that necessitates an announcement to you as my friends and loyal subjects. I have been requested by the Council to make their declaration of war official by my consent. An emergency meeting over sudden developments has made it imperative that we begin immediate action against our most hostile enemies across the barrier. Therefore, before you all, I do declare the empire of Toromon to be at war!'

In the silence, Jon looked for his sister, but she was gone. Someone near the microphone cried out, 'Long live the king!' The cry came again. The musicians started the music once more, partners found one another, and the talking and laughing grew in his ears like waves, like crumbling rock, like the cutter teeth clawing in the rock face. . . .

Jon shook his head. But he was in his own house. Yes, his room was on the second floor and he could go up and lie down. And by his bed would be the copper night table, and the copy of *Delcord the Whaler* which he had been reading the night before. . . .

He'd left the ballroom and got halfway down the hall before he remembered that his room was probably not his room any longer. And the night before was five years ago. He was standing in front of the door to one of the sitting-rooms that open off the hall. The door was ajar, and from it he heard a woman's voice:

'Can't you do something about his index of refraction? If he's going to be doing any work at night, you can't have him popping on and off like a flashlight.' There was silence. Then: 'Well, at least don't you think he should be told more than he knows now? Fine. So do I, especially since the war has been officially declared.'

Jon took a breath and stepped in.

Her emerald train whirled across the duller green of the carpet as she turned. The bright hair, un-tonsured save by two coral combs, fell over her shoulders. Her smile showed faint surprise. Very faint. 'Who were you talking to?' Jon Koshar asked.

'Mutual friends,' the duchess said. They were alone in the room.

After a moment, Jon said, 'What do they want us to do? It's treason, isn't it?'

The duchess' eyes went thin. 'Are you serious?' she asked. 'You call this treason, keeping those idiots from destroying themselves, eating themselves up in a war with a nameless enemy, something so powerful that if there were any consideration of real fighting, we could be destroyed with a thought. Do you remember who the enemy is? You've heard his name. There are only three people in Toromon who have, Jon Koshar. Everyone else is ignorant. So we're the only ones who can say we're fully responsible. That responsibility is to Toromon. Have you any idea what state the economy is in? Your own father is responsible for a good bit of it, yet it's got to the point that if he closed down his aquariums the panic he caused would equal the destruction their being open already causes. The empire is snowballing towards chaos and its going to take it out in war. You call trying to prevent it treason?'

'Whatever we call it, we don't have much choice, do we?'

'With people like you around, I'm not so sure it isn't a bad idea.'

'Look,' said Jon. 'I was cooped up in a prison mine at the edge of nowhere for five years. All I wanted was out. All I wanted was to get free. Now, I'm back in Toron and I'm still not free. But I still want it.'

'First of all,' said the duchess, 'if it wasn't for them, you wouldn't be as free as you are now. After a day of clean clothes and walking in fresh air, if you're not on the road to what you want, then I better change some ideas of my own. I want something too, Jon Koshar. When I was seventeen, I worked for a summer in your father's aquarium. My nine hours a day were spent with a metal spoon about the size of your head scraping the bottoms of the used tank tubes. I cleaned out the stuff that even the glass filters were too finicky to take out. Afterwards I was too tired to do much more than read. So I read. Most of it was about Toromon's history. I read a lot about the early mainland expeditions. Then, in my first winter out of school, I lived in a fishing village at the edge of the forest, studying what I could of the customs of the forest people. I made sketches of their temples, tried to map their nomadic movements. I even wrote an article on the architecture of their temporary shelters that was published in the University journal. Jon Koshar, what I want is for Toromon to be free, free of its own self-entanglements. Perhaps coming from the royal family, I had easier emotional access to a sense of Toromon's history. Even at its best, that's all an aristocracy is good for. But I wanted more than a sense, I wanted to know what it was worth. So I went out and looked. And I found, found it was worth a great deal. Somehow Toromon must pick itself up by the back of the neck and give itself a shaking. If I have to be the part that does the shaking, I will. That's what I want, Jon Koshar, and I want it as badly as you want your freedom.'

Jon was quiet a moment. Then he said: 'To get what we want, we more or less have to do the same thing. All right, I'll go along. But you're going to have to explain some things to me. There's a lot I still don't understand.'

'A lot we both don't,' the duchess said. 'But we know this: they're not from earth, they're not human, and they come from very far away. Inconceivably far.'

'What will they do?'

'They'll help us help Toromon if we help them. How, I don't understand for sure. Already I've arranged to have Prince Let kidnapped . . .'

'Kidnapped? But why . . .?'

'Because if we get through this, Toromon is going to need a strong king. And I think you'll agree my cousin Uske will never quite be that. Also, he's ill, and under any great strain might die in a moment. Also the underground groups of malis are springing up to undermine whatever the government decides to do, once the war get's going. I am working through one now. Let is going where he can become a strong man, with the proper training, so that if anything happens to Uske, he can return and there will be someone to guide the government through its crises. After that, how we're to help them, I'm not sure.'

'I see,' said Jon. 'How did they get hold of you, anyway? For that matter, how did they get me?'

'You? They contacted you just outside of Telphar, didn't they? They had to rearrange the molecular structure of some of your more delicate proteins and do a general overhaul on your sub-crystalline structure so that the radiation wouldn't kill you. That, unfortunately, had the unpleasant side effect of booting down your index of refraction a couple of points, which is why you keep fading in dim light. In fact I got a description of your entire escape from them. It kept me on the edge of my seat all night. How was I contacted? The same way you were, suddenly, and with those words: *The Lord of the Flames*. Now, your first direct assignment will be . . .'

In another room, Clea was sitting on a blue velvet hassock with her hands tight in her lap. Then suddenly they flew apart like springs, shook beside her head, then clasped again. 'Tomar,' she said. 'Please excuse me, but I'm upset. It was so strange. When I was dancing with the king, he told me how he had dreamed of my brother this morning. I didn't think anything of it. It was just small talk. Then, just after I changed partners for the third time, there I was, staring into a face that I could have sworn was Jon's. And the man wasn't dancing. He was just staring at me. Then he said my name. Tomar, it was the same voice Jon used to use when I'd hurt myself and he wanted to help. Oh, it couldn't have been him, because he was too tall, and too gaunt, and the voice was just a little too deep. But it was so much like what he might have been. That was when the king made his announcement. I just turned and ran. The whole thing seemed supernatural. Oh, don't worry, I'm not superstitious, but even though I know it could not really have been him, it unnerved me. But that plus what we were talking about this morning . . .'

'What?' asked Tomar. He stood beside the hassock in the blue conservatory, his hands in his pockets, listening with animal patience.

'About drafting all the scientific students into the war effort. Maybe the war is good, but, Tomar, I'm working on my own project. All at once, the thing I want most in the world is to be left alone to work on it. And I want you, and I want to have a picnic. I'm nearly at the solution, and to have to stop and work on bomb sightings and missile trajectories . . . Tomar, there's a beauty in abstract mathematics that shouldn't be dulled with that sort of thing. Also, maybe you'll go away, or I'll go away. That doesn't seem fair either. Tomar, have you ever had things you wanted, had them in your hands, and suddenly a situation came up that made it look as if they might fly out of your grip forever?'

Tomar rubbed his hand across his hair and shook his head. 'There was a time, once, when I wanted things. Like food, work, and a bed where all four legs touched the ground. So I came to Toron. And I got them. And I got you, and so I guess there isn't anything else to want, not that bad.' He grinned, and the grin made her smile.

'I guess,' she started, '. . . I guess it was just that he looked so much like my brother.'

'Clea,' Tomar said. 'About your brother. I wasn't going to

tell you this until later. Maybe I shouldn't say it now. But you were asking whether or not they were going to draft prisoners into the army; and whether at the end of their service, they'd be freed. Well, I did some checking. They are going to, and I sent through a recommendation that they take your brother among the first. In three hours I got a memorandum from the penal commissioner. Your brother's dead.'

She looked at him hard, trying to hold her eyes open and to prevent the little snarl of sound that was a sob from loosening in the back of her throat.

'In fact it happened last night,' Tomar went on. 'He and two others attempted an escape. Two of their bodies have been returned. And there's no chance that the third one could have escaped alive.'

The snarl collapsed into a sound she would not make. She sat for a moment. Then she said. 'Let's go back to the party.' She stood up and they walked to the door. Once she shook her head and opened her mouth. Then she closed it and went on. 'Yes. I'm glad you said it. I don't know. Maybe it was a sign ... a sign that he was dead. Maybe it was a sign ...' She stopped. 'No. It wasn't. It wasn't anything. No.' They went down the steps to the ballroom once more. The music was very, very happy.

CHAPTER V

A FEW hours earlier, Geryn gave Tel a kharba fruit. The boy took the speckled melon around the inn, looking for Alter. Unable to find her, he wandered on to the street and up the block. Once a cat with a struggling grey shape in its teeth hurtled across his path. Later he saw an overturned garbage can with a filigree of fish bones ornamenting the parti-coloured heap. Over the roofs the towers of Toron paled to blue. Sudden yellow rectangles of window light scattered over their faces.

Turning down another block, he saw Rara standing on the corner, stopping the occasional passers by. Tel started up to her, but she saw him and motioned him away. Puzzled, he went to a stoop and sat down to watch. As he ran his thumbnail along the orange rind, and juice oozed from the slit, he heard Rara say to a stranger:

'Your fortune, sir. I'll spread your future before you like a silver mirror . . .' The stranger passed. Rara turned to a woman now coming towards her. 'Ma'am, a fragment of a unit will unfold your life like a patterned carpet where you may trace the designs of your fate. Just a quarter of a unit . . .' The woman smiled, but shook her head. 'You look like you come from the mainland,' Rara called after her. 'Well, good luck here in the New World, sister, the Island of Opportunity.' Immediately she turned to another man, this one in a deep green uniform. 'Sir,' Tel heard her begin. Then she paused as she surveyed his costume. 'Sir,' she continued, 'for a single unit I will unravel the threads of your destiny from eternity's loom. Would you like to know the promotion about to come your way? How many children you'll . . .'

'Come on, lady,' said the man in the uniform. 'It's illegal to tell fortunes here.'

'But I've got my licence!' declared Rara. 'I'm a genuine clairvoyant. Just a second . . .' Her hands plunged into the seams and pockets of her grey rags.

'Never mind, lady. Just get moving.' He gave her a push.

Rara moved.

Tel peeled back the strip of rind he'd loosened, licked the juice from the yellow wound, and followed Rara.

'Son of an electric eel,' she said when Tel reached her, her birthmark scarlet. 'Just try to make a decent living, just try.'

'Want a bite?'

Rara shook her head. 'I'm too angry.' They walked back to the inn.

'Do you know where Alter is?' Tel asked. 'I was looking for her.'

'She's not in the inn?'

'I couldn't find her there.'

'Did you look on the roof?' Rara asked.

'Oh,' said Tel. 'No.' They turned into the tavern and Tel went upstairs. It was not until he was halfway up the ladder on the second floor and unfastened the trap door in the ceiling that he wondered why Alter was on the roof. He pushed the hatch back and hoisted himself to the dusty rim.

Alter hung head and white hair down from a pipe that went from the stone chimney to a supporting pipe that was fastened by a firm collar to the roof.

'What are you doing?' Tel asked.

'Hi,' she smiled down at him. 'I'm practising.'

'Practising what?'

She was hung double over the pipe. Now she grabbed the bar close to her waist and somersaulted forward, letting her feet evenly to the floor, her legs perfectly straight. 'My stunts,' she said. 'I'm an acrobat.' She did not let go of the bar, but swung her legs up so that her ankles nearly touched her hands, and then whipped them down again, ending the skip by supporting herself upright on the bar. Then she flung her legs back (Tel jumped because she looked like she was going to fall) and went out and down, then under, swung up, arched over, and went down again in a giant circle. She circled once more, then doubled up, caught one knee over, reversed direction, and suddenly was sitting on top of the rod.

'Gee,' Tel said. 'How did you do that?'

'It's all timing,' Alter said. Suddenly she threw her head back and circled the bar once more, by her hands and one knee. Then the knee came loose, and her feet swung to the ground. 'You've just got to be strong enough to hold up your own weight. Maybe a little stronger. But the rest is all timing.'

'You mean I could do that?'

'You want to try something?'

'Like what?'

'Come here. Grab hold of the bar.'

Tel came over and grabbed. He could just keep his feet flat on the tar-papered roof and still hold. 'All right,' he said.

'Now pull yourself up and hook your left knee around the bar.'

'Like this?' He kicked up once, missed, and tried again.

'When you kick, throw your head back,' she instructed. 'You'll balance better.'

He did, pulled up, and got his foot through his arms, and suddenly felt the bar slide into the crook of his knee. He was hanging by his left knee and hands. 'Now what do I do?' he asked, swaying back and forth.

Alter put her hand on his back to steady him. 'Now straighten your right leg, and keep your arms fairly stiff.' He obeyed. 'Now swing your right leg up and down, three times and then swing it real hard.' Tel lifted his leg, dropped it, and at once began swinging back and forth beneath the pole. 'Keep the leg straight,' Alter said. 'Don't bend it or you'll lose momentum.'

He got to the third kick, and then let go (with his thigh muscles, not his hands) and at once the sky slipped over him and his body swung upward away from the direction of the kick. 'Whoooo,' he said, and then felt her hand steady his wrist. He was sitting on top of the bar with one leg over it. He looked down at Alter. 'Is that what was supposed to happen?'

'Sure,' she said. 'That's how you mount the bar. It's called a knee mount.'

'I guess it's easier than climbing. Now what do I do?'

'Try this. Straighten out your arms. And make sure they stay straight. Now straighten your back leg behind you.' As he tried, he felt her hand on his knee, helping. 'Hey . . .' he said. 'I'm not balanced.'

'Don't worry,' she said. 'I'm holding you. Keep those arms straight. If you don't obey instructions you'll have tar-paper all over your brains. Seven feet isn't very high, but head first it's sort of uncomfortable.'

Tel's elbows locked.

'Now when I count three, kick the leg I'm holding forward and throw your head back as hard as you can. One——'

'What's supposed to happen?' Tel demanded.

'Follow instructions,' replied Alter. 'Two . . . three!'

Tel threw and kicked, and felt Alter give his leg an extra push. He had planned to close his eyes, but what he saw was too interesting. Sky and then roof were coming at him, fast. Then they fell away, along with Alter's face (upside down), till an instant later the pale blue towers, all pointing in the wrong direction, pierced his sight. Righting themselves, they jerked out of his line of vision and he was looking straight up at the sky (there was a star out, he noted before it became a meteor and flashed away) until it was replaced by the roof and Alter's face (laughing now) and once more everything swept into its proper position.

He clamped his stinging hands tightly on the bar. When he felt sure he'd stopped, he hunched forward and closed his eyes. Mmmmmmmmm,' he said. Alter's hand was on his wrist, very firm, and he was sitting on top of the bar again.

'You just did a double back knee circle,' she said. 'You did it very well too.' Then she laughed. 'Only it wasn't supposed to be double. You just kept going.'

'How do I get down?' Tel asked.

'Arms straight,' said Alter.

Tel straightened his arms.

'Put this hand over here.' She patted the bar on the other side of his leg. Tel transferred his grip. 'Now bring your leg off the bar.' Tel hoisted his leg back so that he was supported by just his hands. 'Now bend forward and roll over, slowly if you can.' Tel rolled, felt the bar slip from where it was pressed against his waist, and a moment later his feet were brushing back and forth over the tar-paper. He let go and rubbed his hands together. 'Why didn't you tell me what I was gonna do?'

'Because then you wouldn't have done it. Now that you know that you can, the rest will be easier. You've got three stunts now in less than five minutes. The knee mount, back knee circle, and the forward dismount. That was good for a first try.'

'Thanks,' said Tel. He looked at the horizontal bar. 'You know, it feels real funny, doing that stuff. I mean you don't really do it. You do things and then it happens to you.'

'That's right,' Alter said. 'I hadn't thought of it like that. Maybe that's why a good acrobat has to be a person who can sort of relax and just let things happen. You have to trust both your mind and your body.'

'Oh,' said Tel. 'I was looking for you when I came up here. I wanted to give you something.'

'Thank you,' she smiled, brushing back a shock of white hair from her forehead.

'I hope it didn't get broken.' He reached into his pocket and pulled out a handful of something: on leather thongs he had strung the shells. There were three loops, each longer than the one before, and the shells were spread apart and held in place by tiny knots. 'Geryn gave me the thong, and I put it together this afternoon. It's a necklace, see?'

She turned while he tied the ends behind her neck. Then she turned back to him, touching the orange brilliance of one frail cornucopia, passing to the mute blue of another. 'Thank you,' she said. 'Thank you very much, Tel.'

'You want some fruit?' he said, picking up the globe and beginning to peel the rest of it.

'All right,' she said. He broke it open, and gave her half, and they went to the edge of the roof and leaned on the balustrade, looking to the street below, then over the roofs of the other houses of the Devil's Pot and up to the darkening towers.

'You know,' Tel said. 'I've got a problem.'

'No identification papers, no place to go. I should say you do.'

'Not like that,' he said. 'But that's part of it. I guess it's a large part of it. But not all.'

'Then what is it?'

'I've got to figure out what I want. Here I am, in a new place, with no way to get anything for myself; I've got to figure a goal.'

'Look,' said Alter, assuming the superiority of age and urban training, 'I'm a year older than you, and I don't know where I'm going yet. But when I was your age, it occurred to me it would probably all take care of itself. All I had to do was ride it out. So that's what I'm doing, and I haven't been too unhappy. Maybe it's the difference between living here or on the seashore. But here you've got to spend a lot of time looking for the next meal. At least people like you and me have to. If you pay attention to that, you'll find yourself heading in the right direction soon enough. Whatever you're going to be, you're going to be, if you just give yourself half a chance.'

'Like a big acrobatic stunt, huh?' asked Tel. 'You just do the right things and then it happens to you.'

'Like that,' said Alter. 'I guess so.'

'Maybe,' said Tel. The kharba fruit was cool, sweet like honey, orange, and pineapple.

A minute later someone was calling them. They turned from the balustrade and saw Geryn's white head poking from the trap door. 'Come down,' he demanded. 'I've been looking all over for you. It's time.'

They followed him back to the first floor. Tel saw that the scarred giant was still sitting at the table, his hands knotted into quiet hammers on the boards.

'Now, everyone,' Geryn called as he sat down at the table. Somewhat reluctantly people left the bar. Geryn dropped a sheaf of papers on the table. 'Come around, everyone.' The top sheet was covered with fine writing and careful architectural drawing. 'Now this is the plan.' So were the other sheets when Geryn turned them over. 'I'll divide you into groups.'

He looked at the giant across the table. 'Arkor, you take the first group.' He picked out six more men and three women. He turned to the white haired acrobat. 'Alter, you'll be with the special group.' He named six more people. Tel was among them. A third group was formed which Geryn himself was to lead. Arkor's group was for strong-arm work. Geryn's was for guard duty and to keep the way clear while the prince was being conveyed back to the inn. 'The people in the special group already know what to do.'

'Sir,' said Tel, 'you haven't told me, yet.'

Geryn looked at him. 'You have to get caught.'

'Sir?'

'You go past the guards, and make enough noise so that they catch you. Then, when they're occupied with you, we'll break in. Because you have no papers, they won't be able to trace you.'

'Am I supposed to stay caught?'

'Of course not. You'll get way when we distract them.'

'Oh,' said Tel. Geryn went back to the papers.

As the plan was reviewed, Tel saw two things. First the completeness of the research, information, and attention to detail (habits of individual guards: one who left at the first sound of the change signal; another who waited a moment to exchange greetings with his replacement, a friend from his military academy days). Second, he saw its complexity. There were so many ins and outs, gears that had to mesh, movements to be timed within seconds, that Tel wondered if everything could possibly go right.

While he was wondering, they were suddenly on their way, each one with a bit of the plan fixed in his mind, no one with too clear a picture of the entire device. The groups were to split into subgroups of two or three, then reconvene at appointed spots around the castle. Tel and Alter found themselves walking through the city with the giant. Occasional street lights wheeled their shadows over the pavement.

'You're from the forest, aren't you?' Tel finally asked the giant.

He nodded.

'Why did you come here?' Tel asked, trying to make conversation as they walked.

'I wanted to see the city,' Arkor said, raising his hand to his scars. He chuckled. After that, he said nothing.

Prime Minister Chargill took his evening constitutional along the usually deserted Avenue of the Oysture at about this time every night. Prime Minister Chargill always carried on him a complete set of keys to the private suites of the royal family. This evening, however, a drunk reeled out of a side street and collided with the old minister. A moment later, making profuse apologies, he backed away, ducking his head, his hands behind his back. When the drunk returned to the side street, his weaving ceased, his hand came from behind his back, and in it was a complete set of keys to the private suites of the royal family.

The guard who was in charge of checking the alarm system loved flowers. He could be (and had been) observed going to the florist's at least once a week on his time off. So when the old woman with the tray of scarlet anemones came by and offered them for his perusal, it is not surprising that he lowered his head over the tray and filled his lungs with that strange, pungent smell somewhere between orange rind and sea wind. Forty-seven seconds later, he yawned. Fourteen seconds after that, he was sitting against the wall, his head hung forward, snoring. Through the gate two figures could be seen at the alarm box . . . had anyone been there to look.

At another entrance to the castle, two guards converged on a boy with black hair and green eyes who was trying to climb the fence.

'Hey get down from there. All right, come one. Where're your papers? What do you mean you don't have any? Come on with us. Get the camera out, Jo. We'll have to photograph him and send the picture to Chief Records Headquarters. They'll tell us who you are, kid. Now hold still.'

Behind them, a white-haired girl was out of the shadows and over the gate in a moment. The guards did not see her.

'Hold still now, kid, while I get your retina pattern.'

A bunch of rowdies, led by a giant had started to raise hell around the palace. They hadn't even got the kid to the guard house yet, but somehow in the confusion the boy got away. One guard, who wore a size seventeen uniform, was knocked unconscious, but no one else was hurt. They dispersed the rowdies, carried the guard to the infirmary, and left. Doctor Wental saw him in the waiting-room, then left him there momentarily to look for an accident report slip in the supply room at the other side of the building. (He could have sworn that a whole pad of them had been lying on the desk when he stepped out for a bite ten minutes ago.) When the doctor returned with the slip, the soldier was still there—only he was stark naked.

A minute later, an unfamiliar guard wearing a size seventeen uniform saluted the guard at the gate, and marched in.

Two strange men behind the gate flung a cord with a weight on one end over a third storey cornice. They missed once, then secured it the second time and left it hanging there.

A guard wearing a size seventeen uniform came down the hall of the west wing of the castle, stopped before a large double door on which was a silver crown, indicating the room of the Queen Mother; he took a complete set of keys to the private suites of the royal family from his cloak, and locked Her Majesty firmly in her room. At the next door, he locked Prince Let securely in his. Then he went rapidly on.

Tel ran till he got to the corner, rounded it, and checked the street sign. It was correct. So he went to a doorway and sat down to wait.

At the same time, Prince Let, getting ready for bed and wearing nothing but his undershirt looked out of the window and saw a girl with white hair hanging head down outside the shutter. He stood very still. The upside down face smiled at him. Then the hands converged at the window lock, did something, and the two glass panels came open. The girl rolled over once, turned quickly, and suddenly she was crouching on the window ledge.

Let snatched up his pyjama bottoms first, and ran to the door second. When he couldn't open it, he whirled around and pulled on his pyjama pants.

Alter put her finger to her lips as she stepped down into his room. 'Keep quiet,' she whispered. 'And relax,' she added. 'The Duchess of Petra sent me. More or less.' She had been instructed to use that name to calm the prince. It seemed to work a trifle.

'Look,' explained Alter, 'you're being kidnapped. It's for your own good, believe me.' She watched the blond boy come away from the door.

'Who are you?' he asked.

'I'm a friend of yours if you'll let me be.'

'Where are you going to take me?'

'You're going on a trip. But you'll come back.'

'What has my mother said?'

'Your mother doesn't know. Nobody knows except you and the Duchess, and the few people who're helping her.'

Let thought. He walked over to his bed, sat down, and pressed his heel against the side board. There was a small click. Nothing else happened. 'Why don't they open the door?' he asked.

'It's been locked,' Alter said. Suddenly she looked at the clock beside the Prince's bed, and turned to the window. Light from the chandelier gleamed on the shells at her neck.

Let put his hand quietly on the newel post of his bed and pressed his thumb hard on a purple garnet that encrusted the crowning dolphin. Nothing happened, except a click.

At the window, Alter reached out, just as a bundle appeared on a lowered rope. She pulled it in, untied it, and shook them out as the rope suddenly flew out the window again. 'Here,' she said. 'Get into these.' They were rags. She tossed them to him.

Finally Let slipped out of his pyjama pants and into the suit.

'Now look in your pocket,' Alter said.

The boy did and took out a bunch of keys.

'You can open the door with those,' Alter said. 'Go on.'

Let paused, then went to the door. Before he put the key in the lock though, he bent down and looked through the keyhole. 'Hey,' he said, looking back at the girl. 'Come here. Do you see anything?'

Alter crossed the room, bent down, and looked. The only motion Let made was to lean against one of the panels on the wall, which gave a slight click. Nothing else happened.

'I don't see anything,' Alter said. 'Open the door.'

Let found the proper key, put it in the lock, and the door swung back.

'All right, you kids,' said the guard who was standing on the other side of the door (he wore a size seventeen uniform), 'you come along with me.' He took Let firmly by one arm and Alter by the other and marched them down the hall. 'I'm warning you to keep quiet,' the guard said to Let as they turned the last corner.

Three minutes later they were outside the castle. As the guard passed another uniformed man at the sentry's post, he said, 'More stupid kids trying to break into the palace.'

'What a night,' said the guard and scratched his head. 'A girl too?'

'Looks like it,' said the guard who was escorting Alter and the prince. 'I'm taking them to be photographed.'

'Sure,' answered the guard, and saluted.

The two children were marched down the street towards the guard-house. Before they got there, they were turned off into a side street. Then suddenly the guard was gone. A black haired boy with green eyes was coming towards them.

'Is this the prince?' Tel asked.

'Un-huh,' said Alter.

'Who are you?' Let asked. 'Where are you taking me?'

'My name is Tel. I'm a fisherman's son.'

'My name is Alter,' Alter introduced herself.

'She's an acrobat,' Tel added.

'I'm the prince,' Let said. 'Really. I'm Prince Let. Don't forget that.'

The two others looked at the blond boy who stood in front of them in rags like their own. Suddenly they laughed. The prince frowned. 'Where are you taking me?' he asked again.

'We're taking you to get something to eat and where you can get a good night's sleep,' Alter answered. 'Come on.'

'If you hurt me, my mother will put you in the mines.'

'Nobody's going to hurt you, silly,' Tel said. 'Come on. Are you a mali too?'

'A what?' Let asked.

'That's what we are, malcontents,' Tel said. 'It means we don't like where we've been, where we are, or where we're going. What about you?'

'I——' The prince looked confused. 'I don't know what you're talking about.' He blinked up at the dark towers that rose to menace the night. 'I don't know.'

'Well, come on anyway,' Tel said. They started through the streets

CHAPTER VI

THE Duchess of Petra said: 'Now your first direct assignment will be——'

The green of beetles' wings; the red of polished carbuncle; a web of silver fire; lightning and smoke. It pulled away from his eyes.

Only one sun now, the larger red one, lipped the horizon. The sand was crimson. The lake flamed. And by the lake—or was it in it—below the clouds that streaked the alien sky, was the . . . city.

Things moved there, turned; form joined with form, caught the sunlight, then joined with other forms, darkened.

A warm, ozone heavy breeze pushed his collar against his cheek, dropped it. Jon tried to see what was going by the lake. And failed; as an unco-ordinated hand might fail the workings of a clock.

The Lord of the Flames.

'There?' Jon asked. 'In there?'

No. That is only a city building.

'This place,' Jon asked. 'Where is this? Where am I? Why do you keep bringing me here?'

You are on the outskirts of a ruined city, an extinct city on a world a universe away from your own. Twelve million years ago, this planet housed the civilization that began constructing that city. Now the civilization is dead. But the city was so made that it goes on building itself.

'And you say the *Lord of the Flames* doesn't live there?'

No. We do. No one else used the city, so we stay here now.

'You——' Jon said. 'Well then why won't you tell me who you are?'

Each time we speak to you, we tell you a little more. Your mind must accustom to us slowly. You live in a bound, circumscribed, and isolated world, and if we broke on your consciousness all at once, you would be too ready to dismiss us as a psychotic fantasy. We come to you, leave you, and let you forget us a little, and come to you again. We have three agents on your world, you and two others. Now that you have made contact with one another, you have something to hold on to in your own world; but we can tell you more.

Jon gazed at the fabulous creation forming across the dunes in twilight while they spoke to him.

We are wanderers from another universe. We have no home. It was destroyed by a war fought on scales you could not begin to conceive. Now we dwell quietly in your universe, staying only in the abandoned cities scattered throughout your worlds. We can traverse the distances between stars or galaxies, ignoring temporal consideration. We do not usually bother with any living species, except to observe.

But recently—recently by our standards though the actual time is longer than your world is old—another living force has come into this segment of the continuum. It has evolved similarly to us. We can both touch the perceptions of life forms on various worlds; this involves a good deal more work and energy than travelling from one side of the universe to the other, for we must convert our own vision in which neither time nor space are of much importance down to the miniature scope of life forms that exist often for less than a century, where an object behind a wall is an unseen one, where the experiences of one individual can create emotions and ideas unknown to the mind and heart of another. But there are differences between us. The new creature is younger than us by cycles of time meaningless to you. We are a triple-lobed intelligence, and can touch up to three minds on any single world at once. The new creature can only have one agent on a world. We never tamper with any civilization's basic structure. While this creature will not hesitate to completely destroy a world by introducing technological, philosophical, or psychological factors that set up destructive resonances that shake worlds apart. We are bound to ride with your minds, guide you, warn you; but we could change your bodies before we could change your minds, and then only to keep you from death as we did with the radiation. So the battle will be won or lost within the framework of your own civilization.

'Battle——?'

'*Yes. We are preparing also for a war, but with the* Lord of the Flames *whom we have just described to you. And the*

Lord of the Flames *has sought refuge in Toromon.*

'You mean,' Jon said, 'that that's what's beyond the radiation barrier? That's what Toromon is at war with? How can we fight something as powerful as you have described him?'

The Lord of the Flames *is in Toromon. He waits at the edge of the radiation barrier, just beyond Telphar.*

'But that's beyond the place where humans can go.'

The Lord of the Flames *has the same resources to make his agent and his agents protegés immune to the radiation as we have. He is on your world, and we must evict him. But we cannot do it without your help. You and our other two agents must corner him and place yourselves where you can all perceive him at once. We will do the rest; but what you cannot perceive, we cannot effect. We will be able to protect you, and any of your friends that you need to bring with you, from the radiation; with your work in matter transmission, your own technology is within a decade of the discovery. But we cannot protect you from human danger, or violent, or any other natural death.*

'But the enemies on the other side of the barrier——'

We have our enemy in Toromon. You have yours. But until you help us expel ours, you will not be able to face your own. And it holds you in, Jon Koshar, keeps you prisoner, and denies your freedom.

Not understanding, he looked back down at the structure by the lake. Figures moved by the water, carrying lumber, driving carts piled with girders. A crane hoisted a wall up a skeletal structure, while a figure at the top signalled to the crane's driver.

'The city,' Jon said.

Yes. It's still building itself.

'But I can see . . .' He squinted to clear the figures. But they stayed vague.

The city responds to the psychic pressures of those near, building itself according to the plans, methods, and techniques of whatever minds press it into activity.

'But——'

It's responding to you. You're concentrating on it. We are concentrating on you, and Toromon.

'Oh,' Jon said. 'A place like that must be very . . . pleasant for you.'

Yes, when we can wander through it, giving our minds to its shaping and development. But now the distraction of The Lord of the Flames *takes all our attention away. Remember, you and our other two agents will have to confront* The Lord of the Flames *at the edge of the barrier.*

'But the forces behind——'

You may use any method you wish to accomplish our ends, and yours.

The city, silhouetted against the maroon sky, changed and grew and changed. The smoke drifted over Jon's eyes; sand fell from beneath his boots with a flash. Silver gave way to red, green——

Jon blinked. The Duchess took a step backward. The green carpet, the rich wood-panelled walls, the glass-covered desk; they were in a sitting-room of his father's house again.

Finally Jon asked, 'Now just what am I supposed to do, again? And explain it very carefully.'

'I was going to say,' said the Duchess, 'that you were to get to the prince, who is being kept at an inn in the Devil's Pot, and accompany him to the forest people. I want him to stay there until this ridiculous war is over. They live a different life from any of the other people of this empire. They will give him something he'll be able to use. I told you I spent some time there when I was younger. I can't explain exactly what it is, but its a certain ruggedness, a certain strength. Maybe they won't give it to him, but if he's got it in him, they'll bring it out.'

'What about . . . *The Lord of the Flames*?'

'I don't . . . do you have any idea, Jon?'

'Well, assuming we get to the radiation barrier, assuming we find what we're fighting, assuming we find who is carrying around *The Lord of the Flames,* and assuming we can all three of us get to him at once—assuming all that, there's no problem. If I'm to accompany the prince, I'll be going to the forest, so I'll be closest to the radiation barrier. I'll try to get through, see what the situation is, and then the two of you can come on. All right?'

'Fine.'

'If nothing else, it'll put me closer to the *Lord of the Flames* . . . and my freedom.'

'How are you not free now, Jon Koshar?' the Duchess asked.

Instead of answering, he said, 'Give me the address of the Inn at the Devil's Pot.'

Going down the hall, with the address, Jon increased his pace. His mind carried an alien mind, that had saved him from death once already. How could he be free of the . . . obligation? That couldn't be the word.

Around the corner he heard a voice. 'And now would you please explain it to me. It's not every day that I'm called on to declare war. I think I did it rather eloquently. Now tell me why.'

(Jon remembered the trick of acoustics which as a child enabled him to stand in this spot and overhear his sister and her girlfriends' conversation just as they came into the house.)

'It's your brother,' came the other voice. 'He's been kidnapped.'

'He's been what?' asked the king. 'And why? And by whom?'

'We don't know,' answered the officer. 'But the Council thought it was best to get you to declare war.'

'Oh,' said the king, 'so that's why I made that little speech in there. What does Mother say?'

'It wouldn't be polite to repeat, sir. She was locked in her room, and very insulted.'

'She would be,' said Uske. 'So, the enemy has infiltrated and gotten my silly brother.'

'Well,' said the voice, 'they can't be sure. But what with the planes this morning, they thought it was best.'

'Oh well,' said the king. There were footsteps. Then silence.

Coming round the corner, Jon saw the coat closet was ajar. He opened the door, took out a great cape and hood, and wrapped it around him, pulling the hood close over his head. He stepped into the foyer and went out past the doorman.

At the edge of the Devil's Pot, Rara, the woman with the birthmark on the side of her face, was tapping a cane and holding out a tin cup. Wearing dark glasses, she wandered up one street and down another. 'Money for a poor blind woman,' she whined. 'Money for the blind.' As a coin clinked into her cup, she nodded, smiled, and said, 'Welcome to the New World. Good luck in the Island of Opportunity.'

The man who had given her the coin walked a step, and then turned back. 'Hey,' he said to Rara. 'If you're blind, how do you know I'm new here?'

'Strangers are generous,' Rara explained, 'while those who live here are too cold to give.'

'Look,' said the man, 'I was told to watch out for blind beggars who aren't blind. My cousin, he warned me before I came . . .'

'Not blind!' cried Rara. 'Not blind? Why I've got my licence right here. It permits me to beg in specified areas because of loss of sight. If you keep this up, I'll be obliged to show it to you.' She turned away with a *huff* and began in another direction. The man scratched his head, then walked off.

A few moments later, a man completely swathed in a grey cloak and hood came around the corner and stopped in front of the woman.

'Money for the blind?'

'Can you use this?' the man said. From his cloak he held out a brocade jacket, covered with fine metal work.

'Of course,' said Rara softly. Then she coughed. '. . . Eh . . . what is it?'

'It's a jacket,' Jon said. 'It's made well. Perhaps you can sell it?'

'Oh, thank you. Thank you, sir.'

A few blocks later, a ragged boy named Kino was amazed when he was handed a silk shirt by the man in the grey cloak. In front of a doorway two blocks on, a pair of open toed boots with gold discs were left and stolen from that doorway exactly forty seconds later by a hairdresser who was returning to her home in the Devil's Pot. She was missing the little finger of her left hand. Once the cloaked figure paused in an alley beneath a clothes-line. He flung up a ball of grey cloth, which caught on the line, unrolled, and became identifiable as a pair of trousers. A block later the last minor articles of clothing were tossed unceremoniously through an open window. As Jon turned another corner, he glimpsed again the figure ducking into a doorway down the dim street. One of the squat neanderthals—there were a few in the city—had been following him.

Jon walked very slowly down the next block, ambling along in the shadow. Then Jeof, the mugger, crept up behind him, then grabbed his cloak, ripped it away, and leapt forward.

Only there wasn't anything there. Squat Jeof stood there for a moment, the cape dangling from his hand, blinking at the place a man should have been. Then something hit him in the jaw. He staggered back. Something else hit him in the stomach. As he stumbled forward now, beneath the street lamp, a transparent human figure suddenly formed in front of him. Then it planted its quite substantial fist into his jaw again, and he went back, down, and out.

Jon dragged the neanderthal back to the side of the alley, fading out completely as he did so. Then he took Jeof's clothes, which were ragged, smelly, and too small. The shoes, he left off. Then he flung the cape back around his shoulders and pulled the hood over his head.

For the next six blocks he was lost because there were no street signs. When he found the next one, he realized he was only a block away from the inn.

As he reached the stone building, he heard a thud in the tiny alleyway beside it. A moment later a girl's voice called softly: 'There. Just like that. Only you better do exactly as I say or you'll break your arms and or legs, and or back.'

He walked to the edge of the building and peered into the alley.

Her white hair loose, Alter stood looking up at the roof. 'All right, Tel,' she called. 'You go.'

Something came down from the roof, flipped over on the ground at her feet, rolled away, and then unwound to its feet: The black-haired boy ran his fingers through his hair. 'Wow,' he said. Then he shook his head. 'Wow.'

'Are you all right?' Alter asked. 'You didn't pull anything, did you?'

'No,' he said. 'I'm all right. I think. Yeah, everything's in place.' He looked up at the roof again, two stories above.

'Your turn Your Highness,' Alter called up.

'It's high,' came a childish voice from the roof.

'Hurry up,' said Alter, her voice becoming authoritative. 'When I count three. And remember, knees up, chin down, and roll quick. One, two, three!' There was the space of a breath, and then it fell, rolled, bounced unsteadily to its feet, and resolved into another boy, this one blond, and slighter than the first.

'Hey, you kids,' Jon said.

They turned.

Jon looked at the smaller boy. His slight frame, less substantial than even Alter's white-haired loveliness, was definitely of the royal family. 'What are you doing out here, anyway?' Jan asked. 'Especially you, Prince.'

All three children jumped.

It looked like they might baulk, and after their descent from the roof, he wasn't sure where they might baulk to. So he said, 'The Duchess of Petra sent me. How did you do that fall?'

His Highness was the only one to relax appreciably.

'And are you sure you're supposed to be outside?'

'We were supposed to stay on the top floor,' Tel said. 'But him,' he pointed to the ragged prince, 'he got restless, and we started telling him about the tricks, and so we went up to the roof, and Alter said she could get us down.'

'Can you get them back up?' Jon asked.

'Sure,' said Alter, 'all we do is climb . . .'

Jon held up his hand. 'Wait a minute,' he said. 'We'll go inside and talk to the man in charge. Don't worry. No one'll be mad.'

'You mean talk to Geryn?' Alter said.

'I guess that's what his name is.'

They started back out of the alley. 'Tell me,' Jon said, 'just what sort of person is Geryn?'

'He's a strange old man. He talks to himself all the time,' said Alter. 'But he's smart.'

Talks to himself, Jon reflected, and nodded. When they reached the door of the inn, Jon pulled his cape off and stepped into the light. A few people at the bar turned around, and when they saw the children, they looked askance at one another.

'Geryn's probably upstairs,' Alter said. They went to the second floor. Jon let the children go ahead of him as they passed into the shadow of the hall. He only stepped up to them when Alter pushed open the door at the end of the hall and bright light from Geryn's room fell full across them.

'What is it?' Geryn snapped. And then, 'What is it, quick.' He whirled around in the chair at the rough wooden desk when they entered. The giant Arkor was standing by the window. Geryn's grey eyes fidgeted back and forth. Finally he said, 'Why are you out here? And who is he? What do you want?'

'I'm from the Duchess of Petra,' Jon said. 'I've come to take Let to the forest people.'

'Yes,' said the old man. 'Yes.' Then his face twisted as he tried to remember something. He shook his head. 'Yes.' Suddenly he stood up. 'Well, go on! I've done my part, I tell you. I've done! Every minute he's in my house he endangers my boarders, my friends. Take him. Go on!'

The giant turned from the window. 'I am to go with you. My name is Arkor.'

Jon frowned. For the first time the scarred figure's height registered. 'Why——?' he started.

'It is to my part of the country that we go,' said Arkor. 'I know how to get there. I can take you through it. Geryn says it is part of the plan.'

Jon felt a knot of resentment tighten. These plans, the Duchess's, Geryn's, not even the plans of the triple beings who inhabited them: they trapped him. Freedom. The word went in and out of his mind like a shadow. He said, 'When do we go then, if you know how to get there?'

'In the morning,' said Arkor.

'Alter, take him to a room. Get him out of here. Quick. Go on.' They backed from the room and Alter hurried them up the hall.

Jon was thinking. After delivering Let to the forest people, he was going farther. Yes. He would go on, try to get through the radiation barrier. But all three of them had to get through if they were to do any good. So why wasn't Geryn coming instead of sending the giant? If Geryn came, then there'd be two people near *The Lord of the Flame*. But Geryn was old. Maybe the Duchess could bring him with her when she came. Mentally he smashed a fist into the thoughts and scattered them. Don't think. Don't think. Thinking binds up your mind, and you can never be . . . He stopped. Then memory flickered in his mind, those five years of glittering hunger.

That night he slept badly. Morning prised his eyes open with blades of light from the window. It was early. He had been up only a minute when there was a knock on his door. It opened, and Arkor directed the dwarfed form of the prince into Jon's room, then turned and left.

'He says to meet him downstairs in five minutes,' Let said.

'Sure,' said Jon. He finished buttoning up the ragged shirt stolen from the mugger the night before, watching the boy by the door. 'I guess you're not used to these sort of cloths,' he said. 'Once I wasn't either. Pretty soon they begin to take.'

'Huh?' said Let. Then, 'Oh.'

'Is something wrong?'

'Who are you?'

Jon thought for a moment. 'Well,' he said. 'A friend of your brother. An acquaintance, anyway. I'm supposed to take you to the forest.'

'Why?'

'You'll be safe there.'

'Could we go to the sea instead?'

'My turn for a "why"?' Jon asked.

'Because Tel told me all about the sea last night. He said it was fun. He said there were rocks all different colours. And in the morning, he said, you can see the sun come up like a burning blister across the water. He told me about the boats, too. I'd like to work on a boat. I really would. They don't allow me to do anything at home. Mother says I might get hurt. Will I get a chance to work some place?'

'Maybe,' Jon said.

'Tel had some good stories about fishing. Do you know any stories?'

'I don't know,' Jon said. 'I never tried telling any. Come on. We better get started.'

'I like stories,' Let said. Then he looked sad. 'I'm just trying to be friendly.'

Jon laughed. 'I can tell you a story. It's about a prison mine. Do you know anything about the prison beyond the forest?'

'Some,' said Let.

'Well, once upon a time there were three prisoners in the mines.' They started along the hall. 'They'd been there a long time, and they wanted to get out. One was . . . well, he looked like me, let's pretend. Another had a limp . . .'

'And the third one was chubby, sort of,' interrupted Let. 'I know that story.'

'You do?' asked Jon.

'Sure,' Let said.

'Then you go on and tell it.' Jon was annoyed.

Let told it to him.

They were outside waiting for Arkor when the boy finished. 'See,' Let said. 'I told you I knew it.'

'Yeah,' said Jon quietly. He stood very still. 'You say the other two . . . didn't make it?'

'That's right,' Let said. 'The guards brought them back and dumped their bodies in the mud so that . . .'

'Shut up,' Jon said.

'Huh?' asked Let.

He was quiet for a few breaths. 'Who told you that . . . story?'

'Petra,' Let answered. 'She told it to me. It's a good story, huh?'

'Yes,' Jon said, 'I'm the one that escaped.'

'You mean . . .?' The boy stopped. 'You mean it really happened?'

The early light warmed the deserted street as Arkor came to the door of the inn and stepped outside.

'All right,' he said. 'We're going.'

CHAPTER VII

THE news service of Toromon in the city of Toron was both a public address system and video threads that could be replayed by the families well enough off to own a re-video. Among the mainland villages it was a fairly accurate brigade of men and women who transported news orally from settlement to settlement. All announced that morning:

PRINCE KIDNAPPED!
KING DECLARES WAR!

In the military ministry, directives were issued in duplicate, returned in triplicate. At eight-forty, the 27B communications sector became hopelessly snarled. This resulted in the shipment of a boatload of prefabricated barracks foundations to a port on the mainland sixty-two miles from the intended destination.

Let, Jon, and Arkor were just mounting the private yacht of the Duchess of Petra which was waiting for them at the end of the harbour. Later, as the island of Toron slipped across the water, Let mentioned to Jon who was leaning with his back against the railing, that there was an awful lot of commotion on the docks.

'It's not always like that,' Jon told him, remembering the times he'd gone with his father in the morning to the pier. 'They're inspecting cargoes. But I don't know why it's so much busier than usual.'

One group of military directives which had been quite speedily and accurately delivered were the offers of contracts, primarily for food for the army. Two distributors of imported fish who had no chance of receiving the contracts sent in a bid accompanied by a letter which explained (with fraudulent statistics) how much cheaper it would be to use imported fish rather than those from the aquariums. Then they commandeered a group of ruffians who broke into the house of old

Koshar's personal secretary, who was still sleeping late after the previous night's party which he had organized. (So far he has appeared in this story only as a hand at the edge of a storage cabinet door, wearing a wide, brass ring set with an irregular shape of blue glass.) They tied him to a chair, punched him in the stomach, in the head, and in the mouth until there was blood in his trimmed beard; and he had given the information they wanted—information that enabled them to sink three of the Koshar Kargo Fleet that was just coming into dock.

The Duchess' private yacht made contact with a tetron-tramp returning to the mainland and Let, Jon, and Arkor changed ships. Coming from the yacht in bare feet and rags gave them an incongruous appearance. But on the new ship, among those passengers who were returning for their families, they were quickly lost.

In Toron, the pilot of the shuttle boat that took workers from the city to the aquariums found a clumsily put together, but nevertheless unmistakable, bomb in the lavatory. It was dismantled. There was no accident. But an authority, Vice-Supervisor T'jones of Koshar Synthetic Food Concerns (one name you do not need to remember; he was killed three days later in a street riot) clenched his jaw (unshaven; he had been called to the office a half an hour early over the sunken cargo boats), nodded his head, and issued a few non-official directives himself. Twenty minutes later, Koshar Aquariums was officially given the government contract to supply fish to the armies of Toromon. The two rival bidders, the import merchants, had ceased to exist about twelve minutes previously. They had been denied warehouse space, and their complete storage dumped into the streets to rot (nearly seven tons of frozen fish) because the refrigeration lockers, and the refrigeration buildings, and the refrigeration trucks had all been rented from Rahsok Refrigeration, and nobody had thought to spell Rahsok backwards.

In the military ministry, Major Tomar, and Captain Clemen were called away from their present job of completing the evacuation of the top four floors of an adjacent office building to accommodate the new corps of engineers, mathematicians, and physicists that the army had just enlisted. Apparently riots had started inthe streets around the old Rahsok Refrigeration Houses. The warehouses were just a few blocks away from the official boundary of the Devil's Pot.

They got there ten minutes after the report came in. 'What the hell is going on?' Clemen demanded from the head of the City Dispersal Squad. Behind the line of uniformed men, masses of people were pushing and calling. 'And what's that stench?' He was a neo-neanderthal only a quarter of an inch taller than the minimum height for the military.

'Fish, sir,' the Dispersal Chief told them. 'There's tons of it all over the street. The people are trying to take it away.'

'Well, let them have it,' Clemen said. 'It'll clear the streets of the mess and maybe do some good.'

'You don't understand, sir,' the head of Dispersal explained. 'It's been poisoned. Just before it was dumped, it was soaked with buckets of barbitide. Half a ton of the stuff's already been carried away.'

Clemen turned. 'Major Tomar,' he said. 'You get back to headquarters and see personally a city-wide announcement goes out telling about the poisoned fish. Call General Medical, find out the antidote, and get the information all over the city.'

Tomar got back to headquarters, got General Medical, got the antidote which was expensive, complicated, and long, and drafted his announcement:

> WARNING! Any citizen who has taken fish from the street in the area of Rahsok Refrigeration is in immediate danger of poisoning. The fish has been treated with BARBITIDE. No fish other than that directly traceable to the Synthetic Markets should be eaten. WARN YOUR NEIGHBOURS!
>
> If fish has been eaten, go directly to the General Medical building (address followed). Symptoms of Barbitide poisoning: intense cramp about two hours after ingestion, followed by nausea, fever, and swollen lymphnodes. Death results in twenty minutes after onset of cramps under normal conditions. Foods with high calcium contents prolong spasms to a maximum hour and a half (foods such as MILK, GROUND EGG SHELL). General Medical has been alerted. There you will receive injections of *Calcium Silicate* and *Atropayic Acid* which can counteract the effects of the poison up until the last five or ten minutes.

Tomar personally sent the directive through Communications Centre 27B, marked urgent and emergency. Ten minutes later he received a re-video call from the Communications Engineer saying that 27B had been snarled all morning. In fact so had 26B, and 25B. Further, said the engineer, the only available Sectors open were 34A to 42A, none of which had access to complete city lines.

Tomar made a triplicate copy of the warning and sent it out, none the less, through Sectors 40A, 41A, and 42A. A half an hour later the secretary of the Communications Engineer called and said, 'Major Tomar, I'm sorry I just got back from my break and I didn't see your message until just now. Because of the tie-ups, we've received instructions only to let authorized persons have access to the available Sectors.'

'Well, who the hell is authorized,' Tomar shouted. 'If you don't put that through and quick, half the city may be dead by this evening.'

The secretary paused a minute. Then he said, 'I'm sorry, sir, but . . . well, look. I'll give it directly to the Communications Engineer when he gets back.'

'When is he getting back?' Tomar demanded.

'I . . . I don't know.'

'Who is authorized?'

'Only Council members, sir, and only those directly concerned with the war effort.'

'I see,' Tomar said, and switched off.

He had just dispatched seven copies of the announcement with an explanatory note to seven of the fourteen Council members in the ministry when the Communications Engineer called again. 'Major, what's all this about some spoiled fish?'

'Look, there are seven tons of the stuff all over the streets.'

'And poisoned, you say here?'

'Exactly. Will you please see that this message gets out over every available piece of City Wide Communication as fast as possible. This is really life and death.'

'We're just allowed to work on getting war messages through. But I guess this takes priority. Oh, that explains some of the messages we've been getting. I believe there's even one for you.'

'Well?' asked Tomar after a pause.

'I'm not allowed to deliver it, sir.'

'Why not?'

'You're not authorized, sir.'

'Look, damn it, get it right now and read it to me.'

'Well . . . er . . . it's right here, sir. It's from the chief of the City Dispersal Squad.'

The message was, in brief, that twenty three men, among them Captain Clemen, had been trampled to death by an estimated two and a half thousand hungry residents of the Devil's Pot, most of them immigrants from the mainland.

A ton and a half of fish was finally removed from the streets and disposed of. But five and a half tons had made its way through the city. The Communications Engineer also added that while they'd been talking, a memorandum had come through that Sectors 34A to 42A were now out of commission, but that the major should try 27B again; it might have cleared up.

The second shift of workers that day was arriving at the aquariums. In the huge pontooned building, vast rows of transparent plastic tubes, three feet in diameter, webbed back and forth among the tetron pumps. Vibrator nets cut the tubes into twenty-foot compartments. Cat-walks strung the six-storey structure, all flooded with deep red light that came from the phosphor-rods jutting from the pumps. Light towards the blue end of the spectrum disturbed the fish, which had to be visible at all times, to be moved, or to be checked for any sickness or deformity. In their transparent tubes, the fish floated in a state near suspended animation, vibrated gently, were kept at a constant 89 degrees, were fed, were fattened, were sorted according to age, size, and species; then slaughtered. The second shift of workers moved into the aquarium, relieving the first shift.

They had been on about two hours when a sweating man who was an assistant feeder reported to the infirmary, complaining of general grogginess. Heat prostration was a frequent complaint in the aquarium.

The doctor told him to lie down for a little while. Five minutes later he went into cramps. Perhaps the proper attention would have been paid to him had not a few minutes later a woman fallen from a catwalk crushing one of the plastic arteries and her skull, six stories below.

In the red light the workers gathered around her body at the end of a jagged tube. In the spreading puddle, fish, fat and ruby skinned, flapped their gills weakly.

The woman's co-workers said she had complained of not feeling well, when suddenly she went into convulsion while crossing one of the walks. By the time the doctor got back to the infirmary, the assistant feeder had developed a fever, and the nurse reported him violently nauseated. Then he died.

In the next two hours, of the five thousand two hundred and eighty people who worked at the aquariums, three hundred and eighty-seven were taken with cramps and died. The only exception was an oddball physical culture enthusiast who always drank two quarts of milk for lunch; he lasted long enough to be carried on to the shuttle and back to General Medical in Toron. He died six minutes after admittance, one hour and seventeen minutes after the onset of the cramps. That was the first case that General Medical actually received. It was not until the sixteenth case that they arrived at the final diagnosis of barbitide poisoning. Then someone remembered the inquiry from the military ministry that morning concerning the antidote.

'Somehow,' said Dr Wental, 'the stuff has got into some food or other. It may be all over the city.' Then he sat down at his desk and drafted a warning to the citizens of Toron containing a description of the effects of barbitide poisoning, antidote, and instructions to come to the General Medical building, along with a comment on high calcium foods. 'Send this to the Military Ministry and get it out over every available source of public communications, and quick,' he told his secretary.

When the Assistant Communications Engineer (the C.E. himself had gone off duty at three o'clock) received the message, he didn't even bother to see who it was from. He balled it up in disgust, flung it into a waste-paper basket and mumbled something about *unauthorized messages*. Had the janitor bothered to count, that evening, he would have discovered that there were now thirty-six copies of Major Tomar's directive in various waste-baskets around the ministry.

Only a fraction of the barbitide victims made it to General Medical, but the doctors were busy. There was just one extraordinary incident, and among the screams of cramped patients, it was not given much thought. Two men near the beginning of the rush of patients gained access to the special receiving room. They managed to get a look at all the women who arrived. One of the patients who was wheeled by them was a particularly striking girl of about sixteen with snow-white hair and a strong, lithe body, now knotted with cramps. Sweat beaded her forehead, her eyelids, and through her open collar you could see she wore a leather necklace of shells.

'That's her,' one of the men said. The other nodded, then went to the doctor who was administering the injections, and whispered to him.

'Of course not,' the doctor said indignantly in a clear voice. 'Patients need at least forty-eight hours rest and careful observation after injection of the antidotes. Their resistance is extremely low and complications . . .'

The men said something else to the doctor and showed him a set of credentials. The doctor stopped, then left the patient he was examining and went to the bed of the new girl. Quickly he gave her two injections, and made an entry below her name—Alter Ronid. Then he said to the men, 'I want you to know that I object to this completely and I will——'

'All right, Doctor,' the first man said. Then the second hoisted Alter from the cot and they carried her out of the hospital.

The Queen Mother had her separate receiving room. She sat on her high seat looking at photographs. In colour, two showed the chamber of the Crown Prince. In one picture the prince was seated on his bed in his pyjama pants with his heel against the sideboard; standing by the window was a white-haired girl with a leather necklace strung with shells. The next showed the Prince still sitting on the bed, this time with his hand on the newel dolphin. The girl was just turning towards the window.

The third picture, which from the masking, seemed to have been taken through a keyhole, showed what seemed an immense enlargement of human pupil: mistily discernible through the iris was the dottings and tiny pathways of a retina pattern. On the broad arm of the Queen Mother's throne was a folder marked: ALTER RONID.

In the folder were a birth certificate, a clear photograph of the same retina pattern, a contract in which travelling circus availed itself of the service of a group of child acrobats for the season, an elementary school diploma, copies of receipts covering a three-year period of gymnastic instruction, a copy of a medical bill for the correction of a sprained hip, and two change of address slips. Also there were several cross-reference slips to the files of Alline Ronid (mother, deceased) and Rara Ronid (maternal aunt, legal guardian).

The queen put the photographs on top of the folder and turned to the guards. There were four of them against the wall. She lifted the heavy sceptre and said, 'Bring her in.' She touched the two buns of white hair on the sides of her head, breathed deeply, and straightened in the chair, as doors opened at the other end of the room.

Two blocks had been set up in the middle of the room, about four feet high and a foot apart.

Alter stumbled once, but a guard caught her. They walked her between the blocks, which came to just below her shoulders, spread her arms over the surface and strapped them straight across the tops at biceps and wrist.

The queen smiled. 'That's only a precaution. We want to help you.' She came down the steps of the throne, the jewelled rod cradled in her elbow. 'We know something about you. We know that you know something which if you tell me, will make me feel a great deal better. I've been very upset, recently. Did you know that?'

Alter blinked and tried to get her balance. The blocks were just under the proper height by half an inch: she could neither stand completely nor could she sag.

'We know you're tired, and after your ordeal with barbitide—you don't feel well, do you?' asked the queen, coming closer.

Alter shook her head.

'Where did you take my son?' the queen asked.

Alter closed her eyes, then opened them wide and shook her head.

'We have proof,' said the queen, 'would you like to look?' She held up the photographs for Alter to see. 'My son took these pictures of the two of you together. They're very clear, don't you think?' She put the pictures back in the quilted pocket of her robe.

'Aren't you going to tell me?'

'I don't know anything,' Alter said.

'Come now. That room had as many cameras as a sturgeon has eggs. There are dozens of hidden switches. Somehow the alarms connected with them didn't go off, but the cameras still worked.'

Alter shook her head again.

'You don't have to be afraid,' said the queen. 'We know you're tired and want to get you back to the hospital as soon as possible. Now. What happened to my son, the prince?'

Silence.

'You're a very sweet girl. You're an acrobat too?'

Alter swallowed, and then coughed.

The queen gave a puzzled smile. 'Really, you don't have to be afraid to answer me. You are an acrobat, isn't that right?'

Alter nodded.

The queen reached out and touched the triplet leather necklace with their scattering of shells in her fingers. 'This is a beautiful piece of jewellery.' She lifted if from Alter's breast. 'An acrobat's body must be like a fine jewel, fine and strong, an exquisite thing. You must be very proud of it.' Again she paused and tilted her head. 'I'm only trying to put you at ease, dear, make conversation.' Smiling, she removed the necklace completely from around Alter's neck. 'This is exquisite too . . .'

Suddenly the necklace clattered to the ground, the shells making a tiny sound on the tiles.

Alter's eyes followed the necklace to the floor.

'Oh,' the queen said. 'I'm terribly sorry. It would be a shame to break something like this.' With one hand the queen drew back her robes until her shoe was revealed. Then she moved her foot forward until her raised toe was over the necklace. 'Will you tell me where my son is?'

There was seven, eight, ten seconds of silence. 'Very well,' the queen said, and brought her foot down. The sound of crushed shells was covered by Alter's scream. Because the Queen had brought down the sceptre, too, the full arc of its swing, on to Alter's strapped wrist. Then she brought it down again. The room was filled with the scream and the crack of the jewelled sceptre against the surface of the block. Then the queen smashed Alter's upturned elbow joint.

When there was something like silence, the queen said, 'Now, where is my son?'

Alter didn't say for a long while; then she couldn't say. What she told them didn't do much good when they had time to check it.

'To the penal mines?'

'What good could she do in a mine, now.' The queen turned back to her seat. 'Take her back to General Medical. We can always get her there if we need her. She's obviously working for something else. Perhaps the enemy.' Suddenly the Queen Mother waved the sceptre above her head. Drops splattered her hair. 'Ahhh! Get her out of here. Get her out!'

Unconscious, Alter was carried to the General Medical building wrapped in a grey blanket.

'Another fish poison case?' asked the clerk.

The man nodded. The doctor, who had been there when Alter was removed from the hospital, had been working steadily for six hours. When he unwrapped the blanket, he recognized the girl. When he unwrapped it further, breath rasped between his lips, and then hissed out again, 'Get this girl to emergency surgery,' he said to the nurse. 'Quickly!'

In the Devil's Pot, Tel had just got over a case of the runs which had kept him away from food all day. Feeling hungry, now, he was foraging in the cold storage cabinet of the Inn's kitchen. In the chest he found the remains of a baked fish, so he got a sharp knife from over the sink and cut a piece. Then the door opened and the barmaid came in. She was nearly seventy years old and wore a red scarf around her stringy neck. Tel had cut a slice of onion and was putting it on top of the fish when the barmaid ran forward and knocked the whole thing from his hand.

'Ouch,' Tel said, and jumped, though nothing had hurt him.

'Are you crazy?' the woman asked. 'You want to be carried out of here like the rest of them?'

Tel looked puzzled as Rara entered the kitchen. 'Good grief,' she declared. 'Where is everybody. I'm starved. I started selling that homebrew tonic of mine that I made up yesterday, and around noon, suddenly everybody was buying the stuff. They wanted something for cramps, and I guess my

Super Aqueous Tonic is as good as anything else. I couldn't even get back to eat. Is there some sort of epidemic? Say, that looks good,' and she went for the fish.

The old barmaid snatched up the dish and carried it to the garbage basket. 'It's poisoned, don't you understand?' She scraped the plate. 'It's got to be the fish that's causing it. Everybody who ate it has been carried off to General Medical with cramps. Lots of them died. The woman who lives across the street and me, we figured it out. We both brought it from the same woman this morning, and that's all it could be. I never eat the stuff myself, but I served it for lunch.'

'Well, I'm still hungry,' Tel said.

'Can we have some cheese and fruit?' asked Rara.

'I guess that's safe,' the woman said.

'Who was carried out?' Tel wanted to know, looking back in the cabinet.

'Oh, that's right, you've been upstairs sick all day.' And then she told him.

At about the same time, an observer in a scouting plane noticed a boat bearing military equipment some sixty miles away from any spot that could possibly be receiving such a shipment. In fact he had sent an order correcting a typographical error concerning . . . yes, it must be, that same boat. He'd sent it that morning through Communication Sector 27B. They were near the shore, one of the few spots where the great forest had crept to the water itself. A tiny port, used as an embarkation for the families of emigrants coming to join people in the city, was the only obvious civilization between the smoke green sea on one side and the deep green tree-tops on the other. The observer also noted that a small tetron tramp was about to dock. But that transport ship . . . He called up to the pilot and requested contact be made.

The pilot was shaking his head, groggily.

The co-pilot was leaning back in his seat, his mouth opened, his eyes closed. 'I don't feel too . . .' the pilot started, reached forward absently to crumple a sheet of tin-foil he had left on the instrument panel, in which, a few hours ago, had been a fillet sandwich that he and the co-pilot had shared between them.

Suddenly the pilot fell forward out of his chair, knocking

the control stick to the left. He clutched his stomach as the plane banked. In the observation pill, the observer was thrown from his chair and the microphone fell from his hand.

The co-pilot woke up, belched, grabbed for the stick, which was not in its usual place, missed. Forty-one seconds later, the plane crashed into a dock some thirty yards from the mooring tetron tramp.

CHAPTER VIII

THERE was roaring in the air. Let cried out and ran across the deck. Then shadow. Then water. He slipped on the boards as the rail swung by. Then thunder. Then screaming. Something was tearing in half.

Jon and Arkor got him out. They had to jump overboard with the unconscious prince, swim, climb, and carry. There were sirens at the dock when they laid him on the dried leaves of the forest clearing.

'We'll leave him here,' Arkor said.

'Here? Are you sure?' Jon asked.

'They will come for him. You must go on,' he said softly. 'We'll leave the prince now, and you can tell me of your plan.'

'My plan ...?' Jon said. They walked off through the trees.

Dried leaves tickled one cheek, a breeze cooled the other. Something touched him on the side, and he stretched his arms, scrunched his eyelids, then curled himself into the comfortable dark. He was napping in the little park behind the palace. He would go in for supper soon. The leaf smell was fresher than it had ever—— Something touched him on the side again.

He opened his eyes, and bit off a scream. Because he wasn't in the park, he wasn't going in to supper, and there was a strange giant standing over him.

The forest man touched the boy with his foot once more.

Suddenly the boy scrambled away, then stopped, crouched across the clearing. A breeze shook the leaves like admonishing fingers before he heard the giant speak. Then the giant was silent. Then the giant spoke again.

The word the boy heard in both sentences was, '... Quorl ...'

The third time he spoke, he merely pointed to himself and repeated, 'Quorl.'

Then he pointed to the boy and smiled.

The boy was silent.

Again the giant slapped his hand against his chest and said 'Quorl.' Again he extended his hand towards the boy, waiting for a name. It did not come. Finally he shrugged, and motioned for the boy to come.

The boy rose slowly, and followed. Soon they were walking briskly through the woods.

As they walked, the boy remembered: the shadow of the plane out of control above them, the plane striking the water, water becoming a mountain of water, like shattered glass rushing at them across the sea. And he remembered the fire. And something tearing——

Hadn't it started in his room at the palace, when he pressed the first of the concealed micro-switches with his heel? The cameras were probably working, but there had been no bells, no sirens, no rush of guards. It had tautened when he pushed the second switch in the jewelled dolphin on the bedpost. It nearly parted with metallic panic when he had to manoeuvre the girl into position for the retina photograph. *Nothing* had happened. He was taken away, and his mother stayed quietly in her room. What was supposed to happen was pulling farther and farther away from what was. How could anybody kidnap the prince?

His treatment by the boy who had told him about the sea and the girl who taught him to fall pulled it even tighter. *If* the prince *were* kidnapped, certainly his jailors should not tell him stories of beautiful seaside mornings and sunsets, nor teach him to do impossible things with his body.

He was sure that the girl had meant him to die when she had told him to leap from the roof. But he had to do what he was told. He always had. (He was following the giant through the dull leaves because the giant had told him to.) When he had leapt from the roof, then rolled over and sprung to his feet alive, the shock had turned the rack another notch and he could feel the threads parting.

If he had stayed there, talked more to the boy and girl, he could have loosened the traction, block the fabric of reality back into the shape of expectation. But then the man with the black hair and the scarred giant had come to take him away. He'd made one last volitional effort to bring 'is' and 'suppose' together. He'd told the man the story of the mine prisoners, the one cogent, connected thing he remembered from his immediate past, a real good 'suppose' story. But the man turned on him and said that 'suppose' wasn't 'suppose' at all, but 'is.' A thread snapped here, another there.

(Over the deck of the boat there was roaring in the air. He had cried out. Then shadow. Then water. His feet were slipping and the rail swung by. Then thunder. Then screaming, his screaming: *I can't die! I'm not supposed to die!* Something tore in half.)

The leaves were shaking, the whole earth trembled with his tired, unsteady legs. As they walked through the forest, the last filament went, like a thread of glass under a blow-torch. The last thing to flicker out, like the fading end of the white-hot strand, was the memory of someone, somewhere, entreating him not to forget something, not to forget it no matter what . . . but what it was, he wasn't sure.

Quorl, with the boy beside him, kept a straight path through the forest. The ground sloped up now. Boulders lipped with moss pushed out here and there. Once Quorl stopped short; his arm shot in front of the boy to keep him from going farther.

Yards before them the leaves parted, and two great women walked forward. Everything about them was identical, their blue black eyes, flat noses, cheek ridges. Twin sisters, the boy realized. Both women bore the triplex of scars down the left side of their faces. They paid no attention to either Quorl or the boy, but walked across into the trees again. The moment they were gone, Quorl started again.

They passed one or two others of the tall forest people, but as with Quorl there were no scars, and no shock at the encounter. Once they met a group of squat creatures with heavy brows, even shorter than the boy.

When the little ones first saw Quorl, some looked as though they were about to speak. But they hung back because the boy was there. Quorl grinned at them, and one waved back. Again there was none of the stiffness that had cooled the first encounter with the women.

Much later they turned on to a small cliff that looked across a valley to another mountain. Near a thick trunk was a pile of brush and twigs. The boy watched Quorl drop to his knees and move the brush away. The boy crouched to see better.

The big brown fingers tipped with bronze nails gently revealed a cage made of sticks tied together with dried vines. Something squeaked in the cage, and the boy jumped.

Quorl in a single motion got the trap door opened and his hand inside. The protracted squeak suddenly turned into a scream. Then there was silence. Quorl removed a furry, weasel-type animal and handed it to the boy.

The pelt was feather soft, still warm. The head hung crazily to the side where the neck had been broken. The boy looked at the giant's hands again.

Crazy veins roped straight ligaments. The hair on the joints grew up to the edge of the furrowed knuckles. Now the fingers were pulling the brush back over the trap. The giant and the boy crossed the clearing and Quorl uncovered a second trap. When the hand went into the trap and the knot of muscle jumped on the brown forearm (Squeeeeee*raaaa*!) the boy looked away, out across the valley.

The sky was smoke grey to the horizon where a streak of orange marked the sunset. The copper disc hung low in the purple gap of the mountains. A fan of lavender drifted above the orange, and then white, faint green . . . The grey wasn't really grey, it was blue-grey. He began to count colours, and found twelve (not a thousand). The last one was a pale gold that tipped the edges of the few low clouds clustering near the sun.

A touch on the shoulder made the boy turn back. Quorl handed him the second animal, and they went back into the woods. Later, they built a small fire and skinned and quartered the animals on the scimitar-like blade that Quorl wore. They sat in the diminishing shell of light with the meat on forked sticks, turning it over the flame. The boy watched the maroon fibres go shiny with juice, then darken, crispen, and brown. When the meat was done, Quorl took a piece of folded skin from his pouch and shook some white powder on to it. Then he passed the leather envelope to the boy.

The boy poured a scattering of white powder into his palm, put his tongue to it. Salt

As they had nearly finished eating, the forest cooled and stilled. Fire made the leaves around them flickering shingles on the darkness. Quorl was cleaning the last, tiny bone with his teeth when there was a sound. They turned.

Another branch broke to their left. 'Tloto,' Quorl called harshly.

It moved closer, the boy could hear it moving. Then he saw the tall shadow at the edge of the light.

With disgust (but without fear, the boy saw) Quorl picked up a stick and flung it. The shadow dodged and made a small mewing sound.

'Go away, Tloto,' Quorl said. 'Go away.'

Only Tloto came forward instead.

Perhaps it had been born of human parents, but to call it human now ... It was bone naked, hairless, shell white. It had no eyes, no ears, only a lipless mouth and nostril flaps. It sniffed towards the fire.

Now the boy saw that both the feet were clubbed. Only two fingers on each hand were neither misshapen nor paralysed. It reached for Quorl's pile of bones, making the mewing sound.

With a sudden sweep of his hand, Quorl knocked the paraplegic claw away. Tloto backed away, turned to the boy, and came forward, nostril slits widening and contracting.

The boy had eaten all he could and had a quarter of his meat still left. It's only a head taller than I am, he thought. If it's from this race of giants, perhaps it's still a child. Maybe it's my age. He stared at the blank face. It doesn't know what's going on, the boy thought. It doesn't know what's supposed to be happening.

Perhaps it was just the sound of the word in his head that triggered the panic (or was it something that caught in his chest?). Anyway, he took the unfinished meat and held it towards Tloto.

The claw jumped forward, grabbed, snatched back. The boy tried to make his mouth go into a smile. But Tloto couldn't see, so it didn't matter. He turned back to the fire, and when he looked up again, Tloto was gone.

As Quorl began to kick dirt on to the coals, he spoke to the boy, about Tloto and a few philosophical concepts. The boy listened carefully, and understood at least that Tloto was not worth his concern. But speech had become indifferent to the prince. There was nothing in this world he was familiar enough with to comment on. He was not homesick for the statues and rotating windows of the palace.

Jerk someone from one location; fling him in another. The elements in one location define the other. But sometimes the shock of transition is so great that the definition does not begin. Let had abandoned words. He listened, carefully, to the giant, but not for meaning. He examined the words for tone and voice quality, the same way he searched the giant's face, the same way he watched the huge body, shoulder, arm, or knee, shifting as he talked. He was trying to pick out, in the firelight, the hints of emotion he could relate to his isolate fourteen years. He found a few. Then a few more.

They lay down beside the cyst of embers, a glowing scab on the dark, and slept.

When the giant's hand shook his shoulder, it was still dark. The boy did not jump this time. He blinked against the night and pulled his feet under him. It had grown colder and the wind brushed his neck and fingered his hair. Then a high sound cut above the trees and fell away. Quorl took the boy's arm and they started through the dark.

Light filtered from the left. Was it morning? No. The boy saw it was the rising moon. The light became white, then silver. They reached a cliff at last, beyond which was the dark sea. Broken rock spilled to ledges below. Fifty feet down (still a hundred feet above the water) was a table of rock. The moon was high enough to light the entire lithic table as well as the temple at its edge.

In front of the temple stood a tall man in black robes who blew on a curved shell. The wail sliced high over the sea and the forest. People were gathering around the table. Some came in couples, some with children, but most were single men and women. There were only tall people there.

The boy started to go down, but Quorl held him back. They waited. From sounds about them, the boy realized there were others watching from the heights also. A few of the neanderthals observed from the rocks, but there were none below. On the water waves began to glitter with broken images of the moon. The sky was speckled with stars.

Now a group of people were led from the temple on to the platform. Most of them were tall children. There was an old man whose beard twitched in the breeze. There was a stately

stopped. It had too much to do with the recognition of luck, and the impossibility of the whole situation. The boy laughed.

He startled himself with the sound, and after a few seconds stopped. Then he turned. Quorl stood behind him.

(Squeeeee ... Squeeeee ... *raaaaaaa*! Then a gurgle, then nothing.)

Quorl was smiling too, a puzzled smile.

'Why did you laugh?'

The boy turned back now. Tloto and the pig were gone.

Quorl walked the boy back to their camp. As they were nearing the stream Quorl saw the boy's footprints in the soft earth and frowned. 'To leave your footprints in wet earth is dangerous. The vicious animals come to drink and they will smell you, and they will follow you, to eat. Suppose that pig had been chasing you, instead of running into the pool? What then? If you must leave your footprints, leave them in dry dust. Better not to leave them at all.'

The boy listened, and remembered. But that night, he saved a large piece of meat from his food. When Tloto came into the circle of firelight he gave it to him.

Quorl gave a shrug of frustration and flung a pebble at the retreating shadow. 'He is useless,' Quorl said. 'Don't waste your food on him. Oh, well, I suppose we're all histosents.'

The boy felt something start up inside again, a question. But he would not let it move his tongue. So he laughed. Quorl looked puzzled. The boy laughed again. Then Quorl laughed too. 'You will learn. You will learn at last.' Then the giant became serious. 'You know, that is the first histosentient sound I've heard you make since you came here.'

The boy frowned, and the giant repeated the sentence. The boy's face showed which word puzzled him.

The giant thought a minute: 'You, me, even Tloto, are histosents. The trees, the rocks, the animals, they are not. But your laugh, that is a histosentient sound. The word means historically sentient; and that means knowing where you've been, where you are, and where you're going. It also means appreciating it.'

The boy looked away through the trees where Tloto had gone.

'You're still wondering about Tloto? I could tell you how

living here on the mainland so close to the radiation forced some of our tribes millennia ahead on the human evolutionary chain, while other tribes were forced back, both to a point where they could maintain some sort of genetic stability. But Tloto—there are very few like Tloto today—is just a random throw-away nowhere on the human spectrum. When I see the neanderthal children plague him, I make them stop. For the same reasons, I would like you to stop giving him your affection. It may hurt him as much as a stone or flung twigs——' He stopped. 'But you don't want these words now.'

The boy thought about it. Histosent? From somewhere before the change, another word came to him, pulled up by the association of rhyme, then by the definitions. For a while he tried to put one before the other, to understand which was necessarily first. The process of definition was beginning. At last he slept.

He laughed a lot during the days now. Survival had come as close to routine as it could here in the forest. He watched Quorl when they met other forest people. Often there were words, often with the friendliness and good feeling the boy could relax around. But if there was someone with scars, Quorl would freeze.

Once the boy wandered to the temple on the platform of rock. There were carvings on the stone. The sun was high. The carvings represented creatures that may have been human, but were deformed, distorted, some nearly unrecognizable. When he looked up, he saw that the priest had come from the temple and was watching him. The priest watched until the boy went back up into the trees.

Now he tried to climb the mountain. That was hard because spring streams had swelled and flooded the rocks, and often footholds gave from under him. At last he stopped before a jutting fragment that stuck out over the rocks and trees. He wiped the sweat from under his chin, stepped out on the stone, and looked down the side of the mountain. He was very high. He stood with hand against the trunk of a near rotten tree, breathing deep and squinting at the sky. (Three or four times Quorl and he had taken hunting trips: one had taken them to the edge of a deserted meadow across which was a crazily sagging farmhouse. There were no people there. Another had taken them to the edge of the jungle, beyond which the ground was grey and broken, and row after row of unsteady shacks sat among clumps of slithering ferns. Many of the forest people living there had scars and spent more time in larger groups.) The boy wondered if he could see to the deserted meadow from here, or to the rows of prison shacks. A river, a snake of light, coiled through the valley towards the sea. The sky was very blue.

He heard it first, and then he felt it. He scrambled back towards firmer ground but not fast enough. The rock tilted, tore loose, and he was falling. (It pierced through his memory like a fire-blade up through canvas: '. . . knees up, chin down, and roll quick,' the girl had said a long time ago.) It was perhaps twenty feet to the next level. Tree branches broke his fall and he hit the ground spinning, and rolled. Something else, the rock or a rotten log, hit the ground a moment later where he had been. He uncurled too soon, reaching out to catch hold of the mountain as it tore by him. Then he hit something hard; something hit him back, and he sailed off into darkness in a web of pain.

Much later he shook his head, opened his eyes, then chomped his jaws. But the pain was in his leg, so chomping didn't help. He moved his face across crumbling dirt. The whole left side of his body ached, the ache that comes when muscles are tensed to exhaustion but will not relax.

He tried to crawl forward, and went flat on to the earth, biting up dirt. He nearly tore his leg off.

He had to be still, calm, find out exactly what was wrong. He couldn't tear himself to pieces like the wildcat who had got caught in the spring trap and who had bled to death after gnawing off both hind legs.

But each movement he made, each thought was a blurred green haze of pain. He raised himself up and looked back. Then he lay down again and closed his eyes. A log the thickness of his body lay across his left leg. Once he tried to push it away but only bruised his palm against the bark, and at last went unconscious with the effort.

When he woke up, the pain was very far away. The air was darkening. No, he wasn't quite awake. He was dreaming about something, something soft, a little garden, with shadows blowing in at the edge of his vision, swift and cool, a little garden behind the——

Suddenly, very suddenly, it struck him what was happening, the slowing down of thoughts, his breathing, maybe even his heart. Then he was struggling again, struggling hard enough that had he still the strength, he would have torn himself from his leg, thinking while he struggled, of the wildcat, not caring if he were less than the beast, only fighting to pull himself away from the pain, realizing that blood had begun to seep from beneath the log again, just a trickle . . .

Then the shadows overtook him, the dreams, and forgetfulness gauzed his eyes.

Tloto had to drag Quorl halfway up the mountain before the giant got the idea. When he did, he began to run. Quorl found the boy just before sunset. He was breathing in short gasps, fists clenched, eyes closed. The blood on the dirt had dried black.

The big, brown hands caught the log, locked, and started to shift it; the boy let out a high sound from between his teeth.

The hands, with their ropes and ridges, strained the log upward; the sound became a howl.

The giant's feet braced against the dirt, slid in the dirt, and the hands that had snapped tiny necks and bound sticks together with gut string, pulled; the howl turned into a scream. He screamed again. Then again.

The log, coming loose, tore away nearly a foot of flesh from the boy's leg. Quorl went over and picked him up.

This is the best dream, the boy thought, from that dark place he had retreated to behind the pain, because Quorl is here. The hands were lifting him now, he was held close, warm, somehow safe. His cheek was against the hard shoulder muscle, and he could smell Quorl too. So he stopped screaming and turned his head a little to make the pain go away. But it wouldn't go. It wouldn't. Then the boy cried.

The first tears through all that pain came salty in his eyes, and he cried until he went to sleep.

Quorl had medicine for him the next day ('From the priest,' he said) which helped the pain and made the healing start. Quorl also made the boy a pair of wooden crutches. Although muscle and ligament had been bruised and crushed, and the skin torn away, no bone had been broken.

That evening there was a drizzle and they ate under the canopy. Tloto did not come, and this time it was Quorl who saved the extra meat and kept looking off into the wet trees. Quorl had told the boy how Tloto had led him; when they finished eating, Quorl took the meat and ducked into the drizzle.

The boy lay down to sleep. He thought the meat was a reward for Tloto. Only Quorl had seemed that night more than usually full of gravity. The last thing he wondered before sleep filled his eyes and ears was how blind, deaf Tloto had known where he was anyway.

When he woke it had stopped raining. The air was damp and chilly. Quorl had not come back.

The sound of the blown shell came again. The boy sat up and flinched at the twinge in his leg. To his left the moon flickered through the trees. The sound came a third time, distant, clear and marine. The boy reached for his crutches and hoisted himself to his feet. He waited till the count of ten, hoping that Quorl might suddenly return and go with him.

At last he took a deep breath and started haltingly forward. The moonlight made the last hundred yards easy. He reached a vantage where he could look down through the wet leaves on to the stone.

The sky was sheeted with mist; the moon was an indistinct pearl in the haze. The sea was misty. People were already gathered at the edge. The boy looked at the priest, then looked among the circle of people. One of them was Quorl!

He leaned forward as far as he could. The priest sounded the shell again and the prisoners came out of the temple: first three boys, then an older girl, then a man. The next one ... Tloto! Marble white under the blurred moon. Its clubbed feet shuffled on the rock. Its blind head ducked right and left with bewilderment.

As the priest raised the three pronged knife, the boy's hands went tight around the crutches. The priest passed from one prisoner to the next. Tloto cringed, and the boy sucked in a breath as the knife went down; the boy felt his own flesh part under the blades. Then the murmur died, the prisoners were unbound, and the people filed from the rock back into the forest.

The boy waited to see which way Quorl went before he started through the bushes as fast as his crutches would allow. There were many people on the paths that came from the temple rock. There was Quorl!

When he caught up, the giant saw him and slowed. Quorl kept his yellow eyes averted, though. Finally Quorl said, 'You don't understand. I had to catch him. I had to give him to be marked. But you don't understand.' The boy hardly looked at all where they were going. He stared up at the giant.

'You don't understand,' Quorl said again. Then he looked at the boy and was quiet for a while. 'No, you don't,' he repeated. 'Come.' They turned off the main path now, going slower. 'It's a ... custom. An important custom. Yes, I know it hurt him. I know he was afraid. But it had to be. Tloto is one of those who know the thoughts of others.' Quorl was silent for a moment. 'Let me try to tell you why I had to hurt your friend. Yes, I know he is your friend, now. But once I said that Tloto was histosentient. I was wrong. Tloto is more. He and the others are marked, somehow these people know things. That was how Tloto survived. That's how he knew where you were, when you were hurt. He knew inside your head. Many are born like that, more of them each year, among the tall people. As soon as we find out, we mark them. Many try to hide it. Some succeed for a long time. Can you understand? Do you? When Tloto showed me where you were, he knew that I would know, that he would be caught and marked. Do you understand?' Again he paused and looked at the boy. The eyes still showed puzzled hurt. 'You want to know why. I ... we ... Long ago we killed them when we found out. We have a greater spectrum of love than you. As well as a greater spectrum of fear. We don't any more. The mark reminds them that they are different, and yet the same as we. Perhaps it is wrong. It doesn't hurt that much, and it heals. Anyway, we don't kill them any more. We know they're important ...' Suddenly, having gone all through it with the boy, it seemed twisted to Quorl, incorrect. Then he gave the boy what the boy had been sent to the forest to receive, what the duchess had found and knew was necessary. 'I was wrong,' Quorl said. 'I'm sorry. I will speak to the priest tomorrow.'

They walked until the dawn lightened the sky behind the trees. Once Quorl looked and said, 'I want to show you something. We are very near, and the weather is right.'

They walked a few minutes more till Quorl pointed to a wall of leaves, and said, 'Go through there.'

As they pressed through the dripping foliage, bright light burnished their faces. They were standing on a small cliff that looked down the mountain. Fog the colour of pale gold, the same gold the boy had seen in the sunset, rolled across the entire sky. The centre flamed with the misty sun, and way below them through the fog were shattered traces of water, the colour of flame on copper foil, without edge or definition.

'That's a lake that lies between this mountain and the next,' Quorl said, pointing to the water. 'Do you see what they are making there? No, there is too much fog. But look.'

'I thought ...' The boy's tongue, loosed by laughter and crying, at last rose roughly against speech. '... I thought it was the sea.'

Quorl smiled.

Beside them appeared the crouching figure of Tloto. Drops from the wet leaves burned on his neck and back, over the drying blood. He turned his blank face left and right in the golden light and, with all his knowing, could communicate no awe.

CHAPTER IX

CLEA KOSHAR had been installed in her government office for three days. The notebook in which she had been doing her own work on inverse sub-trigonometric functions had been put away in her desk for exactly three minutes when she made the first discovery that gave her a permanent place in the history of the Toromon's Wars as its first military hero. Suddenly she pounded her fist on the computer keys, flung her pencil across the room, muttered, 'What the hell is this,' and dialled the military ministry.

It took ten minutes to get Tomar. His red hair focused on the visaphone. He recognized her and smiled. 'Hi.'

'Hi yourself,' she said. 'I just got out those figures you people sent us about the data from the radiation barrier, and those old readings from the time Telphar was destroyed. Tomar, I didn't even have to feed them to the computer. I just looked at them. That radiation was artificially created! Its increment is completely steady. At least on the second derivative. Its build-up pattern is such that there couldn't be more than two simple generators, or one complexed one . . .'

'Slow down,' Tomar said. 'What do you mean, generators?'

'The radiation barrier, or at least most of it, is artificially maintained. And there are not more than two generators, and possibly one, maintaining it.'

'How do you generate radiation?' Tomar asked.

'I don't know,' Clea said. 'But somebody has been doing it.'

'I don't want to knock your genius, but how come nobody else figured it out?'

'I just guess nobody thought it was a possibility, or thought of gratuitously taking the second derivative, or bothered to look at them before they fed them into the computers. In twenty minutes I can figure out the location for you.'

'You do that,' he said, 'and I'll get the information to whoever it's supposed to get to. You know this is the first piece of information of importance that we've got from this whole battery of slide-rule slippers up there. I should have figured it would probably have come from you. Thanks, if we can use it.'

She blew him a kiss as his face winked out. Then she got out her notebook again. Ten minutes later the visaphone crackled at her. She turned to it and tried to get the operator, but was not able to. She reached into her desk and got out a small pocket tool kit and was about to attack the housing of the frequency-filterer when the crackling increased and she heard a voice. She put the screwdriver down and put the instrument back on the desk. A face flickered on to the screen and then flickered off. The face had dark hair, seemed perhaps familiar. But it was gone before she was sure she had made it out.

Crossed signals from another line, she figured. Maybe a short in the dialling mechanism. She glanced down at her notebook and took up her pencil when the picture flashed on to the screen again. This time it was clear and there was no static. The familiarity, she did not realize, was the familiarity of her own face on a man.

'Hello,' he said. 'Hello. Hello, Clea?'

'Who is this?' she asked.

'Clea, this is Jon.'

She sat very still, trying to pull two halves of something back together (as in a forest, a prince had felt the same things tear). Clea succeeded. 'You're supposed to be ... dead. I mean I thought you were. Where are you, Jon?'

'Clea,' he said. 'Clea ... I have to talk to you.'

There was a five second silence.

'Jon, Jon, how are you?'

'Fine,' he said. 'I really am. I'm not in prison any more. I've been out a long time, and I've done a lot of things. But Clea, I need your help.'

'Of course,' she said. 'Tell me how? What do you want me to do?'

'Do you want to know where I am?' he said. 'What I've been doing? I'm in Telphar, and I'm trying to stop the war.'

'In Telphar?'

'There's something behind that radiation barrier. I'm about to break through and see what can be done. But I need some help at home. I've been monitoring phone-calls in Toron. There's an awful lot of equipment here that's more or less mine if I can figure out how to use it. And I've got a friend here who knows more in that line than I gave him credit for. I've overheard some closed circuit conference calls, and I'm talking to you by the same method. I know you've got the ear of Major Tomar and I know he's one of the few trustworthy people in that whole military hodge-podge. Clea, there is something hostile to Toromon beyond the Dead City, but a war is not the answer. The thing that's making the war is the unrest in Toromon. And the war isn't going to remedy that. The emigration situation, the food situation, the excess man-power, the deflation: that's what's causing your war. If that can be stopped, then the thing here can be dealt with quickly and peacefully. There in Toron you don't even know what the enemy is. They wouldn't let you know even if they knew themselves.'

'Do you know?' Clea asked.

Jon paused. Then he said, 'Whatever it is, it's people with something wrong among them. And war won't exorcize it.'

'Can you?' Clea asked.

Jon paused again. 'Yes. I can't tell you how; but let's say what's troubling them is a lot simpler than what's troubling us in Toromon.'

'Jon,' Clea asked suddenly, 'what's it like in Telphar? You know I'll help you if I can, but tell me.'

The face on the visaphone was still. Then it drew a deep breath. 'Clea, it's like an open-air tomb. The city is very unlike Toron. It was planned, all the streets are regular, there's no Devil's Pot, nor could there ever be one. Roadways wind above ground among the taller buildings. I'm in the Palace of the Stars right now. It was a magnificent building.' The face looked right and left. 'It still is. They had amazing laboratories, lots of equipment, silvered meeting halls under ceilings that reproduced the stars. The electric plants still work. Most houses you can walk right in and turn on a light switch. Half the plumbing in the city is out, though. But everything in the palace still works. It must have been a beautiful place to live in. When they were evacuating during the radiation rise, very little marauding took place. . . .'

'The radiation . . .' began Clea.

Jon laughed. 'Oh, that doesn't bother us. It's too complicated to explain now, but it doesn't.'

'That's not what I meant,' Clea said. 'I figured if you were alive, then it obviously wasn't bothering you. But Jon, and this isn't government propaganda, because I made the discovery myself: whatever is beyond caused the radiation rise that destroyed Telphar. Somewhere near Telphar is a projector that caused the rise, and it's still functioning. This hasn't been released to the public yet, but if you want to stop your war, you'll never do it if the government can correctly blame the destruction of Telphar on the enemy. That's all they need.'

'Clea, I haven't finished telling you about Telphar. I told you that the electricity still worked. Well, most houses you go into, you turn on the light and find a couple of sixty-year-old corpses on the floor. On the roads you can find a wreck every hundred feet or so. There're almost ten thousand bodies in the Stadium of the Stars. It isn't very pretty. Arkor and I are the only two humans who have any idea of what the destruction of Telphar really amounted to. And we still believe we're in the right.'

'Jon, I can't hold back information . . .'

'No, no,' Jon said. 'I wouldn't ask you to. Besides, I heard your last phone call. So it's already out. I want you to do two things for me. One has to do with Dad. The other is to deliver a message. I overheard a conference call between Prime Minister Chargill and some of the members of the council. They're about to ask Dad for a huge sum of money to finance the first aggressive drive in this war effort. Try and convince him that it'll do more harm than good. Look, Clea, you've got a mathematical mind. Show him how this whole thing works. He doesn't mean to be, but he's almost as much responsible for this thing as any one individual could be. See if he can keep production from flooding the city. And for Toromon's sake, keep an eye, a close eye on his supervisors. They're going to tilt the island into the sea with all their cross-purpose intrigues. All I can do is start you on the right track, Clea, and you'll have to take it from there. Now for the message. The one circuit I can't break in on is the Royal Palace system. I can just overhear. Somehow I've got to get a message to the Duchess of Petra. Tell her to get to Telphar in the next forty-eight hours by way of the transit-ribbon. Tell her there are two kids she owes a favour to. And tell her she owes four or five favours to the girl. She'll be able to find out who they are!'

Clea was scribbling. 'Does the transit-ribbon still work?' she asked.

'It was working when I escaped from prison,' Jon said. 'I don't see why it should have stopped now.'

'You used it?' Clea said. 'That means you *were* in Toron!'

'That's right. And I was at your party too.'

'Then it was . . .' She stopped. Then laughed, 'I'm so glad, Jon. I'm so glad it was you after all.'

'Come on, Sis, tell me about yourself,' Jon said. 'What's been happening in the real world? I've been away from it a long time. Here in Telphar I don't feel much closer. Right now I'm walking around in my birthday suit. On our way here we got into a shadowy situation and I had to abandon my clothes to keep from getting caught. I'll explain that later, too. But what about you?'

'Oh, there's nothing to tell. But to you I guess there is. I graduated, with honours. I've grown up. I'm engaged, to Tomar. Did you know that? Dad approves, and we're to be married as soon as the war's over. I'm working on a project, to define the inverse sub-trigonometric functions. Those are about the most important things in my life right now. I'm supposed to be working on the war effort, but except for this afternoon, I haven't done much.'

'Fine,' Jon said. 'That's about the right proportions.'

'Now what about you? And the clothes?' She grinned into the visaphone, and he grinned back.

'Well—no, you wouldn't believe it. At least not if I told it that way. Arkor, the friend whose with me, is one of the forest people. He left the forest to spend some time in Toron, which is where I met him. Apparently he managed to accumulate an amazing store of information, about all sorts of thing, electronics, languages, even music. You'd think he could read minds. And here we are, through the forest, across the prison mines, and in Telphar.'

'Jon, what were the mines like? It always made me wonder how Dad could use tetron when he knew that you were being whipped to get it.'

'You and I'll get drunk some evening and I'll tell you what it was like,' Jon said. 'But not until. When you're trying to convince Dad, bring that up about me and the mines.'

'Don't worry,' she said. 'I will.'

'Anyway,' Jon went on, 'we had to get through the forest without being seen and with all those leaves it was pretty dark. Arkor could get through because he was a forest man and nobody would stop him. But because they'd have seen me, I had to go most of the way naked as a jaybird.'

Clea frowned. 'I don't understand. Are you sure you're all right?'

Jon laughed. 'Of course I'm all right. I can't really explain to you just yet. I'm just so happy to see you again, to be able to talk to you. Sis, I've wanted to be free for so long, to see you and Dad again, and . . . there's nothing wrong with me except the sniffles.'

It welled up in her like a wave and the tears flooded her lids, and then one overflowed and ran down the right side of her nose. 'You see what you're doing,' she said. And they laughed once more. 'To see you again, Jon, is so . . . *fine*.'

'I love you, Sis,' Jon said. 'Thanks, and so long for a little while.'

'I'll get your message out. So long.' The phone blinked dark and she sat there wondering if perhaps the tension wasn't too much. But it wasn't, and she had messages to deliver.

CHAPTER X

DURING the next couple of hours, two people died, miles apart:

'Don't be silly,' Rara was saying in the Inn at the Devil's Pot. 'I'm a perfectly good nurse. Do you want to see my licence?'

White-haired Geryn sat straight in his chair by the window. Blue seeped like liquid across the glass. 'Why did I do it?' he said. 'It was wrong. I . . . I love my country.'

Rara pulled the blanket from the back of the chair and tucked it around the trembling shoulders. 'What are you talking about?' she said, but the birthmark over her face was deep purple with worry.

He shook the blanket off and flung his hand across the table where the old news directive lay:

PRINCE KIDNAPPED!
KING DECLARES WAR!

The trembling in Geryn's shoulders became violent.

'Sit back,' said Rara.

Geryn stood up.

'Sit down,' Rara repeated. 'Sit down. You're not well. Now sit down!'

Geryn lowered himself stiffly to the chair. He turned to Rara. 'Did I start a war? I tried to stop it. That was all I wanted. Would it have happened if . . .'

'Sit back,' Rara said. 'If you're going to talk to somebody, talk to me. I can answer you. Geryn, you didn't start the war.'

Geryn suddenly rose once more, staggered forward, slammed his hands on the table, and began to cough.

'For pity's sake,' Rara cried, trying to move the old man back into his chair, 'will you sit down and relax! You're not well! You're not well at all!' From above the house came the faint beat of helicopter blades.

Geryn returned to his chair. Suddenly he leaned back, head back. His adam's apple shot high in his neck. Rara jumped forward and tried to bring his head up. 'Dear heavens,' she breathed. 'Stop that. Now stop it, or you'll hurt yourself.'

Geryn's head came up again. 'A war!' he said. 'They made me start the . . .'

'No one made you do anything,' Rara said. 'And you didn't start the war.'

'Are you sure?' he asked. 'No. You can't be sure. No one can. Nobody . . .'

'Will you please try to relax,' Rara repeated, tucking at the blanket.

Geryn relaxed. It went all through his body, starting at his hands. The shoulders dropped a little, his head fell forward, the wall of muscle quivering across his stomach loosened, his back bent. That frail fist of muscle that had jarred life through his tautened body for seventy years, shaking inside his chest, it too relaxed. Then it stopped. Geryn slid on to the floor.

The shifting body pulled Rara down with him. Unaware that he was dead, she was trying to get him back into the chair when the helicopter blades got very loud.

She looked up to see the window darken with a metal shadow. 'Good lord!' she breathed. Then the glass shattered.

She screamed, careened around the table, and fled through the door, slamming it behind her.

Over the flexible metal ramp that hooked on to the window-sill two men entered the room. Fire-blades poised, they walked to the crumpled body, lifted it between them, and carried it back to the window. Their arm bands showed the royal insignia of the palace guards.

Tel was running down the street because someone was following him. He ducked into a side alley and skittered down a flight of stone steps. Somewhere overhead he heard a helicopter.

His heart was pounding like explosions in his chest, like the sea, like his ocean. Once he had looked through a six-inch crevice between glassy water and the top of a normally submerged cave and seen wet, orange star-fish clutching the wet stone, their reflections quivering with his breath. Now he was trapped in the cave of the city, the tide of fear rising to lock him in. Footsteps passed above him.

Nearby was a ladder that led to a trap door which would put him in the hall of a tenement. He climbed it, emerged, and then turned up the regular steps to the roof. He walked across the tar-paper surface to the edge, leaned over, and peered down into the alley. Two men, who may have been the people following him, approached from opposite ends of the alley. The sky was deepening towards evening and it was cool. The two men met, and then one pointed to the roof.

'Damn,' Tel muttered, ducked backward, and bit his tongue with surprise. He opened his mouth and breathed hard, holding the side of his jaw. The helicopter was coming closer.

Then something very light fell over him. He forgot his bitten tongue and struck out with his hands. But it was strong. It jerked at his feet and he fell forward. It was not until it lifted him from the roof that he realized he was caught in a net. He was being drawn up towards the sound of the whirling helicopter blades.

When the order came through, he didn't even have time to say goodbye to Clea. Two other mathematicians in the corps had shown appropriate awe at Clea's discovery and proceeded to locate the generator. The next-in-charge General, working on a strategy Tomar did not quite understand, decided that now was the time for an active strike. 'Besides,' he added, 'if we don't give them some combat soon, we'll lose (and I mean lose in the sense of "misplace") this war.'

The shadow of the control tower fell through the windshield and slipped across Tomar's face. He pulled up his goggles and sighed. Active combat. What the hell would they be combating? The disorder, the disorganization was beginning to strike him as farcical. Though after the poisoned fish, the farcical was no longer funny.

The buildings on the airfield fell back and down. The transit-ribbon gleamed below him as the six other planes in the formation pulled up behind. A moment later the island was a comb of darkness on the crest of the evening sea.

Clouds banded the deep blue horizon. There were three stars out, the same stars that he had looked at as a boy when his sun-up to sun-down work day ended. Between hunger and hunger there had been some times when you could look at the stars and wonder, as there were now between times of work and work.

The controls were set. There was nothing to do but wait for land to rise up over the edge of the world.

As the end of the metal ribbon was a transparent crystal sphere, fifteen feet in diameter which hovered above the receiving stage. A dozen small tetron-units sat around the room. By one ornate window a bank of forty-nine scarlet-knobbed switches pointed to off. Two men stood on the metal catwalk that ran above the receiving stage, one young man with black hair, the other a dark giant with a triplex of scars down the left side of his face.

In another room, corpses, stiff and shrivelled, sat on green velvet.

It was evening in the solarium on top of the General Medical building. The patients were about to be herded from their deck chairs and game tables under the glass roof back to their wards, when a woman screamed. Then there was the sound of breaking glass. More people screamed.

Alter heard the roar of helicopter blades. People were running around her. Suddenly the crowd of bathrobed patients broke from in front of her. She touched the cast that covered her left shoulder and arm. People cried out. Then she saw.

The glass dome shattered at the edge, and the flexible metal ramp ran a dark ribbon from the 'copter to the edge of the solarium. The men that marched across had the insignia of the royal guards. She clamped her jaws together and moved behind a nurse. She had a cast on one arm and shoulder. The men marched in, fire-blades high, among the overturned deck-chairs. There were three stars visible, she noted irrelevantly, through the bubble dome.

Good lord! They were coming towards her!

The moment the guards recognized her, she realized the only way to get out was to cross the suddenly immense metal floor to the stairwell. She ducked her head, broke from the crowd of patients, and ran, wondering why she had been fool enough to wait this long. The guard tackled her and she heard screams again.

She fell to the hard floor and felt pain explode along the inside of her cast. The guard tried to lift her, and with her good arm she struck at his face. Then she held her palm straight and brought the edge down on the side of his neck.

He staggered and she felt herself slip to the floor. Then someone grabbed a handful of her hair and her head was yanked back. At first she closed her eyes. Then she had to open them. Night was moving above her through the dome of the solarium. Then the cracked edge of the glass passed over her, and it was colder, and the blur and roar of helicopter blades was above.

'On course?'

'Dead on course,' said Tomar back into the microphone. Below, the rim of land slipped back under them. The moon bleached the edges of the vari-coloured darknesses beneath them, then went down.

'What are you thinking about Major?' came the voice from the speaker again.

'Not thinking about anything,' Tomar said. 'Just about waiting. It's funny, that's most of what you do in this army, wait. You wait to go out and fight. And once you go out, then you start waiting to turn around and come back.'

'Wonder what it'll be like.'

'A few bombs over that generator, then we'll have had active combat and everyone will be happy.'

A laugh, mechanical, through the speaker. 'Suppose they "active" back?'

'If they cripple our planes like they've done before, we'll make it to the island again.'

'I had to leave a hot cup of coffee back at the hangar, Major. I wish it was light so we could see what we were doing.'

'Stop bitching.'

'Hey, Major.'

'What?'

'I've invented a new kind of dice.'

'You would.'

'What you do is take fifteen centi-unit pieces and arrange them in a four-by-four square with one corner missing. Then you take a sixteenth coin and shoot it within forty-five degrees either way of the diagonal into the missing corner. It works out that no matter how you do it, if all the coins in the square are touching, two coins will fly off among the seven on the far edge. Each of those has a number and the two numbers that fly off are like the two numbers that come up on the dice. It's better than regular dice because the chances are up on some combinations. And there's a certain amount of skill involved too. The guys call it Randomax. That's for *random numbers* and *matrix*.'

'I'll play you a game some day,' Tomar said. 'You know, if you used a smaller coin than a centi-unit for the one you fire into the missing corner, say a deci-unit, the chances that it would hit both corner coins would go up, that is your randomness.'

'Really?'

'Sure,' Tomar said. 'My girlfriend's a mathematician, and she was telling me all about probability a few weeks ago. I bet she'd be interested in the game.'

'You know what, Major?'

'What?'

'I think you're the best officer in the damned army.'

Such was the conversation before the first battle of the war.

Such was the conversation Jon Koshar monitored in the laboratory of the Palace of the Stars in Telphar. 'Oh damn,' he said. 'Come on, Arkor. We'd better get going. If the duchess doesn't get here with Geryn soon . . . Well let's not think about it.' He scribbled a note, set it in front of one visaphone and dialled the number of another that was on a stand in front of the receiving platform of the transit-ribbon.

'There,' he said. 'That's got instructions to follow us as soon as she gets here. And she better not miss it.' They went down the metal steps to a double doorway that opened on to a road.

Two mechanical vehicles stood there, both with pre-controls set for similar destinations. Jon and Arkor climbed into one, pushed the ignition button, and the car shot forward along the elevated roadway. White mercury lights flooded the strip as it wound through the dead city.

The road dipped and houses got lower on each side. The horizon glowed purple and above that, yellow clouds dropped into late evening. There was a sound of planes overhead.

As the car halted at the barren limits of the last suburb of

Telphar, a sudden white streak speared from the horizon. 'Uh-oh,' said Jon. 'That's what I was afraid of.'

Something caught fire in the air, twisted wildly through the sky, and then began to circle down, flaming.

'Major! Major! What happened to D-42?'

'Something got him. Pull over. Pull over everybody!'

'We can't spot it. Where'd it come from?'

'All right, everybody. Break formation. Break formation I said!'

'Major, I'm going to drop a bomb. Maybe we can see where that came from in the light. I thought you said "cripple".'

'Never mind what I said. Drop it.'

'Major Tomar. This is B-6. We've been . . .' (unintelligible static).

Someone else gives a slow whistle through the microphone.

'Break formation, I said. Damn it, break formation.'

Over the plane a sheet of red fire flapped up, and Jon and Arkor pulled back from the railing that edged the road. Another white streak left the horizon, and for a moment, in the glare, their shadows on the pavement were double.

The sound of the explosion reached them a moment later, as broken rocks leapt into silhouette like a rotted jaw gnawing red fire.

Another sound behind them made them turn. The lighted roadways of Telphar looped the city towers like strands of pearls on skeleton necks. A car came towards them.

Another wailing missile took the sky, and a moment later a screaming plane tore down the night. It turned as its flaming motors caught once more and careened above their heads so close that they ducked as it disappeared among the city towers: an explosion, then falling fire drooled the side of a building. 'I hope that's nowhere near the Palace of the Stars,' a voice said next to Jon. 'We'll have a great time getting back if it is.'

Jon whirled. The duchess had got out of the car. The red light flared a moment in her hair, died.

'No. That was nowhere near it,' Jon said. 'Am I glad to see you.'

Tel and Alter, still in her cast and hospital robe, followed the Duchess out of the car.

'Well,' he said, 'you brought the kids too.'

'It was better than leaving them back in Toron. Jon, Geryn is dead. I asked what to do, but I didn't get any answer. So we lugged his body along just in case.'

'But what do we do now?'

From the railing Arkor laughed.

'It's not funny,' Jon said.

The Duchess looked overhead as another missile exploded. 'I had hoped this wouldn't happen. This means a war, Jon. A real one, and unstoppable.'

Another plane crashed, too close this time, and they ducked behind the cars. 'Gee,' breathed Alter, which was the only thing anybody said.

Then Arkor called, 'Come on.'

'Where to?' asked Jon.

'Follow me,' Arkor repeated. 'Everyone.'

'What about Geryn?'

'Leave that corpse behind,' Arkor told them. 'He can't help.'

'Look, do you know what's going on?' Jon demanded.

'More than Geryn ever did,' the giant returned. 'Now let's get going.' They sprinted out along the road, then ducked under the railing and made their way across the rocky waste.

'Where are we going?' Tel whispered.

Jon called back over his shoulder. 'That's a very good question.'

The plane got tipped, and for seven seconds, while the needles swung, Tomar didn't know where he was going, east or west, up or down. When the needles stopped, he saw that it hadn't been any of the first three. Suddenly the green detector light flashed in the half darkness of the cabin. The generator! The radiation generator was right below him. Then he was blinded by a white flare outside the windshield. Oh, God damn!

He felt the jerk and the air suddenly rushed in cold behind him. There was a hell of a lot of noise and the needle quietly swung . . . He was going down!

Land lit up outside the front window; a small blockhouse set in the wrecked earth. There were three whirling antenna on the roof. That must be it! That must!

It happened in his arms and fingers, not in his head. Because suddenly he pushed the stick forward, and the plane, what was left of it, turned over and he was staring straight down, straight ahead, straight below him. And coming closer.

It must have been his arms, because his head was thinking wildly about a time when a girl with pearls in her black hair had asked him what he had wanted, and he had said, 'Nothing . . . nothing . . .' and realized he had been wrong because suddenly he wanted very much to . . . (The blockhouse came up and hit him) . . . Nothing.

Tel and the Duchess screamed. The rest just drew breath quickly and staggered back. 'He's in there,' Arkor said. 'That's where your *Lord of the Flames* is.'

The landscape glowed with the encroaching light of the plummeting torch. They saw the blockhouse now with its whirling antenna on the roof. Before the plane hit, a darkness opened in the side of the blockhouse and three figures emerged and sprinted among the rocks.

'The middle one,' said Arkor. 'That's him, face him, concentrate on him . . .'

'What do you——' Tel began.

'You ride along with me, kids,' Arkor said, only he didn't move. Two of the figures had fallen now, but the middle one was running towards them. The torch hit, and his shadow was suddenly flung across the broken earth to meet them . . .

CHAPTER XI

THE green of beetles' wings . . . the red of polished carbuncle . . . a web of silver fire, and through the drifting blue smoke Jon hurled across the sky.

Then blackness, intense and cold. The horizon was jagged, maybe ten feet away. He reached a metal claw out and crawled expertly (not clumsily. Expertly!) across a crevice, but slowly, very slowly. The sky was sharp with stars, though the sun was dim to his light sensitive rind. Like a sliding cyst, he edged over the chunk of rock that spun somewhere between Mars and Jupiter. Now he reached out with his mind to touch a second creature on another rock. *Petra,* he called. *Where is he?*

His orbit should take him between the three of us in a minute and a half.

Fine.

Jon, who is the third one? I still don't understand.

Another mind joined them. *You don't understand yet? I was the third, I always was. I was the one who directed Geryn to make the plan in the first place for the kidnapping. What made you think that he was in contact with the triple beings?*

I don't know, Jon said. *Some misunderstanding.*

There was the laughter of children. Then Tel said, *Hey, everybody, we're with Arkor.*

Shhh, said Alter. *The misunderstanding was my fault, Jon. I told you that Geryn talked to himself, and that made you think it was him.*

Get ready, Petra said. *Here he comes.*

Jon saw, or rather sensed the approach of another spinning asteroid, whirling towards them through the blackness. But it was inhabited. Yes! *The Lord of the Flames!* The three of them threw their thoughts across the rush of space.

There. . . .

Roaring steam swirled above him. He raised his eye-stalks another twenty feet and looked towards the top of the cataract some four miles up. Then he lowered his syphon into the edge of the pool of pale methane and drank deeply. Far away in a beryl sky, three suns rushed madly about one another and gave a little heat to this farthest of their six planets.

Now Jon flapped his slitherers down and began to glide away from the methane-falls and up the nearly vertical mountain slope. Someone was coming towards him with shiny red eye-stalks waving in greeting. 'Greeting to the new colony,' the eye-stalks signalled.

Jon started to signal back. But suddenly he recognized (a feeling way at the back of his slitherers) who this was. *The Lord of the Flame*——! He leapt forward and flung the double flaps of leathery flesh across his opponent and began to scramble back up the rocks. Jon had him tight but was wondering where the hell were . . .

Suddenly his eye-stalk caught the great form that he knew must be Arkor coming down over the rocks (with Alter and Tel. Yes, definitely: because the creature suddenly did a flying leap between two crags that could have only been under the girl-acrobat's control), and a moment later he saw Petra had arrived at the other shore of the methane river. Using her slitherers for paddles, she struck out across the foaming current.

Think at him, concentrate . . . *There*——

The air was clear. The desert was still, and he lay in the warm sand, under the light of the crescent moon. He was growing, adding facets; he let the light seep into his transparent body, decreasing his polarization cross-frequencies. The light was beautiful, too beautiful—dangerous! He began to tingle, to glow red. His base burned with white heat and another layer of sand beneath him melted, fused, ran, and became part of his crystalline body.

He stepped up his polarization, his body clouded, and cooled once more. Music sang through him, and his huge upper facet reflected the stars.

Once more he lessened his polarization, and the light crept farther and farther into his being. His temperature rose. Vibrations suffused his transparency and the pulsing music made the three dust particles that had settled on his co-axial face, seven hundred and thirty years ago, dance. He felt their reflection deep in his prismatic centre.

Then it came. He tried to stop it. But the polarizaton index suddenly broke down completely. For one terrific moment of ecstasy the light of the moons and the stars poured completely through him. Chord after chord rang out in the desert night. Back and forth along his axis, colliding, shaking his substance, jarring him, pummelling him, came the vibrations. For one instant he was completely transparent. The next, he was white hot. Before he could melt, he felt the crack start.

It shot the length of his forty-two mile, super-heated body, He was in two pieces! The radio disturbances alone covered a third of a galaxy. Twelve pieces fell away. The chord crashed again, and the crack whipped back and forth, vivisecting him. Already he was nearly thirty-six thousand individual crystals, all of which had to grow again, thirty-six thousand minds. He was no more.

Jon! the voice sang through crumbled silicate.

Right over here, Petra, he hummed back. (The note was a perfect quarter-tone below A-flat. Perfect! Not clumsy! Perfect!)

Where's Arkor?

To their left the triple notes of an E flat minor chord (Arkor, Tel, and Alter) sounded: *Right here.*

Just as they had made contact, before the music stopped (and once more their thoughts would become separate, individual, and they would lose awareness of each other and of the hundreds of other crystals that lay over the desert, under the clear perpetual night)—just then a strident dissonance pierced among them.

There, sang Petra.

There, hummed Jon.

There, came the triad in E flat minor. *The Lord of the Flame.* They concentrated, tuned, their thoughts against the dissonance.

Jon rolled over and pushed the silk from his white shoulders and stretched. Through the blue pillars, the evening sky was yellow. Music, very light and fast, was coming from below the balcony. A voice sounded beside him: 'Your Majesty, Your Majesty! You shouldn't be resting now. They're waiting for you downstairs. Tltltrlte will be furious if you're late.'

'What do I care,' Jon responded. 'Where's my robe?'

The serving maid hastened away and returned with a sheer, shimmering robe, netted through with threads of royal black. The drape covered Jon's shoulders, draped across his breasts, and fell to his thighs.

'My mirror,' said Jon.

The serving maid brought the mirror and Jon looked. Long sloped eyes sat wide spaced in the ivory face over high cheekbones. Full breasts pushed tautly beneath the translucent material, and the slender waist spread to sensual, generous hips. Jon almost whistled at his reflection.

The maid slipped on the tiny clear plastic slippers over his feet, and Jon rose and walked towards the stairs. In the lobby, the throng hissed appreciatively as he descended. On one column hung a bird-cage in which a three-headed cockatoo was singing to beat the band. Which was difficult to do: the band was fourteen copper headed drums. (Fourteen was the royal number.)

Across the lobby wind instruments wailed, and Jon paused on the stairs. 'Don't worry,' the maid said, 'I'm right behind you.'

Jon felt the terror rise. *Hey,* he called out mentally, *is that you, Petra?*

Like I said, right behind you.

Incidentally, how did I come up with this body?

I don't know, dear, but you look devastating.

Thanks, he said, projecting a mental sneer. *Where's Arkor and Company?*

The music had stopped. There was only the sound of the three-headed bird.

There they are.

The winds screeched again, and at the entrance to the lobby, the people fell away from the door. There was Tltltrlte. He was tall, and dark, in a cloak in which there were many more black threads than in Jon's. He unsheathed a sword, and began to come forward. 'Your reign is through, daughter of the Sun,' he announced. 'It is time for a new cycle.'

'Very well,' said Jon.

As Tltltrlte advanced, the throng that crowded the lobby clapped their hands in terror and moved back farther. Jon stood very straight.

As Tltltrlte came forward, his shoulders narrowed. He pushed back the hood of his cloak and a mass of ebony hair cascaded down his shoulders. With each step, his hips broadened and his waist narrowed. A very definite bulge of mammary glands pushed up beneath his black tunic. As Tltltrlte reached the bottom of the steps, she raised her sword.

Think at him, came Arkor from the bird-cage.

Think at him, came from Petra.

Jon saw the blade flash forward and then felt it slide into his abdomen. *At her,* he corrected.

At her, they answered.

As Jon toppled down the steps, dying, he asked, *What the hell is this anyway?*

We're inhabiting a very advanced species of moss, Arkor explained, with the calmness that only a telepath can muster in certain confusing situations. *Each individual starts off male but eventually changes to female at the desired time.*

Moss? asked Jon as he hit his head on the bottom step and died.

There....

The wave came again and thundered on the beach. He staggered backwards, just as the froth spumed up on the sand. The sky was blue-black. He raised his fingers to his lips (seven long tines webbed together) and whined into the night. He lifted his transparent eyelids from his huge, luminous eyes to see if there wasn't some faint trace of the boat. Spray fell on them, stung the rims, and he snapped all three lids over them, one after another. He whined again, and once more the wave grew before him.

He opened the two opaque lids, and this time thought he saw them far off through the spray. The pentagonal sail billowed, blue, wet, and full. It dipped, rose. He pulled back his transparent eyelid again, this time when the wave was down, and thought he saw figures on the fibrous hammock of the boat. On the blue sail was the white circle of a Master Fisherman. His parent was a Master Fisherman. Yes, it was his parent coming to get him.

Another billow exploded and he crouched in the froth, digging his hind feet deep into the pebbly beach.

The cross-hatch of planking scudded on to the shore, and

they swarmed off. One wore a chain around his neck with the Master Fisherman's seal. Another carried a seven-pronged fork. The two others were just boat-hands and wore identifying black belts of kelpod shells.

'My offspring,' said the one with the seal. 'My fins have smarted for you. I thought we would never swim together again.' He reached down and lifted Jon into his arms. Jon put his head against his parent's chest and watched water beading down the pentagonal scales.

'I was frightened,' Jon said.

His parent laughed. 'I was frightened too. Why did you swim out so far?'

'I wanted to see the island. But when I was swimming, I saw . . .'

'What?'

Jon closed his eyelids.

His parent smiled again. 'You're sleepy. Come.' Now Jon felt himself carried to the water and into the waves. The spray fell warm on his face now. Unafraid, he relaxed his gill slits while water fell across him. They climbed on to the boat.

Wind caught the sail, and the open-work planking listed into the sea. Long clouds swung rapidly across the twin moons like the tines of the fishing forks with which the fishermen saluted the sacred phosphors when they returned from their hunting. He dreamed of this, a little, in the swell and drop. His parents had tied him to the boat, and so he floated at the end of a few feet of slack. Water rolled down his shoulders, slipped beneath his limp dorsal fin, and tickled. Then he dreamed of something else, the thing he had seen, glowing first beneath the water, then rising. . . . He whined, suddenly, and shook his head.

He heard the others on the boat, their webbed feet slipping on the wet planks. He opened his eyes and looked up. The two boat-hands were holding on to stays and pointing off into the water. Now his parent had come up to them, holding a fishing spear, and they were joined by the Second Fisherman.

Jon scrambled from the water on to the plank. His parent put an arm around him and drew him closer. (*Here he comes,* Arkor said.) His other hand went to the seal of authority around his neck, as though it gave him some sort of protection.

'There it is,' Jon cried. 'That's what I saw! That's why I was afraid to swim back.' (*There it is,* Jon said.)

A phosphorescent disc was shimmering under the surface of the water. The Second Fisherman raised his spear higher. 'What is it?' he asked. (*What is it this time?* Petra wanted to know.)

Indistinct, yet nearly the size of the ship, it hovered almost three breast strokes from them, glowing beneath the surface.

(*I'll have a look,* said Petra.) The Second Fisherman suddenly dived forward and disappeared. Still holding to the frame of the boat, Jon and his parent went under the water where they could see better.

One of Jon's eyelids, the transparent one, was actually an envelope of tissue which he could flood with vitreous solution when he was submerged to form a correcting lens over his pupil.

Through the water he saw the Second Fisherman bubbling towards the immense, translucent halfsphere that dangled ahead of them. The Second Fisherman stopped with an underwater double-reverse and hovered near the thing. (*It's a great jelly-fish,* Petra told them.) 'Can't figure out what it is,' the Second Fisherman signalled back. Then he extended his fork and jabbed at the membrane. The seven tines went in, came out.

The jelly-fish moved, fast.

The tentacles hanging from the bottom of the bag ravelled upward like threads. The body bloated and surged sideways. Two tentacles wrapped around the Second Fisherman as he tried to swim away. (*Ow!* said Petra. *These things hurt!*)

Jon's parent was on deck, shouting orders to the boat-hands. The ship swung towards the thing which had now surfaced.

(*Look, let's finish this thing up for good. Concentrate.* That was Arkor. *There. . . .*)

(From beneath the water they felt Petra reach her mind into the pulsing mass: *There. . . .*)

(As the tentacles encased her and she jammed the spear home again and again through the leaking membrane, she felt Jon's mind join in: *There. . . .*)

The boat rammed into the side of the jelly-fish, the planks tearing away the membrane and the thick, stinging insides fountaining over them. Now it nearly turned over, and tentacles flapped from the water in wet, fleshy ropes. The Second Fisherman was caught in one of the snarls.

Their green faces were lighted from beneath by the milky glow.

Suddenly it tore away from the planks, going down beneath the water. The Second Fisherman's head bobbed to the surface, shook the green fin that crested his skull, and laughed.

3 to 6, 3to 6, (Jon's frequency oscillated from 3 to 6 as he drifted through clouds of super-heated gas) 3 to 6, 3 to 6.

7 to 10! (Someone was coming:) 7 to 10, 7 to 10, (It was getting closer: suddenly:) 10 to 16! (Then:) 3 to 6, 7 to 10, 3 to 6, 7 to 10, (they had passed through each other. *Hi*, Petra said. *Have you any idea where we are?*).

(*The temperature is somewhere near three quarters of a million degrees. Any idea?*)

9 to 27, 9 to 27, 9 to 27 (came puttering along and passed through both Jon and Petra:) 12 to 35, 10 to 37, (and then, again) 3 to 6, 7 to 10, 9 to 27, 9 to 27, 9 to 27, (*We are half-way between the surface and the centre of star not unlike our sun,* said Arkor. *Note all the strange elements around*) 9 to 27, 9 to 27, 9 to 27.

7 to 10, 7 to 10, 7 to 10 (*They keep on turning into one another,* Petra said) 7 to 10, 7 to 10, 7 to 10.

3 to 6, 3 to 6, 3 to 6, (*At this temperature you would too if you were atomic,* Jon told her) 3 to 6, 3 to 6, 3 to 6.

9 to 27, 9 to 27, 9 to 27 (*Where's The Lord of the Flame?* Arkor wanted to know)

π to e, π to 2e, 2π to 4e, 4π to 8e, 8π to 16e, 16π to 32e

(*Speak of the* . . . Jon started. *Hey, we've got to do something about that. Not only is it transcendental, it's increasing so fast he'll eventually shake this star apart*) 3 to 6, 3 to 6, 3 to 6.

(*So that's what causes novas,* said Petra) 7 to 10, 7 to 10, 7 to 10.

(At the next oscillation, Arkor, acting as a side-coefficient, passed through the intruder) $36^2\pi$ to 64e (Arkor got out before the second extremity was reached. The wave cycle shuttered, having been reversed end on end). 642π to 32e (It tried to right itself and couldn't because Jon spun through the lower end divisibly) 642π to 16/9e (then Arkor jumped in, tail first it recovered and it resolved into:) 642π to 4/3e, 642π to 4/3e, 642π to 4/3e (it quivered, its range no longer geometric).

(*Watch this,* said Petra. *About face ...* She gave it a sort of nudge, so that when it whirled to catch her she was gone, and it was going the other way:)

$4/3\pi$ to 640e, $4/3\pi$ to 642e, $4/3\pi$ to 642e.

(*I hope no one ever does that to me,* said Petra. *Look, the poor thing is contracting.*)

$4/3\pi$ to 640e, $4/3\pi$ to 622, $4/3\pi$ to 560, $4/3\pi$ to 499.

(Somehow the *e* component slipped through 125. Jon moved in like a shower of anti-theta-masons and extracted a painless cube root so fast that the intruder oscillated on it three times before it knew what had happened:)

$4/3\pi$ to 5^3e, $4/3\pi$ to 5^3e, $4/3\pi$ to 5^3e (Under high gravity—two to three million times that of earth, such as inside a star—in such warped space there is a subtle difference between 5^3 and 125, though they represent the same number. It's like the notes E♯ and F, which are technically the same, but are distinguished when played by a violinist with a fine ear. When the root came loose, therefore, the variation threw the wavelength all off balance:) $4/3\pi$ to 5e, $4/3\pi$ to 5e, $4/3\pi$ to 5e. . . .

(*All right, everybody, concentrate*——)

For one moment, the intruding oscillation turned, ducked, tried to escape, and couldn't. It contracted into a small ball with a volume of $4/3\pi e^3$, and disappeared.

(*There. . . .*)

Jon Koshar shook his head, staggered forward, and went down on his knees in white sand. He blinked. He looked up. There were two shadows in front of him. Then he saw the city.

It was Telphar, stuck on a desert, under a double sun.

As he stood up, something caught in the corner of his eye.

His eyes moved, and he saw a woman about twenty feet away. Her red hair fell straight to her shoulders in the ozone heavy heat. He blinked as she approached. She wore a straight skirt and had a notebook under her arm. 'Petra?' he said, frowning. It was Petra, but Petra transformed.

'Jon,' she answered. 'What happened to you?'

He looked down at himself. He was wearing a dirty uniform. A prison uniform. His prison uniform!

'Arkor,' said Petra, suddenly. (Her voice was higher, less sure.)

They turned. Arkor stood in the sand, his bare feet wide over the white hillocks. The triple scars down his face welled bright blood in the hot light.

They came together now. 'What's going on?' Jon asked.

Arkor shrugged.

'What about the kids?' asked Petra.

'They're still right here,' Arkor said, pointing to his head and grinning. Then his finger touched the opened scars. When he drew it away, he saw the blood and frowned. Then he looked at the City. The sun caught on the towers and slipped like liquid along the looping highways. 'Hey,' Jon said to Petra. (Now he realized; it was Petra with fifteen years lopped off.) 'What's the notebook?'

She looked down at it, surprised to find it in her hands. Then she looked at her dress. Suddenly she laughed, and began to flip through the pages of the notebook. 'This is the book in which I finished my article on shelter architecture among the forest people. In fact this is what I was wearing the day I finished my article.'

'And you?' Jon asked Arkor.

Arkor looked at the blood on his fingers. 'My . . . mark is bleeding, like the night the priest put it there.' He paused. 'That was the night that I really became myself. That was the time that I realized how the world was, the confusion, the stupidity, the fear. It was the night I decided to leave the forest.' Now he looked up at Jon. 'That was the uniform you were wearing when you escaped from prison.'

'Yes,' said Jon. 'I guess it was what I was wearing when I became me, too. That was the time when freedom seemed most bright.' He paused. 'I was going to find it no matter what. Only I felt I'd got sidetracked. I wonder whether I have.'

'Have you?' asked Petra. She glanced at the city. 'I guess when I finished that essay, that's when I really became myself, too. I remember I went through a whole series of revelations about myself, about society, and about how I felt about society, about being an aristocrat, even, what it meant and what it *didn't* mean. And I suppose that's why I'm here now.' She looked at the City again. 'There he is,' she nodded. '*The Lord of the Flames.*'

'That's right,' said Jon.

They started down the sand. They reached the lake quicker than they thought, for the horizon was very close. The double shadows, one a bit lighter than the other, lay like two inked brush strokes over the page of the desert. 'But how come we're in our own bodies?' the Duchess asked, as they reached the shadow of the first building. 'Shouldn't we be inhabiting the forms of . . .' Suddenly there was a sound, the shadow moved. Jon looked up at the ribbon above them and cried out.

As the metal tore away, they jumped back, and a moment later a length of curtain-wall splashed into the sand where they had stood. They were still for a handful of breathes.

'You're damn right he's there,' Jon said. 'Come on.'

They started again. Petra shook white grains from her notebook cover and they walked. A road seeped from under the desert, now, and began to rise towards Telphar. They mounted it and followed it towards the looming city. Before them the towers were dark streaks on the rich blue sky.

'You know, Petra's question is a good one,' Arkor said a few minutes later.

'Yeah,' said Jon. 'I've been thinking about it too. We seem to be in our own bodies, only they're different. Different as our bodies were at the most important moments of our lives. Maybe, somehow, we've come to a planet in some corner of the universe, where three beings almost identical to us, only different in that way, are doing, for some reason we'll never know, almost exactly what we're doing now.'

'It's possible,' Arkor said. 'With all the myriad possibilities of worlds, it's conceivable that one might be like that, or like this.'

'Even to the point of talking about talking about it?' asked Petra. She answered herself. 'Yes, I guess it could. But saying all this for reasons we don't understand, and saying, "Saying all this for reasons we don't understand . . ." ' She shuddered. 'It's not supposed to be that way. It gives me the creeps.'

There was another sound, and they froze. It was the low sound of some structure tumbling, but they could see nothing.

Another fifty feet, when the road had risen ten feet off the ground and the first tower was beside them, they heard a cracking noise again. The road swayed beneath them. 'Watch!' Arkor cried.

Then the road fell. They screamed out, they scrambled; there was cracked concrete around them. They had fallen. Above them was a jagged width of blue sky between the remaining edges of the road.

'My foot's caught!' Petra cried.

Arkor was beside her, tugging on the concrete slab that held her.

'Hold on a second,' Jon said. He grabbed a free metal strut that still vibrated in the rubble, and jammed it between the slab and the beam it lay on. Using the wreck of an I-beam for a fulcrum, he pried it up. 'There, slip your foot out.'

Petra rolled away. 'Is the bone broken?' he asked. 'I got a friend of mine out of a mine accident that way, once.' He let the slab fall again. (And for a moment he stopped, thinking, I knew what to do. I wasn't clumsy, I knew. . . .)

Petra rubbed her ankle. 'No,' she said. 'I just got my ankle wedged in that crevice, and the concrete fell on top.' She stood, now, picking up the notebook. 'Ow,' she cried. 'That hurts.'

Arkor held her arm. 'Can you walk?'

'With difficulty,' Petra said, taking another step and clamping her teeth.

'Alter says to stand on your other foot and shake your injured one around to get the circulation back,' Arkor told her.

Petra gritted teeth, shook, and stepped again. 'A little better,' she said. 'I'm scared. This really hurts. This may be a body that looks like mine, but it hurts, and it hurts like mine.' Suddenly she looked off into the city. 'Oh, hell,' she said. 'He's in there. Let's go.'

They went forward again, this time under the road. The sidewalks, deserted and greying, slipped past. They passed a shopping section; teeth of broken glass gaped in the frames of store windows. Above, two roads veered and crossed, making a black, extended swastika on white clouds.

Then a sudden rumbling.

Silence.

They stopped.

Now a crash, thunderous and protracted. An odour of dust reached them. 'He's there,' Arkor said.

'Yes,' said Jon.

'I can . . .'

Then the city exploded. There was one instant of real agony for Jon as the pavement beneath his feet shot up at him, and he reached his mind out as a shard of concrete knocked in his face (all the time crying, No, no, I've just become Jon Koshar, I'm not supposed to . . . as a lost prince had cried out a universe away) and at the same time. *There. . . .*

Petra got a chance to see the face of the building beside them rip before the air blast tore the notebook from her hands, and at the same time she welled her thoughts from behind the bone confines of her skull. *There. . . .*

And Arkor's thoughts (he never saw the explosion because he blinked just then) tore out through his eyelids as fragmented steel tore into them. *There. . . .*

It was cold, it was black. For a moment they saw with a spectrum that reached from the star-wide waves of novas to the micro-micron skittering of nutrinos. And it was black, and total cold. A rarefied breeze of ionized hydrogen (approximately two particles per cubic kilometre) floated over half a light year. Once, a herd of pale photons dashed through them from a deflected glare from some dying sun a trillion aeons past. Then silence, save for the hum of one lone galaxy, turning eternities away. They hovered, frozen, staring into nothing, above, below, behind, contemplating what they had seen.

Then, the green of beetles' wings, and they flailed into the flood of sensation from the blackness, whirled into red flame the colour of polished carbuncle, smoothly through the nerves and into the brain; then, before the blue smoke, burning through the lightning-seared axion of their corporate organisms, they were snared within the heat and electric imminency of a web of silver fire.

CHAPTER XII

In the laboratory tower of Toron, the crystal above the receiving stage brightened. Shimmering on the platform, the figures solidified. Then Tel slipped beneath the rail on the stage and dropped to the floor (Alter still wore the hospital robe and the cast) while Alter, Arkor, Jon, and Petra used the metal stairway to descend. A battery of relays snapped somewhere and the scarlet heads of forty-nine switches by the window snapped to off. The globe faded.

'A bit more explanation,' Petra was saying. 'Hey kids, keep quiet.'

'Well, as far as *The Lord of the Flames* goes, on earth anyway, it's more or less trivial and irrelevant,' said Arkor. 'You're still right. This war is in Toromon.'

'My curiosity is still going,' Jon said. 'Give.'

'I gathered while I scanned the minds of those two who came out of the generator building with *The Lord of the Flames* (I should say the host of *The Lord of the Flames*), they were forest people. *The Lord of the Flames* got into one of them just about when he was at age four. Then he gave the boy about six hundred years worth of technical information. So he began building all sorts of goodies, forcing others to help him, using some equipment from Telphar. That's how the generators and the anti-aircraft guns got constructed.'

'Our war is still going on,' Jon said.

'Well, *The Lord of the Flames* is no longer with us,' said Petra. 'We've chased it to the other end of the universe. Now that we've removed what external reason there was for the war, we've got to think about the internal ones.'

'What are you going to do immediately about the kids?' Jon asked.

'I think the best thing for them to do is to go off to my estate for a little while,' Petra said. 'We'll all go.'

'It's on an island, isn't it?' Tel asked.

'That's right,' Petra said.

'Alter, now I can teach you how to fish, and we'll be right

by the sea.'

'What about Uske?' Arkor asked. 'You can either walk into his room and interrupt an obscene dream he's having, and present your case and be arrested for treason, or you can leave well enough alone at this point and wait till the opportunity comes to do something constructive.'

Suddenly Jon grinned. 'Hey, you say he's asleep?' He turned and bounded for the door.

'What are you going to do?' Petra called.

Jon looked at Arkor. 'Read my mind,' he said.

Then Arkor laughed.

In his bedroom, Uske rolled over through a silken rustle, opened one eye, and thought he heard a sound.

'Hey, stupid,' someone whispered.

Uske reached out of bed and pressed the night light. A dim orange glow did not quite fill half the room.

'Now don't get panicky,' continued the voice. 'You're dreaming.'

'Huh?' Uske leaned on one elbow, blinked, and scratched his head.

A shadow approached him, then stopped, naked, faceless, transparent, half in and half out of the light. 'See,' came the voice. 'A figment of your imagination.'

'Oh, I remember you,' Uske said.

'Fine,' said the shadow. 'Do you know what I've been doing since the last time you saw me?'

'I couldn't be less interested,' Uske said, turning over and looking the other way.

'I've been trying to stop the war. Do you believe me?'

'Look, figment, it's three o'clock in the morning. I'll believe it, but what's it to you?'

'I think I've succeeded.'

'I'll give you two minutes before I pinch myself and wake up.' Uske rolled back over.

'Look, what do you think is behind the radiation barrier?'

'I think very little about it, figgy. It doesn't have very much to do with me.'

'It's something that can't possibly harm us, especially now that its . . . its generators have been knocked out. All of its artillery it got from a source that is now defunct. Look, Uske,

I'm your guilty conscience. Wouldn't it be fun to really be king for a while and stop the war. You declared war. Now declare peace. Then start examining the country and doing something about it.'

'Mother would never hear of it. Neither would Chargill. Besides, all this information is only a dream.'

'Exactly, Uske. You're dreaming about what you really want. How does this sound: make a deal with me as your guilty conscience and representative of yourself; if this dream turns out to be correct, then you declare peace. It's the only logical thing. Come on, stand up for yourself, be a king. You'll go down in history as having started a war. Wouldn't you like to go down as having stopped it too?'

'You don't understand . . .'

'Yes, I know. A war is a bigger thing than the desires of one man, even if he is a king. But if you get things started on the right foot, you'll have history on your side.'

'Your two minutes have been cut down to one; and it's up.'

'I'm going; I'm going. But think about it, Uske.'

Uske switched off the light and the ghost went out. A few minutes later Jon crawled through the laboratory tower window, buttoning his shirt. Arkor shook his head, smiling. 'Well,' he said. 'Good try. I hope it does some good.'

In the morning, Rara got up early to sweep off the front steps of the inn (windows boarded, kitchen raided, but deserted now save her; and she had the key): she swept to the left, looked right, then swept to the right, looked left, and said, 'Dear Lord, you can't stay there like that. Come on, now. Get on, be on your way.'

'. . . Oh, I'm sorry.'

'For pity's sake, woman, you can't go around cluttering up the steps of an honest woman's boarding house. We're re-opening this week, soon as we get the broken windows repaired. Vandals didn't leave a one, after the old owner died. Just got my licence, so it's all legal. Soon as we get the windows, so you move on.'

'I just got here, this morning. . . . They didn't tell us where to go, they just turned us off the ship. And it was so dark, and I was tired. . . . I didn't know the city was so big. I'm looking for my son. . . . We used to be fishermen back on the mainland.

I did a little weaving. . . .'

'And your son ran off to the city and you ran off after him. Good luck in the New Land; Welcome to the Island of Opportunity. But get up and move on.'

'But my son——'

'There are more fishermen's sons down here in the Devil's Pot than you can shake a stick at, fishermens' sons, farmers' sons, blacksmiths' sons, sons' sons. And all of their mothers were weavers or water carriers, or raised chickens. I must have talked to all of them at one time or another. I won't even tell you to go down to the launch where they take the workers out to the aquariums and the hydroponic's gardens. That's what most of the young people do when they get here . . . if they can get a job. I won't even tell you to go there, because there are so many people that work there, you might miss him a dozen days running.'

'But the war . . . I thought he might have joined . . .'

'Somewhere in the ridiculous mess,' interrupted Rara, her birthmark darkened, 'I have misplaced a niece who was as close to me as any daughter ever was to any mother. All reports say that she's dead. So you just be happy that you don't know about yours. You be very happy, do you hear me!'

The woman stood now. 'You say the launches to the factory? Which way are they?'

'I'm telling you, don't bother to go. That way, down two streets, and left until you hit the docks. Don't go.'

'Thank you,' the woman was saying, already off down the street. 'Thank you.' As she reached the middle of the block, Tel rounded the corner a moment later, sprinting. He brushed past the woman and ran towards the door of the inn.

'Tel,' whispered Rara. 'Tel!'

'Hi, Rara.' He stopped, panting.

'Come in,' she said. 'Come inside.' They stepped into the lobby of the inn. 'Tel, do you know anything about what happened to Alter? I got a weird story from General Medical. And then you disappeared. My lord, I feel like a crazy fool opening this place. But if somehow she wanted to get to me, where would she go if I wasn't here . . . And then, what am I to do anyway? I mean I have to eat, and . . .'

'Rara,' he said, and he said it so that she stopped talking.

'Look, I know where Alter is. She's safe. But as far as you know, you don't know where she is, if she's alive or dead. But you suspect she isn't alive. Understand? I'll be going to her, but you don't know that either. I just came to check on some things.'

'I've got all her things together right here. They gave me her clothes at the hospital, and put them all into a bundle in case we had to make a quick getaway. We had to do that once when we were working in a carnival where the manager suddenly took a liking to her and made himself a pest. She was twelve. He was a beast. Maybe you should take——'

'The fewer things I take the better,' Tel said. Then he saw the bundle on the table by the door. On top was a leather thong to which some shells still clung. 'Maybe this,' he said, picking it up. 'What shape is Geryn's room in?'

'The place has been ransacked since they took him away,' she said. 'Every mali and his brother has been picking at the place. What about Geryn, how is he . . .?'

'Dead,' Tel said. 'What I really came about was to burn his plans for the kidnapping.'

'Dead?' Rara asked. 'Well, I'm not surprised. Oh, the plans! Why I burned those myself the minute I got back into his room. They were all over the table; why they didn't take them all up right then, I'll never . . .'

'Did you burn every last scrap?'

'. . . And crumbled the ashes, and disposed of them one handful at a time over a period of three days by the docks. Every last scrap.'

'Then I guess there's nothing for me to do,' he said. 'You may not see me or Alter for a long time. I'll give her your love.'

Rara bent down and kissed him on the cheek. 'For Alter,' she said. Suddenly she asked, 'Tel?'

'What?'

'That woman you brushed by in the street when I saw you running up the block . . .'

'Yes?'

'Did you ever see her before?'

'I didn't look at her very carefully. I'm not sure. Why?'

'Never mind,' Rara said. 'You just get on out of here before . . . Well, just get.'

'So long, Rara.' He got.

Not so high as the towers of the Royal Palace of Toron, the green tile balcony outside Clea's window caught the breeze like the hem of an emerald woman passing the sea. There was water beyond the other houses, deeper blue than the sky, and still. She leaned over the balcony railing. On the white marble table were her notebook, a book on matter transmission, and her slide rule.

'Clea.'

She whirled at the voice, her black hair leaping across her shoulder in the low sun.

'Thanks for getting my messages through.'

'This is you,' she said slowly. 'In person now.'

'Un-huh.'

'I'm not quite sure what to say,' she said, blinking. 'Except I'm glad.'

'I've got some bad news,' he said.

'How do you mean?'

'Very bad news. It'll hurt you.'

She looked puzzled, her head going to the side.

'Tomar's dead.'

The head straightened, the black eyebrows pulled together, and her lower lip tautened across her teeth until her jaw muscles shook. She nodded once, quickly, and said, 'Yes.' Then, as quickly, she looked down and up at him. Her eyes were closed. 'That . . . that hurts so much.'

He waited a few moments, and then said, 'Here, let me show you something.'

'What?'

'Come over to the table. Here.' He pushed aside a folded paper bearing a strange picture on the front. The paper flapped open; he hardly noticed the poem printed there. All he saw was that his sister had used the margin to make mathematical notes. He moved her books and slide rule on top of the paper, and took a handful of coins from his pocket. He arranged fifteen copper centi-units in a square, four by four, with one corner missing. Now he took a smaller coin and put it on the table about a foot away from the missing corner. 'Shoot it into the gap there,' he said.

She put her forefinger on the silver disc, was still, then snapped her finger. The silver circle shot across the marble, hit the corner, and two pieces of copper bounced from the far side of the square. She looked at him, questioningly.

'It's a gambling game, called Randomax. It's getting sort of popular in the army.'

'*Random* for random numbers, *max* for matrix?'

'You've heard of it?'

'Just guessing.'

'Tomar wanted you to know about it. He said you might be interested in some of its aspects.'

'Tomar?'

'Just like I monitored your phone-calls, I overheard him talking to another soldier about it before he—before the crash. He just thought you'd be interested.'

'Oh,' she said. She moved the silver circle away from the others, put the displaced copper coins back in the square again, and flipped the smaller coin once more. Two different coins jumped away. 'Damn,' Clea said, softly.

'Huh?' He looked up. Tears were running down her face.

'Damn,' she said. 'It hurts.' She blinked and looked up again. 'What about you? You still haven't told me all that's happened to you. Wait a moment.' She reached for her notebook, took a pencil up, and made a note.

'An idea?' he asked.

'From the game,' she told him. 'Something I hadn't thought of before.'

He smiled. 'Does that solve all your problems on . . . what were they, sub-trigonometric functions?'

'Inverse sub-trigonometric functions,' she said. 'No. It doesn't go that simply. Did you stop your war?'

'I tried,' he said. 'It doesn't go that simply.'

'Are you free?'

'Yes.'

'I'm glad. How did it come about?'

'I used to be a very hard-headed, head-strong, sort of clumsy kid, who was always doing things to get me into more trouble than it would get the people I did it to. That was about my only criterion for doing anything. Unfortunately I didn't do it very well. So now, still head-strong, I've at least picked up a little skill. I've had to do some things whose main point wasn't whether it hurt me or not. They just had to be done. I had to go a long way, see a lot of things, and I guess it sort of widened my vision, and gave me some room to move around—some more freedom.'

'Childhood and a prison mine doesn't give you very much, does it.'

'No.'

'What about the war, Jon?'

'Let's put it this way. As far as what's at the radiation barrier, which is pretty much out of commission now, there's no need for a war. None. If that gets seen and understood by the people who have to see and understand it, fine. If not, well, then it isn't that simple. Look, Clea, I just came by for a few minutes. I want to get out of the house before Dad sees me. Keep on talking to him. I'll be disappearing for a while, so you'll have to do it. Just don't bother to tell him I'm alive.'

'Jon . . .'

He smiled. 'I mean I want to do it myself when I come back.'

She looked down a moment, and when she looked up he was going back into the house. She started to say good-bye, but bit back the words.

Instead, she sat down at the table; she re-read Vol Nonik's poem; she opened the notebook; she cried a little bit. Then she started writing again.

The Towers of Toron

CHAPTER ONE

ENGRAVED on a four by five card in graceful letters that leaned like dancers:

To Her Grace the Duchess of Petra
You are invited to attend a ball at dawn
Given by His Royal Highness
King Uske
to honour the patriotic efforts of
Tildon Aquariums
"We have an Enemy beyond the Barrier"

Two things caught the eye about this invitation: first, "Tildon Aquariums" had been printed slightly lopsided in a type face a fraction different from the rest. Second, there was a ten-inch coil of wire taped to the lower righthand corner.

She tore loose the message coil, threaded it into the re-video and pressed the button; it was drawn into the machine. On the screen dots of colour became the face of a blond young man with unhealthy features. "Well, there you are, dear cousin," it spoke with languid insolence. "You see, I'm attaching this personal entreaty with your invitation. Do come away from your little island to my big one. You were always my favourite cousin, and life has been passionately dull since you went into – what else can I call it – seclusion. Please, dearest Petra, come to my party and help us celebrate our coming victory. So much has happened in the three years since I saw you last. So much has happened – So much has happened – So much has happened –"

The Duchess made a disgusted sound, banged the shut-off button, and the face disintegrated. "A nick in the message wire," she said and looked up. "Is Tildon a subsidiary of your father's company, Jon?"

"It's one of the few left that isn't."

"I wonder how much Tildon gave him. My poor cousin really thinks he can seduce the money he needs to keep up the war by the promise of official parties given at the palace."

"Royal patronage still holds its magic, Petra. Your family has wielded power in Toromon for centuries, but my great-

great grandfathers, – and Tildon's – were farmers ploughing by hand on the mainland, or pulling their fish in over the edge of their rowboat. When the council decided that these parties should be given, it knew what it was doing."

She ran her fingers across the mother-of-pearl inlay on the desk. "We're such a disparate land. There are still people living like cavemen on the mainland; yet we have planes, matter transmission, and a university that can produce scientists like your sister." She shook her head. "Don't people like your father, Tildon, and the others, realize they have the real power now? I have enough to live sumptuously here on this island, but I couldn't make more than a token gift to the war effort compared with what these industrial families can – assuming I would want to support the war in the first place."

Jon smiled. "Still, they want the Dukes and Barons to nod on them when they give. Not to mention the King."

The Duchess looked at the invitation again. Suddenly her face twisted. "He prints these by the thousands and just fills in the name of the next moneybag to be honoured, right on the dotted line. I'm afraid the thing that still upsets me more than anything else is the vulgarity."

"But your family is the standard of good taste, Petra. That's what the rest of us have been taught all our lives." There was slight mockery in his voice.

She accepted it. "Yes," and put down the card. "We have been taught the same thing. But there must be some standards – even during a war."

"Why? They're learning, Petra; my father and the others, they're beginning to learn just how much power they do have. After all, the war is being fought for them. As long as their products are used in the war, as long as those malcontent with life and Toromon can be funnelled into the war, everyone will stay happy and in his place. If the war stops, then the royal family – you topple."

Petra spoke back shortly. "As long as they are blind enough to seek royalty's favour, they are not fit to guide something as complexed as Toromon. That's why I spirited off Prince Let to the mainland, so there would be someone with a sense of the scope of this country who would be safe to govern after these intrigues, working around us now, come full circle."

Jon's face lost some of its cynicism. "With the set up of the council and the government, Petra, the King can still hide much of his power. While it is hidden, no one can judge what it is. Is he a madman? Or is he very, very clever?"

"He is my cousin. You were his schoolmate. What do you think?"

"There are great secrets involved in this war. But great secrets have kept the royal family in power since it established itself and set itself at the head of this chaotic fragment of the world."

The Duchess touched her fingers together, nodding. "My great-great-how-many-greats grandfathers with their ships looted the coasts, Jon Koshar, pillaged their neighbours on these islands, using the fragmentary remains of the technology that survived the Great Fire. The radiation on the mainland stopped their expansion inland and the hot currents out from shore did the same. But when they were stopped, they decided that organized government could accomplish more efficiently what piracy had accomplished up till then. There's great variation over the land of Toromon, but it's bounded. They learned not to exhaust what lay within those boundaries, and became a line of Kings and Queens. Now the power is about to shift; but these others must learn the same thing."

"However your ancesters learned it, Petra, today people like Tildon and my father will pay exhorbitantly for your approval. Perhaps because they suspect what you know." Now Jon picked up the card. "Or perhaps because they are vain and ignorant. My father," he repeated, turning the card over. "His greatest disgrace was that I should offend the King and go to the penal mines for it. His greatest triumph was that the King himself should honour my sister when she came from the university with his royal presence at her ball. As long as these are the limits of his happiness, the King can get money for his war, and fill in the names on the dotted line."

"I wish I could allow myself such intellectual clumsiness." She lowered her chin to her finger tips.

Jon looked surprised.

"You call your hysterical murder merely an offence."

Jon clamped his jaw.

"And you have not spoken to your father since the 'offence'

to find out exactly what he feels."

Jon's jaw unclamped and words started in his throat.

"And it is too easy for you to call your father, who was astute enough to build a fortune through brilliant, if unscrupulous, economic exploitation, a puppet of these petty vanities. No, attacking the problem this way leaves too many questions –"

"Petra!"

The Duchess looked up, surprised. She brushed her hand across the sunrise copper hair pulled back by a burnished cluster of gold sea-serpents, "I'm sorry, Jon," and her hand went out and took his. "We have all been here together too long. But when I see how my family, how my people can fool themselves, it hurts. There is a sense of decency that's like a barometer to a man's or a country's health. I don't know. Perhaps I'm too much in love with some idea of the aristocracy: I was born into it. I turned away from it when I was young. Now I find myself back in it again. I think we shall accept that invitation, Jon Koshar."

"I see," Jon said. "With Arkor as well?"

"Yes. The three of us will be needed again." She hesitated. "You were contacted by ... them also, weren't you? The Lord of the Flames ..."

Jon pushed his black hair back from his forehead. "Yes."

They turned at a sound behind them. Doors shaped like double mollusk shells fanned apart. In the doorway stood the giant seven feet and a handful of inches tall. On the left side of his face three scars jagged down his cheek and neck, darker parallel welts in dark skin. "When wil we leave?" Arkor asked. The triplex of scars was the brand with which the frequent telepaths among the tall, mainland forest people were marked.

"Tonight," Petra said.

"You're going to take Tel and Alter," said Arkor. It was a statement, not a question.

Jon frowned. "Are you, Petra?"

"We're all going to pay my cousin the King a visit," she told them. "We've received warning. The *Lord of the Flames* is loose somewhere on earth once more."

"We drove him across the universe three years ago," Jon said.

"Well, we may have to do it again."

*

Across the evening salmon-coloured clouds strung out like floating hair. Red light caught on the polished brass that ran around the yacht deck. Water flopped at the side of the boat. "Everyone's aboard," Jon told the Duchess.

"Then we can start." She turned and issued an order. Engines rang out like plucked cords on a musical instrument. The ship mounted, then plunged forward towards the night. As blackness washed the sky and stars stuck diamond-tipped pins into evening, Jon and Petra lingered at the rail. "Somewhere out there is the war. In which direction?" she asked.

"Who knows?" Jon motioned towards the horizon. "Somewhere beyond the radiation barrier, somewhere out in the mist of our planet."

One of the motormen cried out from the yacht bridge. "Toron ahead!"

"We're nearly there," said Petra. They looked over the prow of the ship, across the water.

Imagine a black gloved hand, ringed with myriad diamonds, amethysts by the score, turquoises, rubies. Now imagine this glittering hand rising slowly above the midnight horizon, in each jewel a flame. Thus the city of Toron thrust over the edge of the sea.

*

The windows of the Grand Ballroom in the royal palace of Toron rose coffin-shaped two stories towards the ceiling. As the panes lightened, the musicians blew windy music from their tuned sea-shells, and above the marine chords, the weaving voice of a theremin dipped and climbed. Emerald and coral gauze swirled from the women's arms, purple and crimson on the jackets of the men.

Through the wide windows, against the ending night, the dark band of the transit-ribbon leapt away from the laboratory tower of the palace and disappeared among the other towers of the city till at last it soared over the sea, over the mainland beach, over the forest of lush titan-palms and descendants of the oak trees of an earth fifteen hundred years in the past, across the penal mines where men and women prisoners toiled the metal tetron from shafts sunk in the twisted rock, across groved plains where only in the past three years had vegetation dared creep, and at last into the mainland city of Telphar. Telphar! – in the past three years it had been converted into the strongest military establishment earth had ever seen, or so her generals boasted.

"A ball in the morning!" the young girl in the ruby silk exclaimed. The shoulder of her dress was fastened with a copper lobster whose beaten tail curved to cover her right breast. "Don't you think this is a wonderful idea, to have a ball at dawn?"

The elderly woman beside her pulled her thin lips tighter. "How ridiculous," she said softly. "I remember when balls were affairs of taste and breeding." A caterer passed them offering hors d'oeuvres. "Just look," the woman continued. On her head she wore a silver wig coiled through with roped pearls. "Just look at that!" Strips of fillet were wound about toasted circlets. "That fish came from the aquariums! Fish from the aquariums served at an affair of state! Why I remember when no one would think of serving anything but imported goods from the mainland. Aquarium grown fish! Why, the idea. What has the world come to?"

"I never could tell the difference between one and the other anyway," the girl in the ruby dress replied, munching into a paté of fish-roe and chopped scallion.

The woman with the silver wig *humphed*.

Jon Koshar moved away and wandered through the hall, over the polished white stone that shimmered with the reflections of fabulous gowns. Isolated on one side of the room and swathed in fur were two representatives of the forest guards, the lonely giants of Toromon's great forest on the mainland. A few feet away stood three squat ambassadors from the neo-neanderthal tribes. They wore bronze wrist bands and leather skirts. Across the floor people clustered around the honoured representatives of Tildon's aquarium. Yes, three years ago it would have been different. But now –

Someone screamed.

Jon whirled round as the scream again crossed the ballroom. Heads turned, people crowded forward on one another, then pushed back. Jon was shoved sideways and someone put an elbow in his chest. More people screamed, backing away from what staggered over the ball room floor.

Something inside that had always made him go against crowds took him forward, and suddenly he was at the edge of the clearing. An elderly man in a bright red suit was lurching across the floor, his hands against his eyes. Behind him a scarlet cape billowed, sagged about his ankles, then billowed once more as he fell forward.

Sticky crimson bubbled between his fingers and dribbled down the backs of his hands staining his scarlet cuffs darker. He cried out again, and suddenly the scream turned into liquid gurgling.

The man went down on one knee. When he came up, there was a smear over the stone and the knee of the trouser leg had deepened to maroon.

Another figure had detached himself from the crowd, slim, blond, dressed in white. Jon recognized the king.

The scarlet figure splattered to the floor at His Majesty's feet and rolled over, his grasping hands falling from his face.

Now more people cried out and even Jon gasped in a breath and bit down on it like metal.

Blood puddled from both cuffs and trouser legs. Red jelly slipped away from what had been a face. Suddenly the barrel chest collapsed and the red cloth that had covered flesh now sagged down till it draped no more than the spikes of meatless ribs. One hand raised two inches from where it lay on the bloody cape, then fell back, tarsals and metatarsals separating, a scattering of tiny bones, as the radial tendon dissolved. At the same time, the skull rolled away from the neck: cheek bone, nasal cartilege, and chin chuckled over the floor.

Through the crowd across from him Jon saw the red-headed figure of the Duchess moving towards the arched ball-room entrance. Immediately Jon turned, made his way to the edge of the room, and in three minutes had skirted the floor to the entrance where the Duchess was waiting. She siezed his shoulder. "Jon," she whispered," do you know who that was? Do you know?"

"I know how it was done," he volunteered. "But not who."

"That was Prime Minister Chargill, the head of the Council." She took a breath. "All right. Now you tell me how."

"When I was in prison at the mines," Jon said, "a not too

close friend of mine was an expert toxologist, and sometimes he used to shoot off his mouth. That was terenide. It's an enzyme action cellular tranquilizer."

"You mean the body cells get so tranquil they can't even hold on to one another?"

"That's about it," Jon said. "The results are what you saw happen to Chargill."

The music, which had stopped, suddenly resumed, and above the twining melodies a casual voice sounded over a loud-speaker system: "Ladies and gentlemen, I am so sorry that this unpleasantry has interrupted my morning party, so terribly sorry. I must request you all, however, to repair to your homes. Our orchestra will now play for us the Victory Anthem of Toromon." The melody on the theremin halted abruptly, then plunged into the soaring theme of the Victory Anthem.

"Come up to my suite immediately," whispered the Duchess to Jon. "There's something I wanted you to see before this. Now it's imperative."

Across the room, the first light stained the panes in the immense coffin-shaped windows. Like violet blades, light slanted through the room, over the heads of the scurrying guests avoiding the scarlet horror drying on the dancing floor.

Jon and Petra hurried through the arched doorway.

The Duchess Petra had secured a family suite among the personal chambers of the palace. A few minutes after they left the ball-room, she ushered Jon through the triple door into the softly lit, purple carpeted room. "Jon," she said as they stepped inside, "this is Rolth Catham. Rolth Catham, this Jon Koshar, whom I told you about."

Jon had stopped at the door, his hand half extended, looking at the . . . the man in the chair. He wanted to close his eyes and rub them, but what he saw was not going to go away. Half of Catham's face was transparent. Part of his skull had been replaced with a plastic case. Through it Jon could see blood boiling along the net of artificial capillaries; metal teeth studded a plastic jaw bone, and above that an eyeball hovered before the ghostly grey convolutions of brain, half hidden by a web of vessels.

Jon's mind thawed from the first surprise, and he said out

loud, "Catham. Catham of *Catham's Revised History of Toromon.*" He jumped at the first familiar thought in his mind, turning it into a pleasantry to battle the surprise. "We used your book in school."

The three quarters of Catham's mouth that was flesh smiled. "And your name is Koshar? Is there any connection between you and Koshar Aquariums or Koshar Hydroponics? Or for that matter with Dr. Koshar who discovered the inverse sub-trigonometric functions and applied them to the random system of spacial co-ordinates – which is more or less the technological reason behind the present conflict in which Toromon has got itself engaged?"

"Koshar Aquariums and Hydroponics are my father. Dr. Koshar is my sister."

Catham's mobile eyebrow raised.

"I told both of you before that I would have surprises for you," the Duchess said. "Professor Catham, we're going to exchange stories this evening. Just a moment. Arkor!" the Duchess called.

In the silence following, Professor Catham caught Jon staring at his glittering visage. The three-quarter smile came again. "I usually announce right off when I meet someone for the first time that I was in an accident fifteen years ago, a freak explosion out at University Island. I'm one of General Medical's more successful, if a trifle bizarre experiments."

"I figured it was something like that," Jon said. "I was just remembering once when I was in the prison mines. There was an accident and a buddy of mine got one side of his face smashed in. Only General Medical was pretty far away, and the medical facilities out there were never particularly famous anyway. He died."

"I see," said Professor Catham. "That must have been the mine disaster of '79. Did they do anything about the safety conditions after that?" . . .

"Not while I was there," Jon said. "I went into prison when I was eighteen and the tetron explosion was in my first year. Five years . . . later, when I got out, they hadn't even changed the faulty cutter machinery."

Just then a door in the side of the room opened and Arkor came in.

At the sight of the triple scars that branded the giant's

neck, the historian's eyebrow raised once more. "Do you always keep a telepath in your service, Your Grace?"

"Arkor is not in my service," the Duchess said. "Nor are we in his. Professor, this is very important. Not twenty minutes ago Prime Minister Chargill was assassinated. I'd like you to go over what you told me when I spoke to you earlier."

"Chargill . . . ?" began the historian. The eyebrow drew down where the other would have met it in a frown. "Assassinated?" Then the half-face relaxed again. "Well, it's either the malis who are responsible, or perhaps the council itself wanted him out of the way . . ."

"Please, Professor," said the Duchess. "Will you repeat what you told me before. Then we'll add what we can."

"Oh, yes," Catham said. "Oh, yes. Well, I was telling Her Grace when she first called me at the University, or rather ferreted me out of . . . Well, anyway." He looked from Jon to Arkor, to Petra, and back. "Anyway," he went on. "Toromon is perhaps the strangest empire in the history of Earth. You have lived in it all your lives so its unique properties do not strike you, but to one who has studied the development of the world before the Great Fire, fifteen hundred years ago, its uniqueness becomes apparent. Toromon's empire consists of the island of Toron, the handful of islands scattered near it, and the fifteen hundred or so square miles of mainland opposite the islands, that of a strip of beach, followed by meadow lands, followed by forests, followed by an uninhabitable rocky crescent that more or less cuts off this fifteen hundred square miles from the rest of the mainland continent, which is still hopelessly radioactive. After the Great Fire more than a thousand years ago, this area I've outlined was completely isolated from the rest of the world by radioactive land and radioactive currents in the sea. Until recently, we never thought that there was anything left on earth to be cut off from. There were several good technical libraries that survived, and some of our ancestors fortunately were literate, educated people, so we have a fairly good picture of what the world was like before the Great Fire. And although there was economic and social back-sliding at first, when a balance was finally achieved, technology began to progress once more and within a comparatively short time, it had equalled that of before the Great Fire, and in many non-destructive areas, surpassed it. Very early in our history, we discovered the metal tetron as a source of power, the one major factor that our pre-Great Fire ancestors seemed entirely ignorant of, from the records we have.

"Now what is unique about Toron is this. No empire that we know of before the Great Fire ever survived for fifteen hundred years, first of all. Nor did any empire exist for over a hundred years or so in complete isolation from any disruptive force. Nor did any empire, country, or even tribe that was in isolation ever develop once it had been isolated.

"Yet, though the strange set of circumstances I have outlined – the surviving libraries, the intelligence of our ancestors, the geographical diversity of our land allowing for interchange between rural and urban cultural patterns – Toromon has existed for one and a half thousand years alone while still managing to preserve a constantly developing technology. The details of this process are fascinating, and I have devoted most of my life to their study, but that is not what I want to explore now.

"The effect of this situation, however, is like a thermite reaction going on inside a sealed bottle – for fifteen hundred years! It doesn't matter how long it takes, eventually the bottle will explode. And the longer the bottle remains sealed, the further the fragments will fly. And, that explosion has taken place." Catham leaned forward in his chair now and brought his fingers meshing together like the tines of a fork. "Sixty-five years ago Toromon's scientists conducted the first experiments in matter transmission. The transit ribbon was built between Telphar, our one city on the mainland, and Toron, our island Capitol. Then Telphar was cut off from us by an increase in the radiation barrier – almost as if the area of Toromon's empire were being diminished to hasten the final explosion. Three years ago we learned that a group of forest people, probably controlled by the enemy had managed to increase the radiation artificially, using some equipment from Telphar itself." Catham turned to Jon now. "Three years ago, as well, your sister, Dr. Clea Koshar, discovered the inverse sub-trigonometric functions and their application to the random system of special co-ordinates. In six months the old transit ribbon was turned into an antenna that could beam matter wherever we wished, and Telphar, inhabitable again, became a military establishment to send men by the thousand to any place on the globe." Catham raised one hand to his transparent cheek. "And the war continues. Why a war? Why not peace? Toromon has been too long held in. That's all I know."

"I thought you would mention what I saw as the most obvious thing about all of this," the Duchess said. "Dr. Catham, do you remember the incident that caused war to be declared three years ago?"

"Yes. The King's younger brother, Prince Let, was kidnapped. That must have been done by some early group of malcontents. The malis go back quite a way, but they were never as strong as they are now. All they actually accomplish is stirring up trouble. Some people think they are connected with the enemy. And no one, so I hear, will even walk through the Devil's Pot after dark."

"It was never a particularly savoury area of the city," replied the Duchess. "But Professor Catham, now I'm going to tell you my story. It's a lot briefer than yours, and more incredible. But it's true. Toromon has had access to matter-transmission on a large scale for three years. There are at least two other races in the universe that have had access to it for billions. They use it to travel among the stars. These races aren't even composed of individuals, but are rather collective consciousnesses. Their method of interstellar travel is more psychic than physical. One seems to be a sort of amoral experimentor. The other, much older, race is benevolent and composed of three centres of consciousness, rather than one, which seems to check and balance one another. We call it the Triple Being.

"You spoke of Toromon's uniqueness, its combination of isolation and development. The experimentor, whom we call the *Lord of the Flames* was also aware of Toromon uniqueness, and from the outside he began to meddle in order to keep it isolated as long as possible. You wonder where the rebels got the equipment and knowledge to close the radiation barrier? It was from the *Lord of the Flames*.

"Myself, Jon, and Arkor here were contacted by the Triple Being three years ago. With their help we rooted out the agent of the *Lord of the Flames*, though too late to stop the major explosion. But he's back again, Professor Catham. What the results of his presence will be this time we don't know. The kidnapping of Prince Let was our doing. For the past three years he's been safely with the forest guards on the mainland. We hope that eventually this hysterical war will end, and then Prince Let can come back and perhaps straighten out whatever's left of Toromon, if there is anything. While he was in the palace with his mother and brother, his very life and sanity were in danger. It was all we could do."

"I see," said Catham. "And you're going to prove all this? Why tell me about it in the first place?"

"Because we need someone with a historical orientation to help us and advise. The Triple Being will only help so much in order not to upset our culture by introducing extraneous upsetting elements. The first advice we need is what to do with two youngsters who helped us in our first effort, a boy and a girl. The boy, Tel, ran away from a small fishing village on the mainland to Toron when he got involved with us. The girl is an acrobat. They were very helpful to us then, but we don't need them any more, and it seems a shame to keep them away from society this long. But they have a tremendous amount of information that might be dangerous, especially to themselves. And there's one more problem." She turned to Arkor. "Bring the kids in, will you?"

Arkor turned from the room. He came back followed by a boy of about seventeen with dark skin and sea-green eyes. After the boy came a girl perhaps a year older and nearly an inch taller. Her skin was tanned the same as the boy's, but her hair was the colour and texture of bleached silk. Both looked surprised at the apparition that was Catham, but they were silent.

"The special problem is this," the Duchess told him, and reached for a button on the arm of her chair. At her touch, the lights in the room dimmed to half their original brightness.

Rolth Catham started forward in his seat. He was sitting alone in the purple carpeted room – with five empty, but animated suits of clothes, a woman's sitting in the Duchess's chair, two men's standing beside it, and the scant garb of the two youngsters hovering by the door. But though the lights were dim, they were still bright enough to see that the bodies inhabiting them had disappeared.

From the chair the Duchess's voice, natural and unruffled, continued. "During the time we were first involved in this affair, the Triple Being went as far as to make us immune to certain frequency's of radiation by re-structuring our crystallization matrix. The side effect, however, was that the index of refraction of our bodies' substance took a nose dive. Which means that when the light gets below a certain intensity, we disappear . . ." The light went up, and the five people were back in the room. "So you see the problem. That demonstration, incidentally, is our only real proof."

"I'm impressed," Catham said. "No, I don't believe you. But I will take it on as a theoretical problem, which might be fun to work on. You want to know what to do with the youngsters? Spray them with pigmented viva-foam, General medical developed for me – but I'm not vain enough to wear it. Turn them out on the world, and leave them to their own devices. The remaining three of you concentrate on the *Lord of the Flames*." Catham rose. "You can contact me back at the University. I must say it's all very interesting. But I seriously don't believe it's anything more than a psychotic fantasy on your part." He smiled his three-quarter smile. "And that's a shame, Your Grace, because you have a terribly vivid imagination. But I will advise you to the best of my ability, however I can." He stopped. "Consider this before I go. You say you're responsible for the kidnapping of Prince Let three years ago? The government finally decided it was malis. Malis probably are responsible for Chargill's death – if he is dead. In your fantasy world, aren't you perhaps responsible for that?" Catham went to the door, opened it, seemed surprised to find it not locked, and went out.

Arkor, Jon, and the Duchess looked at one another.

"Well," said Arkor. "He is serious about advising us, but he doesn't believe it."

"That's better than nothing," Jon said.

"Arkor find out what in the world viva-foam is, and get hold of some as soon as possible," the Duchess said.

CHAPTER TWO

FIFTEEN copper centi-units, on top of an empty cardboard crate, had been arranged into a square – minus one corner.

A hairy fist whammed the surface, the coins leapt, and the three men who had been kneeling around the box fell backwards spluttering. "What's the idea?" demanded one with curly brown hair.

"Hey! Hey, you look at me!" A grin slashed the wide face of the interrupter. Squat, barrel-broad, with no neck and little chin, he had hair and eyebrows the colour of unravelled hemp. "Look at me!" he bellowed again, threw back his head, and laughed.

"Aw, cut it out," whined the green-eyed, heavily freckled kid they called Shrimp. "Why don't you pick on someone your own size?"

Lug's squat torso rolled back on his pelvis and his brachydactylic hands slapped at his low, heavy stomach. "I pick on . . ." He turned to the third man. ". . . you!"

Waggon, the third man around the crate, had the same thick physique, only his hair was wiry and black and his forehead even lower.

"Aw, leave Waggon alone," Shrimp complained. "We're trying to teach him to play a game."

"He's my size," grunted Lug, giving Waggon a playful whack on the shoulder.

Waggon, who had been concentrating on the coins, looked up surprised, his wide eyes blinking. Very little white showed around his pupils.

"Leave him alone, Lug," Shrimp said again.

A second time Lug belted Waggon's shoulder. Suddenly Waggon rolled to his feet, ropes of muscle knotting along his shoulders, arms, and thighs. He leaped, and they tumbled to the floor. The other recruits looked up from their bunks or where they sat reading military pamphlets. One seven foot forest guard who had been leaning by the double-decker bed peeled himself from the olive drab wall, and walked towards the two scuffling neanderthals. Suddenly he reached for them. There was a howl, another howl, and then Waggon and Lug were dangling by their collars from the forest guard's fists. "Why don't you apes learn to do a passable imitation of human beings?" the guard asked in a reasonable voice.

Big pupilled eyes blinked, fists folded like cats' paws, and the big toes sticking through the open-toed boots curled in. The forest guard let go, and they bounced to the floor, catching themselves on their knuckles. They shook themselves and lumbered off, at once seeming to have forgotten the incident.

"Watch it," came a voice from the door.

Everyone snapped erect as the officer entered, followed by three new recruits: a forest guard with a shaved skull, a dark skinned black-haired boy about seventeen with vivid sea-green eyes, and an unusually squat neanderthal who kept blinking.

"New men here," the officer said. "Watch it! Ptorn 047 AA – F." The shaved guard stepped forward. "Tel 211 BQ – T." Tel, green-eyed and silent, stepped forward. "Kogg 019 N – H." The blinking neanderthal moved up now. "All right you guys," the officer said, "don't forget there's an orientation meeting in . . ." He looked at the ceiling chronometer. ". . . eleven minutes. When that gong sounds, hustle!" He left the room.

The three newcomers tried to smile as half a dozen men called out a perfunctory, "Hello."

Green-eyed and freckled Shrimp came over. "Hey, any of you fellows interested in a game of chance? Why don't you come over with me and get to know some of the guys. My name is Archibald Squash. Really. Imagine a mother naming a kid Archibald. But you can call me Shrimp." He seemed to be directing his attention more and more towards the neanderthal. Now he turned directly to him and said, "Your name is Kog, right? Well, come on over and join the game."

Tel and Ptorn looked at each other, then followed Shrimp and Kog to where another man was arranging coins on top of the cardboard crate.

"Hi, Curly," Shrimp said. "This Kog. Kog, Curly. Kog wants to play a little game with us, Curly. That right, Kog?" His enthuiastic friendliness seemed forced to Tel. But the neanderthal grinned and nodded. "You just sit down here," and Shrimp, his hand on Kog's shoulder, pushed him to a squat beside the crate. "Now this is the way we play – you got any money? – you arrange the coins in a square, four by four, but with one corner missing. Then you take this here deci-unit and just flip it across the box-top so that it hits the corner, see? And two coins fly off the far edges of the square, like that. Now we number the coins on the far side – one, two, three, four, five, six, seven. (Get your money out, Kog) and you bet on two of them. Let me show you. I bet on two and six. Now I flip the coin and . . . two and five fly off. Here, you get half a unit. That's 'cause only half my bet came in." He placed a half-unit piece in Kog's hand. "Now. You want to try."

"Eh . . . yeah." Kog nodded. "What do you call this?"

"Randomax, randy, double-dice, cut-coin, seven-down, take your pick.

"Randy . . .?" Kog asked.

"Randy," repeated Shrimp. "All right. Now put your money down. Fine. Your bet?"

"Huh? Oh. Eh . . . two and six."

Kog flipped, the coin struck the vacant corner, and two coins that were neither two nor six flew from the edge.

Shrimp made a regretful sound and Curly picked up Kog's unit note.

"Huh?" asked the neanderthal.

"Oh, it's not over," Shrimp said. "That's just a first try. Now we all go again."

Crumpled notes landed on the box-top and the coin was flipped again; then again; and then again.

A bewildered frown had chiselled itself into Kog's face when suddenly Ptorn, the smooth skulled forest guard leaned over the makeshift table and said levelly, "How about giving me a chance at that?"

Shrimp looked up, at first surprised, then uneasy. "I was just gonna suggest we broke up the game. I mean . . ."

"Come on," insisted Ptorn. His long arm reached across Tel's shoulder and his brown fingers squared the coins, Shrimp and Curly exchanged worried looks.

"Money," Ptorn said and put a unit note beside the coins.

Curly said, "I think I'll throw in my rag right now . . ." From around the box Shrimp kicked him and Curly's hand which had started leisurely for his winnings jerked back like a lengthened spring released.

"Three and five," Ptorn said. His wide ivory yellow index nail struck the milled edge.

Three and five leapt away from the square.

Ptorn picked up the money. "Two and six," he said, moving the corner coin back for another shot.

Click-click.

Two and six shot away.

Again Ptorn crumpled unit notes in his fingers. "Two and four."

"Now wait a minute . . ." Shrimp interrupted.

"Two and four."

Click-click.

He waited while they placed the final bills in his double width palm. Then he dropped the money in front of Kog. "This is yours, ape," he said, and walked away.

Shrimp sucked air between his teeth. "Them god damn big boys," he muttered looking after the guard. "How do they do it, huh? How? It's a perfectly fair game, but they win it every time." Suddenly he looked directly at Tel and smiled. "Hey," he said. "I bet you're from one of the mainland fishing villages."

"That's right," Tel said, smiling back. "How did you know?"

"Your eyes," Shrimp said. "Green. Like mine. You know, us fishermen got to stick together. What made you hitch up with the army?"

Tel shrugged. "Nothing else to do."

"That's the truth," Shrimp said. "Oh, this here is Curly, my partner in crime. He's a farmboy."

Curly was still brooding over his randomax losses. "I'm no farmboy," he grunted. "I ran with a mali gang in the Devil's Pot for almost a year."

"Sure, sure," Shrimp said. "You know, this *is* a perfectly honest game. On His Majesty's yellow locks, I swear. But somehow . . ."

A gong broke the air like china and a metallic voice hit their ears: "All new recruits report to the Stadium of the Stars. All new recruits report to the Stadium of the Stars . . ."

"That's us," Shrimp said, and with the others he and Tel, Curly behind them, started for the door.

Among the central buildings of Telphar to which the activity of the recruits was restricted was one structure that sank into the city like an inverted blister. Large enough to hold ten thousand beneath its canopy of flood-light simulated constellations, only one section was filled with restless, rangey soldiers.

On the dais glinting officers looked like toys. One approached the microphone, coughed into it, and as the echo staggered from wall to wall through the arena, he began: "We have an enemy beyond the barrier, so hostile and abominable to every principle that mankind . . ."

Among the six hundred new soldiers, Tel sat, and listened, with more questioning than some, and not as much as others.

Then there was free time for the recruits until the next day when they would move to training headquarters. Tel still tagged after Shrimp and Curly. "How does that game really work?" he finally asked when they were walking back to the barracks over the raised highway.

Shrimp shrugged. "Actually I don't exactly know. But somehow, the apes just don't have a chance. Oh, it's honest. But they just don't seem to win more than one out of ten. Regular people like you and me, well, we do all right and get better with practice. But those big guys . . . just forget it when they're around. Aren't you coming inside with us?"

They'd stopped at the barracks door. "Naw," Tel said. "I think I'm going to keep walking and see what's around."

"I can tell you it's not much," Shrimp said. "But suit yourself. See you later."

As Tel went off, Shrimp started in, but Curly looked after the figure disappearing down the twilit roadway.

"What are you waiting for?" Shrimp asked.

"Shrimp, what colour are that kid's eyes?"

"Green," Shrimp said. "A little darker than mine."

"That's what I thought too, this afternoon. But I was looking at them all the way back here, and they're not any more."

"What colour are they then?"

"That's just it," Curly said. "They're not nothing. They're just like he's got two holes in his head."

"Hell, it's halfway dark. You just couldn't see."

"Oh yes I could. And I swear there wasn't a thing behind his eyelids. Just holes."

"This evening air's no good for you, boy," Shrimp said,

shaking his head. "Come on inside and I'll play you an honest game of randy."

Tel wandered up the darkening roadway. He took a covered ramp that mounted from one spiralling highway to the next and came out above most of the surrounding buildings. Only the central palace was noticeably higher than this one. As the roadway wound round the dark tower, he could look across the triple railing over the smaller buildings of Telphar.

Below, the city stretched towards the plains, and the plains towards the mountains which still flickered faintly purple from the radiation barrier along their snaggled edge. It was all familiar to him. Mercury lights suddenly flicked on and bleached away the shadows on the ramp. Looking up, he saw a figure perhaps twenty yards away, another recruit out exploring.

As Tel approached, he realised the man was shaved bald. Then, coming closer, he recognized the forest guard who had arrived with him that afternoon.

Ptorn saw him and waved. "How you doing?"

"Fine," Tel said. "You just out walking too?"

Ptorn nodded and looked back over the railing. Tel stopped beside him and leaned on the top bar. A breeze pulled their sleeves back from their wrists and tugged at their open collars. "Hey," Tel said after a minute. "How did you work that thing with the randomax game?"

"You wouldn't understand."

"Huh?" said Tel. "Sure I would. Try me."

Ptorn turned sideways against the railing. "If you really want to know, try and follow this: suppose you're in the city, in Toron, and you're on the sidewalk. Now let's say one of those big trucks Koshar Hydroponics uses to ship stuff from the docks to the warehouses is coming down the street. And let's say it stops about a quarter of the way from the end of the block. What happens?"

"It stops?"

"Well, no, I don't mean stop exactly. Let's say it just cuts its motor."

"Then it goes on rolling."

"How far?"

Tel shrugged. "That depends, doesn't it, on how heavy the truck was, or how fast it was going?"

"Right," Ptorn said. "But if you were crossing the street, you could judge pretty accurately whether you'd have time to get over, or even just about where the truck would stop – once you saw it start to slow down."

"I guess so," Tel said.

"Well, do you realise that when you do that, you're doing subconsciously a problem that would take a mathematician with pencil and paper who knew the exact weight of the truck, speed, rate of deceleration, and friction component of the wheels at least a couple of minutes to solve? Yet you do it in under half a second with only the inaccurate information your senses can gather in a moment or two."

Tel smiled. "Yeah, that's pretty amazing. But what's that got to do with the game?"

"Just this. You and I can do that. But if you put one of the apes on that street corner, he'd have to stand there until the truck came to a dead stop before he'd dare cross over. Oh sure, if you taught him the mathematics and gave him a pencil, paper, and all the factors, he could figure it out in about the same time any other mathematician could. But he couldn't just glance at the decelerating truck and figure where it would stop."

"I still don't quite see," Tel said.

"Well look: the way you men can just figure out by looking things that the apes could never perceive, we can figure out things with just a glance that you men couldn't see either, like what angle and how hard to shoot that coin to make the ones we want fly off the edges of the randomax square. If you can judge the direction and the velocity of the coin, you can figure the give and play of forces in the matrix and how it'll work out by the edge."

"I think I understand," said Tel.

"I can't explain the mathematics to you, but you can't explain the mathematics of your slowing lorry to me."

"I guess not," Tel said. Suddenly he looked up at the forest guard and frowned. "You know when you said 'men' just before, you made it sound like something that . . . wasn't you."

Ptorn laughed. "What do you mean? The apes are part of you, just like you men are part of us . . ."

"There," Tel said. "Even just now. Can't you hear the way you say it?"

Ptorn was quiet a moment. Then he said, "Yes. I hear it."

And the quietness suddenly repelled the youngster. "About the game," he said. "Could any of . . . us men, do what you did just guessing?"

Ptorn shrugged. "I suppose some exceptional minds among you can. But it's really not important, is it?"

"I guess not," Tel said. "Us men," he repeated. "What do you call yourselves, if you don't think of yourselves as men?"

Again Ptorn shrugged. "We think of ourselves as guards, forest guards. Only the 'forest' isn't so important."

"That's right. Sometimes you're referred to as forest guards, sometimes as forest men."

"As 'guards' we guard your penal mines at the edge of the forest and return escaped prisoners."

"Oh yes," Tel said. "I'd forgotten." Again he looked over the dark buildings. "I knew an escaped prisoner once, before I joined the army." He was quiet for a moment.

"What are you thinking about?" Ptorn asked.

"Huh?" said Tel, looking up again. "Oh. As a matter of fact I'm thinking about a necklace."

"A necklace?"

"Yeah," Tel said. "It was made of shells, polished shells that I strung on leather thongs."

"What's that got to do with the escaped prisoner?"

"The girl I gave it to knew the prisoner too. It got broken once, stepped on. But I fixed it later. It was a pretty necklace. I polished the shells myself."

"Oh," Ptorn said, a little softly, a little gently.

"What do you suppose all those lights are, way over there at the edge of the city?" Tel asked.

"I'm not sure. Maybe they have something to do with the basic training camp. That looks like it's out in the restricted part of the city, though."

"Yeah," said Tel. "But then why would they have lights on if there weren't any people there?"

"Who knows." Suddenly he stood straighter ."Hey, look."

"What is it?" Tel asked.

"Can you see? Some of them are going off, just flicking out."

"Oh yeah, I just saw one. I wonder how far away they are?"

"I'm not sure," Ptorn said. "The ones that go out aren't coming on again. I wonder what it might have to do with basic training. You know it's supposed to be a pretty tough six weeks."

"I hear it's rough."

"Yeah," said Ptorn. "But so is the enemy."

"You know," said Tel, hunching his shoulders, "I haven't seen any of . . . you guards in the recruits who can read minds, the ones with the triple scars."

Ptorn stood up from the rail. "Really?" he said. "What do you know about the telepaths?"

"Nothing," Tel said. "I just know . . ." He stopped. "Well, I knew a guy once, I mean a guard, who could read minds. And he'd been scarred . . ."

"You know a lot of interesting people, don't you," Ptorn said. "Did you know that very few of you men know about the telepathic guards? Very, very few. In fact I'd say there were only about forty outside the forest who knew. Most of them are on the council."

"You're . . . not a telepath?" Tel asked.

Ptorn shook his head. "No. I'm not. And you're right. There're none in the army. They don't draft any."

"I don't usually talk about them," Tel said, warily.

"I think that's good," said Ptorn. "That's good." Suddenly he put his hand on Tel's shoulder. "Come on back to the barracks with me, boy. I want to tell you a story."

"About what?"

"About a prisoner. I mean about an escaped prisoner."

"Huh?"

They left the railing and walked towards the ramp that would take them back to barracks level. "I used to live near the penal mines, Tel. Not all of the forest guards patrolled the mines, but if you were born near them, chances are you would. We're organized there into squadrons, platoons, a miniature army. Further away the tribes of guards are much more informal, but near the mines where there's a job to do they have to be fairly strict. The guy in charge of our platoon was a quiet guard, with three scars banding his cheek and neck. We would sit around the campfire, talking or wrestling, but Roq – that was his name – would stand against a tree and watch. At the time I speak of, it had just got dark, and the sticks on which we had roasted our meat still leaned against the rock-rimmed fireplace, their tips shiny with grease. I could feel rain in the air hanging behind the still leaves.

"Then a branch snapped, leaves brushed one another, and Larta entered the clearing. Larta was a lieutenant in Frol's platoon that patrolled the woods a mile away. The left side of her face was also run with triple scars. She pushed a black pelt from her shoulder so that the swinging fur shimmered with orange firelight. Silently she and Roq conversed for perhaps ten seconds. Then, still without looking at the rest of us, they spoke so we would understand. 'When will they try to escape the mine?' she asked.

" 'Just before dawn,' Roq said.

"We all listened now.

" 'How many will try to run?' asked Roq.

" 'Three,' said Larta. 'There is the old man with the limp. He has been at the mines fourteen years. His right leg was smashed in the cave-in five years ago. He holds hate in his brain like a polished ruby, flickering behind his eyes. He is crouching beside the guard-house steps, rolling a twig between his fingers while he waits, trying not to think of the pain in his leg. He feels very old. Beside him is the heavy one. The texture of his mind is like iron and mercury. He is very conscious of his body, and as he crouches, he is thinking of the roll of fat where his legs bend at his waist and his stomach rolls across itself under his prison uniform. He is conscious of the six freckles on his right cheek and the ten on his left. There is an appendectomy scar across the right side of his belly, and he thinks of that now, briefly seeing the white walls of the General Medical building with their chrome handles. He has always tried to give the appearance of an easy, adaptable person around the prison camp, flowing quietly and precisely into the few new situations that arise. But the determination with which he worked on this escape – the dirt under his nails is damp and crumbly, and feeling it roll out between his fingers, he remembers how he was nearly caught in the tunnel they dug with spoons and shoes and hands even to get so far as the guard-house – the determination is cool and hard. The third one, the youngest one, with the shocked black hair and the stunned eyes crouches behind the other two. Think of a smooth pool of water. Then think of something bright thrust up from below, a fire-blade, its sparks glittering in the surface ripples. This is how the idea of freedom thrusts from his young, arrogant mind.' As Larta spoke, the rain began, thin and gentle through the night.

"Roq said, 'They huddle closer. A cord is tied across the guard-house steps in front of the entrance that faces back towards the shacks. The rear guard always leaves this way a moment before the forward guard leaves by way of the entrance facing the jungle. The first guard will trip on the cord and cry out. The second guard will run back to see what happened, and they will dash across the spot-lit strip into the trees. Mercury and Iron planned it. The flickering Ruby tied one end of the string, and the Sparkling Blade tied the other. They are waiting, alone with their breathing and the thin rain.' We sat still and waited too. Larta returned to her platoon.

"That's primarily the story," Ptorn said. "The actual escape, how they heard the first guard cry out and the second run, how they sped across the strip and got separated among the dark wet trees; or how in the darkness I tracked beside the Secret Ruby, heard him limping over the damp leaves not seven feet away, heard him stop, hesitate, then whisper, 'Hank, Jon, is that you? For the love of . . .' and then I flicked the hilt of my fire-blade, and wet leaves shone with sudden green, and he staggered back and screamed, the Ruby of hate confounded in the corners of his eyes; he screamed again, then fell full face on the soft earth. I drew the blade away, flicked the hilt again, and the sparks died, and his body went out. Or how the chubby one screamed, and screamed, and clutched himself to the dripping trunk, his cheek pressed against bark, and screamed. And the mercury vaporized, and the iron flooded him with hot liquid fear. And at last he cried, still clutching the tree, 'Who are you! God damn it, where are you! No! God damn it, come out and show yourself! It's not fair! Oh please, it's not fair . . .' And we circled him, and circled closer. Or, how we carried the bodies back at dawn, in the rain, and left them in the mud outside the shacks – that is really beyond the story, the real story of the escape."

They had almost reached the barracks. "Why . . . ?" began Tel. "Why did you say this to me . . ."

Ptorn smiled. "We only brought back two bodies. The third one, the youngest, got detoured into the radiation fields where we couldn't follow him. He should have died. But he didn't. He escaped. Now you said something about knowing an escaped prisoner, and there's only been one escapee in the past sixteen years. Also you know about the telepaths. And besides, your eyes are funny. Did you know that?"

Tel blinked.

"I'm not a telepath," Ptorn said again. "But any forest guard would have told you that story if you had said what you did. We trust each other with information a lot more than you men do. We ... perceive things a little more clearly."

"But I still don't understand . . ."

"Look. We're going into basic training tomorrow. In six weeks we'll be facing the enemy. Until then, friend, keep out of any more random games. They may not be as random as you think. And keep your mouth shut."

They turned into the barracks.

CHAPTER THREE

THE island city of Toron is laid out in concentric circles. In the centre along colonnaded streets are the Royal Palace and the towering mansions of the wealthy merchants and industrialists. Buildings stare wide windowed at one another, many of the windows composed of layers of stained glass rotated across one another by hidden machinery. Brass or marbled balconies lip the upper stories. Leisurely people dressed in bright colours wander along the streets.

The outer ring is the water-front, the pier, wharves, public buildings and warehouses. Clinging just inside is the section knows as the Devil's Pot, a ravelled webbing of narrow streets where furious grey alley cats stalk wharf rats through over-turned garbage. Living here is the vast labouring population of Toron, and the less vast but vicious underworld of the city, many of them in the roving gangs of malis that ranged inward from the island's rim.

Between the inner and outer rings is a section of indistinct apartments, rooming houses, and even occasional private dwellings, for clerks and craftsmen, salesmen and secretaries; doctors, engineers, lawyers and supervisors: those who had worked hard enough and had been lucky enough to rise out of the confusion of the Pot, and those too weak to cling to the centre who had been flung from the whirling hub.

In a two-room apartment in one of these houses, a woman lay on her back, her eyes closed, her mouth opened, her fingers twined in the bed sheets. She was intensely conscious of the city on both sides of her. And she was trying not to scream.

She clamped her jaws and her eyes snapped open like a doll's stare. On her door was a name-plate that said – black letters on yellow metal – Clea Rahsok. Rahsok was her real name spelled backwards. Once her father, at her suggestion, had called a branch company of refrigeration equipment "Rahsok" She had been twelve when she suggested the spelling to him. Now she used the disguise for herself. Until three years ago she had lived between her father's house and the University. But then she made three discoveries.

Now she lived alone, and did very little but walk, read, figure in her note-book, lie on her back, and try to keep from screaming.

The first thing Clea had discovered was that someone she loved, loved with an aching passion that made the back of her neck tingle, that made her jaws clench and her stomach suddenly flatten itself whenever she thought of him (his short red hair, his broad taurine body, his sudden grin and the deep inside laughter like a bear's growl) – this someone was dead.

The second thing she had discovered (she had been working on it for half her stay at the university and nine tenths of the time that she was supposed to be spending on the government project she had joined right after she received her degree) was inverse sub-trigonometric functions and their application to random spacial co-ordinates. The result was a paper presented to the university and then again before a select board of government councillors. The conclusion still threaded through her mind: "... and so, gentlemen, it is more than conceivable that by converting the already extant transit-ribbon, we may send between two hundred and three hundred pounds of matter anywhere on the globe with a pin-point accuracy of microns." Anywhere! Anywhere at all!

The third thing she had discovered –

Something first about her mind. It was a hard, brilliantly honed mathematical mind. Once she, along with fifty other mathematicians and physicists, had been handed three pages of radiation data in order to discover a way over, under, or around it. She had looked at it for three minutes (having put off picking it up for three days while she scribbled in her note-book on her own pet project) and announced that the radiation was artificial, generated by a single projector that could be destroyed, and had thus solved the problem. In short it was a mind that cut through information to the correct answer even when the incorrect question had been asked.

– she had discovered this third thing when she had been assigned to work on a small section of a top secret government project after the presentation of her paper on sub-trigonometric functions. She was not told what the project was nor the significance of her part, but her mind, extrapolating from her fragment, had carved and carved at the mystery. It was part of some immensely complexed computor, whose purpose, apparently, must be . . . must be . . . !

Her body jerked upright in the bed, the sheets fell from her breasts, and she was breathing very fast in the darkness.

When she made this discovery, she disappeared. Easiest was the trivial disguise of her name. Hardest was convincing her father to let her take this apartment. Between them, the careful destruction of some government records: all copies of her contracts to work for the crystallizing war effort, and the record of her retina pattern on file from her birth. She banked on the general war confusion to keep them from searching her out. After she was established in her two small rooms, she methodically began to dull the edge of that amazing mind.

She went for longer and longer periods away from her books, tried to ignore the war propaganda that flooded the city, made as few decisions as possible, and if she did not succeed in actually blunting it, she sufficiently blurred its keenness to accomplish the same end.

She thought a lot about the person who had died, less about sub-trigonometric functions, and when she came anywhere near the third thing, she would think immediately of something else, about not screaming, not screaming, keeping silent and still.

Crumpled on her desk was a poster she had once peeled from a board fence. Across the green paper, scarlet letters proclaimed:

WE HAVE AN ENEMY BEYOND THE BARRIER

Clea put on her bathrobe, walked to the desk, and reached for the poster. Suddenly she went into the front room without turning on the light. Her clothes were over the back of a chair. In the dark she put them on. Then she went to the door, stepped into the hall, and went to the stairs. Blue-grey dust wedged into the corners.

At the front door she saw Dr. Wental trying to get in. When she opened it for him, he grinned at her, scratched his thin, wrapping-paper hair, and crashed into the door-jamb.

"Dr. Wental!" Clea said. "Are you all right?"

Still smiling, the doctor nodded vigorously. "Spirits . . ." he said. "You be quiet, now. We have to get up stairs quietly so my wife won't. . . ." His adam's apple gave a little leap and he tapped his lips with his fist, guiltily. ". . . won't know. Quietly." His extended arm landed on Clea's shoulder and he sagged against her as his knees gave in different directions. "Beautiful green spirits, Miss Rahsok. If you will excuse a terrible pun, I am in really fine . . ." But he hiccoughed again. "But many too many, much too much. Will you help me upstairs, Miss Rahsok, quietly?"

Clea sighed, and supported Dr. Wental along the hall. "So my wife won't know," he said again. "Oh, this war is a dreadful thing. We have an enemy beyond the barrier, but what it's doing to us back here, in Toromon . . ." He shook his head. "You have to work so hard to get ahead and get the better things in life. But it's hard." He paused to shake his head again. "Occasionally you just have to let go . . ." At the word "go" he slipped back down two of the six steps they had negotiated. Clea whispered "*damn*" and clutched the handrail. "You know," continued Dr. Wental, "all this increased production, of all sorts of equipment? And a good civilian just can't get a hold of any of it. I've got a man coming to me tomorrow with a case of lupus erythermatosis. He was recommended to me by a specialist. I did some research in it a few years ago, and I came up with a few things too. But how can you treat lupus erythermatosis without adrinocorticotropic hormone? You look in the General Medical catalogue and there should be enough around to treat an army – if I can coin a phrase. But try to get it and somebody in a white smock tells you, 'I'm sorry. Private doctors can only get minimum rations during this period.' What am I going to tell this man. Go away? I can't treat you? I can't get the drug? And he has as much money as the sea has salt. One of the Tildons. I'm an honest man, Miss Rahsok, just trying to get the better things for my family. That's all, really." They had reached the doctor's door when the doctor fell against the wall. The forefinger of his left hand pressed against his lips for quiet, while he tried to put his thumb into the print lock.

As Clea went down the hall again, she heard the raspy whisper behind her, "Quietly, quietly, so my wife won't know."

Outside, the breeze from the sea lapped the houses and wedged into the streets. Clea's black dress was snapped tight around her neck, and her black hair (once it had been braided with silver chain, and she had danced in a white dress with a man who had short red hair, whose shoulders were box broad, whose words were quietly wise, whose laugh was like a bear's growl, who wore a military uniform . . . and who was dead) – her black hair was tight back in a bun that took her fifteen minutes each morning to brush, comb, and roll up so straight and lacquer stiff.

Carefully, so carefully she unsnapped her collar, and as the flap fell open, she sucked coolness into her chest, deep against her diaphragm. She walked on more easily.

"Hey, lady."

She jumped, but it was an officer. As he approached, his uniform changed from the dull colour of the under-sides of oak leaves to olive as he stepped into the ring of light from the street lamp.

"Isn't it sort of late for you to be wandering the streets like this? Malis from over in the Pot beat up a man and near killed him last night just six blocks from here. You'd better go on home."

"Yes sir," Clea said.

The officer walked on, but Clea stood a moment. Then she turned and started away. When she had gone twenty steps, she glanced back, perhaps to see if the officer was watching.

Under the street lamp where she had been a minute before was a girl with white, silken hair. Clea frowned just as the girl dodged to the side – and vanished!

Clea opened her mouth. The moment the girl had stepped out of the direct beam of the lamp, she had disappeared, gone out like a candle flame. Clea blinked. Then she turned and hurried towards home.

Halfway she stopped. About three blocks away, she recalled, was an all night bar with a monumental array of pin-ball-, slot-, and bowling-machines.

She came home at six o'clock the next morning. The bartender for the last two hours had simply leaned on the counter and watched the woman with the tight bun and the high black dress who drank only soft drinks and amassed phenominal scores on the gaming machines. A woman with a scarf around her head was setting out a garbage can in front of the building.

"Up bright and early, Miss Rahsok?" asked the woman, wiping her hands on her check house dress. "It's good to get up early and take a walk. Shows a proper attitude. With this war on it's so hard to stay cheerful. I just wish we could send letters to our boys, or hear what it was like, or send packages. Then it would be so much easier. Sometimes I just wish I had a son to be proud of ... But it's still hard on a woman with daughters. Now you take my oldest daughter, Renna. You think she would appreciate how hard it is? What with all the really eligible young men off beyond the barrier a girl has to be particularly careful who she knows, who she goes with. I keep trying to introduce her to nice boys, but she will just pick up with anybody. Oh, it's awful. If a girl's going to get ahead, she's got to be careful. Renna has been seeing some dreadful boy for years named Nonik. Vol Nonik. And do you know where his parents live?" She pointed towards the Pot. "And he doesn't even live with them."

"Excuse me," Clea interrupted. "I ... I have some work to do and I've got to get upstairs. Excuse me."

"Oh, of course, of course," said the woman, stepping back from the doorway. "But you know a girl can't be too careful."

Inside the apartment, Clea stood by the closed door, thinking, "His arms were strong. He caught me from behind once when we were walking single file along the stone wall by the wharf. His laugh was like a bear's growl; he laughed when we watched the two squirrels chattering at one another on the campus lawn the day he came to visit me at University Island, and his words were quiet and wise. He told me, 'You have to decide what you want.' And I said, 'I want to work on my project with the sub-trigonometric functions, and I want to be with you, but if this war –' And suddenly I realised how profound a thing he'd told me then, and realised that having said what I wanted out loud, to him, they were so much easier to have, even though the war ... the war! He's dead!" – and stopped thinking.

On the desk she saw her slide-rule and her note-book

sticking from under the crumpled poster, and she remembered, "... in brief, what all this mathematical hodge-podge boils down to, gentlemen, is that these inverse sub-trigonometric functions do apply to the random spacial coordinate system I've outlined and define it precisely; and so, gentlemen, it is more than conceivable that by converting the already extant transit-ribbon, we may send between two hundred and three hundred pounds of matter anywhere on the globe with a pin-point accuracy of microns." Anywhere! Anywhere at all! – and stopped thinking.

She closed the window, lay down on the bed, and again memories flooded her mind. She had begun work on the computor not long after the paper. "Something for an input that will take information from one and a half to three and a quarter killo-specs, and can handle at least forty thousand data, that's the first thing you can work on." Quite idly she assumed that it must be an input that takes information directly from the human brain, seeing as the neo-neanderthal's brain energy had just been measured at one and a half killo-specs while the strange cortex of the brains of the forest guards produced up to three and a quarter. No, it was not an obvious co-relation to make. But she had the information and made the connection as someone else might reason that a thermometer whose specifications stated that it read at least ten degrees higher than ninety-eight point six would be employed taking abnormal human temperatures. Later on she saw on a colleague's desk a schematic for a switch over circuit for the same voltage differential that would change an input to an output. Removing or establishing up to forty thousand bits of information directly into a human mind, she pondered. She solved the problem of the forty thousand data by getting tri-fasceted tetron crystals to respond to a frequency/multi-frequency hum and coding the overtones. With ten crystals – each about the size of a pinhead – she achieved a sorting system that would handle sixty-seven thousand, one hundred and forty-nine data (three to the tenth power) and was quite proud of her margin. Once, while exploring the far wing of the building where she worked, she saw through an open door where an artist had left pinned to the wall several sketches of grotesque, imaginary marsh-scapes, and some structurely impossible anatomical dissections. Two weeks later rumour got around that two artists working in the building had undergone prefrontal lobotomy at the insistence of the government psychiatrists. Some other tiny things: a messenger carrying those same sketches and a spool of magnetic tape into an office two flights down; what might have been the same spool changing hands between a white smocked technician and a military official; her own inquiry after the pictures: "Oh those? They were burned. They weren't needed any more," said the violet-eyed lab technician; what seemed like the sudden disbandment of the entire project and she was set to something else; the first reports from the conversion of the transit-ribbon from wire- to wireless-matter transmitter; and then a conversation at lunch with an acquaintance from an entirely different department: "... doing work on a weird computer. It puts information right into the brain with tapes. I can't imagine what a human brain is going to do with sixty-seven thousand bits of information, but that's what it's output is. Can you imagine?" Clea imagined. One or two other minor details came along. Then one day she was walking by the wharves late one evening when the sky was the hue of split sapphires between the long red clouds, when it hit her: one – he was dead! Two – Anywhere! Anywhere at all! Three – .... She stopped thinking. She was going to scream.

Think about something else, about not screaming, about being still, about nothing ... Slowly the tension eased from her throat, from her fists, from her calves, and she slept.

Late that afternoon she got up, washed her teeth, hands, wrists, neck, and face. She ate. Then she went out to buy the next day's food. Somewhere among all this she had worked out a novel way of calculating every other place of pi, but she had forgotten it by the time she again wandered along the evening streets with darkness rolling towards her.

The first sound that jerked her mind to the surface was a cry to her left. There were footsteps in the alley beside her, a thud, another cry, then several sets of footsteps. At first she started to turn away, but something made her go forward.

She looked around the corner, then pressed back against the wall. Malis! Two men and then a woman ran forward to where an already indistinguishable number of people were brawling in the street. Someone jumped back, a man was kicked hard in the stomach and rolled over the pavement. A woman screamed, cursed, and staggered with hands over her eyes.

Someone broke loose from the fray, a girl – with white hair!

Clea felt something catch in her gut. The girl ran in a diagonal taking her vaguely in Clea's direction. Then two men were suddenly in front of her. Something fanned white sparks as one man raised his arm.

A power blade!

As the arm descended, Clea saw the reflection near her feet, a thin white line against a disc of water. She reached down, grabbed the bucket from beneath the drainpipe at her side and dashed the contents over the figures. The power-blade shorted, steamed, and went out, falling harmlessly across the white haired girl's arm.

But now her safe position behind the drain was known. The girl, dancing back, looked at Clea, and Clea looked back. Her eyes! she thought. Good Lord, she has no eyes!

But someone was coming towards her, now: the man with the powerblade. His grin looked like the split rind of a rotten kahrba fruit. She kicked at him and dodged, thinking (the way she would think of the fluxuation in the second derivative of a fourth degree log function, sharply, coolly) he supports his weight mostly on his left foot and uses his right to propel himself, and when she was about to be overtaken, she whirled to face him and brought the side of her shoe down hard on the top of his right foot – he was barefooted – at the same time jamming her elbow in the darkness that was his stomach.

As he went down under her double attack, she fled, hearing her own footsteps, then others in counterpoint, lighter, overtaking hers. Again she whirled, thinking, I will throw myself at whoever it is and bite for the neck; they won't expect that.

But she stopped when she turned, the thought ludicrously rising in her mind like a thin blade from beneath a smooth surface: but she does have eyes, bright blue eyes!

They were under a street lamp.

"Come on," the white haired girl said. "Down this way. They're still coming!"

They turned the next corner, ran the block, dodged down two more alleys, then slowed.

Clea jerked the air into her lungs, trying to form the words, *All right, who are you?* her tongue working over them as over an anticipated taste when the girl said:

"Hey, you fight good."

Surprised, Clea looked at the girl and said instead, "Thank you." Then she said. "Your arm! What's wrong with your arm?"

"Huh?" She was holding her left hand across her right shoulder. "Oh, nothing."

"You're hurt," Clea said. She looked up at the sign. "Look, I live eight blocks from here. Come on up and I'll put something on it," and find out who you are, she remembered to add, silently.

"Sure, Dr. Koshar," the girl said. "Thanks."

Clea jumped, or something inside her did, but she started walking.

In front of her door, her finger poised before the print lock, Clea asked, "Who sent you after me? And call me by my first name."

"All right," the girl said.

The door swung in and Clea turned on the light. "What's your name?"

"Alter," said the girl.

"Sit down over there, Alter, and take your blouse off."

Clea went into the bathroom and returned with three small bottles, a roll of tape, and one of gauze. "You haven't told me who sent you yet. Ehhh . . . That looks as if someone took a vegetable grater to your shoulder."

"I guess you shorted the blade, but it was still a little hot. My arm was hurt badly once before and I'm always a little wary." She added, "You haven't let me tell you yet."

"I wonder where they get those weapons anyway. Only the guards and the military are supposed to have them."

"From the guards and the military," Alter said. She winced as transparent liquid flowed across the raw skin and relaxed as red liquid followed it. "Nobody sent me here, really."

"Maybe I don't want to know." Suddenly the brittle tone she was trying to maintain broke and warmth flooded from beneath. "What's this?" she asked, fingering a loop of leather thongs from the girl's neck on which were strung polished shells of green, red, and golden browns.

"A boy gave it to me," Alter said. "It's just a necklace."

"It's been broken once," Clea said. "But it's been fixed.

"That's right. So was my arm." Alter said. "How did you know?"

"Because there're cuts in the surface of the leather around the shells on the right hand side, as if something heavy came down on it and crunched the pieces on that side against the leather. And your shoulder's slightly enlarged. But I'm sure it works well."

Alter looked up, her wide eyes like turquoises behind her tanned face. "That's right, someone stepped on it . . . once." Then she asked, "Why did you tell me that?"

"Because I'm astute. And I want you to know it." Criss-cross, criss-cross, four strips of tape went over the gauze padding on Alter's shoulder. Clea went to the freezer, took out some fresh fruit, and brought it to the table. "You hungry?"

"Um-hm," Alter said, and fell on the fruit, looking up once to say a full *Thank you.* When she was about half finished, Clea said, "You see if the government sent you, there's no reason for my even trying to get away. But if somebody else did, then . . ."

"Your brother," Alter said. "And Arkor, and the Duchess Petra."

"What about my brother," Clea said softly.

"He didn't send me," said Alter biting into the fruit, "exactly. But they told me where you were, and so I decided to come and see what kind of person you were."

"What kind of person am I?"

"You fight good," Alter grinned.

Clea smiled back. "How's Jon?"

"Fine," said Alter. "All in one piece."

"In three years I heard from him only twice. Did he have a message?"

Alter shook her head.

"Well, I'm glad he's alive," said Clea, moving the bottles together on the table.

"What they're trying to do with the war –"

"I don't want to hear about it." Clea stood up, and took

the bottles back in the bathroom. "I don't want to hear anything about the damned war." When she closed the medicine chest, she looked in the mirror for the length of a held breath.

When she came out, Alter had gone to the desk, pushed aside the crumpled poster, and was looking through the notebook. "What's all this?"

Clea shrugged.

"You invented the thing that sends you over the barrier, didn't you?" Alter asked after a moment.

Clea nodded.

"Is that what this is about?"

"That's just fooling around."

"Can you explain how the barrier thing works?"

"It would take me all night, Alter. And you wouldn't understand it anyway."

"Oh," Alter said. "I can't stay up all night because I have to see about a job tomorrow."

"Oh?" asked Clea. "Then I guess you can sleep here. What were those Malis after you for?"

"I was out," Alter said. "And so were they. That's how they work."

Clea frowned. "And you don't have anywhere else to stay?"

"There was a place I thought I could sleep at, an inn over in the Pot, but it's been torn down. So I was just wandering around. I've been away for a while."

"Away where?"

"Just away." Then she laughed. "You tell me about how that over the barrier thing works, and I'll tell you about where I was. Your brother was there."

"It's a deal," Clea said. "But in the morning."

Alter went over to the sofa and lay down with her face to the back so that her bandaged shoulder was up. Clea went to her bed. Before she sat down, without turning, she said, "I thought I saw you following me last night."

"That's right," came the voice from the sofa.

"And suddenly you disappeared."

"That's right."

"Explain."

"Ever heard of viva-foam?"

"No."

"Neither had I until four days ago. And until this morning I never had my hands on any. It's a plastic pigmented spray with pores. I'm covered with it. Otherwise, in dim light you couldn't see me."

"You'll have to go into that in more detail tomorrow."

"Sure."

Clea sat down on the bed. "Those Malis were just out? Where do they come from? What do they want . . .?"

"Aren't you sort of a Mali too?" Alter asked after a moment.

"How do you mean?"

"A malcontent," Alter said. "Why are you holed up here, hiding from everybody like this? With some people it turns inward, with others it turns out, I guess."

"You know everything, don't you." She chuckled.

The sound of a yawn came from the sofa.

What am I doing here? Clea wondered, and thought about that, instead of screaming.

Early morning light slapped red-gold across the wall. Someone was in the bathroom. Water splashed against the porcelain washbowl.

Then Alter walked out. "Hi," she grinned.

"Where are you off to?"

"The circus," Alter said. "To get a job. Want to go with me?"

Clea frowned.

"Come on," Alter said. "Getting out will do you good."

Clea stood up, went into the bathroom, washed her face, and came out coiling the hank of black hair laboriously into a tight, black bun.

"Braid it," Alter said from behind her.

"What?"

"Why don't you braid it. It'll take half the time and it won't look so . . ." She gave a nameless little shudder.

Clea let her hair fall to her shoulders again, then reached up and divided it into three.

When they came out in the street, Clea's collar was open and her hair hung in a thick black braid over her shoulder.

Only a few people were out. The sun set crowns of light on the towers of the city. Gold caught on a balcony railing, snagged on a bright window as the sun descended to street level.

"Which direction?" Clea asked, pausing to look at the towers.

"This way."

They walked between the buildings towards the Devil's Pot.

In that crushed together rim of the city a vacant lot was a rare thing. The Triton Extravaganza ("The Greatest Spectacle of Entertainment on Island, Sea, or Continent") had commandeered a two block area and set up its emporium. Criss-cross ropes webbed green and purple canvas against the sky. Cage upon cage lined one side of the lot: pumas, an eight legged bison, a brown bear, a two headed fox, a giant boar; and a five thousand gallon acquarium housed a quivering albino squid. In another, tiger sharks nosed the glass corners, while further on an octopus ravelled and unravelled over blue sand.

A covey of bright aerial artists ran from one tent, broke about them, and disappeared into another. "Who . . .?" Clea began.

"Trapeze workers," Alter said. "They call themselves the Flying Fish. Corny. Come on; I've got to see Mr. Triton."

"What's over there?" Clea asked as they started towards the large wagon at the end of the lot with its great papier maché neptune bearded, big bellied, and beaming from the roof.

"Huh? That's the chow wagon. Hey, why don't you go over there and get something to eat while I see Mr. Triton? I'll join you later but I have to audition on an empty stomach, or there'll be hell to pay."

"Well, I . . ." But Alter was up the steps of the big wagon; and Clea was alone. The morning was noisy and cool.

She turned towards the cook-tent where a green and yellow awning overhung wooden tables. Grease sizzled on the grill. Clea sat down across from a man sipping chowder from a terracotta mug. He gave her a grin that pulled the sudden net of wrinkles tight around his smokey eyes.

A waitress at her shoulder said, "What'll it be, come on now, I don't got all day, please?"

"What do you have?"

The waitress frowned. "Fried fish, boiled fish, broiled fish, fish roe, fish and chips – special is eggs and fried fish, fifty centiunits."

"The special," Clea said.

"Fine," the waitress smiled. "Surprise! It's edible today."

The man across the table grinned again and asked, "What sort of act do you do?"

Just then a woman in a spangled jumper sat down beside the man and said, "Is she one of the new auditions?"

"I'm a clown," the man volunteered.

"Oh . . . I . . . a . . . don't have an act."

Both the man and the woman laughed.

"I mean I don't have an act in the circus."

They laughed again and the woman nodded. "I just train seals, honey, so don't hassle."

Just then the waitress slipped a plate of fillet and scrambled eggs, with butter streaming through the yellow hills, down to the white crock plate. Clea picked up the fork, and the clown said, "Honey, you enjoy eating, don't you?"

Surprised, Clea looked at him, and then down at herself.

"No, I don't mean your weight. I mean the way you look at food. Someone who looks at food like that, like it was the very special experience it is, that sort of person never has to worry about their figure." He turned to the seal trainer. "You know what I mean? With their look, you know why they're fat as a tug. Or if their eyes get slightly narrow and their mouths purse in, then you've got the reason for their rail thin bodies. But the look you gave –" he said, turning back to Clea.

"Oh, shut up," the seal trainer said. "You start talking and we'll be here all day." Clea and the two circus folk laughed. Then the clown said, "Hey," and was looking over Clea's shoulder and far behind.

She turned.

Across the lot someone had set up a trampoline. In regular bounds the white haired girl vaulted and spun against the sky: back triple somersault, front triple somersault, half gainer, recovery, full gainer, recovery, jack-knife opening backwards in a reverse swan, triple back, then triple front again . . .

"She's good!" the clown said.

The seal trainer nodded.

Triple forward, triple forward, swan, triple back. Then a straight candle through a quadruple back into a full gainer, closing with a double forward before she hit the elastic for the last time.

People over the entire lot had stopped to look. Now roustabouts, sidewalls, and performers set up a scattering of applause.

Alter was coming towards the cook tent. Beside her a man had his arm around her shoulder. He was elderly, rotund, and a great cotton-ball beard fluffed across his chest.

Clea rose to make room for them at the table, then glanced around and saw to her surprise that everybody else at the table was standing too. There was a sudden, uneven, but cheerful chorus of, "Hello, Mr. Triton. Good morning Mr. Triton."

"Sit down, sit down," proclaimed Triton expansively, and chairs slid back into place. Now he continued talking to Alter. "So you'll join us the day after tomorrow. Very fine. Very fine. Do you have a place to stay, because you're perfectly welcome to sleep on the lot."

"Thank you," Alter said. "Oh, this is my friend I was telling you about."

Surprise pulled down the corners of Clea's mouth before she caught them back up in a defensive smile.

"You're an accountant, right? Well, I could use somebody to get the books in order. We'll be doing quite a business on the mainland tour. Be here with the kid –"

"But I. . . ." Clea began, looking to Alter who was grinning again.

"– the day after tomorrow," finished Mr. Triton," and the job's yours. Good morning, everybody. Good morning." Then he paused, looked hard at Clea, and said, "You know, I like the way you look. I mean the way you look *at* things." Then he called again, "Good morning."

"What did I tell you," said the clown to the seal trainer.

"But I . . ." Clea repeated. Mr. Triton was walking away. ". . . I don't want a job – I don't think . . ."

Alter was shaking hands with the seal trainer, the clown, and even the waitress who were congratulating her. A moment later she looked around to say something to Clea; but Clea was gone.

She walked, looking neither at the smoky faces of the clapboard buildings on her left, nor the screaming boy hurling chunks of pavement at a three-legged dog to her right. She looked neither at the littered gutters nor at the pale towers that rose in the centre of the City. She walked straight ahead until she reached her apartment building.

"Oh, Miss Rahsok, there you are. Out early as usual." It was not yet eight-thirty.

"Oh . . . hello."

"Like I always say," said the woman, adjusting her head scarf, "it's always good to get out bright and early." Suddenly the expression on the woman's face reversed itself, and she repeated. "Speaking of bright and early, do you know what my daughter Renna . . . well, she sneaked out of here at sunrise this morning, and I know she's run off to spend the day with that Vol Nonik character. We were arguing about him last night. What are his prospects? I asked her. After all, I'm a reasonable woman. What does he intend to do with himself? And do you know what she told me? He writes poems! And that's all! Well, I had to laugh. But I have a surprise for her that I'm sure will drive this Nonik individual out of her head. I got an invitation for her to the Victory League Ball. I had to wrangle with Mrs. Mulqueen half an hour. But if Renna goes she'll meet some nice young man and forget this idiot boy and his idiot poems. Why isn't a young man like Nonik off in the army? We have an enemy beyond the barrier, and I ask you . . ."

"Excuse me," Clea said. "Excuse me, please."

"Oh, of course. I didn't mean to keep you. Good morning."

But Clea had already pushed past and was walking up the stairs. We have an enemy beyond the barrier. She thought of the poster crumpled on her desk, and like the stimulus of a condition reflex, it released:

His arms strong, confident around me as his laughter and wisdom were confident, his bright eyes blinking in sudden sunlight, and the bear growl tenderness – he's dead;

". . . we may send between two hundred and three hundred pounds of matter anywhere on the globe with a pinpoint accuracy . . ." Anywhere at all;

That computer, what else could they use it for, that insanely programmed, crazy, random . . .

Then she had slammed the door behind her, razoring the scream building in her throat. She leaned against the door, tasting the breaths that plunged again and again into her lungs so hard they hurt.

She did not go out again all day. It was not until midnight that she managed to make herself leave the room for a walk. But as she reached the stairs, she heard a crash. Someone had just fallen at the foot.

Frowning, she hurried down the steps. The someone uncrumpled, grinned at her, and put a finger to his lips. "Shhhh. Please, shhhh. So my wife won't know!"

"Are you all right?"

"Of course I'm all right." Then his adam's apple lunged upward. "Oh, excuse me. I'm perfectly all right. Really in very fine . . ."

"So I gather. Just a moment. Here you go, Dr. Wental."

They started up the stairs, the doctor chuckling. "Oh, the trials and tribulation that a man must go through. Oh, the trials." He gave another burp. "Got that poor old lupus erythermatosis case in this afternoon. Did I say poor? Excuse me. I meant 'bloody rich'. In a month he'll be swollen as a blow-fish. But what can you do when General Medical won't give out any adrinocorticotropic hormone? Gave him a shot of good old saline solution with a bit of food colouring. It certainly won't hurt him and I charged him fifty units. He'll be back tomorrow. Maybe I'll be able to get some by then. But it's terribly hard, Miss Rahsok. I could almost cry."

As they reached the door, Dr. Wental motioned for silence a final time. She left him fumbling for the print lock. When she reached the front door, she stopped.

This time she did not think of her three discoveries. She thought instead, very briefly, about Renna's mother, Renna, and Vol Nonik. She knew that name from somewhere – then she thought about Dr. Wental, Dr. Wental's patient, and Dr. Wental's wife. Outside night pressed against the glass door, but beyond she could just hear the last faint tinkle of the calliope from the circus blocks away. She came back up to her room early.

The next morning, her hair in a braid, her collar opened back from her throat, she walked along the street toward the circus lot. Morning chill cooled the shadowed half of her face while the sun stroked the other with yellow fingers. The sea smell came strong from the wharves, and she was smiling.

As she walked by the fence that rimmed the already bustling lot, she saw someone coming toward her. A flash of silver hair, and Alter, laughing, ran toward her and caught her hand. "Gee, I'm glad you came back!"

"Why shouldn't I?" Clea said. "Though it was touch and go for a while. Why didn't you come back to my place? You could have stayed there. You had me worried."

Alter looked down. "Oh," she said. "I thought you might be angry. It was sort of a funny thing to pull." With one hand Alter was fumbling with her necklace.

"What possessed you to tell Mr. Triton I wanted a job?"

"It just hit me that it might be fun. And maybe you would get a kick out of it."

"Well thanks. Hey, I hope your friend who gave you that comes around some day. Did he put them logarithmically increasing distances on purpose?"

"Huh?" asked Alter. "No, I don't think so. He's off in the war now . . . Hey, did I say something?"

"The war? No – He can't . . ."

"What is it?"

"Nothing," Clea said. Suddenly she put her arm around Alter's shoulder and gave a friendly squeeze.

"Are you sure you're all right?"

Clea took a breath and let her arm fall away. "I'm sure," she said.

They walked together into the lot.

CHAPTER FOUR

THE next day Tel began basic training:

"All right, you guys. Split up into your respective groups and report to your instruction rooms."

He came into a large classroom the far wall of which was covered with charts of machinery. There were no labels on the charts. Across the front wall stretched a full colour swamp-scape, wreathed in mist and spiked with serpentine, leafless vegetation. A loudspeaker in the front of the room suddenly announced in a friendly voice (friendly, though oddly ambiguous as to sex, he noticed): "Take your seats everyone. We are beginning your basic training."

The recruits shuffled to their places at the metal desks.

"You are in the wrong seat, Private Rogers," said the loudspeaker affably. "Two to your left."

A baffled blond boy looked up, then dutifully moved two seats over.

"I am going to read a list of names out loud," continued the speaker. "Everyone whose name I call must leave here and report to room 46–A. That is two flights up and along the corridor to your right. Now: Malcon 831 BQ – N, Motlon 601 R – F, Orley 015 CT – F . . ." Everyone looked a little puzzled, but the named recruits rose and went out the room.

When nearly half the room was emptied, the loudspeaker said: "Now, those of you who are left take your earphones and put them on. Now look into your vision-hoods."

Tel slipped his earphones over his ears and rested his forehead on the support above the masked hood on the table. The magnified screen before him flickered with merging light, misty and indistinct, mostly blues and greens, faint red blushes here and there, a tide drifting slowly, too slowly.

Windy music came through the phones. Then a gruff but pleasant, masculine voice began: "We have an enemy beyond the barrier. We have been able to reach past the radiation barrier only a few years, but already we have discovered a menace of such inhuman and malignant design . . ."

The voice droned and the colours coalesced, forming at

last a recognizable beach. Sand arched away to the horizon, blue waves broke into white froth that scudded over the beach. A girl with a remarkable figure, wearing a skimpy bathing suit, came to the water's edge, touched her toe to the foam, then turned, seemed to see him, and began to run, laughing, towards him. The breeze tossed her auburn hair. Her lips parted and he could hear waves.

Dr-r-r-r-r-r-r – !

Tel jumped back from the masked screen, slamming his spine into the back of the chair. He tore the earphones from his head. The relief as they clattered to the desk was as if two needles of pure sound had been ripped from his ears. His eyes still flickered with the after image of a blinding white light that had suddenly flooded the screen. Around him the room was in confusion, and somewhere a woman was laughing.

The laugh articulated itself, became a voice. "All right. All right. Resume your seats in an orderly manner. Resume your seats." Many of the soldiers had leapt from their chairs.

The feminine voice continued over the loudspeaker. "Your reaction to that last problem was not what we hope it will be at the end of your six week course. You men who just came in –" Tel now realized that a group of completely bewildered recruits had just come in and were standing by the door. "– did they look to you like anyone ready to fight the enemy beyond the barrier?"

Tel felt confused and uncomfortable.

"All during your basic training," continued the lilting alto, "you will be presented with problems of this nature. We want calmness, alertness, and quick reactions; not confusion and disorder. Now sometimes the problems may not be as obvious as that, but watch for them. Remember, we want calmness, alertness, and quick reactions. Will you recruits who have just arrived please take your seats. Everyone reguard your screens and place your head phones on."

Tel noted as he bent forward that the half of the class who had been in the room the whole period were a lot slower in putting on their earphones than the new-comers.

On the magnified screen an explanation was in progress concerning a piece of equipment called 606–B. He was shown in detail how to take it apart, put it together, and keep its numerous parts, mechanical and electronic, in smooth order. But somehow (perhaps he missed it during the twenty seconds at the beginning when he'd hesitated over the earphones) no matter how hard he concentrated, he hadn't the faintest idea what 606–B was used for. But by the time the film had continued for forty minutes, he was sure he could have put one of the damn things together in his sleep.

A gentle bell signalled the end of the period, and everyone raised his head. Tel checked his programme card for his next room and got up to go. Apparently all the new-comers were assigned to stay in the same room.

"Hey," someone whispered, and Tel turned at the door. In the corner seat among the remaining recruits sat Shrimp. Tel nodded to him, but Shrimp looked perplexed. "Hey," he whispered again. So Tel went over to him. "What the hell did they do to you when we came in? You guys looked like . . ."

"No talking back there!" The voice from the loudspeaker this time was definitely masculine. "You in the back there, get a move on! Proceed quietly and quickly to your next class."

Tel left the room.

Two flights up he entered a room nearly identical to the one he'd left. Again the walls were covered with charts of nameless machines. The marshscape spread across the front of the room. He was looking for the 606–B when a fatherly, middle-aged voice announced from the loudspeaker: "Everyone sit down. I am going to read a list of names out loud. All those I call will please report to room 51 – D. Now, Ritter 67 N – T, Ptorn 047 AA – F, Tynan 811 NA – T . . ."

Tel hadn't even realized Ptorn was in the same room with him.

After lights-out they talked for a while in the dark:

Shrimp: "Hey, Lug, what did you learn today?"

Lug (grunting from the bunk beneath): "To put it together, take it apart, keep the central shaft vertical . . . Aw, go to sleep."

Tel: "Hey, was that the 606 – B?"

Lug: "Seven thirty something or other. Go to sleep. I'm tired."

Shrimp (calling upward to Ptorn): "What did you big boys learn about today?"

Ptorn: "Not enough to talk about now. We've got to be up at six tomorrow. We have an enemy beyond the barrier, remember?"

Shrimp: "Yeah, I remember. G'night."

Ptorn: "Night."

Tel: "Hey Lug, what's the seven thirty something used for, huh?"

Lug: (A yawn from the lower birth; then snoring.)

There is the gentle sound of breathing. Someone coughs. Someone turns over and the snoring stops. Then silence as Tel's ears filled with sleep.

The next week the platoon was shown a documentary film. The men filed into the auditorium and took their seats. A few put their knees up against the back of the chair in front of them, others puffed on the plankton cigarettes they had been issued. Tel had never found their taste particularly pleasant. They contained some mildly tranquilizing drug that only made him dizzy. The lights darkened, the screen flickered, and without titles the movie began.

The opening shot Tel recognized as a foggy swampscape similar to the ones at the head of so many of the classrooms. Green mud sucked and bubbled around the stalks of twining plants. Mist scarfed over the silt and writhed about the tines. The scene shifted to a more solid stretch of land, passed by a boulder, a depression in the ground, a fragment of machinery (was it the 606 – B? The camera moved too quickly for him to be certain), at last stopped in front of the ruins of an army barracks. One of the walls was burned away and the roof sagged. The camera dollied through the charred opening into the hut.

A man sits in a chair. His intestines fall over the arm. He has no head. Several bunk beds are overturned in the corner. On a crumpled pile of bedding is a pile of, approximately, two corpses. The camera dollies out of the shack. Propped against the outside wall, his legs at insane angles is a grinning soldier. His eyes are dark holes. An insect scurries over his lip and down his chin.

The camera moves on past a wall composed of burlap

gravel sacks. Through the thickening mist Tel could make out barbed wire strung across the wall. Fog closes across the camera lens. Then the scene cut.

Through the haze Tel could see a row of huts similar to the gutted one in the previous scene. A few men were walking around.

Close-up shot of a young soldier in need of a shave. He smiles at the camera, blinks, and rubs his chin with greasy fingers. Full shot of the same soldier. He is standing beside a complicated looking machine (that certainly wasn't the 606–B, Tel thought. Or was it?). He scratches his chest, looks embarrassed, then goes back to fixing the machine.

Cut to shot of barracks building. A group of men have spread boards over the muddy ground. They squat or sit crosslegged on the boards in an irregular circle. Close-up shot of the centre of the circle: someone is setting up a square of fifteen centiunit pieces with the corner missing. (There is relieved laughter through the auditorium. "Two and six," someone calls out. Tel laughs too.) At some signal which the audience cannot hear, the men look up from their game. Someone scrapes the coins into his palm, and they run off. Shot of the men running across the clearing before the shacks. Shots of men climbing into squat, caterpillar-tread tanks. Shot of tank's plastic observation bubble as driver takes his seat inside. Shot of four tanks starting one after another. Shot of tanks rolling away through the mist, which closes behind them.

Around the twining plants the green mud bubbles. The barracks' shacks are empty. The clearing is deserted.

Cut to:

A tank has stopped in the middle of a thickly overgrown section of swamp, one corner sunk in the mud. Twenty feet away another tank is lying on its side. The camera approaches the first tank. The observation dome has been smashed. One metal side-plate has been twisted away like foil. The camera dollies towards the rent to peer inside the gutted interior where torn and broken . . .

The screen flickered. The lights went on. They had seen nothing through the black gash, but Tel found when he released the armrests of the auditorium chair that his palms were wet. The seat of his pants and backs of his thighs were soaking.

"All right," came the loudspeaker's voice, "report to your assigned work-shops."

Ten minutes later Tel was dismantling a machine very like the one the young soldier had been fixing in the film. He removed an oily plate, wiped it on his apron, and looked at it in the bluish light from the work lights on the ceiling. In the right-hand corner neatly inscribed was: 605–B.

He looked at the machine, then he looked up, coughed, and said, "Eh ... I think there's been a mistake." He felt uncomfortable addressing the thin air. When others asked, they received answers less than half the time.

But the loudspeaker clicked and a man's voice asked, "What is it, Private Tel 211 BQ – T?"

"Wasn't I supposed to be working on a 606?"

There was a long silence. Then a woman's contralto said, "The correction will be made when and if necessary."

Suddenly he felt confusion as a dozen ideas that he was trying to set straight all knotted together like snarled fishing lines. The confusion became rage which immediately retracted into fear. What were they trying to do to him? What was the damn machine used for anyway? And if he didn't know, how could he fight the enemy beyond the ...

Dr-r-r-r-r-r-r-r ... !

They flung their hands over their eyes at the blinding flash that came from the blue fixtures. Before the buzzing stopped the words had leapt into his mind so clearly that at first he thought they came from the speakers: calmness, alertness, quick reaction. He froze, beating back the questions that tried to squirm up into his mind.

Slowly he relaxed. He was calm. He was alert. Two or three people in the shop had already gone back to work, so he picked up a connective bar from the parts rack on the table. For one sudden moment he wanted to heave it at something. Instead he fitted it carefully between the busser plates and twisted the helical pin into place.

That evening some of them went out on the rampway and set up a game of randy.

Shrimp: "O.K. big boy, I'll take my chances with you. Come on, hunker down here, and play me a round."

Ptorn (shaking his head): "I'm just watching."

Shrimp: "Say, how come you big guys have all been so

quiet for the last couple of days? What gives up there in your superior noggins?"

Ptorn: "I'll just watch."

Waggon: "Come on. I got money to lose."

Curley: "Play him, Shrimp. The ape's got better. Won fifteen units off me yesterday – before I won back twenty."

Tel: "Hey, Ptorn, why have you guys been so quiet?"

Ptorn (shrugging): "I don't know." (He pauses) "What do you think the enemy beyond the barrier looks like?"

Lug (leaning against the railing, now looks up and scratches his head): "You know, I never thought of that before."

Tel watches the guard and the neanderthal looking across the railing over the City. Far away the meaningless lights blink in their random pattern.

The third week they put him in a dark room.

"What's your name and number?"

"Tel 211 BQ – T."

Dr-r-r-r-r-r-r...!

He staggered back and covered his eyes. But there had been no flash, he realized a moment later. Calmness, alertness, quick reaction.

"Turn around."

He turned.

"Walk forward."

He walked. He walked a long time, figuring at last that he must have entered a tunnel...

Dr-r-r-r-r-r-r...!

Calmness, alertness, quick reaction; he kept walking, though the tension in his back and shoulders almost made them hurt. And there had been a flash, this time. But it was green and not that bright. He had glimpsed mist, and sharp plants without leaves, and mud was bubbling someplace... No. That was in the front of the room where he had his classes. Or was it someplace else, with the strange machine...

"What is your name and number?"

"Eh... Tel 211 B... eh... BQ – T."

"Describe what you see."

"Eh... where..."

"Describe what you see in front of you. Keep walking."

There was another green flash. "I think ... the sea?" He

said. "Yes, the sea, and there are waves breaking over the sand, and the little boat . . ."

Dr-r-r-r-r-r-r-r . . . !

"Describe what you see." The light flashed again.

"No. I mean the 605–B, or maybe the 606–B, I'm not sure . . . I have to put it together. I can put both of them together . . . that's right . . . either one. They're almost the same, but they're different down in the drive box. I fix them so . . ." And a sudden thought welled warm and comfortable into his mind, and with it amazing relief that started in his shoulders and washed down to his feet. ". . . so we can fight the enemy beyond the barrier. That's what it's for. It must be. It's the 606–B, and I can take it apart and put it together, take it apart and put it . . ."

There was another green light.

"There, yes, the mud, and the plants that haven't any leaves on them, all the mud, and it's foggy. And those are pebbles over there. No, they aren't pebbles. No, they're shells, very pretty, red and brown and milky shells, like somebody polished them for a long –"

D-r-r-r-r-r-r-r!

"– for a long –"

Dr-r-r-r-r-r-r-r!

"– a long –"

Dr-r-r-r-r-r-r-r!

"– pebbles . . ."

The pain that built in his back, his thighs, his arms, nearly made him collapse before he knew it was there. He stopped talking, staggered back, and put his hands over his eyes, though again there had been no flash.

"What is your name and number."

"Eh . . . Te . . . My name is Tel 60 . . . 5 . . . 6 . . . Tel . . ."

"What is your name and number."

Something gripping at the back of his tongue suddenly released and a scream let loose that had been lodged somewhere in his stomach, "606–B! . . . 605–B! . . . I don't know! I don't know! They wouldn't tell me which one . . . ! They wouldn't tell me!"

"What is your name and number."

"Eh . . . eh . . . Tel 211 BQ – T."

"Describe what you see."

"I see . . . I see the mud, and the plants, and the shacks

where the soldiers are. They are sitting in front of the shacks, playing randy. I have to fix it while they play with the coins because ... the enemy ... yes, the ..." and beyond the mist, something moved across the mud, something was knocking aside the plants; at first he thought it might be one of the tanks returning, only it wasn't ... No! "No!" he cried, "it isn't fixed yet! The 606–B, I haven't fixed it yet, and it's coming. Oh Lord, it's ..."

Dr-r-r-r-r-r-r-r-r!

Afterwards, when they took him out of the room, the loudspeaker told him (a soothing female voice), "You did well. Very well indeed. You will be an asset against our enemy beyond the barrier." Already he wasn't sure what had happened in the room. But he had done well, and that made him feel good.

That evening, however, the apes played randomax among themselves. Everyone else sat on their bunks and watched the clumsy games of the neanderthals, speaking very little.

CHAPTER FIVE

JON KOSHAR walked down one of the radial streets of Toron, past the merchants' mansions, past the hive-houses, into the sprawling rim of the Devil's Pot, past the lot where the Triton Extravaganza was folding its tents to begin its mainland tour, past the wharves where the Shuttle Boat was pulling in with its load of workers from the Hydroponics Gardens. A breeze caught in his black hair, his black eyes were calm as he moved through the surge of men and women erupting from the launch pier. Further down were the private yachts. He walked to the royal pier. The sun across the water snagged in the polished chains. The double mollusc shell, insignia of the Duchess Petra dipped and dofted in the water. A long shadow fell across the dock as Arkor appeared at the railing.

"Hi," Jon called. "What's the news from the University?"

He stepped over the chain and walked to the end of the gang-plank.

"I've spoken to Catham," Arkor said, coming down to meet him. "He was a bit surprised to see me, I think. You give me the news here and I'll give you mine."

"Apparently Alter is with my sister, so the Duchess reports. And Tel finally went into the army, off to fight the enemy beyond the barrier."

"Catham simply says to find the *Lord of the Flames* and to expel him as fast as possible. Then ask questions."

"Why?"

"He says it's historical necessity. If Chargill hadn't been assassinated already, we could conceivably spend more time figuring this thing out."

"Sounds reasonable."

They left the pier and started up the waterfront street.

After a few minutes of silence, Jon asked, "Arkor?"

"Yes?"

"What do you hear?"

"With my mind?"

"Yes."

"In you?"

"Around me, and in me too."

Arkor smiled. "You must think that's very important, you who can't see what I see, hear what I hear. It isn't though." He paused. "I can sense – that's a better word than hear – about a block in every direction, at least clearly." They rounded a corner. "There's a worker who's remembering how her brother died eating poisoned fish. In that building over there a neanderthal named Jeof who runs a mali gang is having a nightmare about someone he beat up a few nights ago . . . there, now he's dreaming about food and has turned over and closed his teeth on the pillow. Over there a guy is sitting at a wobbly table in the corner room of the top floor. The late sun through the window strikes his bare chest. He's trying to write a poem about a girl and runs his fingers over the paper. He glances at a sketch of him the girl drew in red chalk and hung on the wall behind him, then writes: *Renna, her brown eyes opening on ocean light* . . . Somewhere in the circus lot I sense a woman with a mind like steel going swiftly through the account books of the Triton Extravaganza . . ." Suddenly he smiled. "It's your sister, Jon." As suddenly a frown replaced it. "Something's wrong."

"What is it," Jon asked, "Is she all right?"

"Yes, but it's something . . . in her mind. It's down very deep." Arkor's frown increased. Then he shook his head. "No, I can't sense it. It's almost as if she's hiding it behind something else. I can see the pattern, hear the sound of it, but it's too deep to sense the meaning."

"What do you sense in my mind?" Jon asked when they had gone a few steps farther.

"A cry," said Arkor, "sharp as a blade thrust up from under a pool of dark waters."

"A cry for what?"

"For . . . a recognition; a recognition of what you call freedom."

Jon smiled. "I'm glad it's still there. You know, Arkor, I'm committed to do as much as possible to end this war. But I didn't exactly choose to become an agent of the Triple Being. It was a choice of dying in the radiation fields after my escape, or joining them. That's no choice, and I won't be free until they leave us."

"Another thing I hear both in your mind and your voice is how much you want me to believe you . . ."

"But it's the truth. Go ahead, read my mind . . ."

"I already have," Arkor said. "I wish you could understand this, Jon. You think the main difference between you and me is that I know what you're thinking while you don't know what I think. That's not it. It's far more a difference in perception that exists between all you men and all us guards. The difference between men and the forest guards is the difference between blind men and men who can see. The difference between the guards who can read minds and the guards who can't is the difference between normal and colour-blind vision."

"Which is to say . . . ?"

Arkor sighed. "Which means that what I hear is not important. And how I interpret it – which is – you can't understand."

They moved among the apartments buildings in the centre ring of the City. The eastern sky was shadowed. Once they paused. "The *Lord of the Flames,*" Jon said.

"Even you can feel it."

Jon nodded. "Can you spot exactly where he is or who he's inhabiting?"

"Not yet."

They moved further through the growing buildings.

"What do you hear now?" Jon asked.

"I hear an Executive Supervisor of one of your father's plants wondering if the assassination of Prime Minister Chargill will eventually affect his salary. He's talking to his wife about it. In the basement of their house is a drunken old woman who has wandered through their cellar door which was accidentally left open. She is hiding in the corner from what she calls the 'jibbies' which actually are memories of the beatings her mother gave her when she was a little girl on the mainland. Neither the supervisor nor the old woman is aware of the other's existence. And even if he were to go into his basement, find her, and drive her out, or if she were to pick up the length of metal pipe in the corner, climb the stairs, sneak into the living room and bash his and his wife's brains out – she has killed two people in her life already – there would still be no awareness exchanged."

"The *Lord of the Flames,*" Jon said again.

"We're closer by a good deal."

"Can you see what he's doing now?"

"Not yet," Arkor said. "But in front of the military

ministry a policeman is standing, waiting for his platoon and darkness. They are going to make a raid on a bar in the Devil's Pot where a mali gang is supposed to hang out." Now they passed by a mansion familiar to Jon. "There's your father," Arkor said. "He's thinking of calling in his secretary and writing a letter to the supply commandant at Telphar expressing his good faith in the war effort with a pledge for half a million units. What will the publicity value of that be? he wonders."

"Does he think about either me or my sister?"

Arkor shook his head. They passed on making their way closer and closer to the Royal Palace of Toron. "The *Lord of the Flames,*" said Arkor.

As night closed finally between the palace towers they turned down the deserted avenue of the Oyster. At last they turned under a stone arch and Jon opened the lock with one of the old fashion keys still used in the centuries old palace. In the corridor they passed a niched statue of the late King Alsen, and turned up a broad flight of marble steps. They reached the fifth floor of the living tower and stopped before the doors of the Duchess' suite. For these inner doors Jon produced a black key, twisted it in the lock, and the doors swung inward over the carpet. Petra was standing by the curtained window, fingering a smoky crystal in a silver chain at her neck and gazing down over the evening City. She turned to them as they entered. "You're back," she said, no smile on her face. "The *Lord of the Flames,* I can feel him as though he were in the room."

"He's in the palace," Arkor said.

"That close?" the Duchess asked. "Arkor, can you tell what he's done this time? I've been dissecting government reports for a week and I can't see any place where he might have stuck his finger in."

"Nothing comes through that clearly yet. Maybe he had something to do with Chargill's assassination?"

"It's possible," said Petra. "I can't throw any light on that either."

"You said he's in the palace," Jon said. "Which direction."

Arkor paused another moment. "There," he pointed.

They went to the door, turned down the hall past the now unoccupied rooms of the Queen Mother and past the other chambers for royal guests. Finally they mounted a short flight of stairs to a hallway lined on both sides with floodlit statues.

"We're going towards the throne room," Petra said.

"That's right," nodded Arkor.

The hall opened into one of the alcoves of the throne room. Heavy draperies sagged towards one another at the fifteen foot windows. Slender isosceles triangles lapped the polished floor where the illumination slipped between the draperies.

"Wait," whispered Arkor. In the quarter darkness Jon and the Duchess saw his forehead crease. He pointed diagonally across the hall towards one of the many other shadowed alcoves.

"We'll spread out," whispered the Duchess. Remember all we have to do is see him all together."

Petra moved off behind the columns to the left and Jon started to the right. Keeping in the shadows of the sea-scaped tapestries he worked his way along the hall towards the empty throne.

Then a voice came, hollow, from across the floor. "What is it! Who's there..."

His eyes froze fast to the alcove.

"Who's there? I'll call the guards..." A white figure moved through one of the spears of light, turning uncertainly and calling, "Who's there.. ?"

The king! Jon felt a twinge of recognition and moved away from the tapestries. At the same time Arkor and the Duchess stepped out of hiding. At first the king saw only the Duchess and said, "Petra. You gave me quite a scare. For a moment I thought that you –"

Then:

The green of beetles' wings ... the red of polished carbuncle ... a web of silver fire. Lightning split Jon's eyes and he plunged into blue smoke. His mind hurled the parsces.

He saw grey, great strips of grey, but tinged with lavender, some with red, others faint yellow, orange. It took him a moment to recognize that he was on a desert, opalescent under a dim, grey sky. A wind pulsed and the tints shifted; orange glinted green, red lightened to yellow, the bluish colour to his left deepened; and the grey gauzed over all, endless and rippling.

His tenticles slithering up his trunk. His roots stretched far into this sand, down to a stream of pure hydrofloric acid nourishing and cool. But here at the surface the thin atmosphere was cold, dry, and grey.

Three heat sensitive slits in his husk registered the presence of two other cactuses near him. He rustled his tentacles again and they rustled back to him. *Watch out*, rustled one cactus (that was Arkor), *There he is . . .*

Another cactus (that was Petra) swayed, tentacles lisping over the sand.

Something raised its head behind a near dune. Three eyes blinked and drew back.

Jon let his feelers hang still.

Now the head, onyx black, raised once more and again the three eyes blinked. The lizard hissed; needle teeth rimmed a spongy gum. It hissed again, and glowing sand swirled before its mouth. On six black legs it climbed the dune, heading in Jon's direction.

Suddenly Jon lashed out and caught the beast around the neck. Rasping, it pulled back, but the tall plant that was Arkor bent forward and three lanky fronds circled the reptilian body. The Duchess snared two beating legs, and together as they all strained back, the hissing turned into a scream in the thin air. The black skin parted and blue oozed over the broken limbs, darkened the sand.

The scream sounded once more, then stopped as the throat caved in beneath crushing tenticles. *There . . .*

It was dark. Moist soil slipped by Jon's rough skin as his boneless body muscled through the earth. There was a vibration to one side and above. (Yes, it was Petra's.) He angled his burrowing until he broke through the ground separating them and was burrowing beside her, their flanks in rippling contact.

Where's Arkor? Jon asked.

He's gone ahead to the temple.

Is he back in good grace with the priestess?

Apparently. She sent a summons for him a heat cycle ago.

His offence was very great, and perhaps she has not forgiven him yet. I wonder if she suspects what part we played in the scheme.

There was a shudder along the length of the great worm

beside him. *I hope not*, she vibrated nervously. *Then we'll be in for it. All we can do is attend the end-of-cycle prayers and hope she makes no denouncement.*

Now, except for their identifying vibrations, they were silent as they pushed towards the temple and the end-of-cycle ceremony.

It was a pocket of soft mud kept moist by perfumed liquids syphoned from every corner of the subsurface world. Jon could sense the exotic odours even before the texture of the earth changed and he broke into the luxuriant silt. They coiled near the back, waiting while the other worms joined them, waiting for the prayers to begin.

At last when the mud was filled, the familiar vibrations of the priestess reached through the temple. She communicated to her congregation through an ingenious amplifying system composed of a pair of metal rings that circled the mud hole, and when she curled around them and spoke, her words carried over the entire volume.

Hail to the great Earth Goddess in whose food track we reside, she began the invocation. *May the mud be pliable always.*

May none under her protection bifurcate until he chooses, responded the congregation, and the prayers began.

At last the rituals ended and the priestess began the announcements. *We have good news for you, my fellows. A member of our herd who previously incurred our displeasure is with us once more.*

Jon felt among the vibrations a new, but familiar pattern. (Arkor, he realised, must have just entered the temple.) But at the same time he realized there was something else present, something that had been there much longer, but was suddenly pressing in on his awareness. With a shudder the length of his intestinal track he realized it was the Lord of the Flames. The Duchess twisted apprehensively beside him. *The Lord of the Flames*, she whispered, touching her flank to his. *It's the priestess!*

I know, he whispered back, as the priestess continued.

This apostate again with us engaged in a plot to end the custom of our cyclic sacrifice to the earth goddess of eleven newly bifurcated children, claiming that to drive them down into the earth until their bodies were shrivelled by the Great Central Heat was beneath our wormlike dignity. But he has come back, said the priestess warmly, *and for his crime of subversion he has agreed to sacrifice himself at the beginning of the next heat cycle, and with him will be sacrificed his two co-conspiritors in the plot. . . .*

They didn't even wait for the identification vibrations to be sounded over the ring-amplifier. Both leapt forward slipping between the other worshippers, sliding through the temple mud. When they reached the priestess, however, the temple was in mayhem. Jon bumped into a sluggish body that was sending out Arkor's identity vibrations, but the form was flaccid. Of course, he must have been drugged and carried here against his will. But the *Lord of the Flames. . . .* Jon leapt for the priestess and coiled around her body only to find she and Petra were already grappling. With his nether end he dragged Arkor towards them. The movement revived the worm a bit, but someone had coiled about the speaker rings and was crying, *Help! Help! The priestess is being murdered!*

Other muscular lengths fell into the struggle, but the *Lord of the Flames: There . . .*

Cataracts of blue gushed from the rocks. Geysers of orange billowed from the burning stones, whipped the dark sky. The fire was beautiful, and the only other light came from the three moons in their shifting triangle in the night.

Jon soared above the fire, exaltation contracting the muscles of his breast. The air beat through his waxed feathers. His whistling wing tips arced the night again and again as he rose. Heat fanned his soft underfeathers. Opening his beak, the breath over his larynx quivered to song. *Arkor,* he called, *Petra, where do you fly. . .* ?

Even before he had completed his question, Petra's voice sang, *I fly over the green flames where the copper burns, now to the yellow where sodium flames . . .*

From further away a third voice joined them, *Hydrocarbons lap currents through orange tides . . .*

From the hundreds of birds around him, two joined him and together they rose through the thickening smoke until the air cooled their wings, beating like hearts, without stop, without rest. The music blended, melodies wove and unwove with one another.

Then cawing cut the smoky air.

Dark wings flapped among the golden. Viciously it tore up at passing under-feathers with a purple beak; swooping down, its scarlet talon struck at an upturned eye. As it beat through the cloud of birds, gold feathers fell, were caught up on a breeze, then dropped again, singeing, charring, at last to burst into fire.

Follow, cried Petra.

We follow, cried Jon and Arkor.

Jon whirled and arrowed towards the marauder. His beak plunged among black feathers. Talons meshed with his own. Arkor was close above him, and the terrible flapping of Petra's wings hammered from below. Then Arkor's beak jabbed a glittering eye, and the great wings shook, then relaxed. They were so entangled that at first they were dragged down nearly a hundred feet before their frantic flapping caught the air. For one moment they held the body in the dusty heat. One wing still shivered uselessly. Then Jon released his hold at the same time as Petra and Arkor, and as they rose, the whirling body fell. They watched the shadow burst into livid fire.

The Lord of the Flames, they sang, *there.* From the corpse smouldering on the rocks a final fire leapt. Then Jon caught one glimpse of movement, soaring from the ashes, heard one bright explosion of melody as this new beast ascended towards the flock, before blue smoke washed into his eyes, only to be swept away by lightning. He was bound in a web of silver fire, he was lost in the red of polished carbuncle, and before his eyes was the fading green of flickering beetles' wings.

Jon stood in the throne room, blinking. To his left he saw Petra and Arkor in the dim light. To his right, at the foot of the throne, one hand clutching the fluke of the gilded squid supporting the arm, was the white cloaked figure of the king sprawled on the polished steps. The other hand still moved over tile. Jon ran up to him and stooped beside him. "He's alive," he called back.

There was a clattering of footsteps. He looked up to see guards all around him, their power-blades poised. Someone turned on the throne room lights. Arkor and Petra stood among the guards. "All right, what happened to His Majesty?"

Jon was flustered, but the Duchess began quickly, "We're not sure. We heard him call out as we were coming towards the throne room. Then suddenly he ran across the floor and collapsed."

"He's alive," Jon repeated. "But you'd better get a doctor to him."

"Move away," the guard said, and Jon stepped back. "Who are you?" the guard demanded.

"I'm the King's cousin," the Duchess said, "and these are my guests."

The guard frowned. "You better return to your suite, Your Grace. And stay there till we get this straightened out," he added.

Just then another guard came from across the room. "Yes sir, he did get a chance to trip the cameras before anything happened."

"Fine," said the chief guard. He glanced from Petra to Jon and Arkor. "This place is combed with cameras, you know, that can be tripped from a dozen places." He waited for some reaction. There was none. "We'll develop these and see what happened. Please go to your rooms."

Jon, Arkor, and the Duchess left the throne room. As they reached the hall, Jon released a breath that he had been holding since his last, *he's alive.*

In their suite, the Duchess dropped into the chair with the wooden back carved like shell, and ran the fingers of both hands through her hair. "I suppose where they have cameras, they have microphones," she said, glancing around the room. Arkor walked to one wall on which was an underwater sea-scape in tones of orange and sienna. He leaned his palm against the right eye of a stylized octopus in battle with a whale. "Now they don't," he said. "Or at least they can't hear anything out of it. Actually they haven't even put a monitor on it yet."

"Those cameras almost foiled us when we kidnapped Prince Let. Thank God this time there won't be anything to see." She turned to the giant now. "Arkor, did you get a chance to see what the *Lord of the Flames* did on this visit?"

"It was more difficult this time," Arkor said. "Human beings' minds are a bit harder to ferret things out of than the neo-neanderthals where he was hiding before."

"Well, could you tell anything?"

"I can tell who murdered Chargill."

"Who?"

"His Majesty."

"Do you know why?"

"That I'm not sure. But there was something else in his mind, something that . . ." Suddenly he turned. "Jon, do you remember when we were coming here, I caught your sister's thoughts, and I said that something seemed to be wrong? I said there was some kaleidoscopic image that I could get the pattern of, but not the meaning? Well that same pattern, that same image was in King Uske's mind too!"

They were silent a moment.

Then Jon asked, "What exactly does the similarity mean?"

"It means that they both know something, the same thing, and even feel the same way about it. But it's hidden, like something you learn and then try immediately to forget. It was a lot stronger in Uske's mind, but it was there in both. And it may have something to do with the *Lord of the Flames*."

"Well then what is it doing in both of their minds?" asked the Duchess.

"That's a good question," Arkor said.

"We'll try it on Catham to see what he comes up with – along with about umpteen others . . ."

There was a knock on the door. At the Duchess' nod Jon opened it. The chief guard stepped in. "Your Grace, gentlemen, the films have been developed. You are free to go and come as you like, but you may be questioned later on."

"Has His Majesty said anything yet?" Petra asked.

The guard looked from under lowered brows. "His Majesty is dead." He turned abruptly, and Jon closed the door slowly after him.

"I guess," said Petra, "that dislodging the *Lord of the Flames* was more of a jolt than he could take." They were silent.

"It's all a healthy man could stand," said Arkor, "and the king was sickly all his life."

Petra placed her long fingers together. "Chargill dead at the King's instigation. Now the King dead through . . ." She didn't finish. "With all this war business streaming about, the government is going to go through quite a contortion. All the little functionaries will start to wiggle and squirm."

"Do you think anyone will try to use the Queen Mother as a rallying point?" asked Jon.

"I doubt it," Petra said. "She's safe in her padded room at the General Medical psyche-ward. I hope she's happy, too. It's a shame she broke down last year. I remember her once being a powerful personality who might well have done the empire good."

It was Arkor who said, "This means it's time for Prince Let to come back."

The Duchess nodded.

"Just who is in line for the throne, I mean after Let?" Jon wanted to know.

"I am," Petra said, shortly. "You and Arkor must start out to the mainland forests this evening and bring him back as fast as possible."

"If we can find him in the forest."

"We'll find him," Arkor said.

Jon pulled back the curtain at the window and looked over the lights of the city, to where the sea spread like black cloth to a moonlit horizon. The transit-ribbon threaded from the palace, streaked with moon-silver, supported by mammoth pylons. The two hundred and twenty-five mile antenna beamed matter around the world. "I don't know," he said. "I wonder now if this is getting out of hand. No one meant to kill – or at least I certainly didn't mean to kill – the King."

"Are you suggesting that I did?" asked Petra quietly. "Ask Arkor if that was my intention."

"No, I won't ask," Jon said. "When I was in prison, I wanted . . ." He stopped.

"Jon, who was responsible for your going to prison?"

"Three years ago I would have said King Uske. But both of us were only children in school when it happened. Yes, something very twisted and sadistic made him dare me to break into the palace and steal the Royal Herald. But something equally foolish and headlong made me go along with it, frightened me so much I actually killed the guard who was trying to stop me. But when I found out the King was dead just now, I waited for the feeling inside me, wondering whether it would be a sense of completed revenge, relief, or freedom. And it was nothing. I'm still not free, not just of the Triple-Being, but of something in myself."

"Everyone has that," Petra began. Then she added more softly, "Perhaps you have it more than most, Jon Koshar."

Without turning from the window, Jon asked, "All right Arkor, you can sense it. Tell me what it is."

Arkor's voice, though not sad, came with a grave emotion Jon had not heard in his voice before: "I can't, Jon Koshar. It's another mask I can't pierce. It's easily the most familiar pattern that I see in your men's minds, almost the identifying mark of a human."

Jon turned from the window, sharply. "Guilt?" he asked. "Is that what it seems to you? Well now I perceive something very finely, and it's not guilt, Arkor. It's something . . . else."

The giant's eyes narrowed in momentary concentration, and when he spoke this time, it was with an uncertainty as new in his voice as the previous grave emotion: "No . . . it is not guilt."

Jon turned to the window again. "I don't understand," he said. "Perhaps Catham was right. Every time we exorcise the *Lord of the Flames* and suddenly go hopping around the universe, I wonder . . ."

"Wonder what?" asked the Duchess.

"I wonder whether this whole thing isn't a psychotic fantasy after all."

The Duchess drew a breath, giving her mind time to disengage from Jon's words. "I only know," she said, "that whatever this means, we can only act as we see. And we must return Prince Let to Toron as soon as possible."

Jon turned back to the room. "All right. Then we will go to the forest and bring him back."

"Shall we leave tonight?" asked Arkor.

"Yes," said the Duchess. "I will try to get the council's ear and see if I can waylay some of the confusion that is going to result."

Jon and Arkor started for the door. A moment before they closed it, Jon repeated, with puzzlement in his voice, "A psychotic fantasy."

The Duchess looked up from the report she had begun.

"You have no time to worry about that," Arkor said to him briskly. "You only have enough to think it once, or perhaps twice, to convince yourself that it is not."

CHAPTER SIX

HIS boot soles hit the mud; he was in enemy territory; beyond the barrier. He hugged his arms tight around his chest and pulled against himself to release the excitement that quivered in his wrists and shoulders. The ground was as soft here as the swampy pools made by the sea's back-wash in those winding inlets. The mist in front of him was as dense and damp as the autumn fogs that used to wrap his fishing boat at dawn. The air held October chill. And the sky, beyond the mist glowed faintly like the polished surfaces of well rubbed . . . shells . . ?

No. Something wouldn't let him think that. You shouldn't think of that. Tel walked forward, trying to see. He felt vaguely unsteady, like the time when he had been lost for six hours in the dinghy one foggy morning when the oar had slipped into the sea. For a moment the mist gave way and he glimpsed the barracks to which he was to report.

He ducked forward, noticing that the ground was firmer, and at last stepped through the door of the shack. "Hello?" he called. There were no lights. He sniffed the fog floating in the darkness. It had the faint odour of sea-weed. The familiarity made everything more real, vivid. Yet he was somewhere in a half dead blister of the irradiated earth, on some protected scab on the wrecked crust of the earth. "Hello," he called again.

"Hello yourself," came back a familiar voice. A face rose, came forward, its features materialising through the haze. "So you made it out here," Ptorn said. The black eyes smiled down at him. "Good for you. Quite a trip, eh?"

"Yeah," said Tel. "You can say that again."

"I think that's your bed over there."

Tel moved inside. Along the wall he could just make out a row of cots. "Hey, where's the enemy in relation to us?" he asked. "And where's everybody else?"

"We're pretty well behind the line of fire," said Ptorn. "And the others will be here soon."

"Sure as hell can't see anything around here," Tel said, squinting towards the door again. "Some of them damned bastards might be hanging around, just sneak up behind you, and burn you out. How are you gonna know?"

Ptorn shrugged.

"Hey, boy!" A shadow filled the doorway.

"Hi," Tel said, not sure if he recognized the newcomer, even though the voice was familiar.

"Glad to see you made it too."

"Certainly looks like you came through all right," Tel said, still unsure of whom it was. ". . . Shrimp? Oh, I thought it was you. How do you feel?"

"Damp," Shrimp said. "Smells like the inside of an old lobster pot."

"Just like home," Tel joked back.

Another shadow darkened the door. "Ugg. Can't see nothing up here."

"There's nothing to see, ape," Shrimp shot back across his shoulder as he went to his bed. He dropped on his back on the mattress. "That transit jump sure takes a hell of a lot out of you." He stretched himself, arched his back, then fell back to the bed. Springs squeaked. "Like rocks," Shrimp mumbled, closing his eyes. "When the enemy comes around, wake me, hear? But not for anything else."

"Hey, Tel," said Lug, stepping into the shack, "I'll play you a game of randy."

"I'll beat you," Tel warned him.

"I don't care," the neanderthal said. "I just want to play. Over here."

"All right," said Tel. "A couple of rounds."

Lug hunkered down in the doorway where the light was bright enough to see and spread a handful of centi-units on the boards. Tel leaned on the jamb watching him. Then he squatted too and helped arrange the coins in the randomax square.

Darkness slipped across his hands, and he and the neanderthal looked up. A forest guard stood before them. Tel squinted through the mist. He could make out nothing distinctive about the features save the yellow eyes.

"Move. I want to get inside." The voice was cold. If sound could have colour, thought Tel, then this voice would shine like oiled steel.

"Can't you step over?" Lug asked affably. "We just got them set –" Suddenly a lot of expression went over Lug's face: they were all types of pleasure. "Hey, Quorl! You're up here too? You're the first person I've met from home. I'm glad to see –"

The booted foot shot out, Lug and Tel snapped their hands back in time, the coins went skittering.

"What the . . ." began Lug. "Hey," he called into the cabin after the guard. "Quorl, what's the matter with you? You don't have no manners, you know that? If you were my size, I'd bust you –"

"Keep quiet, Lug," Tel said. Something in that voice bespoke a tautness he did not want to cut. Remembering what he had said about perception, he wondered whether or not Lug felt it too.

"But I knew that guy in the forest." The neanderthal was gathering up the coins. "Quorl, he was my friend. But now he's acting just like an ape that ought to be pounded around a little." He made a disgusted sucking sound.

"Hey, you guys are new up here, right?"

The squat hulk of a neanderthal stepped into the doorway. Lug blinked.

"You guys are new?"

"That's right," said Ptorn from inside.

"Then come on," the neanderthal said. "I have to show you something."

Ptorn joined Lug and Tel as they followed the other man out. "My name is Illu," he introduced himself as he led them over the soft ground outside the cabin.

"What do you want to show us?" Tel asked.

"You'll see," said Illu. "We show it to everybody who comes here. It makes them feel better. Some of them, anyway."

"What is it?" It was Lug who asked now.

"You'll see," Illu repeated.

They entered a clearing among the cabins. A post was stuck in the ground at the centre. As they approached, Tel saw that there was a sign nailed to it, pointing into the fog:

TOROMON – THIS WAY HOME

"The Scout put this up," Illu said.

"The Scout?" asked Tel. "Who's that?"

"A forest guard in our cabin, named Quorl," Illu said. "He's the guy who came in just before I did." He looked at the sign. "Doesn't it make you feel better?"

Tel was puzzled. But Lug put his ham-like hands against the post and growled with satisfaction. "Ummm," he said, looking from Tel to Ptorn. "Now we know which way home is. That means we know where we are. That makes me feel better."

Illu grinned. "I told you. We show it to all you new people."

"Quorl put this up?" Lug asked. He thought for a moment. "That's like Quorl. Back in the forest, a lot of times he made me feel better. Why is he so funny acting though?"

Illu shrugged. "A lot of people act funny out here. After a while you just sort of accept it, when you've been here long enough."

"How long have you been out here?" Lug asked.

"Aw . . . too long." He spat in the mud. "You knew the Scout back home, huh? Tell me what's happening back home."

"It's all crazy," Lug said. "All everybody talks about is the war. Nothing but war."

Illu nodded. "And now you're in it yourself. The Scout is a pretty important guy up here. Tell me about Quorl when you knew him back in the forest."

"Well," said Lug, "he was certainly different from now . . ." And the two neanderthals, having struck up a friendship, wandered off together, leaving Ptorn and Tel.

"I wonder how he figured it out?" Tel said, looking at the sign up close.

"He must know his math," Ptorn said.

The split plank that formed the post was grey and weathered, and the grain was separating. The nails had rusted quickly in the damp, leaving brown rings around the heads, like the nails in the weather-beaten boards of his father's boat-house. He was about to say something, but before the words formed in his mouth, Ptorn nodded his head and said, "Yes, it does."

When they got back to the barracks, most of the beds were taken with soldiers already in the regiment. In the lightless cabin, the figures looked like shadows through the thick mist hanging even inside. Tel went to his bed. As he sat down, the figure on the bed next to him suddenly rolled over. "Hey, you're one of the new guys that's come to fill up the holes."

"What holes?" asked Tel.

"You know; replacements."

Tel couldn't make out the face and for a passing moment was reminded of one of the featureless voices that had issued from the loudspeakers during basic training.

"What happened to the others, the ones we're replacing?" Tel asked warily.

"You really want to know?" responded the shadow.

"Not really." Tel ran his palm across the blanket, to detect the texture of the weave. "Do your eyes ever get accustomed to all this fog?"

"No. But you do."

"How?"

"After a while you get used to being half blind."

"Oh. Just exactly what do you guys do here?" Tel wanted to know.

"Well," mused the bulky shadow, "it depends on what you've been trained for."

"I'm a maintenance mechanic for the 606–B. And I know the 605 pretty well too."

"Oh, then you won't have any problem here with finding something to do."

Tel grinned through fog and felt a glow of usefulness, a warm reassurance.

"I gotta get some sleep," the shadow said.

"Hey, just one more question." Tel lowered his voice. "What's with that big yellow-eyed guard?"

"You mean Quorl, the Scout?" the voice came back.

"Yeah, the one who put up the sign-post."

"How do you mean 'what's with' him?"

"Well," said Tel, "he acts sort of funny."

"Sure he does," replied the voice. "He's the Scout. You'd be funny too if you had to do what he does." The springs squeaked again as the figure turned over. "Look, talk to me some other time about it, soldier. I gotta get some sleep."

"Oh, Yeah," said Tel. "Good night." He sat back on his cot, alone, looking this way and that through the murky cabin. He wondered what Quorl's function was; then he wondered who he was a replacement for. Maybe he should have asked what happened to the person he was replacing, but . . . He was glad there was work for a 606–B repair man. Very glad; because he could take it apart, put it together, replace any worn part, tell when the slip plates had too much oil, or when the plumb coils were about to give. If only he knew what . . . if he knew what it was . . . No. He mustn't think that. Instead he thought about how good it made him feel.

A few hours later, when Tel was wandering outside the barracks, he stopped, bent down, and looked at his boots. They were coated with mud to the ankles. As he stood up, sucking breath between his teeth, someone called, "Who's that?"

"Eh . . . Tel 211 BQ – T."

"Oh, hi. It's me, Lug."

"Hey there, ape. I thought you were a sergeant or something."

"Hell no," Lug said, solidifying in the mist as he came forward. "You surprised me too." He came only a bit above Tel's shoulder, but his smile showed through the haze.

"Did your friend Illu tell you anything about what's going on?"

Lug scratched his head and fell into step beside Tel. "I don't know if I understand it."

"What did he say?"

Lug brought his hands together in concentration and his craggy face furrowed. "First he says we're in front of the main line of enemy forces. We're part of a string of bases thirty miles in front of that line. But what Illu said is that they're afraid they'll circle us and attack from behind." He looked up puzzled at Tel.

"What don't you understand?"

"How can they attack us from behind if they're in front of a string, a line of bases?"

"Simple," Tel began. Then he paused, remembering what Ptorn had told him about perception. "Look, Lug, how long is a string?"

"Huh? I don't know."

"How far does a string run?"

"From one end to the other," said Lug, shrugging. "How long is that?"

"That's as long as it needs to be: from one end to the other. Now suppose the enemy comes around the ends of the string. Won't they be behind us then?"

Lug pondered a moment. "Oh. I guess they will. I hadn't thought of going around." They went on a few more steps. "That means we're in some danger, or we may be, huh?"

"I guess so," said Tel, feeling at once apprehensive, and at the same time affably superior for having solved Lug's topological conundrum. Perhaps that was what Ptorn felt like towards him, he reflected. Examining his own feeling, he was relieved to find in it nothing that the ape might resent. "Just by being here, we're in danger, Lug."

"Yeah. We have an enemy beyond the barrier," Lug quoted. "Only now we're beyond the barrier too."

They were nearing a rise.

"Hey, rocks," said Lug, moving to place his hands on the broken surface. "Makes me think of . . ." He did not finish his sentence, and Tel remembered his own first thoughts about the colours behind the mist, putting them out of his mind as quickly as before. He folded his arms, leaned against the rocky wall, and gazed through the fog. "What do you think we're looking at?"

"Nothing," answered Lug.

"Mist, fog, water vapour . . . nothing. Lug, what's it like where you come from?"

"You mean . . ." Tel could sense the words came from deep in Lug's mind. ". . . home?"

"Yeah. What was your home like?"

"Home," mused Lug, "was . . . the place I lived." He turned to Tel and grinned. "Yeah," he said. "That was what was best about it. It was the place I lived!"

Tel laughed, and again wondered how his own insights seemed to Ptorn.

"And Mura," Lug's voice became quieter, "and Porm, and Kuag; those are the people I lived with. Porm," he explained, "was my daughter."

"You have a daughter?" He hoped his surprise did not come through the mist. "How old is she? How old are you?"

"She's four summers old," Lug said. "I'm nineteen winters."

From somewhere Tel remembered that the average age of the neo-neanderthals was forty-five. To think of your life so short must make things appear very different. Yet a daughter, a family. Someplace in him, like an efflorescent crystal, he felt respect growing for this condensed, alien image of himself. "What was your home like?" he asked again.

"It was in the forest," Lug said.

"What else?" asked Tel.

"It was in a broken stone building, a 'ruin' they called it. From before the Great Fire. The big trees had pushed most of the buildings down, and there were stairs that led up and just stopped over open air. Children played with rocks and sticks on the stairs, and sometimes the wind came and we all went inside the stone building and stayed in the corner, and sometimes sang to the wind; or when the water fell from the sky, we sang to the water. When it was very hot, we danced for the sun." He stepped back and began to raise one foot and then the other with a little hop. "Like that, only with lots more people, and faster, with beating and shouting. Once a month we did that for the moon, only different. That's because the moon and the sun are different, and not like rain and wind. You understand?"

"I understand," Tel said.

"Sometimes we'd mend the leather over the hole in the sunward wall. But then you have to go out and catch a boar, or an elott – and outside, that's not home anymore. That's . . ." He paused.

"The rest of the wide world," Tel supplied.

"Yes," said Lug, screwing up his eyebrows and nodding. "And it's very, very wide, you know. Very wide."

Now Tel nodded.

"The rest of the wide world," repeated Lug. "That's very different from home. That's something else entirely. Home . . ." He paused once more, and at last took refuge in his previous revelation. "Home is where I live." Suddenly Lug grinned slyly. "All you very tall, very wise men who can get around the ends of strings, you must think this is silly. You must know where home is."

"Do you think it's silly?"

"No," said Lug, "but . . ."

"Then don't worry about it," said Tel. "It just may not be silly after all."

Lug pondered, then seemed satisfied. Now he moved back from the wall again and did his little dance. He stopped and looked up. "No sun," he said. "No moon. Home is where I live, and then there is the rest of the wide world. But where is this?" He gazed forward through the mist. "Noplace."

Tel looked down at Lug's feet. "Don't your feet get muddy?" he asked. Because their big toes were comparatively opposable, the neanderthals felt uncomfortable in boots that prevented them from picking up things with their feet.

"They get too muddy," Lug said, wriggling his toes in the soft earth, "I wash them."

"I guess that's the way it goes," Tel shrugged.

"What's your home like?" Lug asked. "Is it the place you live?"

"It isn't," Tel said. "At least I haven't lived there for a long time, almost three years. I left when I was fourteen and went to Toron."

"Some of my people go there," Lug said. "I don't know if they like it very much. Those that come back say it's very complicated."

"It is," Tel said.

"What did you do in the city?"

"Just knocked around," Tel answered evasively. "Got into trouble here, got out of it there, couldn't get a job because there weren't enough jobs to go around, and ended up in the army." They leaned back against the rocks once more. "Say, did Illu say anything to you about your friend Quorl."

"The guard who put up the sign-post?"

"That's right. And kicked up our game."

"Oh, the one with no manners. He's not my friend no more. All I know is he's a real important person around here. I don't know what he does, though."

"Maybe he goes out spying on the enemy. That's what I'd guess from the name. I wonder if he knows what the enemy looks like."

"You know you're right," said Lug, his face furrowing. "How are we gonna fight them if we wouldn't even recognize one if it came up to you and said hello?"

"We'd recognize it."

"Yeah." Lug said after a moment. "I guess we would."

CHAPTER SEVEN

ABOVE the yacht the stars were still. Water rushed the hull, whispering and lisping. At the horizon the jewelled towers of Toron diminished and sank down.

"Do you think after these three years that you'd recognize the Prince if he came up to you right now and said hello?" Jon asked Arkor. The wind was a cold palm against his cheek, cold fingers playing with his hair.

"I don't know," Arkor said. "His mind will have changed. His body will have grown."

Jon leaned into the wind, his eyes narrowing to pry between the two sheets of blackness, sky and sea, that joined before them. Finally he stood up. "Perhaps we'd better get some sleep," he said. "We'll be there by dawn." Together Jon and Arkor turned from the rail.

Sun broke through one layer after another of the night, till at last it burst bloody over the water. Already the shore was in sight. The forest came nearly to the beach. Once it had been an immigration port from the mainland to the island City. Now a burned dock sagged like a blackened limb into the tide, where a war plane had crashed there three years ago.

As Jon mounted the deck through the chill, he saw there were no other boats at the piers. Overhead a thin whine razored the sky. High above him, the sudden gleam of planes. They were army craft, carrying recruits from Toron to Telphar. The whine died, and he looked back towards the port which swung towards the boat through the lightening morning.

When Arkor joined him on deck, the wooden pilings were already thumping the side of the boat. The motor cut, reversed, and the space between the bow and the dock foamed with backwash.

A few dock-hands appeared to catch the hawser that the crewmen tossed. One boatman appeared by Arkor's side, but the giant had already picked up the huge coil of rope. "I'll secure it," he said, dismissing the man, and flung the line across the closing slip.

They leapt aboard, Jon catching himself a moment by one

of the near-rotten pilings, looking after Arkor who had already started towards the board walk.

A half hour later they stood among the trees. Arkor was listening, one brown hand against a barrel-thick oak.

"You're home now," Jon said. "What does it feel like?"

The giant shook his head. "Not what you think it should feel like." His eyes narrowed. "I don't hear anyone yet. Come on, let's go this way."

With surprising rapidity they made their way for the next hour through the forest. Abruptly the trees thinned, and in front of them Jon saw a glitter that must have been sun on the sea. They reached a cliff where broken rock spilled to ledges below. Fifty feet down, still a hundred feet above the water, was the largest table of rock. The sun burned white across the whole lithic expanse, and the small temple at the edge cast a sharp shadow.

"The priest is there," Arkor said. "Follow me down."

Before they reached the plateau, a man emerged from the door of the temple. Black robes caught the breeze that moved across the rock towards the sea. A trumpet shell hung by a leather strap over one shoulder. His face showed age more than any other guard Jon had ever seen.

"Why have you come back?" the priest asked.

"To take the young king to reign in Toron. His brother, King Uske, is dead."

"There are no kings in the forest," the priest said. "You have left us; why do you come back?"

Arkor was silent a moment. Then he said, "Three years ago, a young, light-haired boy came into the forest. He was the King's younger brother. The King is dead. He must rule now."

Jon noted that the priest was not marked with the triple scars of the telepath.

"Do you wish anything of him? Are you going to take anything from his mind? You know that is not allowed."

"I will take nothing from his mind," Arkor said. "His consent will be given, not taken."

"He is not of the forest people?"

"No," answered Arkor. "He came here and chose to avail himself of our people's hospitality. It is his right to choose to leave. May I have permission to search for him?"

The priest was silent for a space in which two waves broke on the crumbling rocks a hundred feet below. "You may search for him along your own ways," the priest said, and turned back into the temple.

Jon and Arkor walked back to the trail that led up into the forest. "What was that all about?"

"How much of it did you understand?" Arkor asked. "I don't mean the words, but what was going on?"

"You were asking him for permission to look for Prince Let... and telling him why you came?"

"Yes, but I was doing a lot more." The giant hoisted himself up around a leaning sapling. "I was – how would you say it – acknowledging the status quo.

"It's like this," Arkor said as they gained level ground again. "Among the forest guards, the telepaths are in an ambiguous and uncomfortable position. In fact that was why I left. You see at once they are realized superior, and feared. It is understood that nature is aiming for the time when all guards will be born telepathic, yet the non-telepaths know that they are threatened by this growing minority. So the telepaths must be marked on discovery and must acknowledge the nominal sovereignty of the non-telepathic priest. It keeps peace and allows nature to go on."

"I hate to think what would happen if telepaths started appearing among us ... men," Jon said. "There wouldn't be peace for long."

Arkor nodded. "That's why we keep the knowledge of our powers from you as much as possible."

"Occasionally I wish I could hear into other men's minds myself," said Jon.

Arkor laughed. "As I said before, it would be like giving colour vision to a man still incapable of distinguishing one shape from another and who could not even judge distances. It might be fun as a game at first, but finally it would become a meaningless, annoying hindrance – to you."

Jon shrugged. "Where do we begin to look for Let? It's your territory."

"First we find some people and check for any knowledge of the boy."

"Is that what the priest meant when he said you could search along your own ways?"

"That's right."

"Maybe your people are more civilized than we are," Jon said.

At that Arkor laughed.

Like capillaries, a dozen paths threaded the body of the forest. They had crossed nearly a dozen before Jon recognized the subtle scattering of crushed leaves on black earth, the broken twigs, the slight compactness of the earth that marked the passage of feet.

"Over there," said Arkor, "two women are napping on a cape of moss by the side of a fallen maple log. One of them has seen the strange light haired boy with the limp, who is not of the forest people." He looked at Jon. "It sounds like Let."

"Where did he get the limp from?" Jon wanted to know.

Arkor shrugged. A bit later he paused again. "A man passing by over there once hunted with the light-haired boy. They made a moose trap together six months ago."

Jon strained to see through the trees in the direction Arkor pointed, but he didn't even hear a rustle. "In six months, Arkor, he could have wandered anywhere."

"True," said the giant. Suddenly he stopped short, and Jon drew up still beside him.

A moment later the leaves before them were pushed aside and a tall guard with a shock of white hair running through the black at his temple stepped forward. Three scars ran down the left side of cheek and neck.

"You have come for the young stranger," said the guard.

"You know where he moves now," Arkor said. "You know that he walks by the high rocks, stops now, leans against the stick he is carrying and squints up at the sky through the leaves like pale blue chips."

"You will follow the webbing of thought that holds him in the centre," said the guard with the white blazed hair. Without further interchange, Arkor continued walking in his direction and the other guard passed on in his.

"Now you know where Let is?" Jon asked.

Arkor nodded.

After a moment Jon said, "Why did you speak out loud?"

"We were being polite."

"You talk loud when you want to be polite to each other?" Arkor glanced down at Jon. "We were being polite to you."

The light that lapped among the leaves grew yellower as

day turned towards noon. Once they heard an animal screech in the distance, and once they walked over a damp stretch of ground through which a mazy stream delved in a rocky cleft. "There's something wrong," said Arkor after a bit.

"With the Prince?"

"No, not with Let, but with the thought pattern I'm following."

"What thought pattern?"

"It's like a radar net that all the telepaths, or most of them, maintain for directions, for information. You have to ask permission to use it. But there's something wrong with it, something down at the very end, dark, and unclear." He stopped and looked at Jon, his eyebrows pulling together. "And Jon, it looks for all the world like the pattern I saw in your sister and in the King."

"What's it doing here in the forest?" Jon asked. "Can you tell what it means now?"

Arkor shook his head. "The prince is through those trees," he said. "Perhaps you better speak to him first alone. It will recall things to him more quickly if a man presents them to him."

"Doesn't he remember?" Jon asked.

"It's been a long time, and he's young."

Jon nodded and stepped forward through the curtain of branches.

The figure turned abruptly and the light eyes narrowed behind the dark face.

"Your Majesty?" Jon said.

The long, naturally fair hair was sun-bleached in uneven streaks.

"Your name is Let? You are the heir to the throne of Toromon?"

The figure stood very still. He held a staff in one brown hand and wore the garb of the forest guards, leather pants, a pelt across one shoulder for a cape. His feet were bare.

"Your Majesty?" Jon asked again.

The eyes widened now, extraordinary bright in the browned face. "Excuse ... excuse me." The voice came rough, yet youthful, "If my speech is ... slow. I haven't spoken much for a ... a long time."

Jon smiled. "Do you remember me? I and a friend brought

you here three years ago. Now we are here to take you back with us. Do you remember, you were sent here by the Duchess of Petra?"

"Petra?" He paused, looking up now as if some answer would come from the trees. "My . . . cousin, Petra? The one who told me the story, about the prisoner who tried to escape. Only it wasn't a story, it was real . . ."

"That's right," Jon said. "I'm that prisoner."

"Why have you come?" the young man asked again.

"Your brother is dead. You must take over the throne."

"Did you know my brother?"

"Only a long time ago, before I went to prison." Jon paused. "I was just about as old as you are now."

"Oh," said the Prince. He took a few steps forward, and Jon noticed the slight limp. "There is a war on," said the Prince, "I hear them talk about it sometimes when they come to take people from the forest to fight the . . . enemy beyond the barrier. I will have to learn a lot, and there will be a lot to do. I remember now." As they went through the trees to where Arkor was waiting, Jon wondered at the speed with which the youth was adjusting to this new situation. Subtleties of perception, he reflected, wondering whether merely living among these people had caused any of it to affect the Prince. Arkor met them on the other side of the trees.

They had nearly reached the shore when Arkor suddenly stopped. "The boat!" he said.

"What is it?" Jon asked. They were still in the woods.

"It's malis," Arkor said, "at the docks, trying to sink the ship!"

"Out here, on the shore?" Jon asked. "For what? I just thought there were malis in the City."

"Gangs have sprung up all over Toromon. There's a forest guard with them, and the . . . the pattern I saw!"

Jon felt the momentary irony of the strange gang that had kidnapped the Prince and brought him to the forest three years past which Arkor had been part of. "Why are they wrecking it?" Jon asked. "Can you get any reason?"

Arkor shook his head. "The crewmen are fighting. One of them tries to start the motor, but a fire-blade slashes across his back and his scream goes all liquid and gurgly before he slumps over the control panel. Fire glints in the eyes of one man who jumps backward from the tilting deck as water sloshes across the boards and hisses against the fire. Smoke obscures the wheelhouse where the crewman lies." Arkor breathed heavily.

"Why?" Jon asked. "Why? Were they sent? Did they have a plan?"

"The malis," Arkor said softly, "the malcontents. No, or at least I couldn't detect any."

"What do we do now?" Let asked.

"We've got to get back some way," Jon said. "I guess we go in another direction."

The strain left the giant's face and he turned with them and nodded. They began to walk again, this time perpendicular to their original route. "We might be able to get back to the Island from one of the fishing villages, or perhaps catch a tetron tramp taking ore from the mines back to Toron." A bird chirped.

Once they came to a field in which a deserted farm house sagged into the slow breeze that waved across the riotous grain. Once more in the woods, night draped the trees until the moon rose and silvered the leaves. They came to another clearing where a great strutwork pylon soared into the air and a black band of metal – the transit-ribbon – made a mark like a pen line across the lightened night sky. They slept at the edge of the clearing, and at dawn they continued.

In the brightening woods, Arkor heard the sound first. Then the two others stopped and listened. Beyond the trees, the tincan wail of a caliope sounded thinly through the morning . . .

CHAPTER EIGHT

"... THEN they started to fire on us from the left. We scrambled back behind those rock bags fast as cuttlefish. We must have splattered mud all the way back to Toromon. They have something that flames like the sun almighty and makes the fog look like powdered fire where it hits. A couple of times I've been to advanced platoons that have gone out to try and establish the beginnings of a permanent encampment but got messed up. It's pretty horrible what they do; nothing but pieces of guys all over the place. They'd told us this particular capture was going to be easy as cutting a kharba melon. They'd told us there probably wouldn't be a shot fired. Well I didn't want to end up like one of those gutted platoons and I swear I was about to take off over the rock bags and just beat it as fast as I could. Suddenly, though, there was a scrambling in the confusion of guys about twenty feet down the line. I remember I heard a rock bag fall, so I took a breath and figured – really sort of calm when you think how much sweating I was doing –, 'Well, they've finally broken into the fortress, and I guess I can expect to be dead in just about six seconds.' But I was wrong. The excitement down the line was growing. Apparently somebody from our side had scrambled back over the wall. Then someone turned on a hand-flood, and for a moment I saw a tall silhouette against the fog. Quorl had got back!

"I was down there in no seconds flat. Everybody else was crowding around too, trying to hear what he was saying. He squatted down in the mud and pulled the guy with the hand-flood down beside him. 'Shine it over here,' he whispered. We were all crouching to see. He began sketching in the soft mud, and you could just see where his finger scarred the ground with the dark and the mist. 'This is our wall,' he said. 'There's a nest here, and here. So they can hit us along the wall pretty hard. But remember, it's only two encampments. If you make a bee line fifteen degrees off twelve o-clock, you'll bypass both of them, and they won't be looking for you there. You've got about ten minutes before their next barrage. So get going.' He pointed over the wall. 'In that direction. It'll take you straight back to the base.' And before we could ask any questions, he was over the wall and gone in black fog. The next thing I know I was over the rocks running after the footsteps of the guy in front of me."

"That was me," Illu grunted. "Running 'after', hell, you nearly ran me down."

The others laughed. They were sitting on a pile of boards that had been laid outside the barracks across the mud. Tel sat cross-legged, his back against the shack wall. Now he leaned forward on his knees to hear the rest of the storyteller's tale.

The fire had almost removed the immediate sense of mist, but along the curve of shacks he could see other fires blurred orange, curving away through the fog.

"That Scout," the narrator concluded from his seat atop the empty machinery crate, "He's a pretty good guy." Now he looked at Tel. "So don't mess with him too much. Yeah, he's a little strange, but . . ." The soldier shrugged. Someone else had asked the question, and Tel inside the cabin, hearing it start, had come out to listen.

Just then a darkness passed the fire near them in the haze. Then fire light touched the long neck, the open collar, the knifelike cheek bones, and the yellow eyes. Quorl swept his glance across them and he went straight into the shack. Shrimp, who was standing in the doorway, quietly moved aside. A moment later there was a creaking of bed springs.

"That's him," the storyteller said.

"He's really seen the enemy close up?" somebody asked.

The raconteur motioned for him to keep his voice down and answered softly, "Well if anybody has, it's him." He dropped his hands to his knees, leaned back in the darkness and yawned. "I'm turning in," he said. "It's just as hard to get up in the morning here as in Toromon."

Tel watched the group break up as some of the men from other barracks who had wandered over started back in the darkness. "Officers will be shooing us inside in a minute anyway," Illu grunted down to Tel.

"Guess so," Tel answered, stretched, and stood up on the boards.

He was just about to go inside when he heard a sound something between chirping, a cheeping, with a twitching melody beneath. It was coming from the other side of the barracks.

Tel stopped, glanced around the corner and held his breath.

Something was beating the mud. Quickly Tel ducked back around the corner and grabbed the shoulder of the first person he saw still outside the hut. "Hey," he whispered. "There's something back there! You can hear it!"

"Probably a spy for the enemy." Then there was a laugh and the shoulder shook under Tel's hand. "Forget it, soldier. It's just one of the flip-flops that come around sometimes." Now Tel recognized the voice. It was the man who had the cot beside his.

"What are they?"

"Who knows. They're animals, I think. But they could be plants. They don't bother the enemy and except for making noise, don't bother us."

"Oh," Tel said. "You're sure?"

"I'm sure."

The sounds came again, a distinct flapping sound, irregular stuttering; then the chirping melody.

Tel went inside the barracks pulling his shirt out of his pants. He shrugged it down his arms, and sat on the edge of his bed. The sagging springs were tight against his buttocks, the air moist on his chin. He'd almost got used to the vegitative odour, but if he took the air deeply into his lungs, he could feel the rank smell far back on his pallet.

He pulled the blanket up from the mattress and slipped into the dark envelope with the warm spot from where he'd been sitting, listening to the sound the material made coming loose from its tucking, bringing a warmth to the surface of his mind by its familiarity. With his cheek pressed against his forearm, he squinted his eyes and listened. Outside in the mud he heard the flapping again, a sound like a loose canvas sail beating against a mast, like the slap of his mother's hand-loom when the treadles struck the leather stops and the threads shifted up and down, like his father's hand beating the water from his slicker as he strode up from the boat house, like his father's belt beating . . .

Flop-flip, flup-flep, flap-flep; he opened his eyes. The mist was bluish between himself and the barracks ceiling. He was lying on his back. It was very early in the morning. Flep-flap. The sound was just outside the door.

Suddenly Tel sat up, stuck his feet in his boots (the leather was damp) and stood up in his underwear. The mist was lighter now and the shadows on the beds were still. He went to the door and narrowed his eyes against the blue morning. Flip-flup. Last night's fire was dead, and the ashes and half burnt boards lay a few feet away. A very neurotic quail was walking among them.

Or maybe it was an extraordinary self-composed feather duster. It was exploring the remains of the fire on three large webbed feet. It poked at a bit of charcoal, circled it three times, then stood over it, squatted, and – injested it!

At first Tel thought he glimpsed a head or a tail, but no, the body was a shapeless ball of feathers. It flapped around another piece of charcoal, then changed its mind and sounded its chirping, whistling chuckle. Tel stooped at the doorway to look more closely. Perhaps the creature noticed him, because it cocked its head (body?), took six flop-flop steps towards him, then leaned its body (head?) the other way and did a couple of demi-pliés.

Tel laughed and the flup-flip twittered.

"Hey, what's that?" someone asked above him.

Tel looked up and saw Lug leaning against the door jamb, clawing at his hairy stomach where his undershirt didn't reach his underpants. Tel shrugged.

"He's sort of cute," Lug said. Then he coughed and ground his fist first into one eye then the other. "Damn mist," he muttered and spat across Tel into the mud. The flap-flip stepped back, then carefully waddled closer to the door. Tel held out his hand and made a rapid snapping sound with his fingers.

"Does it bite?" Lug asked.

"I'll find out in a minute."

At the sound the flep-flep leapt ten inches backwards, nearly lost its balance and began to plié again.

"Reveille hasn't rung yet. Why are you up?"

Both Tel and Lug turned quickly at the steel voice behind them. The Scout had come to the door. As he stepped forward the blue light slowly defined his equine features.

"Either shut up or go outside," Quorl said. "Men are trying to sleep in here, Lug. One or two of them even worked hard enough to deserve it." He stepped through the door, then looked back over his shoulder. "Go on. Get out of there if you're going to jabber." Then he glanced down and saw the flip-flap.

Tel and Lug had stepped outside and were standing uncomfortably by the wall when Quorl looked back at them, smiling. Tel met the smile with a puzzled frown.

Quorl pointed to the flop-flup who was now doing an arabesque with two of its legs, and perhaps listening. "Is that a friend of yours?"

"Huh?"

"Do you want a pet?"

Tel shrugged.

Quorl bent down, picked up a piece of charcoal and held it towards the flup-flop. The creature lowered its feet, scurried to Quorl's hand, straddled it, and squatted. Then it quietly wrapped its flippers around the Scout's wrist. As Quorl stood up, the flap-flop sagged over and dangled from his forearm like a feather pocket book.

"Hold out your arm," Quorl said.

Tel extended his arm alongside Quorl's and the forest guard began to flex his fist. The flop-flip suddenly got nervous and, one flipper at a time, transferred to Tel's arm.

"He likes charcoal and he likes warmth," Quorl said. "Give him both and he'll stay with you." Then he turned and strode off through the mist, buttoning his shirt.

"I wonder if he's going off to sneak a look at some enemy encampment," Lug said. "What are you gonna do with that thing?"

Tel looked at the flip-flep. Then the flop-flap did something. It opened an eye and looked back at Tel. The boy laughed out loud.

The eye was the milky hue of a polished shell, streaked with veins of gold. Another eye opened to reveal mother of pearl. Then a third (as the other two closed) shone through the feathers, streaked, like the first, but with red. "Will you look at that?" Tel said.

The third eye closed.

"At what?"

"Aw, it just stopped."

Lug yawned. "Let me get back inside and catch my last five minutes," he said. "I just got up to see what you were looking at anyway." He frowned after the Scout. Then he went back to the door and made his way to bed.

Tel raised the flop-flap and stared at it. Seven eyes appeared in the feathers; without pupils, their muted silver surfaces swirled with pastel lustres. A warm feeling uncoiled through him, fighting the coolness of the mist. He was beyond the barrier, gazing into friendly, familiar – so familiar pastel eyes.

That afternoon he checked over the 606–B. The asbestos washer on one clutch plate had worn down, so he stripped it as neatly as the rubber gasket would allow and took it to the quarter-master's station. He got a new one in under thirty seconds which was a relief after the time it took to get replacement parts on the training base back in Telphar. Once the flup-flup tipped the lubricant can and black oil spilled onto his arm and got all over his hand; after washing most of it off at the spiggot, he resigned himself to black-rimmed nails.

Once a tank rolled by close enough to see Shrimp riding in the open bubble. "How's it going?" Tel hailed him.

"I can almost turn this thing on a deci-unit," Shrimp called back.

"Good for you," Tel called.

"Hey, guess where I saw Curly. . . ." But the tank swerved away and the mist closed behind.

It was not until after the knock-off whistle pierced the fog that Tel realized the flup-flup had left its perch on top of the assembly rack. Quickly he looked around.

Flap-flup came from somewhere behind him. He wiped his hands on the seat of his pants, turned, and started off through the mud. Once he hit a pot-hole, staggered, and nearly fell. When he got his balance he was just outside the semi-circle of cabins.

He listened and heard a twittering from the left. He turned and followed it. He had climbed over a three-foot wall of rock before it occurred to him that maybe it wasn't his flep-flop he was following. He stooped down and made the snapping sound with his fingers. Instantly the twittering began again, but still too far away for him to see. He took a few running steps forward and heard the sound of paddle feet receeding. "Hey, come on," he called. "Come back and stay with me." Maybe he should have brought some charcoal. He'd put some in his pocket that morning, occasionally feeding the animal all afternoon. But now when he ran his hand into the envelope of his back pocket, the cloth was just gritty. "Come on back here," he called again.

Flep-flop, flip-flip, flop-flep.

He ran forward ten, fifteen, twenty steps. When he stopped, the flup-flap stopped too and chuckled. "Oh, the hell with you," Tel said and turned around.

He walked maybe half a dozen long strides though the thicker mud before he slowed down and a frown deepened into his face. He turned right, took five steps, and stopped when a clump of leafless trees appeared before him. He frowned again and walked in the other direction. Five minutes later he noticed that the ground was extremely firm under his feet. He didn't remember crossing any ground of this consistency.

To his right the mist was bluer. He tried to recall: from which side had night approached the encampment? There was the grey afternoon, when he had met all the guys in the barracks. Then there was the night, sitting around the fire, listening to the stories the soldiers told. But how went the change between them?

He had started walking again when something brushed his cheek. He jumped and saw that he had walked blindly into another grove of spikey trees. The twig that had brushed his cheek had not been sharp and scratchy but wet; it bent like rubber. He rubbed his jaw, then reached out to touch the branch again.

Just then the idea of what being lost meant slipped into his brain and galvanised his spinal column, like a hot wire through his vertibrae. His hand drew back, and the rear of his thighs, his neck, and the small of his back felt like crinkled foil pulled slowly tight. He backed away from the skeletal trees. His legs felt soft, his joints all a-wash on one another. The mist was thick and very close . . .

Something twittered on his left. Violently he turned right and ran. The mud splashed, and it was darker to his left. The ground was hard, then soft under his shoes. He ran. The mist clawed into his lungs and made the inside of his nostrils sting. He ran.

Then his hands snapped up just in time to keep him from crashing face first into a sudden rise of rock. He kept his cheek pressed against the veined stone biting into tiny, terrified breaths for nearly three minutes, when he realised he was at the bottom of a cliff. The rock disappeared above him and faded away right and left. He turned his back to the wall at last and tried to keep his eyes closed and not think; but they kept on opening and darting about of their own volition. Hysterically they tried to fix on some form in the dark haze. Yet he was afraid to take his hands away from the rock behind him (where he had nearly rasped away his finger tips) and look at them for fear he wouldn't see them even if he held them in front of his eyes.

And something was coming towards him.

He mashed the air out of his lungs, his ribs strained like crushed springs. Mother, he thought, waiting for white fire; oh, mother, father . . .

"You pick a hell of a time to go off on a stroll," Quorl said. As Tel nearly collapsed from the wall, the forest guard's hand struck his chest sharply. "Breathe," Quorl said, in the dark.

Tel began to breathe. He wanted to cry, but choking down the rank damp air was more important. He peeled himself from the rock. The back of his shirt and pants were soaked.

"Don't fall down," Quorl said, "because I won't carry you."

Tel didn't fall.

"Come on. We don't have all night."

His legs didn't want to work. His first steps were irregular. "Where . . . where are we?"

"About forty yards from an enemy nest," came the slow, figuring voice.

That stopped Tel. "Wait a minute . . ." he managed to pant. "I thought they were . . . were thirty miles away. I couldn't have come that far."

"They don't wait for us to come to them. Get a move on. We're nowhere near safe."

"Wait a minute . . ." Tel got out again. "You mean they're really camped only . . . I mean you've seen them, really looked at them. You could take me close enough so I could look. . . ."

"In this light with this mist," the Scout's polished voice came back, "you'd have to get awfully close to see anything." Then, with the same amusement in his voice as when he'd shown Tel how to coax the flap-flap, he said, "Do you want to go over and take a look?"

Tel had to clamp his jaw to keep from making the hysterical

noise that ached and flooded up behind the prison of his teeth. All he did was shake his head. Whether Quorl sensed his answer, or actually saw his wagging head in the near black, his only words were, "Let's get going." Then, after a minute of silence, he added, "I've never seen them either."

Finally the camp-fire glow pierced the mist ahead of them. Chills still raced Tel's back but he said, "Eh . . . thanks. What . . . made you come out after me?"

"You're a good mechanic. The 606–B is a pretty important machine."

"Yeah," said Tel. "I guess so."

As they passed the sign-post, there was a twittering chuckle, then a whistling chirp. Something went flep-flup by his left boot.

"It's been wandering around here all night trying to figure out where you were," Qurol said. "It's been lonesome."

"Huh?" said Tel. He stood still and blinked. Then he let his body drop to a stoop and extended his arm. The flip-flop's paddle-feet wrapped trustingly about his wrist.

"You mean to tell me you've been waiting here all this time? You mean you're just going to hang there and blink at me with those pretty eyes of yours and tell me you were here all along, while I was out running around in that . . . You ought to be ashamed of yourself! Why you ought to be ashamed!"

Like pure relief, like the upward thrust at the removal of pressure, the affection welled. And there were tears running down his cheek when he looked up.

Quorl had disappeared into the fog, by the barracks.

The nightly game of randy was breaking up. He fished a piece of warm charcoal out of the fire, fed the flop-flip, and set it to warm itself by the embers. "Man," said Illu when he saw Tel, "we thought you'd had it. What were you out looking for?"

"Just exploring," said Tel.

"Just don't explore yourself right into an enemy encampment. You know they've moved closer."

"Yeah," said Tel. "I heard."

When Tel got into bed, he was just about to go off to sleep when the soldier next to him raised up on his elbow and whispered, "You back alive?"

Tel laughed. "I guess I am."

The shadowed figure whistled. "I'm surprised. I admit it. You hear about the enemy moving in?"

"I know they moved."

"There may be a major blast soon."

"You mean a battle?"

"I don't mean a game of randy." Tel heard his head drop back to the pillow. "Well, good night soldier. And I am glad to see you back, kid."

"Thanks," Tel told him, and rolled over. Outside, once, he heard the tiny whistling, chirping chuckle before exhaustion struck him into dark slumber.

CHAPTER NINE

FLAP-FLAP, flap-flap, flap-flap: in the breeze from the meadow, the canvas cover that she had pushed from the calliope beat against the back of the key-board console. Her note-book was open on the music rack and a strange graph of multiple lines waved over the page, cut here and there by single, double, and triple dashes. She struck a fourth, an augmented fifth. On the lower right hand corner of the page was a meticulous pencil drawing of a leaf. The model for the drawing had blown across the field and settled on top of the calliope bench for the eight minutes she had needed to trace its serried edge and fine veining, then tilted away on another gust.

She struck a third chord.

"What are you scribbling at?"

Clea turned, smiling. "Hello, Mr. Triton."

The rotund, bearded gentleman leaned against the console and looked back over the tents, wagons, aerial rides, and the metal runways between them. "Not too much business this afternoon. I remember when we'd travel through the farm lands here and have more yokels out than you could shake a stick at. When it came time for the Big Show you'd have to turn them away." He made a clicking sound with his teeth. "This war is a bad business. Still, we have an enemy beyond the barrier. What's all that scratching?"

"It's a new and totally useless method of musical notation. It's much too complicated for sight reading, though it's able to catch a lot more nuances in the music than the present system."

"I see," said Mr. Triton, burying one hand in his beard. With the other he began an arpeggio over the tinny notes. "I started out playing one of these things twenty-seven years ago." He took his hand from the keys and made a gesture over the entire park. "Now I own the whole thing myself." Then he let his arm fall and a disappointed look darkened the wrinkles already there. "This slack we're in, though; we've had slack seasons before, but never quite like this. We'll be heading back to Toron before the end of this week. At least there we'll be sure of a steady crowd. The war hasn't left people in the mood for circuses. And everyone's migrated to the City anyway."

Just then Clea looked over the top of the calliope wagon at the grassy meadow. Then she stood up.

"What is it?" Mr. Triton asked. "Who are they?"

Clea slipped out from behind the bench, jumped from the platform and began to run across the field. The warm stems brushed her legs. Once she ran through a clearing in the grain and from the yellow stubble, twenty locust snapped up before her. "Jon!" she cried. Stalks flicked her forearms.

"Clea!" He caught his sister in his arms and whirled her.

"Jon, what are *you* doing here?"

He set her down between them. Arkor and Let stood back.

"We came to pay you a visit. What are you doing?"

"So many things I couldn't begin to tell you. I've discovered a new overtone in the tetron vibration series. And did you know that the density of leaf veins, as they get further away from the stem is a constant, and a different constant for each leaf? You can put that in your useless information file. Then I'm working on something a lot bigger than all that, but I can't really go into it yet. Oh, and mornings I do the accounting." As they began to walk back towards the calliope wagon, she asked, "Who are your friends?"

"Arkor, this is my sister, Dr. Koshar. And this is . . ."

"Excuse me," Clea interrupted. "I'm travelling under an alias. They know me as Clea Rahsok."

Jon laughed. "We've got a secret too. Clea, this is His Royal Highness, Prince Let. We're taking him back to Toron for coronation."

Clea stopped and looked hard at Let. "It's possible," she said. "But I thought he was dead. At least that's the official information the News Service let out when he was kidnapped. You're still working with the Duchess Petra?"

"That's right."

"Oh," she said. "Well, come on and I'll introduce you to Mr. Triton."

"What sort of show have you got?"

"A good one," Clea said. "But no business." It was not until they had passed into the shadow of the calliope wagon that Clea stopped again and looked from Jon to Arkor. "Your eyes," she said. "Jon, can I talk to you later and ask some questions?" Then the volume of her voice raised as she looked up to the platform. "Mr. Triton, this is my brother Jon and two friends of his."

"Really?" asked Mr. Triton. "You don't say."

"We're travelling back to Toron along your route. We saw your posters up at the fishing village and decided to come by," Arkor volunteered. "It's a fine poster, too. It really catches your eye. Who designed it?"

Mr. Triton folded his hands over his belly, beamed, and said, "Why, I did it myself. You like it? I even designed the mast head for the wagons back there. It's my circus from toupee to toe-nail."

"Would you show us around?" suggested Arkor.

"Well," said Mr. Triton. "Well. I believe I will. Come along. I believe I'll just do that." The flattered impresario climbed down the wagon steps and led them towards the tents, past the various stands and along the metal walk-ways.

A tongue of sunlight fell between the tent flaps. Jon stood just inside the door, breathing the warm odour of sawdust. Clea leaned against the dressing table.

"That isn't all your stuff, is it, sis?" He pointed to the open wardrobe.

"I share this dressing room with a friend of yours," she told him. "Now just what's going on, brother of mine?"

"I'll show you," he said, grabbing a piece of skin at his neck. He twisted it, and suddenly it tore loose. He peeled it upwards, and his jaw and half his neck and cheek came away. "You mean the acrobat. She's a good kid, Clea." He peeled away another slab of his face so that only the mouth and one eye socket were left. There was nothing underneath.

"I know she is," Clea said. "I wouldn't be here if it wasn't for her. I asked her to tell me what was going on, once, but she said that the more people who knew, the more people who would be in danger. So I've let it lie. But I'm still curious."

The rest of Jon's face disappeared. "She was in a group, Clea, that today would go by the name of Malis. I was a member too, you might say. Unfortunately we were marked, just like the forest guards you see with their triple scars. Our mark, though, was that we disappeared in dim light – like creatures of the imagination, if you will." He ran his fingers roughly through his hair which vanished as though a hanging wig had rubbed away. "Like psychotic fantasies," the headless voice came from above the empty collar.

Then his hand reached into his pocket, brought out a tiny capsule, and held it up to where his face should have been. The thumb pressed a tiny stud on one end and a fan of spray jetted out and caught the form of his skull, a transparent face, then swiftly opaque again.

"But there's a solution to everything." His face, though still wet, was almost complete again. "Now the job is to get a king back on the throne as soon as possible, and to end this war." The other end of the capsule produced a black spray which covered his hair. "Will you help us, Clea?"

"I'm impressed. But Alter showed me already," she said. "Maybe you can do an act in the side show. That stuff doesn't clog your pores?"

"No," explained Jon. "When it dries, it perforates and allows air and sweat to get through. But we've got to get Let back."

"Which faction are you working for?" she asked. "Or has the Duchess got her hand in for the throne herself?"

Jon shook his head. "Clea, it's bigger than any political hassling. It's even bigger than our enemy beyond the barrier; because we may have an ally among the stars."

Necklaces of light loop by tent and gambling stand. Couples stroll, eating fried fish from paper bags. A wonder-wheel rings the darkness and children scuttle under the railings along the walks. At the bottom of the glass aquarium wagon, the octopus stretches over green rocks. The calliope hails notes against the neon night.

Alter came out the back exit of the big tent, lifting her white hair from the back of her neck with both hands. The breeze was cool across her nape and under her arms. She felt slightly light-headed from her bout on the trampoline before the applauding crowd. She ran down the passage-way thick with clowns and sawdust.

She stopped when she saw the scarred giant. "Arkor?" she smiled. "How've you been? How's the Duchess, and Jon. And is there any word from Tel?"

"No word," he said. "But everybody's alive and kicking.

Jon is here with me. So is Prince Let."

"You're taking him back to claim the throne? Good." She frowned. "What are you looking so hard at?"

"I'm listening." They had started walking beside the tent, Alter ducking under the slanting guy ropes, Arkor stepping over. "Alter, there's something in Clea's mind that I can't quite understand. It was the thing that was keeping her to herself. It was the thing that somehow you helped to break through. But I can't see it enough to understand it."

"It's Tomar," Alter said. "He was the soldier that she was engaged to at the very beginning of the war. And he died. She told me about it just before she got to work on this new project of hers. She says this one should be even more important than the matter-transmission projection."

Arkor shook his head. "It's not that, Alter. It's something much further down. It was something she figured out once, and it was so terrible, she uses Tomar's death to avoid remembering the other thing. It has something to do with the *Lord of the Flames*, too."

"Clea?" asked Alter in surprise.

"As I said, I still don't know exactly what it is. But for one thing, all the telepathic forest guards also know about it, and they're using their combined forces to keep it away from me. They apparently know about my contact with the Triple Being and they're unsure of what to do about it. The information is in the minds of all the important councilmen, but the guards are protecting it in their minds. Clea seems to have figured it out all by herself, and then rejected it as too unbelievable. Alter, just listen to anything she has to say and see if something pops up."

"I thought I'd retired from this intrigue business," Alter said. "But I'll listen." Her fingers went to her throat to touch the leather necklace strung with polished shells.

Chains of lights dangle between tent and gambling stand. Couples stroll, crumpling their greasy bags. A merry-go-round whirls light over the hides of sea-horses and porpoises, and the children crawl from under the tent flaps again and scurry back to the walk-ways. Dolphins nose the corners of the aquarium wagons and the calliope plays faster.

"How do you like it, son?" Mr. Triton came up behind

the blond boy in the forest dress who was leaning against a stay and looking up at the glittering trapeze act.

"It's fine," Let said. "I've never seen anything like that before."

"Never?" Mr. Triton ran his eyes over the boys erect figure. From his height, he certainly wasn't a guard. "Well, then I guess it must be quite a sight for you." Beside them in the stands, the audience applauded.

"It must be hard to do that up there," said Let.

"It certainly is. But you know what the hardest thing of all is? It's managing all these people, each with his own individual act."

"How do you mean?"

"Well, I've done just about everything in this business, from play the damn calliope to training wild sharks." He paused and looked up at figures spinning in the aerial spot. "Come to think of it, I never was anything where I had to stay up in the air too long." Applause swept the dark tent once more. "But the hardest thing I ever did was trying to get them all to work together. You've got to listen to everybody's say, and try to keep everybody happy and alive at the same time."

"How do you do it?"

"You don't. At least never as well as you want to," Mr. Triton said. "You hold votes, sometimes; or sometimes you look ahead and put your foot down hard when there's disagreement. And when you're wrong, you admit it as fast as possible, and change to right if you can."

"Then what?" Let asked.

"Then you hope everything goes all right and that you'll be around next season to hold your show."

The Prince looked up at the spinning artists. "They're beautiful," he said. "All that strength and delicacy at once; it's worth trying to keep that up there, isn't it."

"Yes," said Mr. Triton, folding his hands over his stomach. "Yes, it certainly is. You'd make a good circus person, boy."

Some of the lights have winked out by the side-show tent. The fried-fish wagon and the gambling stand, however, are still open. Couples stroll arm pressed against arm, hand in hand, head against shoulder. The bumpercars on the wooden arena still collide amidst laughter. The children stand on the walk-ways, knuckle their eyes and yawn. The manta-ray ruffles the sand at the bottom of the aquarium tanks, and the calliope player has stepped down from the wagon for chowder.

Clea decided to walk once more around the circus grounds before she went to bed. She passed the darkened side-show tent and was going towards the wonder-wheel when she caught a look, or a feeling, she wasn't sure. She turned her head and saw the scarred giant who had come with her brother looking at her from about fifty feet away.

He looks like he's trying to see inside my head, she thought. Then she shook the thought away. Under everything she had been thinking of recently, was her new project. It was an amazingly beautiful, subtle, and profound unified field theory. It was far neater than any she knew – or would be when she finished it. It rose in towers of logic, plumbed oceans of reverberating overtones among syeogistic rhythms, and encompassed all her previous work on random spacial co-ordinates – "... gentlemen, it is more than conceivable that by converting the already extant transit-ribbon, we may send between two hundred and three hundred pounds of matter anywhere on the globe with a pinpoint accuracy of microns."

No, don't think about it. Brush that thought away with the other. But you haven't thought about it for so long, so long ...

And then she remembered his quiet smile, his bull-like body, the red hair, his sudden grin, and the inside laughter like a bear's. And then she stood, stunned, surprised, because the memory was so much clearer in her mind, now, so that she did what she had never let herself do before, and whispered his name, "Tomar ..." and waited for the pain, that *should* come only it didn't. Sometime in the last few months the wound had healed, and in healing he had not slipped away, but come closer, if only because she was in the world of life where he had lived, instead of the retreat world of death that was her own projection.

As she stood shocked motionless by the discovery, something from the deeps of her mind began to boil, to surge upward towards her consciousness, like a pattern clearing, a kaleidoscopic mayhem resolving into a recognizable, meaningful thought....

No! She threw herself upon it, grappled with it, struggled to keep it out of her mind. No! No! Oh, please help me. No!

And . . . and . . . oblivion received it again.

She was panting, and the wonder-wheel, rimmed with lights circled the black. The calliope was playing again. She blinked, and looked at Arkor. She saw him frown once, shake his head slightly, and turn away.

The bulbs were black along the wires that dangled from tent to gambling stand. The couple threw a crumpled bag into a trash receptacle. The moon laid out a template of the wonder-wheel and the merry-go-round across the grass. The octopus, the porpoises, and the manta-ray had settled on the bottom of the tanks. The calliope was still.

They met by the darkened wonder-wheel, and the late moon turned her hair silver. Their eyes were hollow darknesses.

Jon smiled. "How do you like normal life now that you've lived it again for a bit?"

"You call a circus normal?" She smiled back. "How's it coming with the war? Will you stop it?"

"We've made another try at it. We chased the *Lord of the Flames* out of King Uske."

"What had he done this time?"

"We don't know yet," Jon said. "Clea knows. At least Arkor thinks she does. But it's too deep in her mind."

"That must be what he meant when he was talking to me earlier," said Alter. "How could Clea know, Jon?"

He shrugged. "It's not exactly 'know'; it's that she seems to have some obscure information that coincides with some that was in King Uske's mind when the *Lord of the Flames* left him."

"I see," she said. "You know, it's funny, I mean Tel and me. We're the only people in Toromon who really know anything about what you're really doing. And both of us have just sort of drifted away from it all. He's in the army and I'm in the circus. He's off in the war you're trying to end, and I'm . . . well, I'm here." She dropped her head and then raised it again. "I hope he gets back soon. I'd like to see him again. Jon, have you got your own thing straightened out, that search for freedom you used to talk about?"

"I won't have it until the war is over and I'm free of the Triple Being. Or so I tell myself. In prison I learned to wait. That's what I'm doing now. And being able to walk about makes waiting a lot easier. And I'm still learning things that will probably be useful to me when it's all over. But sometimes I envy you kids, I really do. I hope the both of you have a lot of good luck."

"Thanks, Jon."

Before dawn the lights were wound up. The new sun shone across the ballooning tents as they collapsed and were folded, the stacked at the side of the dismantled gambling stand. A few children had come to watch the wonder-wheel, the merry-go-round, and the bumper-car arena dismantled. By six thirty, the circus carts were rolling towards the shore and the docks where the red and gold circus ship, would take them back to Toron.

CHAPTER TEN

THAT morning reveille sounded early. Tel gave the 606–B a thorough check before it was hauled off into the tank. Though the mist lay thick, the weather was warm.

"The King is dead."

"Huh?"

"In Toron, King Uske died at the palace. The report came through this morning!"

"Do you think it was an assassination?"

"I don't know. I didn't see the report."

The rumour washed over the camp like a wave. Though no one could be sure, it was assumed that the King's death had something to do with this sudden move they were making. And it was comforting, if only because it established some reason.

Tel was coming from the supply cabin with a number-three plumbing coil for the 605 (nobody had ordered him to, but he'd checked it on his own and found the number-three nearly burned through) when he saw Illu carrying something over his shoulder. "What's that?" he hailed the neanderthal.

"It's the sign-post," Illu said. "I asked Quorl if he was taking it with us, and he said, 'What for?' and walked away. So I'm bringing it."

"Good for you," Tel said.

When he got back to the 605, he had to argue with the two guys who had just come to take it away and who didn't want to give him time to fix the coil. But then one of them saw the flup-flep and said, "Hey, you must be the fellow that they been talking about that's got one of them things for a pet." And during the time they were fooling around with the feathered animal, Tel got the coil in place. Then they went off, wheeling the 605 in front of them on a bearing-dolly.

When he was on his way back to the barracks, he passed Ptorn and Quorl at the corner of the cabin. "Perhaps this battle will be the final one," Ptorn said. "You mentioned there was talk of a truce?"

"Of a victory or a truce," said the Scout, "now that the King is dead."

Inside the shack, Tel was reaching under his bed for his

rucksack when someone said, "Well, it looks like this is it."

"Huh?" said Tel, looking up.

The mist hid the man sitting on the next bed.

"Oh, how are you?" Tel grinned. "I guess there's no way to know where we'll be assigned in our next camp. I wish we'd gotten a chance to talk some." Tel gave an embarrassed chuckle which the other man returned.

"You heard anything about a truce?" the man asked.

"Just rumours. Do you think they'll end the war?"

The man shrugged.

"Well, I have to get to my departure detail. I hope we run into each other again some day." He picked up his sack and slogged out into the mud. He could hear the wheezing tanks lining up at the other end of the encampment. His order-plate said he should report to tank number three.

He was wondering if he would have any problem taking flap-flep along when a familiar voice called, "Hey." Shrimp solidified in front of him. "Tel? Yeah, I thought it was you." There was someone else with him. "Tel, here's Curly. How do you like that."

"Oh, hi," Tel said, shaking hands.

"How've you been?" Curly asked. "I'm over in Camp D–2. You guys working any good randy deals?"

"Hell no," Shrimp interjected. "Everybody in this camp's honest." He shifted his weight. "Hey, Tel, we were having a little argument about you. And we wondered if you'd help straighten it out for us, if you don't mind."

"Sure," Tel said. "What is it?"

"Just exactly what colour are your eyes?"

Tel drew his eye-brows together and shifted uncomfortably. "Green," he said. "Why?" And then wished he hadn't.

"Can we take a look?"

"I . . . I guess so."

Shrimp came very close to him and Curly looked over his shoulder.

"See, I told you," Shrimp said. "They're green, just like mine. That's cause we both come from the shore. On the shore almost everybody's eyes are green –"

"That's not what I meant," said Curly. "What I'm talking about only happens when it was darker, and not as much light as now. Come on, let's get in the shade."

"Hey, look," said Tel, "I gotta get going. I'm supposed to be at my tank and ready to pull out."

"What tank do you take?"

"Eh . . . three."

"Good. That's the one I'm driving. Come on."

Tel jutted his mind out in five different directions for an escape but struck brick at the end of each; so he walked with them through the fog towards the dark row of tanks.

"Here's my baby," Shrimp said, whacking the black metal hull. It rang hollowly as they went around to the side.

"Inside'll do it," Curly said, opening the door. The hydraulic ladder dropped its rubber casters into the mud. "Now I'll show you what I mean."

Tel mounted to the tank behind Shrimp and in front of curly.

"No, don't turn on the light. That's the whole point."

In the three-quarter dark tank whose only illumination came from the pilot bubble at the other end, Tel stood against the wall while Shrimp and Curly peered into his eyes. Tel's heart was going like snapped fingers.

"All right," Shrimp said. "Now what colour does that look like to you?"

Curly frowned. "I don't understand it," he said. "Back in basic training, whenever it was half dark, they always used to look like they just weren't there."

"But . . . but my eyes are green," Tel said. Something was turning inside him, like a smoky crystal full of memories he could not see. "My eyes are green."

"Of course his eyes are green," Shrimp said. "What other colour would the eyes of a fisherman be, or the eyes of the son of a fisherman."

"Yeah. I guess so," Curly said. He looked again. "They're green all right. Maybe I'm crazy."

Yes, thought Tel, my eyes are green, always have been, and always will, and wondered why he had felt so nervous when they had asked to look. Why should they be any other colour, he wondered. Why?

"The King is really dead back home?"

"Yeah. I heard it at the report office. Do you think that means the war may be over soon?"

"Who knows. They say this is going to be the big battle. Maybe this will decide it."

"I hope so. I'd give my eye-teeth to get back to Toron, hell, just to see what it looks like."

"Me too."

As the tank whined through the mud, the mist struck in gusts against the oval portals. Tel sat at the end of the bench. In the bubble-seat at the front, Shrimp jogged right and left, his hand on the steering rod, his head and shoulder in silhouette on the fog. They had been going for an hour when there was a sudden burst of sound to their left, like rocks smashing.

The men looked at each other. "What was that?" someone called up to the driver.

Shrimp shrugged.

The rising and falling of the tetron motor sizzled beneath them. Tel leaned his head back on the wall. The vibrations had nearly put him to sleep when there was another crash. He came awake to see light flare through the right window.

"What the hell was that?" somebody bellowed. "Are we under attack?"

"Shut up," Shrimp called from the driver's seat. "Shut up back there."

Then, through the instruction speaker in the corner, a voice came: "Be calm, alert, remember your training. Drivers proceed as scheduled. Stand by for orders."

Tel waited, trying to pull down the beating blood that filled his body. The tank rolled forward.

Half an hour later someone said, "This is a hell of a way to fight a war, all trapped up in a damn clam-crate."

"Shut up," the officer with them said.

The flep-flap was sitting quietly under the bench. Now Tel reached down and gave it a piece of charcoal. As he bent forward and his cuff pulled up, feathers brushed his wrist.

The next time he looked at the oval windows, it was getting dark. They had been going a long time.

"All drivers halt," said the speaker.

Shrimp's shoulder jerked as he jammed on the brake stick. The tank lurched. Tel reached under the bench and set the bundle of feathers on his lap. All its eyes were tightly closed.

The men began to scrape their boots back and forth over the floor. The benches squeaked. "Come on, relax," the officer said. "You guys'll get your chance."

"Convoy disembark," came through the speaker.

The men stood up, stretched their legs, and punched at the ceiling to stretch their arms.

The door clinked open, the ladder dropped, and Tel, in his turn, climbed out. Except that the mist was darker and thicker, it might have been the same place they had left. As the group at the ladder's foot grew, Tel noticed that the ground was a little firmer here. Just then there was a crashing noise through the evening.

Their eyes snapped left; fire, fifty feet away, rose white and billowing through the mist. A momentary silhouette of spiky trees –

Suddenly there were orders breaking in the air all around them. "Tank-four to your left." "Despatch convoy report to Major Stanton." "Convoy from tank three follow me."

Tel followed at a half run as they left the tank. Two men joined them from another platoon. Suddenly they were stopped, the group split in half, and Tel was herded off left while the others went right.

They had just passed a group of tanks when there was another hit, this time on the far side. Tel squinted. Heads turned as the deep blue evening flamed, then darkened. "Throw those rock bags up!" someone was calling. "Throw those rock bags up!"

Tel turned in time. A heavy burlap sack scraped into palms, yanking at his shoulders. It nearly pulled him to the ground. A man on the other side was waiting for it, and Tel tossed it on, turned back, and caught another. They were making a chain of rocks across the area.

"You and you –" (neither one was Tel, but the order made him turn his head and almost miss a sack) "– climb that rise back there and report on D–T platoon."

Something metallic jingled to his left.

"Watch out! It's prickly!"

Three men were unrolling barbed wire over the rock-bags. Coils spiralled over the burlap. The flip-flup jumped back just in time to avoid being stepped on and the coil rolled along the wall.

"Hey, you! They need you down the line about fifty feet."

Tel sprinted off. A handful of men, running to the same destination, joined him when there was thunder and another flash. He clamped his eyes shut and nearly tripped over something. Someone steadied him and as he looked up a voice said, "Hold on there, Green-eyes."

Curly was one of the men.

They were ordered after one another to a new section of the wall. The rhythm was working its way into his shoulders, his body: steady yourself, catch, swing around, and toss.

Splat! He'd been too self-confident. He was bending down to pick up the bag when somebody yelled, "Get down!" He went down onto his knees in the mud and clutched the sack. His eyelids turned orange in front of his eyes and he felt heat all along his right side. When it went away, he staggered up, and nearly tripped over Curly.

Curly grabbed his arm and together they went as fast as they could back up along the wall. Suddenly Curly pulled him into a depression in front of the rocks. The flop-flop rolled in after them and twittered. The fog was deep blue, but through it Tel saw the sweat on Curly's face. They were both panting.

Behind them was the whine of a tank shifting position, a coughing stutter, a sizzling hiss of tetron units, then silence. Twenty feet away some men were hauling a machine.

"Is that the 606–B they're setting up?" Curly asked. "I thought I heard it humming. That's your machine, isn't it?"

"Yeah, it is," said Tel, trying to catch his breath. "But I don't think I could tell a tank from an electric razor right now." Another hit caught them to the left. They ducked, and then Curly raised his head and peered around. "Looks like they're giving us hell," he whispered.

"I guess they are. What are you looking for?" Tel asked. "I can't see a thing."

Curly pulled back into the pit. "Just to see if anybody's real close." His voice was suddenly grave. "Hey, I . . . I want to explain something, well, I meant something about me. To you."

"Huh?" said Tel.

"I felt sort of funny with that business about your eyes today. So, I got to thinking. And I figured I might as well tell this to you, about me; like an apology."

Tel's first surprise turned over in his belly, and though unsure of what was on the other said, he said, "Yeah, I see."

Curly smeared a muddy hand across his forehead. "Damn," he said, with an embarrassed laugh. "There used to be this guy, in this mali gang I ran with back in Toron. He wrote these strange poems. His name was Vol Nonik, a sort of funny guy. Anyway, I wish I was showing this to him, because then he'd make a poem out of it. But he couldn't get into the army because there was something funny with his back. So I guess you'll have to do..." He laughed again, then looked down at his hands. "You've never seen anybody do this before, have you?"

"Do what?"

"Look." Curly said. "At my hands. Look."

"I don't under –"

"We may not get out of this thing alive," Curly said. "So look at my hands!"

Tel gazed at the soldier's cupped palms.

They began to glow.

They were bluish at first through the fog, but then the blue became red, a red fire flickering in his hands, a ball of red fire glittering just above his palms, shot with green, suddenly yellow. "Look," Curly breathed. "You see..." The ball of light lengthened, became slenderer, bifurcating at the bottom and top. The waist thinned, the head raised, fingers articulated themselves at the ends of tiny, flaming hands. She bent, miniature, and swayed on tip-toe, wavering on his palms. Blue, copper, and gold flames like pin-points raced her body. A breeze (Tel felt it on the back of his neck) and her hair, a bell of sparks, shimmered behind her. She raised her arms and whispered (a voice like the whisper of water over sand): "Curly, I love you. I love you, Curly, I love you..."

"Isn't she ... beautiful..." Curly's own whisper came like two rasps against one another over the voice of the miniscule homuncula. Curly breathed deeply now, and she faded.

When Tel looked up from the muddy fingers, Curly was staring at him. "You ever see anyone do that before?"

Tel shook his head. "How . . . how do you do it?"

"I don't know," Curly said. "I . . . just do. I used to dream about her, before I came to the army. But once, I thought: what would happen if I just made her happen. And there she was, like you saw, in my hands. I never showed anyone else. But with all this . . ." He made a motion around them. ". . . I thought I ought to show it to someone. That's all." Suddenly he seemed embarrassed. "Well," he grunted.

Tel glanced at his pet; the flup-flip's polished eyes were open, and he wondered if it too had seen the flaming girl, so vivid, so sparkling, so real.

The whine of a tank motor grew behind him. Suddenly Tel whirled in the mud, and saw the looming machine. "Get out of here!" he cried to Curly who looked flustered and then dived right. Tel scrambled left. The tank careened towards him, passed within inches. He whirled to stare at the moving side and staggered backwards; for one moment he was close enough to see through the bubble dome, the tall, yellow-eyed figure of Quorl at the steering rod. Then the tank was past him, crashed through the rock wall. Fog closed behind it and swirled into the gap in the wall.

What the hell's going on? Tel wondered. A bunch of people were running towards them. An officer's voice stopped them. "Get the hell on down the line! Are you waiting for them to come in after you?"

Tel was running again when the next hit came – not close enough to blind him, but not far enough away to ignore. He caught himself short in the middle of a breath. In the harsh light he saw against the wall, tangled in the barbed wire, Shrimp: His left side was charred black. The mud had kept the rest of his uniform from burning. There was very little of his left leg, only the burnt stick of his left arm, and one cheek looked like crinkled carbon paper. The remainder of his face was vividly recognizable. Aflame and panicked from a former hit, he must have tried to climb the wall, forgetting where he was going and fallen back into the tangles of . . .

Then the light went out, and Tel was still running. He wasn't breathing; perhaps his heart had stopped; but his feet kept beating down into the mud. It was too dark to see anything now, but on the screen of night before him, blinking on and off, was the after image of the glittering flakes of burnt uniform, the red of drying blood, and a net of iron wire.

They did a lot of fighting after that. During one lull, the first stories began to trickle back:

"Did you hear what happened about the Scout?"

"What?"

"He was in that tank."

"The one that went beserk and busted the damn blockade?"

"Yeah. And they found him. He'd driven the thing smack through our wall into an enemy nest. He just crushed the whole installation."

"What about him?"

"They said the tank exploded when it hit. He knew that nest was there and that they would get us if they weren't destroyed. He saved the whole company."

"He sure picked a hell of a way to get rid of them. Where's Quorl now?"

"Are you kidding? They found pieces of that tank over half a mile radius."

In the darkness Tel pressed his cheek against the wet burlap, feeling the gravel through the cloth, and listening to the men talking beside him. His fingers moved through the flap-flip's feathers. They tickled the skin on the inside of his knuckles. He thought about Quorl, and Shrimp, and wondered why . . .

CHAPTER ELEVEN

"MISS RAHSOK! Where in the world have you been?" The woman with the headkerchief set down her garbage pail beside the stoop. "I'm so glad to see you. Isn't it all terribly exciting, the coronation and everything? You'll never know what I've been going through. I'm so upset I don't know what to do. You know how concerned I am about my daughter, Renna. I don't even know how to begin telling you . . ."

"Excuse me," Clea said, "I'm in an awful rush . . ."

"What happened? I actually managed to get a ticket to the pre-victory ball the council gave last week in memory of His Majesty. That was just before Prince Let had been found. I had to lie myself perfectly green to that atrocious woman on the committee about why my daughter hadn't been sent a ticket through the regular debutante channels. But I got it, and we made the most beautiful dress, all white and silver. What girl wouldn't love a white and silver dress. It was gorgeous. Well, you would have thought she was going to a funeral, the way she moped around. Renna does a little drawing, nothing great mind you, but suddenly her pictures turned completely morbid, skulls lying in the branches of trees, dead birds, and one perfectly hideous little boy crouched on the sand about to be swept away by a wave. I should have known something was wrong right then. She kept on saying she didn't really want to go to the ball, she wasn't interested. Go for your mother's sake, I told her. You may meet some Duke or Baron, and who knows – Well, she thought that was silly, and laughed. But anyway, at four o'clock in the morning, she set off in her beautiful white and silver dress. Oh, she looked so beautiful, Miss Rahsok, I nearly cried. In fact I did cry, after she was gone. She never came home. That evening I got a letter that she had married that awful boy Vol Nonik. I told you about who writes poems and lives in the Devil's Pot. Do you know he was even expelled from the University. She invited me to visit them, but I just couldn't go. She said that she would tell me about the ball, and that it hadn't been so bad after all. Imagine, a pre-victory ball, not so bad: Isn't it awful? Isn't it terrible." The woman drew up her shoulders.

"Excuse me," Clea said. "I'm sorry, but I've got to get upstairs and get some things. Excuse me." She hurried past the woman into the hall. Then she slowed; she was trying to remember something about the names Vol Nonik and Renna. Had she heard of them before? Without resolving it, because it dated from a time before those three discoveries, she hurried on.

She opened the thumb-print lock and stepped into the apartment. The shutters were closed.

It's like a cave, she thought, where I spent so much time. There's not enough room for an acrobat to turn a cartwheel, it's too dim to see the grease paint on a clown's face even if he were standing just across the room, and you can't hear any . . . any calliope music.

She had come back to pick up her notebook with the odd radical fotmulae she'd never thought she'd look at again. But then I never thought I would want to look at anything again, she reflected. She went to the desk, thinking of Alter, Mr. Triton, and all the red and gold that was the circus. As she opened the drawer, she rested her other hand on the desk, and her fingers brushed a crumpled piece of paper. She frowned, stood up, and spread out the sheet. Yellow letters blazed across green:

WE HAVE AN ENEMY BEYOND THE BARRIER

Viciously she tore the paper across, tore it across again. She flung the pieces into the waste basket, snatched up her notebook from the opened drawer, and left the apartment.

Around the corner of the hall from her, something crashed to the floor, bringing her up from the pit of unformulated anger. She ran forward to see what it was.

"Oh . . . oh . . . good morning, Miss Rahsok."

"Dr. Wental, it's three o'clock in the afternoon!" exclaimed Clea. "Isn't it sort of early to be . . . in this condition?"

The doctor raised his finger to his mouth. "Shhhh . . . I don't want my wife to know. I'm celebrating."

"What in the world are you celebrating?"

"The young King's coronation. What else?" As he tried to get to his feet, Clea took his arm. "Oh, the bars are filled to bur – (urp) – sting. Everyone's celebrating! The war will be over! The war will be over and all our boys will be back. Hold on a minute there, will you?" The doctor shook his head and steadied himself against the wall. "A new king, and a new age, I tell you. You have no idea how good an age it will be. But then, you have no idea how good an age it has been. Who knows where I'll go, what heights I'll have scaled . . ."

"What *are* you talking about?"

"My medical practice," said the doctor, and chuckled. "I get new recommendations everyday, everyday."

"Your lupus erythermatosis patient got better?"

"Eh . . . which one?"

"The first one, the one you had difficulty getting the medicine for."

"Him? Oh, him. He died. There was a very small stink about it, when someone accused me of not using the proper medicine or something. But they couldn't prove a thing. I have acquaintances on the Council; they couldn't prove a thing. The important part is that people heard about the recommendation, and every day, every day . . ."

"I think you can make it the rest of the way by yourself, Dr. Wental," Clea said.

"Oh, yes, of course. But when things go so well, sometimes you just have to break out and celebrate . . ."

"Not that door," Clea said. "The next one."

"Oh, thank you." He moved unsteadily to the next apartment entrance. "Yes, thank you so much. But be very quiet now, because I don't want my wife . . ."

Clea left him fumbling at the thumb-print lock.

The entertainers, supplied by Mr. Triton, were waiting in the palace garden for the festivities to start. Clea strolled over the plots of grass cut by stone walks, set granite benches. Multicoloured canvas had been stretched over tent poles, and the circus people wandered back and forth in their spangled costumes, talking.

"Dr. Koshar?"

Clea turned to see the giant Arkor. "What is it?"

"We need your help."

"What do you want?"

"Some information." He paused. "Will you come with me?"

Warily she nodded.

"I don't want to frighten you," Arkor said. "And some of what I want to talk about will be frightening." They walked into the palace entrance. "Will you help us?"

"What do you want the information for? So far I haven't any idea what you're talking about."

"You do have an idea," Arkor corrected her. "Why else did you quit your government job three years ago, and shut yourself off from the world."

"Because I was unhappy, and confused."

"I know why you were unhappy," Arkor said. "What confused you?"

"I don't think I understand your distinction."

"The distinction was yours," Arkor said. "You have a very precise mind, and you usually mean what you say. I ask again, why were you confused?"

"You haven't answered my question," Clea said. "Why do you want ths information?"

"Fair enough," Arkor said. "It's a piece of information that a number of people have, among them, most of the council, and the late King Uske. Many of the people of the forest have it also. Yet it is being protected very well. You are the only person we have found who possesses this information who is outside this protection."

"You are being very imprecise," said Clea. "You're going to have to be honest with me if you want my help."

"I said it would be frightening."

"Go on."

"First of all I can read your mind." He waited for a moment and then went on. "There are many telepaths among the forest guards. They have a constant mental net that spreads all over Toromon. Now though I can read minds, I have been excluded from this net. I assumed it was because I was somewhat of an apostate; my interests were not theirs, and among the telepaths there is little ... I suppose you would call it nosiness. This piece of information I'm looking for concerns the war, is perhaps the most important thing about it, maybe the secret of ending it, of winning it, or losing. The first thing that conceals it in most minds is an incredible layer of guilt. I should have been able to break through that, but I can't. It is under the further protection of the telepathic net I spoke of. I tried to get some explanation from my people, in the forest, but though I was not discouraged from seeking along my own ways, I was given no clue. You are the only person in whom I can detect this information who is not under the protection of the net. That's because you figured it out yourself whereas these others have all been informed of it by one another, and have had to deal with it somehow on an official level. The guilt is there even more strongly in you, but what I want is still there, glowing beneath the surface of your mind." Arkor paused one final time. "The last person we tried to explain any of this to insisted it was a psychotic fantasy. But he agreed to help us as though it were a hypothetical problem. So you have a positive precedent even if you don't believe me."

They turned down the hall.

"If I'm not being protected," Clea asked. "why haven't you dug it out of my mind already?"

"You're working on a unified field theory," Arkor said, "that you believe might be a great discovery; I have a great deal of respect for your opinions, Dr. Koshar. If I dug it out, it would leave your mind terribly shaken, and some of your creative faculties might be impaired. You'll have to fish it out yourself, with just a little prodding from me, and perhaps some verbal assistance as well."

"As a hypothetical problem," Clea said, "– and no, I don't know if this is real or not –" She smiled, "I'm game."

"Fine," said Arkor. "Now, as I said before, don't be frightened. But about an hour ago you tore up a piece of paper and threw it away, very angrily. Why?"

"How did you ... I didn't tear." The confusion caught her with complete surprise. "Oh you mean ... well, it was a stupid war poster, and I suppose ..." Why was she so upset –

"Why are you upset now?"

"I'm not – I mean I just wondered how you knew I tore it – the paper, the poster – up. I was in my apartment with the door locked –"

"That's not what upset you. Why did you bring the poster into your home in the first place?"

"Because ... because I just don't like this whole war business in the first place. I don't like the idea of our people dying beyond the barrier for –" She stopped.

"For no reason?"

"No." She took two breaths. "For something I did, something I discovered."

"I see," Arkor said. "And that's why you quit your job?"

"I . . . yes. I felt responsible."

"Then why did you bring the poster into your house in the first place? And why did you wait all this time, until you were about to leave that house for good, to tear it up?"

"I don't know. I was . . ."

". . . confused, yes. Now what confused you?"

"I was confused because I felt guilty. I felt somehow responsible for . . ." Anger started somewhere. What right had he –

"For the war? But we have an enemy beyond the barrier, Dr. Koshar. You mean that you personally felt responsible for this whole governmental and economic flux that produced the war? You must know that there were many more factors than just your discovery at work."

"For personal reasons!"

"You mean the death of your fiancé, Major Tomar?"

"I mean for the death of my fiancé Major Tomar in the war!"

Arkor waited a moment. Then he said, "I don't believe you."

Clea looked up at him. "That's your privilege."

"Shall I tell you why?"

"I don't know whether I want to hear."

"When did Major Tomar die?"

"I don't think I want to talk about it!"

"He died in late spring three years ago on a mission to wreck the radiation generators just beyond Telphar. You didn't make your discovery of the inverse sub-trigonometric functions and their application to random spacial co-ordinates until three months after he was dead. Major Tomar didn't die beyond the barrier. He died in military service here in Toromon. Now how could your discovery have had anything to do with his death?"

"But I was working for the government –"

"Dr. Koshar, if you were half a dozen other people – half a dozen other brilliant people – you might be capable of falling into that sort of sentimentality. But you have a hard, resilient, supremely logical mind. You know that's not why you feel guilty . . ."

"I don't *know* why I feel guilty then!"

"Then answer these: why did you bring the poster into your house if you didn't *want* to be reminded of the war? And if you were angry, if you disagreed with this 'whole war business', why didn't you tear the poster up the day you peeled it so carefully from the fence? Why did you leave it crumpled on your desk for nearly a year and a half? What *were* you trying to remind yourself of, something you had discovered but couldn't, wouldn't believe; something that today you thought you wouldn't have to remind yourself of again; tear it up, jam it into the waste-basket, push it out of your mind . . ."

"But there won't be any war now," she interrupted him. "Remind myself! There's a new King now! There'll be a truce declared, they'll all come back, and there won't be any . . ." She was talking very loudly, very fast, and they had nearly reached the throne room. There was nobody in the palace hall.

Light through a rotating window passed over a random pattern that caught Arkor's attention for just a second.

Clea looked shocked. Something had been prying at her mind; she had been resisting, pulling down. But as the pressure lifted a moment, her mind relaxed.

It happened. It surged from the bottom of her brain like a tide, a geyser, errupting into her consciousness as an undersea volcano throws off mud, sand, and steam. She fell against the wall and whispered, "The war . . ."

But Arkor had taken a step forward. It hit his mind almost as violently as it hit hers. He tried to crawl away from it. "But we'll win the war! We have an enemy beyond the barrier. But we can –" He turned right and left, dazzled, confused.

From the wall, Clea shrieked back, "What war! Oh, don't you see! *What war!*"

CHAPTER TWELVE

Among the soldiers, Illu pounded the signpost into the mud. "How do you know if it's pointing right?" someone asked.

Illu shrugged. "It don't really make much difference, does it."

Tel turned away with Ptorn beside him. The barrack cabins at the edge of the new encampment were dim and distant through fog.

"It's good to be camped again."

Tel looked around at the men in the mist. "Yeah," he said. "Makes you feel like you've got your feet on the . . ." He pulled his boot from the mud. ". . . ground again."

Ptorn laughed.

"You know, I've been thinking. I've been thinking about it a long time, too."

"About what?" asked the guard.

"About the Scout."

"You and a lot of other people," Ptorn said, gesturing back to where the group of soldiers were breaking up around the sign. "What's your particular thought?"

"It's: 'Why?' "

"I can think of six 'whys' I'd like the answer to," said Ptorn. "Which one's yours?"

"Just why he did what he did: why he smashed that tank into the enemy nest to save us."

"That's a pretty good one. Maybe he figured that if somebody didn't do it, we'd all go up in flames."

"Maybe." Tel hunched his shoulders. "You know, I suppose I could understand it better if the whole regiment was made up of guards. But it wasn't."

Ptorn laughed. "Look," he said, "we're all the same phylum, same genus, same species. All histosents. That's not the part to wonder over."

"Well, I do," Tel said. "You guards live a completely different life from the rest of Toromon. But you're fighting here. What about the neanderthals? How did they adapt so fast?"

"Have you asked any of the apes about it?"

"I will," Tel said. After they had walked on a few more steps, he said again, "But I still don't know 'why'."

Someone was running towards them through the fog. He nearly bumped into them, steadied himself on Tel's shoulder, and cried. "A truce! Did you hear? They're crowning the new King and there's going to be a truce! We'll all be going home! We'll all be going back to Toromon!"

He took off towards a group of soldiers standing around the barrack's door. Tel and Ptorn looked at one another. The forest guard grinned. "We'll go back!" he said. "We'll go back!" They turned and looked at Quorl's sign.

They were called in later, and as they stood around the little room, the speaker announced to them through the mist:

"... does not go into effect until six o'clock this evening. Until then we are still at war. We are quite near several enemy encampments. There will be no wandering off base. Until the truce is actually consummated, the enemy defence will be doubly active. Anyone who strays beyond the camp limit-line will be considered guilty of aggressive action. When the truce conditions are concluded, we will begin preparations for decamping."

First whispers, then talk, then laughter spread through the men. They burst from the door into the clearing. Somebody took his shirt off, knotted it, and flung it into the air. Somebody else fell down, laughing hysterically. There was a lot of running around, and more laughing, and some crying. Tel saw Lug coming out of the barracks.

"What is it?" the neanderthal called. "Huh? What's the matter?"

"What do you mean what's the matter?" Tel called back.

Lug came up rubbing his eyes. "What's everybody shouting about?"

"Where were you?" Tel asked. "Weren't you there for the announcement?"

"I was..." Lug rubbed his eyes again and looked – it was in the way he hunched his shoulders a little – embarrassed. "I was asleep."

"A truce!" Tel explained, getting excited all over again.

"Huh?" His fists fell slowly from his face. He shook his head. "Huh?"

"Lug, they signed the truce! The war's over!" He gave the neanderthal a playful whack. "Ape, how do you manage to sleep through something like that?"

"I was tired," Lug said. He looked up at Tel and drew in the thick ropes of his brow. "The war's over?"

Tel nodded vigorously. "Finished, over, ended; don't you see everybody cheering and jumping around?"

Lug looked at the rollicking men. "That means we can go home?"

"That's right. Home."

Lug smiled and yawned. "That's good," he said with his eyes still closed. "That's good."

"Lug, what are you going to do when you get home?"

He shrugged his shoulders up; then, as they began to go down, an idea suddenly flooded up behind his broad face and burst out in words: "I know! I'm going to teach."

"Teach?" Tel asked.

"That's right," Lug said; excitement lifted his heavy features. "I'm going to teach them things."

"You mean your people in the ruins?"

"That's right. I learned a lot of things just coming here that they should know. Like how to write down talking. Quorl taught me to do that, before he ... Well, he taught me; and to read it too."

"The Scout taught you to write?" Tel asked in amazement.

"That's right," Lug said. "I started to teach my woman, and my girl child, and the others. Now I can go back. And we could plant kharba fruits in rows where the land was clear instead of picking them wild. You can take care of them better and can have a lot more of them that way. I was talking to a guy who lives on one of the coastal farms and he said that's the way they do it there. I've learned a lot of things. Some of them here, too. And if I teach, then everything will be better for us. Right?"

"Sure," said Tel.

"Hey," asked Lug, looking down at Tel's feathery, flippered pet that was slapping back and forth and twittering a few feet away, "will they let you take that thing back with you?"

"I don't know," Tel said. "I hadn't thought about it."

"Do you think he'd be happy back in Toromon? It isn't very muddy back there, is it."

"No, it isn't. I'd like to take him, though. I like him."

Lug squatted down and made the snapping sound with his fingers. The flep-flep waddled over and climbed onto his hand. Lug stroked the feathers and chuckled. "Maybe if you had two flip-flaps to keep each other company, it wouldn't be so bad. But one by itself would get lonely."

"I'd like to keep him around up until I go, anyway, even if I couldn't take him back. He can sort of wave good-bye to me just as I leave."

"That would be nice. Going home," Lug said. "I remember a nice thing about home." His thick fingers halted in the feathers. "Near the place where I lived, there was a mountain, and on the far side, at the bottom was a lake. Some people came there and began to build, houses, paths, docks on the lake."

"It sounds very nice," Tel said. He wondered what they were building.

"When it rained," Lug went on, "just before morning, there would be fog – not like this fog – but if you stood on the ledge and looked down the mountain, you could hardly see the water, until the dawn cut through to the lake. The fog hid everything they were making on the shore. But the centre of the lake was like gold fire." He sighed. "That was nice."

"I guess so."

"Quorl, when I knew him in the forest, he went with me there once. It's funny how he acted here in the army."

"You've been thinking about the Scout too?" Tel decided his curiosity about the building would not be answered right now.

"Yeah." Lug nodded. "I guess I have."

"Guess we all have," Tel said. "Say, Lug. You want to look after the beast for a bit? I'm going to check my tools and see if everything's ready to go back. It'll take me about half an hour to run through them all."

"I'll watch him," Lug said. Tel walked off towards one of the barracks, calling back over his shoulder: "Thanks a lot."

Tel had been blundering under what he'd thought was his bed for five minutes when it dawned on him he'd probably wandered into the wrong cabin. The arrangement of the barracks was a little different from the old camp and he still hadn't got it down right. As he got up, he nearly bumped into the figure of another soldier about to sit down on the next bed. "Oh, hey, I'm sorry," Tel began.

"That's okay pal," the other soldier said. "Say, aren't you the guy who used to be in my cabin back in the other camp?"

Then Tel recognized the voice. "Yeah, that's right. Glad to run into you again. I thought you'd been transferred to another company. How've things been treating you since we moved?"

The figure shrugged.

In the darkened cabin they sat now on opposite beds, The fog had thickened. The soldier was still a faceless shadow to Tel's eyes.

"Fair, I guess." The shadow chuckled. "It hasn't been too bad."

"I guess if you got through this damn war you can't complain about too much. Isn't it great about the truce? What's the first thing you're gonna do after you get back to Toromon?"

The soldier let out a sigh. "I don't know if it's all that great. Maybe for you guys it is. But me? I really don't have anything to do when I get back. I was hoping it would go on a little longer. I used to be in company forty-four. Now that was a great company. It really was. Now I'm here. I'd just as soon go someplace else after this and fight a little more. This ain't a bad life. Just risky. And I guess for me the risk's just about over."

"Oh," Tel said, not quite understanding. "Well, what did you used to do back in Toromon?"

The shadowed head shook slowly. "You know, I don't remember. I've been away so long, somehow I just don't even remember."

Tel frowned as the figure lay back on the bed. He stood up and went outside, stepping over the burned out logs from last night's fire. He was just about to go into his own cabin, when somebody hailed him, "Hi there, Green-eyes?"

"Curly?"

"In person. All ready to leave?"

"Just about. I still gotta check my tools. Hey, Curly, I wanted to ask you about that thing you showed me –"

"Shhhh." Curly's forefinger sprang to his lips. "Somebody might hear you talking about it."

"I just wanted," Tel lowered his voice, "to know how you did it."

"Have you tried it yet?"

"No, but . . ."

"Well, then don't bother me." Curly's annoyance got cut off when somebody cried out halfway across the muddy flat: "Hey you, come back." There was a distant, double flop-flup, flup-flop: one was the tiny flippered feet, the other, the open-toed neanderthal boots.

"That's Lug!" Tel said. "He must be chasing my –"

The form was just visible thirty feet away and moving further off.

"Where does he think he's chasing it?" said Curly.

"Oh, hell," Tel said, "I forgot to tell him about the boundary!" He ran across the mud shouting, "Come back here, you stupid ape! Get back here!"

He caught up to Lug some forty feet outside the camp limit, grabbed his shoulder and whirled him around.

Lug looked surprised. "It got away, and I just –" he began to explain.

"Just get back as fast as you can run."

"But the truce . . ."

"It doesn't take effect until six o'clock and the enemy's doubled its watch. Get going." As they started back at a trot, Tel felt his first panic break and found relief in a flow of friendly abuse directed towards the neanderthal's jogging back. "I used to wonder why the Scout would break his neck for us guys. Maybe I should know now, but I'm damned if I do. Come on, move." Lug speeded up. Then Tel heard the sound of flippers at his feet. He stopped and dropped to a crouching position. "Well, there you are!" He held out his hand and snapped his fingers. "Come on, baby," Tel said, "you can have a nice piece of charcoal when we get back."

Lug who was already inside the boundary line turned around and called, "Hey, I thought you said run?"

"Come on," Tel called once more at the flap-flop who opened four shell polished, pastel eyes and blinked at him. "Come –"

That was the last sound he made.

Lug staggered backward from the thunder, his lids clamped shut before the column of white fire that spurted where a moment before Tel had crouched.

"What the hell was that?" someone cried from across the flat. Ptorn ran up and grabbed the neanderthal's arm. "Lug, what happened?"

"I don't know ... I don't know –" His eyes were still closed and he was shaking his broad head back and forth.

One of the officers was shouting: "God damn it, this war isn't over yet! Now who was outside the boundary! Who was it?"

By the barrack wall, Curly looked up from his cupped hands where a flaming woman danced on his palms and frowned.

CHAPTER THIRTEEN

"... PRONOUNCE you King Let of the Empire of Toromon."

Jon, standing in the first gallery below the raised throne, watched the councilman back away from the blond youth who was now King. There were not more than sixty persons in attendance: the twelve councilmen, members of the royal family, their guests, and several other important or highly honoured state personages. Jon was there as Petra's guest. Among the others was the grotesque imposing figure of Rolth Catham, the historian. The King paused while he looked over the people in the room, and then sat upon the throne.

Applause rippled among the participants.

A man in the back of the room looked over his shoulder at another noise, louder than the clapping. It came from the antechamber. Someone else turned, then still more people. The guard's attention was alerted by now. Jon and Petra both received mental nudges at the same time. "It's Arkor," Petra whispered, but Jon had already begun to make his way back through the guests. The Duchess paused just long enough to get Catham's attention, then followed.

When Jon pushed into the smaller chamber there was confusion. Guards were holding Arkor. Clea was leaning against the wall.

Arkor was saying calmly but loudly, "No, we're all right. Yes, thank you. We're all right. But we must speak with Her Grace."

The sentries looked, the council members stared. A moment later Jon saw the King push through the door with a guard on either side. "Now what's going on," one of the guards was demanding.

It was Petra who suggested the private meeting in the council room. The members sat along one side. At the head of the room the young King sat on a slightly raised chair. On the other side sat Jon, Petra, Arkor, Catham, and Clea.

"Now what is it you want to say?"

The Duchess nodded to Arkor who stood up and faced the council. "I have somebody here who is going to tell you something that you all know, but have insulated yourselves from. Something you all did, decided consciously was the only way out of a problem, but took that decision only at the assurance that you would not have to remember making it." He turned to Clea. "Now, will you tell the council what you were about to tell me, Dr. Koshar?"

Clea stood up. Her face was pale. "They won't believe it," she said. Then her voice grew firmer and she spoke directly to the council. "You won't believe it. But you know it anyway." She paused. "I spoke to many of you three years ago when I first made the discovery that enabled you to send people, equipment, and supplies off to war. You were incredulous then. And you will not believe this at all: there is no war."

The council members looked at one another and frowned.

She repeated, "There is no war. You know it."

"But..." spluttered one of the council members, "then what... I mean where... are all our soldiers?"

"They are sitting –" she took a breath "– in tiny metal cells stacked up like coffins in the vast section of Telphar where recruit soldiers are not allowed."

"And what are they doing there?" demanded another council member.

"They are dreaming your war, each one desperately trying to dream his way back to what he knows is reality, somewhere deep in his mind. Sodium pentathol drugs keep them in a foggy, highly suggestive state; three years of constant propaganda keep their minds trained on the subject of war; six weeks of basic training formally designed to make a psychotic of the steadiest mind lends the final unquestionable patina of reality to the dream in which every sensation of the real world, the sound of wrinkling sheets, the glitter of sun on water, the feel of wet cloth, or the smell of rotten wood, are fitted into a mosaic defined by whatever each one fears and loves most, and is called war. A computer with an information sorting mechanism that can take whole sensory patterns from one brain and transpose them to another keeps all these dreams co-ordinated with one another."

"Oh, that's ridiculous..."

"It's impossible..."

"I don't believe all this..."

It was as if the doubt released a mental flood gate. It was

as though Jon had suddenly acquired another sense, sharp as sound or sight.

In terms of sight, it was like standing before a vast pattern of bright lights rising around him yet still before him. In terms of sound it was as if a symphony's opening phrase had begun and he was waiting for the cadence to resolve. In terms of touch, it was as if a storm of frozen and heated winds swirled towards him but had not yet struck. But it was neither sight, nor sound, nor feeling; because he still felt the ridged back of his chair, could hear the rustling of the councillors' robes, and could see their worried faces, their narrowing eyes and pursing lips.

"Why did the telepathic guards protect this secret in their minds?"

The answer came back like fire-works, music, waves of tingling foam: Arkor said, "Because they did not know what else to do with it. It was an idea, this war, which sprouted in the late King's mind, yet the seeds of it are in every mind in Toromon. The one man who opposed the King, and that even after the plan was well under way, was Prime Minister Chargill, who was assassinated. They felt they could neither help nor hinder you in your effort because they did not understand it. The government asked their help in obliterating the knowledge from the minds of those officially connected with the project, and since it was a solution to the economic problem, they consented; because we could not refuse."

Jon and Petra both stood now beside Arkor. "Then understand our effort now," Jon said.

"Our intent was to save our country," said Petra.

"And to salvage the freedom of each man in it," said Jon, "freedom from such oppressive . . . dreams!"

"Then what must we do?" asked the collective mentality of the telepathic guards.

"You must go into every mind in Toromon and release the knowledge of war. You must band them to one another for one moment, so that they both know themselves and each other, whether they be in the royal palace or the coffin-cells of Telphar, or the stone ruins beyond. Do that, and you will have served this breed of ape, man, and guard called Human."

"Some minds may not be ready."

"Do it."

There was a wave of consent.

And a doctor in the General Medical building dropped his thermometer against the desk and realized, as the mercury beaded over the white plastic that his anger at the head nurse who always put the progress tags on backwards was hiding his knowledge of war;

Vol Nonik drinking at a Devil's Pot bar ran his finger around the wet ring his glass had left on the stained wooden counter and saw his frustration at being expelled from the University for cheating on an examination that he had worked for six hours arranging microfilm crib sheets flogging him to ordered speech;

Councilman Rilum, caught the thirty-year-old memory that spun in his mind of the time that a clothing industry that he had been vice co-ordinator of had burned down, and realized his rage at the lax enforcement of fire regulations;

A man who worked in the aquariums paused on his way across the wharfs, took his hands out of his back pockets, looked at the scars beneath the black hairs on his forearm, and realized his fury at the woman who had whipped him with an iron rod when he had been a child on a mainland farm;

Councilwoman Tilla caught a fold in her robe and squeezed it with her old fingers as she remembered the catastrophe at Letos Island where her father had been killed when she had gone to help him collect fossils as a girl, and realized that the child's fright had been hiding the adult's knowledge of war;

Captain Suptus stood on the bridge of a tetron-tramp that was pulling away from the dock, blinked his eyes against bright sunset, remembering how a man with white hair had stood up behind a desk in the office of a shipping company (another company than the one he worked for now) and sworn, "You'll never set foot on another ship as long as I am alive!" and suddenly understood his terror at that dozen years dead man;

A woman named Marla dived from the coastal rocks and felt the waters close her in a fist of shadows. The rims of her goggles pushed against her face, and in the last light she tore the oyster from the shale and soared towards the surface again. Sitting on the rocks a moment later she worried her knife between the crusty valves. Crack, scrape, crackle; and the tongue of flesh, without pearl, shone wetly in the blue evening. And for a moment she remembered another, larger oyster in which had lain an immense, milky sphere, that had rolled away from her fingers, across the edge of the rock, and dropped with a miniscule splash twelve feet into green water. And her stomach had caught in a furious knot, and in that knot were tied such anger, such frustration;

A forest guard stopped by a tree and pressed his palm against the rough bark, and remembered the morning seven years ago when he and two others had been sent to catch a girl that was to be marked as a telepath, and how she had fought him with silent, maniacal indignation, and how his momentary anger had risen, connecting with a score more of tiny streams;

A prisoner stepping from the mine-shaft lift spat in the footsteps of an overseer who had turned his back and was walking out into the ferns, then frowned, remembering her older brother years ago walking away from her down a dark hallway, and there had been tears running down her own face as she crouched in the corner; and she suddenly understood those tears.

Councilman Servin pressed his heel hard against the leg of his chair, glancing from one face to the other in the council room and thought: "Harsh, and uncomprehending, like my uncle's face the day he called me down from my room and in front of the whole family accused me of stealing wine from the green stall in the pantry, and even though I had done nothing, I was mute with fright, and was punished by being ignored completely by the whole family for a week and had to take my meals alone," and knew what had kept him from speaking then;

Across Toromon, a military recruiting officer suddenly lifted his pen from his paper. At the same time, across the desk from him, the young neanderthal who had been about to mark the application raised his broad head, and the two stared at one another, each recognizing his own knowledge of war;

And in the palace garden, among clowns and acrobats, Alter sat on the ground against a marble urn. Wind over grass and through leaves tugged at her white hair. She moved her fingers along the leather strands of her necklace, from the milky shell streaked with gold, to the one that was plain mother of pearl, then to the one with veins of red, and thought, "Oh, he tried, he tried to dream some fragment of me into that terrible dream, dream himself back into reality," as another had dreamed his mother's face was always on the bottom of a certain kind of rock, as another had been able to converse with his dead father when the breeze made the leafless foliage shiver and speak to him, or as another had found all beauty and love in a flaming figure dancing on his fingers. "But he didn't know, he didn't . . ."

"How did you know?" Jon asked.

Clea moved her hand over the polished table-top before she looked up at the council members. "Because I worked on the computer. Because I knew from the reports on the conversion of the transit ribbon that progress couldn't be going that fast. Because there was a minor mistake in calculation in the working condensation of the theory due to a typographical misprint that would have rendered the whole process invalid and that no one ever caught but me. Because I knew what the economic situation of Toromon was, and I knew it had got into that bind of great excess and little mobility that must mean war. Because of a dozen things which meant this was the only answer possible. Because it was assumed that war would become such a reality in everyone's mind that it would never be questioned; and because they did not realize that reality must prove itself again and again to questioners, and that it is the fantasy which goes on without contradiction, without having to prove itself under logical rigour. The idea of asking questions was almost impossible; but only almost."

Rolth Catham stood up, sunset through the window striking the plastic case of his skull. "I have one more question, Dr. Koshar. How do the soldiers die?"

"Do you really want to know?" Clea asked. "Do you know the game randomax that has become so popular recently? The computer has a selector that works on a similar principal only with a much larger matrix, singling soldiers to be killed by random choice. Then, when the choice has been made, by controlled suggestion the dream is manoeuvred into some situation that will allow death. Then the cell in which the soldier is lying is electrified, his body is incinerated, and the cell is ready for another drugged madman who is prepared to fight the enemy beyond the barrier.

"Oh, the planning that must have gone into this," Clea said, "The probing and discovery. The complete slaughter of company forty-four with not one left alive, then the detailed report of the death of two men under the torture by the enemy. Simply turn them loose in the haze of their own injured psyches and they will create an enemy, greater and more malignant than any a psychologist could create for them, always hidden behind their own terror.

"They were stultified by horror, incapable of questioning law or reality, or any other facet of existence. Because after this training, the six weeks and before, no questions could be asked."

Catham raised his head slowly, and the young King stood up. "Perhaps," said King Let, "now, there will be peace."

Later they filed from the chamber to attend the coronation festivities. Jon started to turn down the stairway that would take him back to the garden when someone touched his shoulder. It was Catham.

"Yes?"

"I have some questions that are not for the rest of the Council," the historian said. "They're about your *Lord of the Flames*."

"Our psychotic fantasy?"

"If you will." The three-quarter smile formed on the human half of his face.

"Why don't you just rack him up to one of those elements of reality that must be questioned to prove the reality real."

Catham shrugged. "I already have. What I want to know is this: do you think the *Lord of the Flames* planted this monstrous idea of a war without an enemy in King Uske's mind?"

"Certainly not the idea," Jon said. "Perhaps the method for turning the idea into such a reality, though."

"I hope it worked the other way around," Catham said.

"Why?"

"Because of what it says about mankind if the idea *didn't* come from something extra-human." Catham nodded, and walked on down the corridor. Jon watched him go, then continued down the steps.

The circus people were all filing into the doorway of the palace auditorium.

Across the garden he saw his sister with her arm around Alter's shoulder. They stood quietly at the end of the line. He thought: *And what have I learned? Look, they all go softly into the doorway towards the spot-lights, even though they know now, the way they went before. Can I detect any difference in the way this one holds her shoulders up, that one has two fingers beneath his belt, the other fumbles with the gold braid on his chest? But what difference should there be? I have waited these years, I have watched. And I will still go pondering on what I have learned. Watcher and prisoner, I wait for freedom. At least from all this I know from which direction freedom will come; I have lived with my observation, and can at last move in to see what effect the observations have had on me. What can I salvage? Whatever is not clumsy and does not hide from war.*

The garden was empty now. Jon stood by himself in the swelling dark, fixed actor and observer in a matrix of matter and motivation.

And a universe away, a triple mind watched him, ordered its own knowledge of war, and made ready.

New York. April 6th, 1963

City of a Thousand Suns

CHAPTER I

WHAT is a city?

There is at least one on the planet earth, isolate among deadly seas, alone on an island near a radiation-pitted continent. Some of the sea and the land at the edge of the continent have been reclaimed: among these silent tides and still plains there is an empire. It is called Toromon. Its capital city is Toron.

Halfway around the universe, in a dispersed galaxy, is another . . . city.

A double sun throws twinned shadows from a tooth of rock jutting in the sand. The gullies sometimes shift in the rare breeze. The sky is blue, the sand lime white. Low on the horizon are streaks of clouds. And down the steep side of one powdery dune is the . . . City.

What is the City?

It is a place in the sand where a field of energy keeps the octagonal silicate crystals in perfect order, lined axis end to axis end. It is a place where a magnetic compass would spin like a top. It is a place where simple aluminium has the attractive capacity of sensitized alneco. And although, at the moment, it housed hundreds of inhabitants, there was not a building or structure of any kind in it. The sand was no longer smooth, and only a microscope could have detected the difference in the crystalline placement.

Responding to the psychic pressures of those who observed it, at times the City seemed a lake, at others a catacombe of caves. Once it had appeared a geyser of flame, and occasionally it looked like buildings, towers, looped together with elevated roads, with double light glinting from thousands of sunward windows. Whatever it was, it stood alone on the white desert of a tiny planet halfway across the universe from earth.

A meeting was being called in the City now; and with merely a turning of attention, the inhabitants met. The presiding intelligence was not single, but a triple entity much older than any of the others present. It had not built the city. But it dwelt there.

We have called you here to help us, it began. *Simply by being here you have already contributed greatly. There are only a few more of you to arrive, but we thought it better to begin now than to wait.* To one group at the meeting, immense, thirty-foot worms, the City seemed a web of muddy tunnels and the words came as vibrations through their hides. *As we have explained before, our universe has been invaded by a strange, amoral creature whom we have called till now the* Lord of the Flames. *So far he has only engaged in scouting activity to find out as much information about life in this universe as possible.* A metallic cyst received the words telepathically; for him the City was an airless, pitted siding of rock. *But even through his methods of experimenting, we know him to be dangerous. He thinks of completely perverting or destroying a culture to gain his information. We have tried to drive him out, and to keep the various cultures of the universe intact. On your several words, as our agents you have all had contact with him. And you have all had brief contacts with each other.* To the fifty-foot eyestalks of one listener the atmosphere of the City was tinged methane green. *He has been gathering information for a full-scale attack, but since we have dogged him to each planet, we have been able to see the information he gathers. Each of your cultures was undergoing some serious political and social upheaval when he chose to examine you. His method of observation in each culture has been to activate the elements that would push the upheaval a little too fast, would bring it to its conclusion a little too rapidly. Then, oddly, his point of concentration would be not the workings of the economic or social upheaval itself but rather an intense study of the personal life of some socially alienated individual, a madman, an upper echelon political figure, often an outlaw, a dispersed genius at the edge of society.* To one living crystal in the City the words of the Triple Being came as a significant progression of musical chords. *Now we wish to discuss one particular incident of his observation.* A sentient cactus shifted its tentacles and beheld the City almost as it was in reality, a stretch of pastel sand; but, then, who can say what was the reality of the city. *You have all arrived here except our agents from Earth, and we want to take this opportunity to discuss their specific situation.* To a casual observer of the meeting, the statement that the Earth representatives had not arrived would have seemed a flagrant oversight;

one of the attendants was an attractive, auburn-haired woman with wide hazel eyes. But a minute examination would have shown her slim almond-nailed fingers, her cream and honey skin to be a bizarre cosmic coincidence. Internal examination and genetic analysis would prove her a bisexual species of moss. *Self-contained and self-providing, the empire of Toromon has rested on Earth for fifteen hundred revolutions about the star Sol. The upheaval that Toromon went through was a complexed economic, political, and psychological reorganization coupled with a tidal wave of technological advances in farming methods and in food production that the degenerate, thousand-year-tired aristocracy was unable to redistribute.* 'Tidalwave' was the metaphor that a web-footed, triple-lidded marine creature from a world all water heard; to others it was 'earthquake', 'sand-storm', 'volcano'. *Their solution was to simulate a situation which existed only in the libraries from the time when the whole planet was populated with nations like theirs: they simulated a war, a war that would rid them of their excesses, in energy, in production, in lives. The vestigial skeleton of a military organization that had survived from before their isolate period (when just such real wars had completely demolished other nations, leaving Toromon alone) was enlarged to a tremendous force, armies were recruited, equipment was prepared, and a vast fantastical war was staged near the radiation-saturated rim of their empire, controlled by an immense random computer situated in the ruined remains of a second City in their empire called Telphar. Because of the radiation around them, evolution has run wild in Toromon, and there is one atavistic section of the population that has regressed to a point that race had passed three million years ago, while another segment has jumped a million years ahead and become a race of giants with many telepaths. The telepaths tried to remain above this war, but were at last dragged into it. Our agents, a telepath among them, convinced them—in an effort to find some other solution less destructive than this mock war—to establish a momentary telepathic link among all the inhabitants of the empire. The fact that the war was not real has come out among the people. The results have been too violent to predict accurately. The whole structure of Toromon was weak; it may have crumbled beyond hope already. Outlaw bands of malcontents—or malis—roam the country. There was an attempt to establish a new, young king, and for a while that worked, but the governmental system had been designed to rule a peaceful, calm nation, not a nation at war.* A strange life-form composed solely of thermal vibrations oscillated pensively in the City, listening, contemplating. *The reason we go into this situation in so much detail is because of the strange action of the* Lord of the Flames *when he encountered Toromon. First of all, his attempts to bring the situation to a rapid termination were immensely more violent and destructive than in any of his previous endeavours with other worlds. We, who can sense the energy of his concentration, realized that the intensity of his observation has quadrupled. Whatever he had been looking for desultorily among your worlds, he found in Earth. Our agents drove him out once and he returned. They drove him out a second time; he still hovers near, ready to invade again. We can only have three direct agents on a planet: we can only house ourselves in three minds. But with the help of the telepaths, we contacted two more—Tel and Alter—who became our indirect agents for a while. One of our indirect agents, Tel, was killed in the mock war, and so there are only four people left on Earth who are our contacts. As I said, we can only inhabit three of their minds at once; this leaves one, already used to contact extra-terrestrials, open for infiltration; this time we are sure that the* Lord of the Flames, *on his third return to earth, will choose one of our own agents, whichever one is left outside our protection. If we let them know directly the results would be disastrous to their own psyches. Therefore, our contact, already rare, will have to cease entirely after our next message.* A great bird ruffled its golden feathers, blinked a red eye, cocked its head, and listened. *The reason for the* Lord of the Flames' *interest in Toromon is clear. He is making ready to begin a war in our universe; he is now trying to find out all he can about how a life form of this universe conducts itself in a war. And this war of Toromon is a pure war, because there is no real enemy. Well, perhaps we can learn something too. We have the advantage of knowing where to look, for everyone in this City is so much more akin to each other and to the earth men than is the* Lord of the Flames *that ideas such as 'intelligence', 'compassion', 'murder', 'endurance' mean nothing to him; he must learn them by alien observation. Similarly, he has characteristics of which we have no idea. To further our own understanding, we have requested our agents to bring with them three documents, products by three of the most sensitive minds on Earth: the* Poems *of Vol Nonik, the* Unification of Random Fields, *by Dr Clea Koshar, and* Looms of the Sea, a Final Revision of the History of Toromon, *by Dr Rolth Catham.*

There was silence in the city, and then a faint life form spoke, a form that existed only as a light-sensitive virus who saw from the star-wide waves of novas to the micro-micron scattering of nutrinos, a life form disturbed occasionally by a fragment of ionized hydrogen, a loose photon, the aethric hum of a spinning galaxy eternities away from its home in cold, inter-galactic space: 'What will stop them from getting these . . . works?'

Then the Triple Being returned: *These works, remember, are by the most sensitive minds of Earth and will never reach the common man as books or periodicals, and among our four agents, there will constantly be a traitor, the* Lord of the Flames *himself.*

And a Universe away . . .

. . . And she was beautiful, beautiful with sun through the cracked window caught in her falling hair, beautiful with her closed eyes, her olive lids, darker than the rest of her face, the rest of her skin, which was beautiful with colours like honey and the blush of kharba fruits going from white to pink, before they become speckled, orange, ripe; beautiful with textures like velvet, like polished, brown stone where her knee was drawn up and the skin tight; and where her body curved slightly towards him, at her side, and the skin was loose—like velvet.

The cracked pane in the window made a jagged line of shadow over the floorboards, up the side of the bed, across the crumpled sheets, a serpent of shadow on her stomach. Her lips were opened and her bright teeth were faintly blued by the shadow of her upper lip.

She was beautiful with shadows, the long violet ones that fell over the waterfront streets where he had walked with her last night, beautiful with light, the glare of a mercury light which they had stopped under briefly to talk to a friend of his——

'So you went and got married after all, Vol. Well, I thought you would, Congratulations.'

'Thanks.' They both said it, and his voice, low tenor, and hers, rich alto, were even musical together. 'Renna, this is my friend Kino. Kino, this is my wife, Renna.' He spoke that solo, like a single instrument after a chord, it implied symphonies to come between them.

'I guess you won't be having so much to do with your old gang any more.' Kino dug a dirty finger in a dirtier ear. 'But then, you never were a gang man really. Now you can sit around and write poems as you always wanted to, and enjoy life.' And when the grimy youth, too old for urchin, too young for derelict, said 'life' he glanced at her, and all the yearning of his restless age flamed in his eyes and lit her beauty.

'No, I'm not a gang man, Kino,' Vol said. 'And what with that stupid feud between me and Jeof, I decided that this was as good a time as any just to drop out of the whole mali business. We're going to be moving to the mainland in a couple of days. There's a place there we've heard about that we'd like to look at.'

Kino moved a bare toe around a cobblestone. 'I wasn't gonna mention Jeof, but since you did first, I guess I can say I think getting out is a good idea. Because he is a gang man, to the root of every rotten tooth in his jaw.' Suddenly he ducked his head and grinned apologetically. 'Look, I gotta go some place. You just don't let Jeof see her.' He made a motion towards Renna, and with the motion Vol looked at her, her dark skin pale under the light of the mercury lamp; Kino was gone, and she was . . .

. . . beautiful with shadow again as they walked through the dark streets of the Devil's Pot and at last turned into the ramshackle tavern-boarding-house, beautiful as they stepped into the hall and darkness closed over her, blackening details. Just then someone opened the door at the end of the hall and a wash of yellow threw her into silhouette as she walked a step ahead of him, and he learned with his eyes as he already knew with his hands that the shape and outline of her whole body—waist, breasts, neck, and chin—were beautiful. They had gone together to his room.

On the wall was an exquisite picture she had done of him, red chalk on brown paper. On the rickety table in front of the window was a sheaf of paper. The top sheet bore the final draft of a poem that was, in its exquisite use of words and bright image, a portrait of her.

He sat cross-legged in the crumpled, body-warmed bedding, now, and looked at her beside him until his eyes ached with

he only stood. But then the cry turned into a long, steady scream. Suddenly Vol was screaming too, and fighting, and their voices had lost all music and become dissonant and agonized. He fought, and nearly killed one of the men who held him, but there were three others around him who broke four of his ribs, dislocated his shoulder, and smashed in one side of his jaw.

'No,' said Jeof, making a calming gesture with his hand—there was blood on his hand, and she couldn't scream now because the cartilages of her larynx were crushed, 'Don't kill him. I just want him to watch what we do to her.' He looked around. 'One of you guys come over here and help me now.' They used their hands, then their whole bodies, and then the double gleam of a fire-blade came from a hidden scabbard, the bottom on the hilt was flicked, and white sparks glittered up the double prongs.

A minute after that, mercifully, Vol lost consciousness. They couldn't even beat him awake. So they left.

Half an hour later Rara, the woman who ran the boarding-house, got up enough courage to look into the room. When she saw the naked man crumpled in front of the table she said, 'Good Lord,' and stepped inside. Then, when she saw what was left on the bed, she couldn't say anything, and just stepped backwards with her hand over her mouth.

The man's hand moved on the grimy floorboards. 'Oh, my good Lord,' she whispered. '*He's* alive.' She ran towards him, beating out of her mind a picture of the two of them together as she had seen them even yesterday (drinking from the same tin cup at the downstairs sink, walking with loosely coupled fingers, laughing at each other's eyes). She kneeled over him, and his hand moved to her foot.

Got to get him out of here before he wakes up, she thought, and tried to lift him up.

Vol was at the point now in drifting unconsciousness where the pain of his cracked ribs jabbing at his lung was enough to wake him. He opened his eyes, and looked blankly at the face of the woman bending over him. It was a strong face, though the other side of fifty. A brown-red birthmark sprawled over her left cheek. 'Rara?' he spoke her name with just a hint of inflection, and the bruised jaw, swelling now, kept all expression out of his face.

'Mr Nonik,' she said. 'Come with me, won't you?'

He looked away, and when his eyes reached the bed he stopped.

'Don't, Mr Nonik,' Rara said. 'Come with me.'

He let her raise him to his feet and walked with her to the hall, despite his agonized arm, despite the fire on the right side of his chest.

Rara saw the limp and recognized the impossible angle at which his arm hung. 'Well,' she began, 'we're going to have to get you to General Medical pretty quick. . . .'

Then he cried out. It was a long cry, wrenched up from inside him; it changed in the middle, rising nearly an octave to a scream (like a trapped boar in a quicksand pool whose cry goes from the hope of struggle, rising through sudden understanding, into final terror and submersion.) Screee*aaaa* . . . Vol sank to the hall floor. He shook his head; tears ran down his face; but he was quiet.

'Mr Nonik,' Rara said. 'Mr Nonik, get up.'

Again he stood. The silence started chills on her back. She supported him down the hall. 'Look, I know this won't mean anything to you, Mr Nonik, maybe. But listen. You're young, and you've . . . lost something.' He heard her through a haze of pain. 'But we all do in some way or another. I wouldn't say this if it hadn't been for what happened a month ago, that moment when we all suddenly . . . knew each other like that. Since then I guess a lot of people have said strange things, that they wouldn't normally. But like I said, you're young. There are so many people that we lose one or another, whom we think are . . . are like everyone who saw you two knew you thought she was. But you'll live.' She paused. 'I had a niece, once, that I loved as much as a daughter. Her mother was dead. Both she and her daughter were acrobats. Then, four years ago, she disappeared, and I never saw her again. I lost her, lost a person I had brought up since she was nine years old. And I'm alive.'

'No . . .' he said, shaking his head now. 'No.'

'Yes,' she said. 'And so are you. And you'll stay that way. At least if we get you to General Medical.' Suddenly the despair that she had been trying to keep out of her voice, keep away from him, broke through. 'Why must they do things like that? Why? How can they do it now, after that moment when we all knew?'

'For the same reason they did it before,' he said flatly. 'Just like you,' he went on, and she frowned. 'They're trapped in that bright moment where they learned their doom. But they won't get me. They won't.'

'What are you talking about?' she asked, but his voice (or perhaps it was the sound of the words themselves, the double oo of doom, a rare word then, that echoed the spuming sea) brought chills again.

'They'll never find me,' he said. 'Never!' He lurched forward —and fell a quarter of the way down the stairs.

'Mr Nonik!'

He caught himself on the banister, and started on again. Rara hurried down behind him, but he was already at the door.

'Mr Nonik, you've got to get to General Medical!'

He stood in the door, naked, shaking his head in animal denial. 'They'll never find me!' he whispered once more, then he was gone into the street.

Bewildered, she hesitated. When she looked she couldn't see him at all. The early morning pavement was deserted. The sun was bright. At last she gave up looking. She found an officer to bring back to the boarding-house and report what had happened.

The twin sun shone on the white sand of the City.

'When will the agents from Earth arrive?' someone asked.

As soon as they have found their three documents, the triple voice said . . . *and if they are still alive.*

An ozone-scented breeze shifted the powdery whiteness down the side of a dune so that the subtle shape of the desert was changed again, and the only thing stable and isolate was the City.

Near the centre of Toron an old merchant sat on his tiled balcony, gazing at the palace towers, then down to the clapboard houses in the waterfront area of the Devil's Pot. 'Clea?' he said.

'Yes, Dad.'

'Are you sure this is what you want? You've had every possible honour Toromon could offer you as a scientist, for your work in matter-transmission, your theoretical studies. I don't think I've ever said it directly to you. But I'm very proud.'

'Thanks, Dad,' she said. 'But it's what I want. Neither Rolth nor I intend to stop working. I have my Unified Field Theory to complete. He will be working on a new historical project.'

'Well, don't stand there. Call him out here.'

She walked back into the house, then emerged a moment later, hand in hand with a tall man. They stopped before the marble table at which Koshar sat. 'Rolth Catham, you wish to marry my daughter, Clea Koshar?'

'Yes.' The answer was firm.

'Why?' And response was quick.

Catham turned his head slightly, and the light glinted on the transparent plastic case of his cheek. The fraction of his face that was mobile flesh smiled, and under it the direct gaze of Koshar wavered. 'That's not a fair question,' Koshar said, 'is it. I don't know. Since that . . . second when we all . . . well, you know. Then, I guess a lot of people have been saying things, asking things, and even answering things that they wouldn't ordinarily.'

The embarrassment, Clea thought. Why must they all speak of that blind moment of telepathic contact that had blanketed the empire that second at the end of the war—with embarrassment. She had hoped that her father would be different. It wasn't embarrassment at what had been seen, but at the newness of the experience.

' "Why?" is never an unfair question,' Catham said. 'It's partly because of what we saw at that moment.'

Catham spoke of it without fear. That was one of the reasons she loved him now.

'Because we'd known each other's work. And because during that moment we knew each other's mind. And because we are the two people we are, that knowledge will serve us for heart and soul as well.'

'All right,' Koshar said. 'Get married. But . . .'

Clea and Rolth looked at each other, smile and half-smile leaping between them.

'But why do you want to go away?'

Faces grave once more, they looked back at the old man.

'Clea,' Koshar said. 'Clea, you've been away from me so long. I had you when you were a little girl. But then you were away at University Island so much, and after that you turned right around and wanted to live alone, and I let you. Now the two of you want to go away again, and this time you don't even want to tell me where you're going.' He paused. 'Of course you can do it. You're twenty-eight years old, a woman. How could I stop you? But, Clea . . . I don't know how to say this. I've lost . . . a son already. And I don't want to lose my daughter now.'

'Dad——' she began.

'I know what you're going to say, Clea. But even if your younger brother Jon were alive—and everything would make it seem that he was dead—even if he were, if he walked in here right this minute: for me he would be dead. After what he did to me, he would be dead.'

'Dad, I wish you didn't feel that way. Jon did something stupid, clumsy, and childish. He was a clumsy child when he did it, and he paid for it.'

'But my own son, in the penal mines, a common criminal . . . murderer!' His voice fell to grating depth. 'My friends do me kindness by not mentioning him to me today. Because if any of them should, I couldn't hold my head up, Clea.'

'Dad,' Clea said, with entreaty in her voice, 'he was eighteen, spoiled. He resented me, you . . . and if he is alive anywhere, eight years will have made a very different man from the boy. After eight years you can't keep this up against your own son. And if you can't hold your head up now, perhaps that's your problem, and has nothing to do with Jon.' She felt Rolth's hand on her shoulder, a gentle warning that her tone, if not her words, were passing into that dangerous field of outrage, like particles moving into a random energy field, darting and unpredictable. She drew back from the feeling.

'I won't forgive him,' her father was saying. He clasped his hands together. 'I can't forgive him.' He averted his eyes from her, staring into his lap. 'I couldn't. I'd be too ashamed——'

'Dad!' she had turned from the outrage now, and the word came with all the love she felt for him. She saw his body, back, neck, arms, fingers, locked in self-protective inward curves. 'Dad!' she said again, and held her hand out to him.

The curves broke, his hands separated, his eyes lifted. He did not take her hand, but he said, 'Clea, you say you've got to go away, and you say you don't want anyone to know where you are. I love you, and I want you to have anything you want. But at least . . . letters, or something. So I'll know you're all right, so I'll know . . .'

'It can't be letters, Dad,' she said. Then she added quickly, 'But you'll know.'

Catham said, 'We've got to go now, Clea.'

'Goodbye, Dad. And I love you.'

'I love you,' he repeated back to her, but they were already entering the wide doors of the house.

'I wish I could tell him,' Clea said when they reached the front door, 'tell him that Jon was alive, tell him why we have to go so secretly.'

'He'll know soon enough,' Catham said. 'They'll all know.'

She sighed. 'Yes, they will, won't they. That great, monstrous computer in Telphar will let them know. They could all know now if they wanted, but they're too embarrassed. Rolth, for three thousand years everyone has tried to find a word to differentiate man from other animals; some of the ancients called his the laughing animal, some the moral animal. Well, I wonder if he isn't the embarrassed animal, Rolth.'

Her husband-to-be laughed, but with half humour. Then he said: 'I've asked you this a hundred times, Clea, but it's so hard to believe: you're sure of those reports?'

She nodded. 'The only ones who've seen them are a handful of people who were intimately involved in the computer construction. I was only allowed in by the skin of my teeth, more because of that final mix-up at the palace than anything else. But it makes me ill, Rolth, ill that I had anything to do with that monster.' She let out a breath as they passed from the shadow of the balcony on to the colonnaded street. 'But then I've worked through that guilt business already, haven't I.' It was a question that needed only the momentary reassurance of his hand tightening around hers. 'Rolth, they've tried four times to start disassembling it. But it won't work. Somehow it's protecting itself. They can hardly get near it.'

She turned, waved to her father on the balcony, and then continued down the street.

'How, I won't question,' Rolth said. 'It's got all the unused equipment, armaments, and so forth for a full-scale war in its control. But, "Why?" Clea. You're the mathematician. You know computers.'

'But you're the historian,' she answered, 'and wars are your department.' She glanced once more at the tiny figure on the balcony that still waved after them. 'I wonder how long it will take him . . . them to learn.'

'I don't know,' he said. 'I don't know.'

Above, the transit-ribbon scribed a thin black line across the sky.

When old Koshar, on the green balcony, saw them disappear he sighed. Then he did something he hadn't done for a long time. He went in, called the taxi service, changed into inconspicuous clothes, then shuttled along the radial streets of the city to the waterfront. He stood around quietly while the launch pulled out with the afternoon shift of workers for the Koshar Aquariums.

Once he paused at a corner while a transport rumbled by with 'Koshar Hydroponics' in large green letters over its aluminium side. He stopped outside a building, the cleanest and tallest in the area; it was the offices of Koshar Synthetics.

Later, walking the thin, dirty alleys of the Devil's Pot, he stopped in front of one of the combination tavern–boarding-houses. He was thirsty, the afternoon was hot, so he entered. A number of people apparently had had the same idea, and the conversation was going at the bar. A friendly voice beside him said: 'Hello, old man. Haven't seen you here before.'

The woman at the table who had spoken to him, close to fifty, had a large birthmark on one side of her face.

'I haven't been here before,' Koshar said.

'I guess that would explain it,' Rara answered. 'Have a seat.' But he was already moving towards the bar. He bought a drink, then turned with it, wondering where to go, and saw the woman sitting by the door. So he went back and sat down at her table. 'You know, a long time ago I used to spend a lot of time in this area. I don't remember this place though.'

'Well, I've only had it here about a month,' Rara explained. 'Just got my licence. I'm trying to drum up some steady business. Being friendly is real important in business, you know. Hope I see you around here often.

'Um,' Koshar said, and sipped green liquid from his mug.

'I tried to start a place some years back. Took it over from a friend of mine who passed away. But that was just when the malis were getting started, and they busted the place all up in a raid one night. Now, here I am just started a couple of weeks and I've had trouble already. Some of them broke in here this morning, one of those gang-feud things. Of course officers are never around when you need them. Killed a girl.' She shook her head.

An argument had started at the bar. Rara turned, frowned, and said, 'Now what do you suppose that's all about?'

A wiry man whose face was cracked from wind and sand spoke loudly, while a woman stood beside him, her green eyes fixed on his face. But he was looking at another man. 'No,' he was saying. He made a sharp, disgusted gesture with his hand. 'No, it's rotten here. Rotten.'

'Who are you to say it's rotten?' somebody laughed.

'I'll tell you who I am. I'm Cithon the fisherman. And this is my wife Grella, a fine weaver. And we say your whole island is rotten!'

The woman put her strong hands on his shoulder, her eyes imploring for silence.

'And let me tell you something else. I used to live on the mainland coast. And I had a son, too; he would have been as good a fisherman as I am. But your rottenness lured him here to your island. You starved him out on the mainland, you seduced him here with the aquarium-grown fish. Well, we followed him. And where is he now? Is he sweating himself to death out in your aquariums? Or is he running with one of your mali gangs? Or maybe he's draining the good sea salt from his body in your hydroponic gardens. What have you done with him? What have you done with my son?'

'Damned immigrants,' muttered Rara. 'Hold on just a second, will you?' She got up and went over to the bar. The man's wife was trying to pull him away, and Rara assisted her. The man got really nasty before they got him out.

Rara came back, brushing her hands on her skirt. 'Immigrants,' she said again, and sat down. 'Now I'm not saying anything against them; some of them are good people, some of them are not so good. But some of them are nuts like that. Funny, that woman looked awfully familiar. Like something I might have swept off my doorstep once.' She laughed. 'But then, all those green-eyed mainlanders look alike. Oh, are you leaving? Well, come back soon. This is a real friendly place here. Real friendly.'

Outside, Koshar stopped once in front of a wooden fence,

scabbed with the remains of peeled posters. Across the remnants of blurred shiboleths someone had scrawled in red chalk:

'You Are Trapped in That Bright Moment Where You Learned Your Doom.'

The wild irregular shape of the letters (or perhaps it was in the words themselves, the palatals of 'that bright moment' clicking against the soft labials, like the click of coins in a random matrix) made him feel strange.

Old Koshar turned up the street, his heart half-broken.

A universe away, white sand blew down the dunes.

What is the City?

It is a place where the time passes as something other than time. It is a place where the mechanical movements of spring, cog, and gear would slow to a veritable stop. The same is true with a clock of blood, bone, muscle, and nerve. Yet the psychic flashing of photon against photon travels at normal if not accelerated speed.

'But why is this isolated empire of Earth so important?'

'Are they so technologically advanced that this paper on Random Fields will give us a weapon to vanquish the *Lord of the Flames*?'

'Will this historical work predict for us the outcome of our own great war?'

'Is there no other art among all our cultures that teaches so much compassion, that fixes life's place in the universe so brilliantly as these poems?'

A score of minds, in their ways and words, formed a barrage of bewilderment. For answer came a triad of laughter. *The earthmen are important because the* Lord of the Flames *is among them now,* and the 'now' is an inexact translation for the reverberating concept of cross-sectioned, inter-gallactic time with past and future patterning implied. *Yet if these earthmen arrive their very arrival will herald our victory over the* Lord of the Flames, *and there will be no need to study their documents, other than for your own edification. If they do not arrive, then we are defeated.*

Bewilderment among them grew to concern.

You will see why, the triad voice said. The double sun dropped towards the horizon, and there was silence in the city.

CHAPTER II

'PUT your head back.'

He put back his head.

'Now bring your knees up and roll backwards.'

He rolled, feeling the torque of his shifting weight from his wrists to his taut shoulders. Slowly his feet came down, his toes brushing the mat.

'Fine,' she said.

He let go of the rings. 'Think that's enough for today?' he asked her, grinning.

'More than enough,' she said. 'You don't want to work at it too hard, Jon. That's no good either. Let yourself ease into it. You're doing superbly already. Where'd you get that co-ordination?'

He stepped off the mat, shrugging. 'The muscle I got first when I was in jail, digging tetron ore at the penal mines. The rest—I don't know.'

'You really amaze me,' Alter said. 'The way you've been sticking to this tumbling business is impressive. And the progress is more so.'

'It's something I wanted to learn,' he said. 'I don't like being clumsy. Let's shower and then get something to eat.'

'Fine.' She smiled.

They left the gymnasium and walked along the tiled hall to the showers as a bunch of youngsters came from an adjoining hall in bathing suits. One girl, thick bodied and low browed, snapped a towel at an extraordinarily tall youth with a flat, equine face. The others laughed, and then continued down the hall.

'Have you seen that girl swim?' Jon asked. 'You wouldn't think it to look at her, but her speed is fantastic.'

'I saw her through the observation porch this morning,' Alter said. 'You're right. That hundred yards was pretty amazing.'

Just then they passed two boys loitering by the wall. One had small features pocked with acne. They were also looking after the swimmers. 'Damned foreigners,' one muttered, his face hardening.

'Catch them walking around the Devil's Pot at night,' the other one said and sneered. Then he made a grinding gesture with his fist against the tile.

Jon and Alter exchanged frowns and separated at the shower rooms.

Ten minutes later, his skin steamed and his hair damp, Jon stepped out on to the concourse. Shifting jets of water from the aluminium fountain clashed in the sun. Alter was already standing there. Her bare tanned shoulders, her long legs and sandled feet moved slightly in the act of waiting. A breeze cooled his face, and at the same time he saw wisps of her white hair leap to the side.

A couple stopped by the fountain, stared at the base, frowned, and moved on. When he reached her he, too, frowned. 'What's that?' he asked.

'Where?' She turned to look. A scowl of surprise formed around her light eyes. 'I didn't see that before!'

Someone had written across the dull metallic surface in whitewash:

YOU ARE TRAPPED IN THAT BRIGHT
MOMENT WHERE YOU LEARNED YOUR DOOM

'What's that supposed to mean?' Alter asked.

Jon read it once more. 'I don't know. But it makes me feel funny.'

Somewhere something buzzed.

Across the concourse one person looked up, three more; then by dozens, eyes turned to the whining sky.

Jutting above the transit ribbon, two, then three, then four silver flashes hurled through the clouds.

'Aren't they awfully low?' Jon said.

'Scouting planes?' Alter suggested.

A small bead of light dropped from one of the airships. When it hit, there was a silent flash among the city towers. Seconds later the sound came, and with it, restraint broke and the screams started.

'What the . . .!' began Alter.

For five seconds the sound came on, a concussive rumbling explosion.

'That's the war ministry!' Alter cried.

'That *was* the war ministry,' Jon said. 'What the hell happened?'

A broken stud of burning masonry, the remains of the tower, flickered above the hem of buildings. Chaos broiled on the concourse. 'Come on,' Jon said. 'Let's go!'

'Where are we going?' Alter asked.

'To get something to eat and to sit down and talk.'

They made their way to a side street. As they reached the corner, the news speaker grill began humming:

Remain calm, citizens. Remain calm. A tragic accident has just occurred at the Military, where, through a grave oversight, planes from Telphar carrying high explosives were re-routed automatically by a failure in the mechanism of the disbandment programme....

By the time they turned into the restaurant the casualty figures were being given out.

The front window of the place they chose was two twelve-foot discs of multi-coloured glass rotated slowly in opposite directions by hidden machinery. Pastel patterns slipped across the tablecloth as they slid into the booth.

'What do you think happened?' Alter asked again.

John shrugged. 'An accidental bombing.'

'That's a strange thing to happen accidentally,' said Alter.

Jon nodded.

There was some disturbance at the restaurant entrance and the two looked up.

A woman with a wealth of fiery hair had just entered. The man with her was a handful of inches over seven feet. The owner of the restaurant apparently did not wish to seat the giant—an example of the behaviour that was becoming more and more common towards the giant forest people and the squat neo-neanderthals since the release of so many soldiers from the war. The owner made his excuses with explanatory gesticulations: 'But we are already full ... my other patrons might not under ... perhaps somewhere else you would receive....' The woman became annoyed. She touched her lapel, turned it over, and revealed her insignia.

The owner stopped in mid-sentence, put both hands over his mouth, and whispered through his pudgy fingers: 'Oh, Your

Grace, I had no idea it was ... I'm so terribly sorry that ... I never realized you were a member of the royal ...'

'We'll sit over there with that couple,' said the Duchess. With the forest guard, she moved across the room to where Jon and Alter sat.

The owner preceded them like a diesel-powered slug. 'Her Grace, the Duchess of Petra, wonders if you would be so kind as to allow herself and her companion ...'

But Jon and Alter were already on their feet. 'Petra, Arkor,' cried Jon, 'how are you? What are you doing here?' And Alter echoed his greeting.

'Following you,' answered the Duchess shortly. 'We just missed you at the Public Gym and then caught you ducking around the corner in all the confusion.'

'May I ... eh ... take your order?' ventured the owner.

They ordered, the owner left, and what little interest from the other diners melted now that altercation was over.

'What did you want us for, Petra?' asked Jon. He looked closely and saw that the Duchess's face was tired.

'The war,' she said. 'The war again.'

'But the war's over,' said Alter.

'Is it?' asked Petra. 'It may be too late already.'

'What do you mean?' Jon asked.

'You saw the "accidental" bombing a few minutes ago?'

Jon and Alter nodded.

'First, it wasn't accidental. Second, there are going to be a lot of other "accidents" unless we can do something about it.'

'But ...' began Alter, 'there's no enemy.'

'The computer,' the Duchess said. 'The reports have just come in. I only saw them in my capacity as adviser to King Let. Apparently the computer that ran the war has gone wild! It's self-repair circuits have made use of the radio-co-ordinators to seize any equipment with automatic controls. Until now it has only defended itself against the military dismantling unit. But today it launched its first attack on Toromon.'

'How?' Jon wanted to know.

'A very imprecise explanation accompanies the report. Remember that thousands upon thousands of minds were controlled semi-hypnotically by the machine, and recorded in complete detail. Even though it killed thousands of men, it still had these mental records in its memory bank. Somehow, between its structure and function, the whole pattern of death and war was lifted from the minds of its victims and internalized by the activity circuits. The result was the bombing of the military ministry. Right now it seems to be spending long inactive periods still digesting the information. But its activity is on the increase, and what the end . . .' She stopped.

'So we're still up against ourselves,' said Jon, after a moment. 'Only this time in a mirror image stored in memory banks and transfer coils.'

'What about our galaxy-hopping friend the triple being?' Alter asked. She glanced about, always feeling odd whenever she mentioned the strange force known only—if it existed at all—to the four of them. 'It kept promising to help if we helped it, and we certainly have.'

'But we have heard nothing from them,' Arkor said. 'All I can think of is when peace was declared and the *Lord of the Flames* was driven from Earth, their interest in us ceased. Whatever we do now will have to be done on our own.'

'But we are going to need help,' said the Duchess. 'Somehow I feel that if we could find——'

It touched them now, but subtly, registering on another level than perception, so that the green light from the window reflected on the silverware held for a moment the faint flicker of beetles' wings, the copper grill over the air vent for an instant was the same red as polished carbuncle, and the general flickering in the eye was a faint web of silver fire: the four were touched, three of them with the presence of the Triple Being; yet one of the four——

'—could find your sister, Dr Koshar, she could be a great deal of help. She worked on the computer for a while and should know something about it; she's got the sort of mind that might be able to cut through exactly this sort of problem.'

'Another person we would do well to consult,' came the measured voice of the giant telepath, 'is Rolth Catham. A war is an historical necessity; I'm quoting him, and he has more understanding of the economics and historical influences on Toromon than any other person alive.'

The others, who had consulted Catham before, nodded, and for half a minute there was silence.

'You know,' said Jon, 'who I would like to find, Alter!'

'Who?'

'The person who wrote that thing on the side of the fountain.'

'I've been wondering myself,' said Alter, 'just who thought that one up.' She turned to Petra. 'It was almost a line of poetry that someone scrawled over the fountain in front of Gymnasium Plaza.'

' "You are trapped in that bright moment where you learned your doom," ' said the Duchess.

'Yes, that's it,' said Jon. 'Did you see it on the fountain when you came looking for us at the gym?'

'No.' She looked puzzled. 'Someone had scribbled it across the palace wall by the gate this morning. But it stuck in my mind. That's all.'

'I guess a couple of people have been writing it,' Alter said.

'I'd like to find the one who wrote it first,' said Jon.

'Well, before that, Jon, let's see if we can't find Catham, and your sister,' the Duchess said.

'Why is there a problem?' asked Alter. The young acrobat brushed back silver hair. Large eyes, blue-grey, blinked in her tanned face. 'We should be able to find them at University Island, right away, shouldn't we?'

Now Arkor spoke. 'Yesterday morning Rolth Catham resigned the chairmanship of the history department of the University of Toromon, left for Toron that afternoon, leaving no indication of what his plans were.'

'And my sister, Dr Koshar?' Jon asked.

'She quit her position with the governmental science combine,' the Duchess said, 'also yesterday morning. After that, nobody can trace them.'

'Perhaps my father knows where she is.'

'Perhaps,' said the Duchess. 'We haven't wanted to ask him without speaking to you first.'

Jon leaned back in his chair, looked at his lap, and then up, 'Eight years,' he said, 'eight years since I've seen my father. I guess it's about time I went.'

'If you'd rather not . . .' the Duchess began.

Jon raised his black eyes quickly, tilting his head. 'No. I want to. I'll find out from him where she's gone—if he knows.' Suddenly he sat up. 'Will you excuse me, please?' He pushed his chair from the table, walked to the entrance of the restaurant, and left.

The three remaining at the table looked after him, then back at one another. After a moment the Duchess said, 'Jon has changed recently, hasn't he.'

Alter nodded.

'When did it start?' asked Petra.

'At that moment . . .' She paused, then gave a little laugh. 'I was about to say "at that bright moment where we learned . . ." ' Now her face furrowed with remembering. 'It was the next day that he asked me to teach him tumbling. And he's mentioned his father an awful lot recently. I think he's been waiting for a reason to go and see him.' She turned to Arkor. 'What did Jon learn when we all saw each other? He's always been so quiet, such a deep person up until now. He still isn't what you'd call talkative, but . . . well, he is working hard at the tumbling. I told him at first he was too old to get really good, but he's making so much progress, I wonder.'

'What *did* he learn?' It was the Duchess who asked now.

'Perhaps,' said the telepath, 'Who he was.'

'You say "perhaps",' said Petra.

Arkor smiled. 'Perhaps,' he repeated. 'That's all I can say.'

'Has he gone to see his father now?' asked Alter.

The giant nodded.

'I hope it goes all right,' she said. 'Eight years is a long time to hold grudges. Petra, Arkor, when you teach somebody something physical, just from the movements of their body, you learn how they feel, what makes them breath deeply when they're glad, or pull their shoulders in when they're afraid; and just watching him for these past couple of months. . . . Well, I hope it goes all right.'

'You and Dr Koshar were very close to each other,' the Duchess said, leaning forward over the table. 'Do you have any idea where she might have gone?'

Alter looked up. 'That's just it,' she said. 'Up until that moment at the end we were always together, talking, laughing about something. Then she went away. At first I thought she'd gone into the same sort of retreat she was in when I first met her. But no, I got a few letters, she hadn't given up working; she was happy over her new field theory, and I thought she was finally getting at peace with herself. From the last letter that's what seemed to be happening. But there hasn't been another one, and this business about her stopping her job: that seems strange.'

'Almost as strange,' mused the Duchess absently, 'as a country at war with its mirror image caught in a steel memory bank.'

CHAPTER III

WHAT do you think when you're about to see your father after five years of jail and three of treasonable adventuring? Jon asked himself that: the answer was a fear deep in his throat that might drag at his tongue when he could speak. As he walked up the radial street of the city, other fears returned. There was the nameless one from childhood that had to do with a woman's face that might have been his mother's, and a man's that was probably his father's, but it was vague. At eighteen there had been a week of fear, beginning with a ridiculous dare by a treacherous friend who happened to be the late king of Toromon (and he wondered now, would he have taken the dare if it had come from another boy?) and finished with clumsy panic, a stroke of Jon's fire-blade, and the death of the palace guard chasing him. Then there were five years in prison (the sentence was life, not five years) in which anger and humiliation and hate for the guards, for the faulty mining equipment, for hot hours underground with rocks scraping his hands, for the sound of tall ferns brushing his dirt-stiffened uniform as he walked to and from the shacks at dawn and sunset; but the only time in prison fear had come undisguised was when the first talk of escape began, filling the night in whispers from bunk to bunk, mouthed behind a guard's back in the infrequent rest periods that punctuated his subterranean labour. It was not fear of punishment, but of the talk itself, of something uncontrollable, the small random thing unplanned for in the tight fabric of prison life, flowering in the unregimented moment, in a free exchange of eyes, in the whispers passed in the washroom.

He had tackled that fear differently, by joining the plans, helping, digging with his hands till his nails were quick-torn, counting the steps a guard took from the office to the sentry-box at the edge of the prison area. When the plan was finished only three men remained: he had been the youngest crouched in the light rain by the guard-house steps, waiting for freedom.

During the dash, in darkness, with wet fronds beating his face, there was no fear. There was no time for it. It culminated and exploded in his brain like the crystalline spears in a disturbed super-cooled liquid after he had got lost from the other two, after he had wandered from the jungle too close to the edge of the radiation barrier, after he had seen the spires of Telphar black on the dawn, when, unexpected, unpredictably, with neither mental nor physical defence, over the distance of a universe he was struck from the stars.

Then came the adventuring. There had been danger and he had been weary, but not afraid in the same way he was now. This small white emptiness was a negative of the black spot of terror from half-remembered childhood.

He climbed the long-ago familiar stairs of his father's house and stopped in front of the door. As he raised his thumb to the print lock he thought, is it through this doorway freedom lies?

It had been a long time since the lock had read the lines and whorls of his thumb: dark wood fell back, and he stepped into the foyer. He wondered if his father had changed as much as he had. If his working habits were the same he would be working in the family dining-room.

Jon walked by the wall hangings of blue cloth, the familiar chronometer embedded in the floor (the crystal had been replaced since he had last seen it), past the turn in the hall that had the strange whispering-chamber effect where you could stand thirty feet away around the corner and hear someone talking, even softly, by the coat closet, past the door to the trophy room (the wood on the panelling had been split before, now it was repaired) and into the ballroom. High, dim, it spread before him to the long, swan's-wing staircase that cascaded from the inner balcony. His sandle heels *clisped* softly, steadily, and for a moment he felt that many ghosts of himself were following him to the dining-room.

The door was closed, He knocked, and a voice said, 'Who is it? Come in.'

Jon opened the door. And hundreds of clocks began to tick.

Startled, the portly man with white hair looked up. 'Who are you? I gave instructions that nobody was to be admitted without . . .'

'Father,' he said, thinking, Am I telling him or asking him?

Koshar pulled back in his chair, his face darkening. 'Who are you and what are you doing here?'

'Father,' Jon said again, thinking, The knowledge is hanging in front of him like a glittering light and he is pulling back, afraid. 'Father, I'm Jon.'

Koshar sat forward again, both hands falling to the desk like weights released. 'No.'

'I've come back to see you, Dad,' Jon said, thinking, Even denying it, he has admitted me. As he stood in front of the desk the old man who was his father raised his head, his jaw moving slightly as if tasting over possible words and finding them bland.

He said at last, 'Where have you been, Jon?'

'I . . .' Then all this perceptions turned inward, and as clearly as he had been observing his father, he was staring at the chaotic emotions that had exploded in himself: he wanted very much to cry, a little boy lost and found in the dark, or a man lost and finding himself in light. There was a chair beside him, so he sat down, and that helped keep tears from coming. '. . . I've been away a long time, a lot of places. Jail, you know about, I guess. Then I've been in the service of the Duchess of Petra for three years, having adventures, doing a lot of growing up. Now I've come back.'

'Why?' Koshar's head shook, shook as though a sledge had just struck the base of his spine. 'Why? Do you want to be forgiven, for disgracing me, making me unable to hold my head up before my friends, my business associates?'

Jon was quiet a moment. Then he said, 'You suffered too?'

'I, suffered . . .?'

'Five years,' Jon said, softer than he meant, 'I saw sunlight less than an hour a day, was yelled at, beaten; I strained in the neon darkness of the tetron pits and called up muscles I didn't know I had. I rubbed my palms raw on rock. You suffered?'

'Why did you come back?'

'I came back to find my . . .' He paused. Suddenly the resentment turned over in him. 'I came back to ask you to forgive me, for hurting you—if you can.'

'Well I——' Then old Koshar began to cry. It began as the dry sound of a man unused to tears, but like an empty cistern before a breaking dam, the sound filled. 'Jon,' he said. 'Jon.'

He went around the desk and put his arm tightly around his father's shoulder, thinking: the dangerous we do by instinct, by relying on training; and the hardest are done quickly, walking a familiar street to a familiar door, that moment in which we must go backward to go on. 'Dad,' he said, 'where's Clea? I came to talk to her too.'

Koshar sucked in his breath. 'Clea? She's gone.'

'Gone where?'

'She's gone with the history professor, from the University.'

'Catham?'

'They were married, yesterday. I asked them where they were going, but they wouldn't tell me. They just wouldn't tell me.'

'Why?'

Koshar shook his head again. 'They wouldn't tell.'

Jon went to the front of the desk, sat down, and leaned over it towards his father. 'They wouldn't give you a reason either?'

'That's right. That's why I got so upset, just now, about you. I think a lot, Jon. I didn't like thinking about you in the mines, and me here, living off the ore you broke your back to pull up from the ground. That embarrassed me more than anything my friends ever could have said.' Koshar looked down, and then up. 'Son, I'm so glad to see you.' He extended his hand across the table, and with the other took out a pocket handkerchief and wiped his face.

Jon took his father's hand. 'I'm glad to see you, Dad.' Just as a whirling blade cuts into the spinning bar on a lathe and hones the blunt end to sharpness, so the blunt confusion of Jon's emotions suddenly honed to a point that scribed a clean line down his being.

His father shook his head again. 'Toron is a very tight, moral little world,' Koshar said. 'I've known that since I was a boy, and more than any other piece of information, using that has helped me become rich. Yet, it's trapped me, and held me away from you.'

'There's a lot of violence outside that world, Dad,' Jon said. 'I hope it doesn't crash in on your world and destroy it.'

His father gave a little snort. 'There's no more violence outside than there is in. If I learned one thing in that moment it was that.'

On the desk-communicater a yellow light blinked. Koshar pressed a button and a mechanically thin voice said, 'Excuse me, sir, but an emergency report came in from the mainland. Somehow a tetron tramp stalled just outside the harbour for six hours. Its control mechanism was hopelessly fouled, and it was unable even to radio for help. While it was stuck malis from a small power-craft overran the boat, dumped the ore, and in the panic two officers were killed.'

'What time was this?' Koshar asked.

'About ten this morning.'

'Were the malis responsible for the stalling? was it their plan?'

'I don't think so, sir. That's the whole thing. The tramp was one of the old radio-control ships. This morning the whole area was blanketed with an incredible interference that seems to have originated in Telphar. There are rumours the military is having some trouble with the Computer, which may have something to do with it. The malis were just passing by and took advantage of the situation.'

'I see,' said Koshar. 'Check directly with the military, will you, and find out what's going on, and if it's going to happen again. Send the answer straight to me.'

'Yes, sir.' The voice clicked off.

'Damned pirates,' said Koshar. 'You'd think they were trying to run me personally out of business. I don't understand this violence for violence's sake, Jon. They don't steal the ore; they just dump it and do as much damage as they can.'

'It's not easy to understand,' Jon said. He stood up. 'If Clea contacts you will you let me know? It's very important. I'm staying at——'

'You're not going to stay here?' Surprise, bewilderment broke in his father's face, and struck through to him. 'Please, Jon; this huge house has been so empty since you and your sister went.'

'I wish I could, Dad.' He shook his head. 'But I'm staying in the middle ring of the City. I have a place there, that's mine. It's easier for me to get to the places I have to go from there.'

An expression wilted in his father's face. Then a deeper one flowered. 'I guess I couldn't expect you to return as if nothing had happened.' Over the shelves the clocks whispered to one another.

Jon nodded. 'I'll see you again soon, Dad. And we'll talk a lot, and I'll tell you a whole lot of things.' He smiled.

'Good,' his father said. 'That's so good, Jon.'

Outside the sun lowered over Toron's towers, filling the deep, empty streets of the city's hub with shadow. Jon walked through the street, feeling both powerful and relaxed. Towards the middle ring of the city the spectacular buildings of the central section gave way to more ordinary structures. Here people walked back and forth, many returning from work, and an occasional transport rolled past. Jon was three blocks from his apartment when he saw something across the street that made him stop.

Barefoot, trousers frayed, black shirt torn across his back, hair wild, a boy was scribbling letters over the wall in long slashes of chalk: *You Are Trapped in That Bright Moment Where . . .*

'You!' Jon called out and started across the street.

Hair flew back on the head, the figure whirled, paused with feet apart, arms out, then ran down the street.

'Wait!' Jon called, and ran after him. Jon caught up after three-quarters of a block, spun him by the shoulder, and pushed him panting against the wall. His forearm struck the boy's chest, and with his other hand he grabbed the boy's wrists. 'I'm not going to hurt you,' Jon said evenly. 'I just want to talk to you.'

The boy gulped and said, 'I didn't mean to be marking up your building, mister.'

'It's not my building,' Jon said, aware of how much better dressed he was than his captive. 'What were you writing? Where did you see it?'

'Uhn?' The grunt was almost a question.

Jon let go. 'You started to write something on the wall. Why? Where did you hear it? Who told it to you?'

The youth shook his head.

'Look,' Jon said. 'I'm not going to bother you. What's your name?'

Black eyes flickered left and right, then stopped again on Jon's face. 'Kino,' he said. 'Kino Nlove.'

'You're from the Devil's Pot, aren't you?'

Kino's eyes dropped and sprung from his own rags again to Jon's clothes and then to his face. 'Going back that way?'

Quick, suspicious nod.

'I'll walk part of the way with you,' Jon told him. They started, Kino still weary. 'You were about to write: *You Are Trapped in That Bright Moment Where You Learned Your Doom*. Right?'

Kino nodded.

'I've seen it scribbled around the City. You must be pretty busy.'

'I didn't write them all,' Kino said.

'I guess you didn't,' said Jon. 'But I want to know where you got it from, because I want to know who wrote it first.'

Kino was silent for a dozen steps. 'Suppose I did write it first,' he said. 'What would that mean to you?'

Jon shrugged.

'I *was* the one who wrote it first,' said Kino, as though he didn't expect to be believed. Then he added, 'I didn't say it first, but I wrote it first. Then I saw a couple of places where it was chalked where I didn't write it, and I thought that was real funny.'

'Why?'

Kino laughed shortly. ''Cause I knew it was going to happen. I knew other people were gonna start writing it too, start thinking it, wondering about it. And I thought that was the funniest damned thing in Toromon. Like you're wondering about it, huh?' His voice at once grew sullen and secretive. 'Didn't know nobody was gonna come slammin' after me though, like you did.'

'I didn't hurt you,' said Jon.

'Naw,' Kino shrugged. 'You didn't.' Then he laughed quickly again.

'Who said it to you?' Jon asked.

'Friend of mine.'

'Who was he?'

'A friend,' repeated Kino. 'A murderer, a thief, a poet: he ran a mali gang for a while, over in the Pot.'

'How did you know him?'

Kino raised a heavy black eyebrow. 'I ran with him.'

'What was his name?'

'Vol Nonik.'

'When did he say this to you?'

'Yesterday morning.'

Jon felt curiosity sharpen. 'What sort of character was this murderer, thief, poet, mali-leader of yours? And what possessed him to say that to you yesterday morning?'

'What do you want to know for?' Kino asked. 'You wouldn't believe it.'

'I don't know why,' Jon said. 'Like you said, it makes you think. But I'll believe it.'

'You're a funny guy,' Kino said. 'You talk strange, like a mali, even.'

'How do you mean?'

'You want to know funny things, believe anything. That's what Vol told me made a person a mali. He said when a guy gets out and gets his face ground into the real world he comes up angry, wants to know how it works, and he'll believe anybody who tells him how, right or wrong.'

'Vol Nonik said that?'

'Yeah. Where you been that's real, pig?'

'What?'

'Where you been in all them fine clothes you got, where hunger hacks your belly and death tells you you ain't free, pig?' Kino laughed again. 'That's mali talk, see?'

'I've been in the penal mines,' Jon said. 'I've puked in the pit, pig, and that tongue you swing in your head and call mali talk is just plain old pick-pocket jabber to me. Thief's lingo's gone up in the world.'

'You were in the penal mines?' Surprise bloomed in Kino's voice. He tapped Jon on the shoulder with the back of his hand. 'Big *man*!'

'Now what about Vol Nonik?'

'I guess it won't do no harm,' Kino reflected over a gnawed hang-nail. 'You know any mali business at all?'

'My time with that was a long while ago,' Jon told him. 'It didn't even have the name then, and that lingo you fling around was pretty rare. I just heard a couple of guys joking with it back in the mines.'

'Oh! Well, once upon a time there were three mali gangs.'

'Spill on,' Jon said.

'The people in these gangs are a funny bunch: lots of guys who were too messed up even to get into the army; then lots of guys who were sharp enough to haggle their way out before they got to the death-tanks; everybody's crazy younger brother; your misfit cousins; and, pig,' here Kino made a fist and shook it, 'we got 'em from all over Toromon. Apes and giants from the mainland, rich kids from the middle of the city, a lot from the edge, and more from in between: you people don't want to know it, but we're growing all over this dead land. Oh, yeah, and girls.'

Kino laughed. 'All them nice sweet pretty gentle little things they wouldn't let go to war. Most of the gangs have at least a handful that run with them, cut with them, kill with them. And there are at least three gangs that don't let no studs in at all. And, pig, you watch out for them witches on a dark night by the waterfront.'

'Where does Nonik float in?'

'Three gangs,' Kino came back, 'Vol's gang, with me there too, see. Then a gang run by an ape named Jeof. You know those apes don't quite have it all in the head, and they know it; so when they get into a gang they make up for it by being *mean.* And Jeof ran one of the meanest. Third was Larta's gang. She was one of them giants from the mainland. Nobody knows why she came, or what she was doing before. She just hit the Pot one week, all scarred down the side of her face, and that was *it.* Some people swear she can read minds.' Kino rubbed his dirty hand down his left cheek. 'Three gangs, see? And one city block in the Devil's Pot that both Larta and Jeof wanted. This was just about a week before that Moment. There was a lot of glitter on that little strip, pick-pockets, gambling, some hard hustling, both A.C. and D.C., and the other stuff a mali can worm his way into and live off. To settle a territory dispute, what they usually do is call in a third gang who fights it out with each of the other two, and the one who wins over the third gang gets all rights. Since you're battling with a disinterested contender, it keeps it from getting too bloody, or boring. If both sides whip the third they get a fourth and start all over again. Well, Nonik was called into the middle. They fought, and Larta got the area. Her witches still have it, too. But Jeof demanded a return match with Nonik. And suddenly there was that Moment where we all knew, about the war, and each other.

'A lot of funny things happened in the malis then. Vol and a couple of others broke up their gangs. Vol had been going with a girl named Renna from the middle ring of the city, and her old lady would have had a fit over his mali gang. They met at the university. She was an artist and some sort of teacher and wanted him to go on writing and stop the violent stuff. I guess he wanted to himself, because right after the gang broke up they got married. Only Jeof didn't like this. He thought Vol was chickening out of the whole business, and he wanted his return match. Then Jeof's gang got smashed by another gang, and he somehow managed to blame that on Vol too. He swore he'd get even with him, and yesterday he did.

'What did he do?'

'Killed Renna. She never had anything to do with any of the mali business, and didn't really want Vol to. For Vol, she was everything that was good and clean and right and orderly and . . .' He paused. '. . . beautiful. You watched them together, and it was like each one was a world in which the other wanted so much to reach, and might some day, and just in trying was beautiful. Jeof crashed into Vol's world and killed her.'

'Just like that?' Jon asked, sensing the outrage that flickered then faded in Kino's tight face. 'What happened then?'

'I guess Vol went crazy,' Kino said. 'He ran out in the street stark naked. I was coming to see him that morning 'cause I had tried to warn him Jeof was after him, and at the corner I saw him staggering down the street with no clothes on. I didn't know what Jeof had done then, but I knew Vol was hurt. I pulled him into an alley, wrapped a sack around him, and got him to my hole—I'm sunk in an old warehouse by the docks, an abandoned refrigeration building—and got some clothes on him. I pulled what had happened out in little splinters that made him howl. He was raving about something being after him, and I thought he meant Jeof. But he meant the universe, pit-worm! That's when he said what you saw me write on the wall.

'Then he laughed. "You tell them that," he said, "then see what happens. You tell them all that, and watch them squirm. But they'll never catch me now." I was trying to hold him up and I steadied myself against one of the burnt beams on the warehouse wall. "I got to get you fixed up," I said. "I've got to get you to General Medical." His arm was all shot and his face bruised. He said, "Let them try and fix themselves up. It's too late. They're trapped. We're all trapped." Finally, I got him outside. Once he had me stop by a fence and told me to write what he had said on the boards. I told him we had to get to General Medical. It was still pretty early and there were hardly any people out, I was going right down the big street to get there as quick as I could when, I remember, I heard a helicopter. I glanced up and saw that it was flying awfully low. Vol was nearly unconscious.

'Suddenly the 'copter began to roar down, and a moment later it sat right in the middle of the street ahead of us. Then this woman and the weirdest guy you ever saw jumped out; half his head is plastic, and you can see all the brains and things! He runs up the street and the woman is right behind him, and he cries out, "Vol! What happened, Vol?"

'Now I really get scared. Then I think maybe this is who Vol dosen't want to find him. The man says, "Clea, help me with him." Then he asked me what happened to him. I can't run, because Vol's too heavy and weak. Vol half wakes up, shakes his head, and then whispers, "Professor Catham," tears himself away from me. The man said, "Clea, help me get him to the 'copter."

'Then I decided to run. Once I turned around, and they were whipping up into the air. I was scared so I went back to the warehouse. But I stopped once, at the fence Vol had pointed out. I had some chalk, and scrawled real big what he had told me. That was all I could do. I didn't understand anything about it. But it made me feel funny when I read it, almost like I didn't even have to know what it meant. I wrote it in a few other places. Pretty soon some other people were scrawling it too. And I thought that was pretty funny. Pretty damn funny.'

They had reached the hive houses of the city now. 'You're not putting me on?' Jon asked. Surprise sounded in his voice.

'I said you wouldn't believe me.' Kino laughed.

'Who said I don't believe you?' Jon's voice gained its evenness once more. 'You say it was a man named Catham with a plastic face and a woman called Clea. You're sure you heard the names right?'

'Sure I'm sure,' Kino said. 'Say, you're not one of the people after Vol, are you?'

'Maybe I am,' Jon said.

'Hell,' said Kino, 'if I'm gonna rat on a friend like that I should've charged you money. What you want him for?'

'For me to know and you to find out,' Jon said. 'Where do you hang out if I want to talk to you again?'

'Around,' Kino said. 'Next time, gimme some money for opening my yapper, you hear?'

'Where's around?'

'Well, there's the place that Vol was staying. Old woman runs it, with a bar on the ground floor. She don't hastle about serving people under twenty-one.' He gave Jon the location.

'I may see you there,' Jon said.

'O.K.' said Kino. 'And remember about the damn money, huh? It's a hard life, pit-worm.'

'Scoot,' said Jon.

Kino grinned, and scooted.

CHAPTER IV

ALTER had left a message tape at his apartment. As he played it through, her grey eyes blinked pertly, she smiled, and said, 'Come and tell me how it went with your father,' and clicked off. Jon put one foot on the desk in front of him, switched the re-video from play back to Intra-city, and called the royal palace. The Duchess of Petra's face now looked into his own. She sat back at her desk too, and pushed her red hair from her forehead.

'Want to hear something funny?'

'What, Jon?'

'I found out where Clea and Rolth Catham are.'

'Where?'

'With the guy who first said that line we were talking about this afternoon: *You Are Trapped in That Bright Moment Where You Learned Your Doom. Right*?'

The Duchess frowned.

'It was a guy named Vol Nonik, a poet of sorts, also an ex-mali leader.' Then he related the story Kino had told him.

'Vol Nonik,' mused Petra. 'Clea, Catham, and Nonik go off somewhere in a helicopter yesterday morning. You couldn't get any idea what there was between this Nonik fellow and your sister and brother-in-law?'

'A blank,' Jon said.

'I'll check in General Records,' the Duchess said, 'and call you if anything turns up there.'

'If you call this evening I'll be over at Alter's.'

'Maybe the two of you can wander over to the inn where Nonik was staying and see if you can find anything about him there.'

'Good idea,' he said.

The night air was warm. The small apartment where the young acrobat had lived since she had left the circus was the same one his sister, Clea, had lived in for the years she had tried to shut herself off from the world. Alter, he thought; Alter, who had managed to burst the shrinking globe of the mathematician's retreat and had pried his sister from the cocoon of her guilt back to reality. Now his sister had disappeared again. Jon shook his head as he knocked on Alter's door.

'Hello,' she said, opening it to him. 'I'm glad you came. Did you find out about Clea from your father?'

He grinned. 'You sure ask loaded questions.'

The smile turned into apprehension. 'Oh, Jon, it did go all right with your father, didn't it? You did speak to him. Was he still very angry?'

'I spoke to him,' he said. 'It worked out a lot better than I thought it would. I still have a father; and my father still has . . . a son.'

'I'm glad,' she said, and took his hand and squeezed it. 'I think of my aunt, sometimes, not being able to see her, not knowing even if she's alive or not. I know what it must be like for you. Or almost, anyway.' They went to the table and Alter sat down. 'What about Clea? Where did she go?'

'I only know this much,' Jon said. 'She and Rolth Catham were married, and then they disappeared.'

'She married Catham?' asked Alter in surprise. Then she laughed. 'Well, I'm glad of that, too. I guess they were the only people who could really understand each other, anyway. Where did they go?'

'Don't know,' said Jon. 'But here's something interesting. Remember that line we saw on the fountain this morning?'

Alter nodded.

'The author was a mali poet named Vol Nonik, and the last person to see him saw Clea and Catham taking him off in a helicopter.' He gave her the details.

Alter whistled. 'That's funny.'

'Sure is. Petra said she would check and call if she——'

The video-phone buzzed. Alter answered, and once more that evening Jon saw the Duchess's face. 'Jon there?' she asked.

'Right here,' he answered from across the room.

'Well, I just made an enemy for life of the night librarian over at Central Records, but I got something on Mr Nonik.'

'Spill.'

'What?' asked the Duchess. 'Spill what?'

Jon laughed. 'Just some gutter slang I'd been remembering. It means go on.'

'Oh,' said Petra. 'Well, first, Nonik was a bright kid in school, though a bit erratic. Bright enough, however, to get a scholarship to the University, where he majored in languages, minored in sociology. Two of his sociology classes were with Rolth Catham.'

'Did they know each other well?' Jon asked.

'Probably,' Petra said. 'He was scheduled for Catham's seminar on Twentieth-century America, which was an honours seminar restricted to six students personally picked by Catham.'

'You say he was scheduled for it?' Alter asked. 'Didn't he take it?'

'No.'

'Why not?' asked Jon.

'He was expelled from the University for "conduct unbecoming to a student". It's unspecified exactly what.'

'Probably writing nasty poems about the teachers on the walls of the john.'

'Do that at universities?' Alter asked.

'At least we know where they know each other from,' Jon said. 'Now we have to figure out what they have to do with each other.'

'I may even have an answer to that,' the Duchess said. 'Arkor is checking something for me right now. Oh, here he is.' She glanced down at something handed to her, then looked up. 'He had a hunch and it paid off,' she said. 'The week that Nonik was expelled there's a record of Catham making a purchase of a transceivicule.'

'A what?' asked Alter.

'A transceivicule,' said Petra. 'It's a small, two-way radio that can be grafted by surgery into the throat. The week-end that Nonik left they both had a pair grafted into them by the University medical department.'

'You mean the two of them have been in radio-contact ever since Nonik was in college.'

'A little over three years,' Petra said. 'Yes, they have.'

'What on earth for?' asked Alter.

The image in the visaphone shrugged. 'That I don't know; but as far as the helicopter picking him up off the street, Catham and Clea were probably looking for him and just following the radio signals.'

'What about Clea and Nonik?' Jon asked. 'Were my sister

and Nonik at the University at the same time?'

'Yes, but she was in the graduate department and he was still at grade level. I gather too that she kept pretty tightly to her own department back then. Well, that's all I have.'

'That's a lot,' Alter said.

'Only it still doesn't tell us why they were together, or where they went. Petra, is there any record at the airport about the 'copter, or for that matter, even anything we could do to stop the enemy—I mean ourselves?'

The Duchess started to say something. Then the firm expression she had held her face in suddenly went. 'I . . . I don't know, Jon. I just don't know any more. The council is trying to pretend it isn't happening and is paralysed with panic because they know it is. Perhaps we'll have to go to Telphar ourselves. But short of that, I just don't know.'

'We'll find them,' Jon said. 'If we don't, then Telphar it is.'

The Duchess regained her composure. 'Try where Nonik lived. Maybe there's some clue there. That's all I can think of now.'

'Will do,' Jon said. Abruptly the Duchess switched off. Jon turned to Alter. 'Ready for a walk?'

'Um-hm.'

Jon eased himself up from the chair and frowned as he turned to the acrobat. 'She's tired,' he said.

Alter nodded. 'I know, Jon.'

'I guess I would be too if I were trying to run a whole country with a panic-stricken bunch of old men, on one hand, and a seventeen-year-old king who spent the past three years away from court. About all you can really say for him is that he's bright and amenable.'

'Let's go to Nonik's inn.'

'Come on,' said Jon, and they went out.

Night stitched darkly between the roofs. The buildings themselves, as Jon and Alter walked towards the Pot, were lower, closer together, and more dilapidated. They turned down one of the stone alleys that marked the oldest section of the city. Though it was evening, there were more people walking in this part of the city than in the central area.

Alter smiled as they passed two men arguing over a bundle. The package was ill wrapped, and under the street lamp they could see if contained old clothing. 'Home again,' Alter laughed. 'I bet they stole it, and now they can't decide who gets what. The inn must be down this way.' They turned another corner. 'When I think about all the times I ran these streets, I get positively homesick. I don't know why, though. It was a hungry life, and whenever I was stuck here I couldn't wait to get out with another carnival.'

On the corner was a fruit stand under a blue canopy. Lights beneath the awning lit a display of hydroponically grown fruit, and in a glass refrigerator case the plump, shiny aquarium-grown fish lay on glittering ice. The seller, in a white apron, was completing a sale.

Alter glanced to see if he was looking, then snatched a melon. As they turned the next corner, she broke it open and handed half of it to Jon. She bit into the sweet pulp, but Jon held his as they walked.

Finally, he smiled and shook his head.

'What is it?' Alter asked.

'I was just thinking. I spent five years in prison, and I've never stolen anything like food or money in my life. Before I went to prison I had everything I wanted, so that when I got there the idea of taking something never occurred to me. Now the Duchess pays me. And you know something else? When I saw you take that my first reaction was surprise and I guess what you'd call a little moral indignation.'

Alter's eyes widened. Then she frowned. 'I guess it was a silly thing to do ... I mean, I was just remembering how we used to swipe fruit when I was little. But you're right, Jon. Stealing is wrong——'

'Wrong or right,' Jon said. 'I didn't say anything about that.'

'But I thought——'

'And the second thing *I* thought was, she comes from the Pot, I come from the hub, and there's a whole set of morals and customs that keeps us apart from one another. And I thought, how do you get around all those things, and really touch?'

She started to say something, but stopped, and only watched him.

'Right or wrong,' he said. 'Hell, I'm a murderer, remember? But how do we touch? I'm a rich man's son, and you're a circus girl from the Pot. Visiting the stage setting for my childhood probably brought all this up. But I have an answer: we've already touched, in all the things you've taught me, telling me when to put my head back, to tuck my chin, roll. And we can still touch, so simply. Like this'—he took her hand—'and like this.' He bit into the sweet fruit.

She gave his hand a little squeeze. 'Yes. Only about not touching, I know that too. Remember the time we spent on Petra's estate, before we came back here to Toron? I spent so much time being uncomfortable over such silly little things, like which fork to pick up first, when to get up and when to sit down, and who I could scratch in front of, and whom it was worth my life to let a *damn* or a *hell* slip out in front of. When you're trying to stop a war those are very silly things to think about. But I thought about them. You know I used to think you could just sit around and wait for things to happen, and all you had to worry about was the next meal. But being around you and the Duchess, I guess it taught me this: you have to go out and do and learn; otherwise you spend much too much time being uncomfortable.' She shrugged. 'That's probably why Tel and I spent so much time together out there. Even though he was from the mainland, he was a lot more like me in that way, we could have run together.' She fingered her necklace of shells for a moment. 'But he's dead now, killed in the war. So what do I do?'

'Did you love him?' Jon asked.

Alter let her head drop to the side. 'I liked him a whole lot.' She glanced back up at Jon. 'But he's dead.'

After a moment Jon asked, 'Then what are you going to do?'

'Learn,' she said. 'You may have to teach me: call it a mutual exchange.' They laughed together now.

A fairly solid building stood in the midst of so much sagging clapboard and rusting sheet metal. As they reached the doorway, Alter said, 'I hope this trip doesn't turn out to be for——'

As she stepped inside, she stopped.

The woman with the purple birthmark, standing behind the counter, glanced up, then stepped back and opened her mouth.

Alter had grabbed Jon's arm. She let go of it slowly and whispered, 'Aunt Rara!'

The woman ran from behind the counter, wiping her hands on her apron. She stopped in the middle of the floor, still open-mouthed, shook her head, then swallowed, and came on again. Alter met her, arms locking about the older woman's shoulders. 'Aunt Rara!'

'Oh, Alter! How ... where ...?' Then she shook her head again, the expression on her face resolved to smile. But there were tears on her cheeks. 'You're back with me,' was all she said, the timbre of her voice rough with relief.

The people in the tavern, many of them in military uniform, looked up.

Alter stood back from her aunt. 'Aunt Rara, you mean you work in this place?'

'Work in it? I own it. I've got my licence. Really I do.'

'Own it?'

'I've been doing all sorts of things and saving all sorts of money, wheedling and conniving here and there. There's very little a practical woman can't do if she sets her mind to it. Oh, Alter, I looked for you, but I couldn't find you!'

'I looked for you too, but Czeryn's old place was torn down!'

'I know. For a while I had a job as nurse's aid in General Medical. I searched every circus and carnival that came to Toron.'

'I wasn't working until a few months ago.'

'Of course! That's when I stopped looking.' Again Rara shook her head, blinking away tears. 'I'm so glad to see you. So glad!' They embraced again.

'Aunt Rara,' Alter said, rubbing her eyes with one knuckle, 'I'd like to talk to you about something. Could you help me? I have to find out about somebody who lived here.'

'Of course,' Rara said. 'Of course.' Now she saw Jon for the first time. 'Young man,' she said, 'will you watch the place while I go and talk to my niece, for a moment.'

'Oh, Aunt Rara,' Alter said, remembering herself, 'this is Jon Koshar, my friend.'

'I'm glad to meet you,' Rara said, nodding. 'Just watch everybody and make sure nothing cataclysmic happens.' She surveyed the figures in the room. 'Don't let anyone leave without paying. Though it doesn't look if anyone's going to leave at all.' She turned towards the back room, holding Alter by the hand. 'Pour yourself a drink if you want.' Suddenly she put her hand over her heart and took a breath. 'Pour everybody a drink!' And she hurried off, dragging Alter with her.

Still grinning, Jon went to the counter, poured himself a drink, and sat next to a soldier at the bar. The man looked up, nodded vaguely, and then looked down again. His emphatic reaction to Alter's reunion with her aunt made Jon expansive. 'You guys seem to be making an evening of it!' he told the soldier. 'How're you doing?'

The soldier looked up again. 'Rather clumsily,' he said. 'How'm I doing? You should have asked, "What am I doing?" ' He nodded sagely at Jon. 'Now that's the question.'

'O.K.,' Jon said. 'What are you doing?'

'I am getting drunk.' He picked up his mug of green liquid and ran his finger around the wet ring. It suddenly struck Jon that something was going on in the soldier's mind, and he tried to catch the tone as the soldier went on, 'I am making a clumsy attempt to hide, if you will, in a glass.' There were a lot of empty mugs in front of him.

'Why?' Jon asked, trying to relate the cynicism to his own good feeling.

The soldier turned so that Jon saw his insignia: a Captain's shield from the Psychological Corps. Since the Moment, many of them had removed their insignia, as had many soldiers discarded their uniforms. 'You see,' the officer went on a little drunkenly, 'I'm one of the ones who knew about the war, who planned it, figured out the best way to make it come off. How do you do, fellow citizen; I'm glad to shake your hand.' But he didn't offer his hand and turned back to his drink.

Ordinarily Jon knew better than to try and pry out someone so wrapped in moodiness. But he wasn't in an ordinary mood. 'You know——' Jon began.

The psyche officer looked up.

'—I wasn't in the army, but sometimes I have the feeling that perhaps I missed out on something by not being there. If nothing else, I think it's an experience that turns boys into men.'

'Yes, I know you do,' the psyche officer said shortly.

'The physical discipline, and the experience in action,' Jon went on, 'even if it was a hypnotic dream, must have meant something, because the death that waited for them was real.'

'Look,' the psyche officer said, 'we did a lot more than plan the combat. We controlled all the propaganda that went to civilians too. I said, "I know what you think." '

Jon was surprised. 'You don't believe that military discipline can be a good experience?'

'An experience is what you make it,' the officer said. 'That's real profound, huh? Boys into men? Look at the guys who like the army, or even do well there. Guys who hate the random inconsistency of their parents so much they are willing to give up love to get a father who hands out his orders by a book of rules you can run and check in the library, even if the rule is go out and die. You'll do a lot better if you come to terms with the father you already have than by running off to the state substitute.'

Despite drunkenness, the man was maintaining logic, so Jon went on, 'But doesn't the army give you a fairly rigorous microcosm to work out certain problems of . . . well, honour and morality, at least for yourself——'

'Sure,' drawled the officer, 'a microcosm totally safe, completely unreal, free of women and children, where God is the general and the Devil is death, and you're playing for keeps—the excuse for conducting everything with high seriousness. It was all set up to make the most destructive and illogical human actions appear as controlled and non-random as possible. By the time the psycho-economic situation of Toromon had reached the point where "war was inevitable" we had to have some place for all the sick minds, wounded by just that psycho-economic situation to fall into. That's the army. But our job was to make the rest of you think it was safe and glorious and good, too. Boys into men? Discipline that isn't self-discipline doesn't mean a thing to a boy. Your hand . . .'

Jon looked down. Whichever way an acrobat turns around a suspended bar, thumbs lead and fingers follow; the reverse grip that must be second nature had got Jon in the habit of laying his hands before him palms up. The calluses from the mine had come back quickly on the bar.

'. . . those hands can move and make and do. You talk like an intelligent man, so you probably do what you do well. When you learned to do whatever made those calluses that was discipline. Can you build, can you follow the rules of some craft, can you submit those hands to order, working along with someone else, or alone? I don't know what you do, but I know that in educating those hands you've had more discipline than any dozen men who know only how to kill in a dream. What you already have in those hands, we had to lie ourselves blue to make you *think* the army could give you. We had it so finely planned! The novels, the stories, the articles, all answering emphatically "Yes!" to the questions you've just asked. The psych corps didn't write them, either.

'We'd done our propaganda job already, laid the grounding for all the uncertain and doubting intellectuals to do the rest; "Yes, yes! The war is a real and valid experience," because they, among you all, might have doubted enough to figure out it was a fake. Make you into a man? Look at them, why don't you? Just look.' He gestured towards the other soldiers in the tavern.

One was asleep across the table in the corner. Two more were beginning to argue near the door, while a fourth looked on anxiously, expecting a fight. A fifth laughed hysterically at something the brown-haired girl with him said, leaned back in his chair, holding his stomach, and fell over backwards. Now the girl began to laugh.

The psychologist wavered on his stool and turned back to the bar. 'Or look at me,' he said. He talked into the glass before him. 'Look at me.'

'You think the whole thing, without any redemption, was meaningless?' Jon asked. His thoughts went to Tel, who was dead, Alter's friend, Tel. 'For all of them, it meant nothing?'

The psychologist shook his head slowly. 'You don't see. You just don't see. You knew someone who went up in cinders inside one of those death-tanks, didn't you. You want like hell to make it mean something. But I knew a lot of guys who died. I trained them. There's not one who wouldn't have become a lot more of a man doing whatever you did to get those hands. I don't care what it is.' The officer made a face. 'Because life ... living'—he reached out with his finger and flipped a coin on the counter against the square of coins that was his change: two other coins shot from the far side of the matrix of metal discs—'is like that. The enemy isn't always somebody you can shoot at over a gravel bag. There isn't always somebody to tell you when to shoot and when to cease fire. The women and children haven't been left conveniently behind, and because they haven't, you're forced to look at them and see that they have their problems, which look surprisingly like you own—a hard fact for too many "mature" men to accept. The army is just too easy and too simple: fight to the death for the cause is just.' The officer looked at Jon. 'You knew somebody who got burned. Well, compared with what you have to live for, he didn't die for a damned thing.' He paused. 'That's hard to take.'

'This is how you take it?' Jon asked. Once out, the words sounded cruel, but he had said them with wonder, a beginning of understanding.

The psyche officer chuckled. 'Yeah,' he said. 'Like this.' The chuckle passed away like gravel from a roof. Now he frowned and shook his head. 'They don't hate me. You know, they still don't hate me. They come in here, drink with me, razz me about not having seen real combat, with all sorts of goodwill, even though they know I was one of the ones responsible. Oh, we did our work so well, well, well. It's easier for them, still, to go along with the feelings we tried so hard to instil. But I'm a psychologist, see, so I know exactly when I'm sitting here getting drunk. I know all that's going on in my mind, making me do it. And I know why I went and got drunk last night. And I know why I got drunk the night before that. I know, they know, and it doesn't help a damn bit.'

Alter and her aunt came from the back room, and Jon turned on the stool.

'Well, here we are,' Rara said, wiping her eyes on her apron. 'Now you come back soon,' she said to her niece. 'Your old aunt is a respectable woman now.'

'I will,' Alter said, and hugged her. She turned to Jon and took his hand.

'Sure the two of you wouldn't like something to eat?' asked Rara, 'or maybe just to stay and talk a little while?'

'That's all right,' Alter said. 'But we can't now. We'll come back soon.'

'Very soon,' Rara said. 'Please make it very soon.'

They walked from the inn slowly. 'Did you find anything about Nonik?'

'Um-hm,' she nodded. In her hand was a folded packet of paper. 'Some of his poems. They were left in his room after ...' She shuddered and handed them to Jon.

'What did your aunt want to talk to you about?' he asked.

She was silent a moment. 'She wanted me to stay there with

her, and live there.'

Jon nodded.

'The whole thing caught me when I wasn't looking. I even think I might have liked to. But I've got my own apartment, and I'm just used to being on my own.' She brushed her white hair from the back of her neck. 'At the same time I realized how much I loved her.'

'You know,' Jon said, 'I guess I have to be hit over the head with something before it takes.'

'How do you mean.'

'I was thinking about what I said to you about customs and morals keeping people apart, making them different from one another. People are so much more alike than different. So much more.'

Slowly they walked from the city's rim, through the pithy strictures of the night, back together to look at the poems.

CHAPTER V

Take rage and twist it through loops of violence; with the circle ring the lipped pit of the brain; set brain in bone, and tell man in the dark he is alone.

Blue water runnelled the cellar floor, and from the corner came the smell of damp fish-sacks. Jeof squatted on a barrel. He turned his hands over in his lap, closing and opening the fingers, a gesture in which he could let drop fragments of the isolate terror. His perception dim, his breathing slow, he sat in the dark as he had for the last hour and a half, not so much thinking as allowing pictures to form in his mind: a girl's face, eyes closed, a line of blood from her mouth, thin as a red pencil mark; a body falling on the wharf as sirens filed at the darkness; a store window shattering brightly before his jutting fist in moonlight. That time his arm had been cut. He still had the scar. He touched the welt under the hair of his forearm. Here, he thought, I can sit quietly within this rage and be alone. The loneliness was painful, but he accepted it because he could think of no other way to be. He closed his fingers again, trying to catch the terror. Perhaps some day he would stop trying. But that was a long time away.

Doctor your wounds with evil. Leave your blood over the wharf cobbles webbed with mud. The ambient heart stalks from the sea into the City's mystery.

Renna's mother watched her living-room door close as the police officer went out, and thought, My eyes will explode, perhaps I shall scream. Maybe the plaster will begin to crack and shatter up the walls. She waited. Nothing happened, so she sucked in a breath and heard herself sob. She turned, thinking, A coin dropped into deep water, spinning as it fell.

Then she went to the visaphone and dialled Dr Wental. He was the only doctor in the building, and even as she finished dialling and the piercing buzz began, she wondered. What am I calling a doctor for? What in the world am I calling a doctor for!

Dr Wental's face focused. 'Yes?'

And something inside her tore apart and she was crying, 'Dr Wental, for the love of . . . help me . . . she's dead, my daughter, Renna, she's been . . . Oh, she's dead . . .' The half phrases stumbled from her tongue. Something burned her lips, her cheeks, seared her eyes blind until only tears could wash back sight.

'You're the woman who lives on the second floor?'

'Yes, I . . . yes . . .'

She wondered what her face looked like. But the doctor frowned a moment and then said, 'I'll be right down,' and switched off. Time passed. Time is always passing, she thought. Where am I going in all this passing time? There was a knock on the door.

Hysterically calm she went to open it, and the doctor stepped inside.

'I'm sorry,' she said. 'I'm so sorry. I didn't mean to disturb you, Doctor. There's nothing you can do, I mean for me. There's nothing . . . why did I get you all the way down here? . . .' She shook her head.

'Don't bother to apologize,' Dr Wental said. 'I quite understand.'

'The officer was just here. He told me. They couldn't identify her till now from her retina pattern because her eyes were all . . .'

'Perhaps I can give you a sedative.'

'No,' she said. 'No I don't want a sedative. I didn't mean to call you down here . . . I mean . . .' Then the embarrassments she had been mouthing for nearly a minute became real. 'Oh, Dr Wental, I just wanted to talk to somebody. I thought of a doctor first, I don't know why. But I just wanted to talk.'

'Are you sure you don't want a sedative?'

'Oh, no,' she said again. 'Here, let me get us both a drink.'

'Well'—he paused—'well, all right.'

She went to the cupboard and got out glasses and the green bottle. Just the movement of walking over the floor, the fall of her wrist as she turned the knob, the smooth pressure of glass against thumb and forefinger brought back the physical part of her she had forgotten. She moved quickly into the kitchenette and pushed the wall treadle with her foot. The table swung out, and she set the glasses and bottle down on the surface of chipped blue stone.

'Let me,' said Dr Wental, pulling up a chair for her. As she sat down, he stepped around the table, opened the bottle, and poured out the drinks. When she picked up hers he seated himself, finished his in one gulp, and poured himself another, but with such self-assurance that she didn't even think about it.

She looked at the green liquid shivering in the wide mouth of her glass, and said, 'Dr Wental, I feel so alone. I want to run some place, crawl under something, be told what to do. When my own parents died I didn't feel anything like this . . .'

'They say that the death of a child,' began the doctor, and finished the statement with a nod. Had he taken a third drink?

'I love her so much, spoil her, I suppose. I sent her to parties, bought her clothes . . . oh, the clothes. I bought her so many clothes,' and she felt something inside her begin to tear again. Catching at the edges, she continued, 'All parents live through their children, Doctor. It isn't wrong. It isn't wrong, is it?' She ran her hand over her hair, and the scarf caught in her fingers. When she brought it before her the silken green with its design of blue and red seaweed was so vivid, and the loose skin of her hand so terribly grey.

When she looked up the doctor was pouring himself still another glass. He smiled apologetically: 'I guess I'm depleting your store here a bit. Forgive me.'

'Oh, that's all right,' she replied vaguely. 'I hardly ever use it. Go ahead, please.'

'Thank you.'

'I feel like I have to give something to somebody, do something for somebody, make believe I'm'—she paused—'I was going to say alive.' She moved the glass back and forth in front of her. The light from the wall fixture struck through the green and fell shimmering on the blue stone. 'Make believe I'm alive,' she repeated.

'Did you start to say, "Make believe she's alive"?' the doctor suggested.

She shook her head. 'No. No, I know what I said.' She looked up. 'I think I will take the sedative. I really don't want anything to drink.'

'Very well.'

'I'll be all right now. Thank you for coming, for letting me feel for a little while that I wasn't alone. But there's . . . nothing I can do about it, is there?'

'There's nothing you can do about your daughter,' Dr Wental said.

'That's what I meant.' She stood up from the table. 'I'll take your sedative and rest now.'

The doctor nodded and started to rise.

She frowned. 'Are you all right, Doctor?' He had grabbed the edge of the table.

He smiled again. 'Perhaps I depleted your store a little too much.' He rose to his full height and stepped unsteadily from the table.

In the living-room he searched in his bag a long time for the amber glass pill bottle. 'I'll leave one . . . two'—he swayed, and the hem of his tan jacket shook against his thigh—'two of these with you. Take one, at first, and if you need more, to settle you, take the other one.' He handed her the pills on a pad of surgical gauze.

She followed him to the door and opened it for him. As he stepped into the hall he seized the door jamb, as before he had caught himself on the table edge. She frowned; then, trying to turn her own concern into a joke, she laughed, 'You'd better not tell you wife how much you've had down here. You wouldn't want your wife to know.'

She saw his back stiffen under the tan cloth. Slowly he turned back. 'I suppose I ought to inform you,' he announced thickly, 'that I gave you those sedatives illegally. As for my wife, she won't know, because she doesn't live with me any more.'

She looked surprised.

'A week ago I was charged and convicted of malpractice. Tampering with drugs—somebody died. Well, my wife does know, and she left me. So I really don't have to bother about keeping anything from her any more.'

He turned again and moved off unsteadily down the hall. Bewildered, she stepped back into the empty apartment.

The image of your eye cased in a jewel. Outside the solitary rooms of sleep observes the acrobat, the thief, the fool, the workings of ambition, death, and grief. Magnificent and isolate, then, dream.

The King watched his cousin by the window, absently fingering a smokey stone set in a silver chain around her neck. Petra let the curtain fall back across the lights of the city and turned to him. Her red hair, loosed from the golden comb shaped like crab claws, fanned across her shoulder. 'What is it, Petra?' he asked.

'What is what, my King?'

'Please, Petra,' he said, 'don't pretend to be formal. Just be my cousin as you used to be, when you would tell me stories.'

The Duchess smiled and shook her head. 'Let, I'm running out of stories to tell.'

'Then tell me the truth. What's bothering you?'

'I told you about the "enemy" going wild,' she said, walking to the couch and sinking down. 'You've been at the council meetings. You've done a splendid job too. You've argued down ministers calmly whom I would have ended up screaming at. Let——'

'—while you sat beside me,' he went on for her, 'as my adviser. I wish they allowed you to speak at official meetings, Petra. All the calm arguing I do is what you've gone over with me beforehand. I can see you aching to speak. That's probably what's rubbed your nerves so raw.'

She laughed. 'You're right about the nerves. But it's just as well you do all the talking at the council meetings. You're a remarkably articulate boy.'

'But I am a boy, only seventeen, and I haven't forgotten it. Neither has the council. Sometimes I can almost hear you thinking, "If protocol only allowed me to say the same thing . . ."' He sighed. 'But that's responsible for only half. What about the other half?'

Petra was silent a moment. 'Sometimes I think you learned to read minds too in the years you spent among the forest guards.'

'I learned to observe carefully,' he said. 'And I've watched you. Now will you tell me?' His voice was both calm and imperative, the voice through which she had made what little progress she had with the council.

She rose again and crossed to the window, and once more pushed back the brocade drape. A breeze waved her blue robes. Let watched half expressions seat themselves in the strong lineaments. 'It's doubt, Let. A great and serious doubt.'

'What do you doubt. Petra?'

'I doubt you. I doubt me.' With her free hand she motioned through the open window towards the pattern of lights on the darkness. 'This island, this empire, spread around us; we are responsible for it. And I doubt us, deeply, Let, deeply.' Again she let the drape swing back.

'How do you doubt, Petra?'

He watched her breathe in, then hold the air as if afraid to release it. 'Let,' she said at last, 'years ago I conceived a plan, before the war was even declared, that I thought might save Toromon. I love Toromon, Let, her ships, her farms, her factories, her forests . . . I knew she was weak. And the plan was to save her strength, and do whatever I could to ease the economic trauma Toromon was passing through by guiding the reins of the council whenever I could. But primarily my hope was in you, getting you away from your mother and your brother, and then restoring you to the throne. I thought Toromon would need a strong and articulate king. The training you received in the forest was all that I could have hoped. Yet now I doubt the whole plan, my part in it, and yours.'

'I still don't quite——'

She turned from the window a last time. 'The aristocracy of Toromon is not even capable of holding the country together. It's too old, too tired, too tied up with the council to make the sweeping changes that might save us; but it's too powerful to die. Maybe I should have spent my efforts trying quietly to control the country. Maybe I should have gone about the whole thing completely differently. Perhaps the answer was to smash the existing government and to let a new, vigorous one grow out of whatever was left healthy in Toromon. Maybe I should have become a mali and destroyed for the destruction's sake. There's so much more evil than good in the whole system. Have I been trying to keep alive something that would have been better dead a long time ago? Let, I doubt deeply how right I was. And if I *have* done wrong, then I have done more wrong than anyone for over a thousand years.' She sat down on the cushions, lifting her long fingers to her neck, bringing them around to rub away the fatigue that had gathered there from holding her regal head so high.

'It is a great responsibility, Petra,' the young king said emptily.

She leaned her head back. When she looked up again he saw tears banked on her lower lids. 'Let, I feel so alone,' she said softly, blinked, and the tears were on her cheek.

'Petra.' The King leaned forward from his chair, urgency in his voice. 'Petra?'

'Yes?'

'If you could do anything in the world you wanted to do, what would it be—I mean something that had nothing to do with Toromon?'

'I don't know,' she said. 'Something that has nothing to do with Toromon—it's been a long time since I could want anything like that. What do you want, my King?'

'Petra, I feel alone too.'

She tilted her head to the side. 'Yes. You must. This is lonely work.'

'It is.' He nodded. 'Everyone I know well is in the forest. Here, you're my only friend. But when I feel very bad, sometimes I think about what I would do if ... and I think some day I'll do it. Then I feel better.'

'What do you want to do?' She smiled.

'It should be different for each person,' he explained, 'but——'

'But tell me.'

Again the King leaned forward, his hands joined tightly in front of him. Already, she saw, they were beginning to lose some of the rich colouring they had gained during his exile to the mainland forest. 'I remember, from a long time ago, even before I was taken to the mainland, I remember a boy—I don't recall exactly how I knew him, but he was from the coast and he was a fisherman's son. He told me all about working on the boats, rocks of all different colours, and in the morning, he said, you can see the sun come up like a burning blister on the water. He told me about fishing too. I'd like to work on a boat, Petra. Oh, not be carried from place to place with other people turning the wheel. I want to be in control, going where I want to go, smacking down the waves as they come up to me, and as they rise about me, I cut through.' He paused a moment, blue eyes glowing. The yellow hair, run with paler streaks from the bleaching mainland sun, was again darkening to gold. 'I'm alone,' he said, 'like you, Petra. But when I feel it very strongly I think. Some day, like that boy—whoever he was—I'll ride on a boat, and steer it into the sea. It helps.'

'Good,' she said. For the third time she went to the window and pushed back the curtain. This time, however she motioned to him. 'Come stand with me, my King.' Let rose and walked to her side. 'Toromon,' she said, and he nodded, gazing across the lights of the city to the midnight sea.

'And we are in the centre,' he said, 'both alone.'

Order these desperate strokes to single lines, separate and tangible, beautiful and real; fish-bones throw their thin shadows on the wall, portending the ideal.

Arkor stood in the laboratory tower in the west wing of the royal palace of Toron. At the end of the metal band was a crystal sphere, fifteen feet in diameter, which hovered above the receiving platform. A dozen small tetron units of varying sizes sat about the room. The viewing screens were dead. On a control panel by one ornate window a bank of forty-nine scarlet-knobbed switches pointed to off. Arkor was walking slowly across the catwalk above the stage. He reached the balcony and paused before the night. A breeze combed through his hair.

He glanced back into the room. Across the catwalks, the platform, and the sphere fell the long shadows from the super-structure of conversion equipment that had turned the transit ribbon into a matter projector for use in the war. It had never been used. He looked out again into the City.

Normally the giant's telepathic receptivity was only a few hundred feet, but recently he had found his range expanding, sometimes for an hour or more, to cover miles. As he stepped on to the balcony, he felt the subsensory tingling that announced one of these attacks. Suddenly the City, as though a veil were pulled away, was revealed to him as a vast matrix of minds, clashing, jarring one another, yet each isolate. I am alone, he thought, adding the millionth repeat to a million-fold echo. The few other telepaths in the City, as well as the non-telepathic guards, flashed on the web of dimmer minds. But even trying to contact them was at best like touching through glass. There was only the image, without warmth or texture. Isolate, he thought, letting the pattern fill him, alone in the palace tower, in the tower of my own perceptions, as a brute neanderthal guilty at the City's rim, as King and Duchess beside me, minds circled and alone, standing together as the drunken doctor and grieving mother part a mile away.

Somewhere a man and woman sat—Jon and Alter, but he identified them only after he picked them out—together in a room, shoulder to shoulder, heads bent together, reading a poem from a crumpled paper, now stopping to ask each other what this line meant, now going back to look at another page. The patterns growing in their minds were not the same, but as they tried to explain what they thought to each other, or bent to read or reread the lines, the images the poem made upon their thoughts were like flames dancing orderly about one another, contrasting or similar, still a single experience, an awareness of unity, unaware of their isolation. Delusion? thought Arkor. No. The now brittle, now flexible, bending and quivering lights danced orderly together. Arkor smiled, alone, as the two bent closer to the paper. Jon held the page, while Alter unfolded a corner that had been bent down across the last stanza:

Bring me to a city gold and grey where the human and the wild can mesh, not where I am gutter-bound by fishbones.

CHAPTER VI

'ALL right,' Alter said. 'You teach me now.' She opened the box where she kept her small collection. 'It's not much, but it's all I've got. What should I wear?'

Jon glanced over the green lining where the few pins, brooches, and necklaces lay. 'First of all, as little as possible.' He grinned. 'It's a formal affair of state, and Toromon is an empire bound up with the sea. That means all your jewellery should take its pattern and substance from the ocean. At a less formal affair you could get away with some of the floral designs. But since it's high state, I'd say just the shell necklace you wear most of the time anyway; then the pearl earrings and the pearl buckle. That'll do it.'

She picked them from the box and went to the chair where the beige silk gown lay. 'I just can't get over this. It's beautiful. I'll never be able to thank Petra for having it made for me. Imagine wearing a dress that probably cost half a year's circus salary.' She held it up in one hand and fanned out the panels with the other. Then she frowned. 'What're these?'

'Where?'

'Here.' She had a look of disappointment.

'Pockets,' said Jon, surprised at her reaction.

'Really fine women's clothing doesn't have pockets!'

'Huh?' Then he laughed.

'What's so funny? Here I thought this was a——'

'Look,' Jon said, 'if you're going to make your entrance into society you might as well do it all the way and know what you're doing.'

Her frown grew puzzled.

'I wasn't born into the aristocracy, but grew up next to it, so I can give you some insights into its working that Petra might never think of mentioning. Toromon's aristocracy can be an amazingly functional group of people; at least they were when they were pirates fifteen hundred years ago. And they have always had pockets, though after a while they didn't advertise them. The pockets in that dress are behind a fold, and no one will know you have them unless you walk around with your hands in them. Now the people who make what you call expensive clothes for women—the ones in the downtown dress shops—imitate what they think they see: they equate aristocratic with decorative, useless, unfunctional. Hence, no pockets. This dress was probably made by the Duchess's personal dress-maker, and if the dresses you've seen cost half a year's salary this is more like five or six years' pay.' Alter's puzzled expression became delighted surprise. 'That's what comes of not having any formal balls out at Petra's estate: you have to wait until you get here to pick that up.' He sat down on the couch. 'It surprises me the things I remember.'

'I'm glad you do,' Alter said. 'At least I feel I've got some chance of getting through the evening without choking on my ankle. Now you won't let me say the wrong thing!' She seized his wrist. 'And if I pick up something in the wrong hand you'll kick me quietly on the shin.'

'Did you ever let me fall off the high bar on to my head?'

'Imagine,' exclaimed Alter, 'and I can't, really—me, even thinking about things like this, a ball at the palace! I'm not supposed to care about silly things like that. But, oh, I do, I do, I do.'

'Be yourself,' Jon laughed, squeezing her hand. 'Keep your conversation light, and remember, the idea is more important than the action to these people. Be gracious; your duty is to take the initiative in gentleness. Speak softly, move slowly, try and spend at least five times as much of your energy listening as talking.'

'Oh . . .' breathed Alter. 'Do you think I'll be all right?'

Jon smiled. 'Hurry up, get dressed.'

The spreading windows rose about the hall, stars shone through the upper panes from the clear night. The musicians wove the old melodies with their polished shells, and with the help of a theramin opened the ball with the familiar anthems of Toromon. 'Mr Quelor Da and party,' announced the loudspeaker. Jon glanced at the entrance as the brightly dressed figures, miniatured by the distance of the palace ballroom, descended from the arched entrance. He pushed back his black cloak and thought, How familiar all this is. But so much else was familiar as well. He recalled swinging the mali tongue in the mines—familiar, as the turn and fall of the dances of royalty, the carriage and etiquette of a ball. Glancing at his tall reflection in one of the mirrored walls, he recalled the boy he had been at eighteen. A bit of that was still there—a familiar energy behind the deepened expression, the gaunter face. He smiled, then turned to the dais where the King and the Duchess were receiving.

Jon touched Alter's shoulder, and she turned, silver brows vaulting above large blue eyes. 'I think they have a moment.' He took her arm. They made their way across the floor to the emerald-clad Duchess. The King's royal white dazzled against the remaining tan from the forest. The pale streaks over his hair were near Alter's semi-albino tresses. Almost, thought Jon, as though they were from the same family. The Duchess held out her hand in greeting. 'Jon, Alter,' she said warmly. 'Here you are! My King? You've all met briefly before.'

'Jon I remember well. But'—the King turned to Alter—'it's been a while since I've seen you this close. I've only watched you glittering in the air at the circus, since you kidnapped me.'

'It's good to see you back at the palace, my King,' Alter said.

'It's boring here,' the King said, confidentially. 'But you give me something beautiful to contemplate.'

'Oh, thank you . . . My King!'

'Do you like the party, Alter?' asked the Duchess.

'It's just . . . beautiful, Your Grace!'

The Duchess bent slightly towards her. 'Petra, as usual.'

Alter flushed a trifle, and said, 'Oh, and Petra, the dress is lovely.'

'You double its loveliness.'

'Petra, just what is the purpose of this ball?' Jon asked while Alter beamed.

The Duchess's voice lowered. 'Primarily to feel out what we can get by way of financial aid from whoever we can. It hasn't changed that much. The war's end has left us in quite a bind.'

'Especially since it hasn't really ended,' commented Jon.

Petra sighed. 'But we must appear as though it has.'

Jon thought back to the last ball he had attended at the palace.

'Petra, shall I open the dancing?' asked the King.

She looked over the guests, then nodded.

King Let offered his arm to Alter. 'Will you dance with a lame man, to open the ball?'

'My King . . .' Alter said, and glanced at Jon, who nodded gently to her. 'Of course I wouldn't mind. Thank you.' And she moved off at his side.

Jon and the Duchess watched as, beige and white, the youngsters reached the musicians. 'The limp,' Jon said, 'it's almost gone.'

'He tries hard to hide it,' said Petra. 'When he dances, hardly anyone will notice—because he is King.' The bitterness that momentarily filled her voice surprised him.

'Alter will notice,' Jon said. 'Her body's a trained, sensitive instrument.'

Music began, and the turning figures of the acrobat and the royal youth opened a path through the other guests, who, at the musical signal, themselves broke into bright whirling couples over the white tile floor. The Duchess's eyes, however, were down. When they did look up Jon saw they were bright. 'We are disguising Toromon's wounds well this evening,' she said softly.

He watched the figures of the dance bloom like a flower. Then the music ended, and petals drifted back to the edge of the floor.

'How did we look?' demanded Let, flushed and a bit breathless, when he and Alter reached the dais.

'Charming,' said the Duchess.

People had again come over for the interminable introductions, and Alter stepped quickly to Jon's side. 'We'll go now, Petra. I hope it goes well.'

'Thank you, Jon.'

'Good evening, my King.'

'Good evening. We'll dance once more before the evening's over, Alter.'

'Oh, yes, my King.'

Jon and Alter left the dais and strolled over the floor. 'How is it to dance with a king?' asked Jon.

Her hand was on his arm, and now she squeezed gently. 'He's sweet. But I had more fun practising with you this afternoon.'

'Dance with me now, then,' he said, as the music for the partner-changing dance began. She came into his encircling arm, her right hand resting, small—and warm—on his left, the tip of her pinky just pressing the knuckle of his index finger.

'Don't go too far away from me,' she whispered. Gowns rustled about them. 'I want to be able to get back to you in a hurry.'

Turn, dip, separate, join again; through the recalled steps, her smile was brilliant. The music rose, she turned away from him, and a girl in blue replaced her in his arms. He nodded graciously and began the figure of the dance again, glancing once at Alter: her new partner was a middle-aged man with short brown hair and heavy lips and whose chest bore the royal insignia of the house of B'rond. Jon exchanged a few civilities with his partner, the music rose again, and a moment later Alter whirled back to him. 'Who were you dancing with?'

'Some industrialist's daughter. Her father's in transport; one of the Tildons.'

'And who was I dancing with?'

'Count B'rond.'

'Do you realize in those two minutes he said I was beautiful, he must see me again, and that I was the most graceful person at the ball, and he would be waiting for me at sunrise at the castle entrance.'

'He and his seven wives?' Jon asked. 'At least he had had seven before I went to the mines. I think he killed a couple of them, though—accidentally of course.'

'That's him!' exclaimed Alter. 'Wasn't there some scandal a few years ago, during that exposé of the aristocracy? It was swallowed up with all the business over the emigration from the mainland. They kept talking about some B'rond.'

Jon nodded. 'Apparently hasn't changed his habits much, either.'

Alter pulled her shoulders in and shivered.

'The blue blood of Toromon isn't in all that hot shape. You remember King Uske. And finally the Queen Mother had to be put away. Both of them were batty. Petra's an exception.'

'I guess so,' Alter said, moving away to the music, coming back, then whirling off. Jon turned to receive his next partner as Alter's beige silk opened like a whispering rose.

Then the windows in the west wall went white: light like swords leapt across the floor. Women cried out; men stepped backwards, throwing their arms over their faces. The shells ceased sounding and the theramin squacked. A moment later thunderous rumbling replaced the music, growing, then fading, as darkness filled the high, coffin-shaped windows once more.

Jon was the first to run forward. Alter was beside him. After them, the others ran to see.

Jon reached the middle window and pushed away the heavy edging. Alter's shoulder jostled against his as others rushed against her.

Far among the city's towers flames flicked through the ruptured skyline.

'What in the world do you... ?'

'Now which direction are we facing... ?'

'It's the General Medical building... !'

'No, no, it couldn't be. Isn't that over... ?'

'They've bombed the General Medical building! Can't you see! That's where the General Medical building used to be!'

Jon pushed his way back through the crowd. Alter, her skirts held to her legs, pressed after him. 'Jon, was it the General Medical?' He nodded shortly to her over his shoulder.

Petra intercepted them from another window. 'Jon!' Reaching him, she caught his arm. 'You saw that!' She shook her head, like a confused beast, red hair leaping sideways brighter than the flames across the night. 'There's no time, Jon. You've got to go to Telphar. That's the only thing left. I would go with you, but somebody must stay to help Let hold the city together. Alter, will you go with him?'

Amazed, she nodded.

'If you can stop this enemy, stop it. If you can find out how it might be stopped, tell me and I'll stop it. Jon, even the records have ceased coming in. The military is threatening to withdraw.'

'Can we take Arkor?' Jon asked. 'Maybe we can use him?'

Petra hesitated, her white teeth catching her lower lip as she dropped her head in thought. It raised quickly. 'No. I can't send him with you. I haven't wanted to, but I may have to use his powers to pry things out of the Council. More attacks like this and we'll have to evacuate the city. I can't let the whole population risk being blown to bits. The council is panic-stricken already, and nothing will get done unless I use every method available.'

'All right,' Jon said, pulling in a breath. About them the

ballroom was frantic. 'We'll leave now.'

'Goodbye, Petra,' Alter said.

The Duchess took her hand with sudden urgency. 'Goodbye,' she said quietly, 'and good luck.'

At the arched doorway Alter, catching up to Jon, said, 'The General Medical building, Jon. Won't that mean——?'

The conversation in the room was rising towards hysteria.

'—It'll mean that the major source of medical supplies for the City is cut off. Let's just hope there isn't a plague before they get it operating again.'

The industrialist's daughter in blue had been accosted by Alter's ex-partner, Count B'rond. 'It's so terrifying,' she moaned. 'It reminds me of something I saw a little girl scribbling on a wall this afternoon, something about being trapped at a bright moment . . . trapped——' The lower voice of the count interrupted as he leaned towards her: 'You are still the most beautiful woman I have seen during the whole evening.' His gloved hand was a moth on her shoulder. 'Will you let me see you again?'

Jon and Alter gained the door and went first to the Duchess's suite. Arkor opened the door for them.

'Yes, I know what's happened,' he said.

'Then what's the best way to get to Telphar?' Jon dropped his black cloak at the feet of the chair.

'The transit-ribbon's out of commission, at least from this end. That conversation nonsense has left this side useless for sending.' From a closet, while he talked, he took two ordinary sets of clothing and handed them out. 'There's nothing you'll need I can't give you here, is there?'

'I don't think so,' Alter said, reaching into the silken folds of her skirt. 'This is all I'd want to take, and I brought them along.' She drew out a sheaf of papers.

'Nonik's poems?' Jon pulled off first one openwork boot and then the other. 'Reading matter for when things get dull?'

Alter reached behind her back, snapped open a snap, and the dress was a ring of silk about her feet. She stepped out, stepped into the green tunic, and belted it about her waist with a leather belt. 'I'd better leave these.' She removed the pearl earrings, started to take off the shell necklace, then bit her lip, shrugged. 'I'll wear this.' Arkor handed them sandals and they began to lace them up.

Jon closed the top buckle around his shin, and stuck the poems in his shirt pocket, before pushing his arms down the loose three-quarter sleeves. 'I'll hold these for you.'

'I miss my pockets,' Alter laughed.

The video-phone buzzed and the Duchess announced, 'All the royal yachts are out. Two reservations are waiting for you on a tetron-tramp at the pier.'

They left the Duchess's suite moments later.

As they rushed from the palace on foot open-topped transports carried the more elegant attendants off through the streets. Shoulder to shoulder against the indifferent night, they made their way towards the city's rim.

CHAPTER VII

A SIREN still gnawed at the dark. A water main had broken and the street was covered with a black, glittering rush. Orange scimitars from reflected flames streets away flashed in the ripples over the curb.

A white figure staggered across the pavement, whirling absurdly, the soaked hem of the large cloth flapping on her legs. The light struck something shiny and askew on her white, ropey hair. As she tottered to the street lamp it was revealed as a strip of tin, ripped edge-ragged from a can and bent in a circle. She turned and called into the alley: splashes followed her into the light.

Several men and women came along hesitantly, blinking, shuffling, flapping through the water. One youngster, whose hair fell into his face, had, stencilled over his pyjama chest: WARD 739. Aimless crying came from his open mouth. With grubby fingers he kept twisting his right ear.

Something struggled among them. They crowded about an odd duo: one beefy man in soaked pyjama pants had a hammer-lock on a frailer figure in white. This white was not a hastily issued nightgown or abruptly snatched sheet, but a short-sleeved, doctor's uniform. It was wet and wrinkled now. The man's arms were tied behind his neck and his squinting attested to a pair of lost glasses. His captor, chuckling, held him by the shoulder and whammed the back of his head with the ham of his hand. The bound figure collapsed to one knee on the streaming pavement. 'Will you please... ?' he began, raising his head, tendon's taut in his brown neck, to watch the tall woman. 'Look, you don't realize you're not well, none of you.... Just let me take you back to...'

The tall woman had begun searching the folds of her bed-sheet cloak. In frustration she cried out, 'Oh, keep him quiet I tell you!' The beefy man flung his foot like a club into the doctor's back and laughed when he splashed forward. Then he hoisted him back up.

'I can't find it!' screeched the woman. Her face went white, then red. 'Oh, I can't find it! Who has stolen it? Will nobody answer me! Don't you know who I am! How dare you treat me like this! Haven't you any respect!'

Despair, like the chill water, gushed over the kneeling physician. 'Help!' he cried into the darkness. 'Help me!' His cry, directed at no one particular, threatened no one, and his persecutor only tilted his broad head curiously to watch him howl. He laughed again and began to chew at the nub of his thumb nail.

Then from the alley splashed a man in green slicker and rubber boots. 'Hey, come on,' he ordered indignantly, 'we're trying to keep this area evacuated till we get the water main fixed. Now clear out and stay away from the flooded area.' The officer cursed, coughed, and flung the rubberized cloak back over his shoulder. 'Hurry up before I run you in!'

'They've taken it away from me again!' screamed the woman, pawing at her sheet. 'I can't find it! They've stolen it again! Oh, why won't they give it back!'

'Help me, *please*,' cried the kneeling man.

The youngster with the hair over his face and WARD 739 over his chest sobbed and twisted his ear.

The officer came up short. 'What are you, some sort of nuts?'

A young woman broke towards him, a pigeon gurgle falling from her pale mouth. When she passed beneath the street lamp the officer saw she would have been pretty had her eyes not been streaked like a puppy's. Cooing, she embraced him, rubbed her head against his wet slicker.

'Hey, what the hell do you think you're——'

The tall woman whirled on him. 'Young man, do you know who you are talking to?'

'The Queen of Sheba for all I know! I was telling her to get——' He staggered as the young woman settled herself from him like a pendulum.

'The Queen!—The Queen? Do you *know* who I am?' demanded the woman again. 'Oh, keep him quiet, will you!' She began clutching at her sheet once more.

The officer was still trying to loose the girl hanging from his neck when he heard a giggle in his left ear. He turned, more from instinct than interest, and saw the full lips with the rim of pink tongue pressing between them, the puffy lids of the dark-brown eyes, hair rough and yellow as hemp on the wide skull, the same coarse hair on the wider chest, tufting the thick collarbone——

—The beefy man smashed in the side of the officer's face with his fist; then he hit the officer on the neck with the edge of his hand.

'They stole it,' cried the tall woman as the officer sagged out of the girl's arms.

'You ... you don't know what you're *doing*!' cried the doctor. He was nearly on his feet. 'Will you please, will you *please* let me take you some place where they can help you. Just listen to me, just follow me to ...'

'*Will* you keep him quiet?' demanded the tall woman. 'How do you ever expect me to find it!'

Smiling, the beefy man dragged the inert officer across the pavement. His bare feet splashed up water like flat stones. When he reached the doctor he tilted his head, blinked like a puzzled monkey, then kicked the man's feet from under him so that he flopped on to the pavement again, called out in pain and surprise.

'Quiet!' screamed the woman, shaking the wet cloth away from her arms and whirling beneath the lamp.

The beefy man kneeled in the water, clamped his fingers over the necks of both conscious and unconscious men, lifted them and looked from face to face, one limp and bleeding, the other contorted and gasping. He licked his lower lip, his upper one. Then he pushed both faces into the water and held them there.

The doctor struggled a while.

Sobbing, the youngster with the long hair bent over the glistening rubber back and tugged at the slicker till it came loose. From the officer's waist he pulled something long and thin and pointed it at the sky. With his dirty thumb he pressed a button on the hilt and sparks glittered up the double prong of the power-blade.

Nail-bitten fingers, like sprung clamps, released bruised necks as the beefy man's face twisted in the light. His lips rolled back from a broken tooth and the corners of his eyes crinkled like paper.

The young woman ceased her moan, and even the old woman paused, groping to straighten the tin circle which dimmed and brightened in the blade's wavering light. 'That,' she said after a whispering exhalation, 'certainly isn't it. But never mind. Bring it along, anyway. Somebody stole it from me, I'm sure. But we'll find it, don't worry. Come along, there! Don't dawdle! Come along now!'

As the boy raised his head the hair fell back from his eyes. Reflected sparks shot from tear to tear on his cheek.

'Through here,' Jon said, motioning her towards the alley.

'What about the broken water main?' asked Alter.

'It can't be that deep. Just wet. They've blocked off almost every other way to the wharf. We'd just have to go around to the airfield to get through.'

'We both know how to swim,' Alter shrugged.

'Come on.' Down the block Jon could see lights gleaming on the flooded street. They looked like sheets of black glass.

'Ever notice how dark alleys make you whisper?' She glanced at the warehouses, and the windows of empty stores drifted past. The feet began to slap water.

As they passed under a light the inverted face of a building, its dusty windows, the black wound of the doorway and lop-sided steps, shattered under their sandals. Their footsteps lisped as they slogged forward. The back of his hand occasionally brushed her wrist; her shoulder gently struck his bicep, a physical assurance of mutual presence.

When they reached the corner Jon stopped. With a hand on her shoulder he halted Alter. She blinked, questioning him in the shadows.

His answer was the rising of his chin, the turn of his head denoting gathered attention.

She turned to face the same direction, listening. There was the distant sound of many feet in water.

'Malis?' asked Alter.

'Keep going,' Jon said. But when they reached the next corner they stopped again. Something was coming towards them from the cross street.

First, a mark of white fire hovered halfway down the block.

Jon dropped his hand on her shoulder again. In surprise she turned to him. 'What is——' Then turned back to see for herself.

The splashing grew, and the white mark became a fireblade,

aloft in the hand of a young man in white pyjamas: WARD 739. Behind him, eyes raised to the bright beacon, a dozen figures staggered, shuffled, and reeled.

When what *is* is congruent to what *is supposed* the reaction is functional and the mental processes competent. When what *is* and what *is supposed* have nothing to do with each other the choice of reactions is random. Something tears. Stay or run, laugh or frown: the decision is chance. Malis are supposed to lurk, vicious and malevolent, in the night streets of the city. But these were like no malis they had ever seen. Jon and Alter stayed and frowned.

So when the tall woman suddenly pointed a furious, quivering finger, crying, 'Of course! They must have it! Quick! Catch them before they get away!' Alter and Jon were off guard. The hesitant half-movements of the figures found focus: someone dived at Jon's legs and pulled them from under him so that he fell. Someone else yanked Alter by the arm, and three hands caught her shoulders.

As their minds worked to pull shredding reality together she cried, 'Jon, look! That woman!' She tried to ignore the fingers holding her, but her hands were still free below the elbow. Her left hand grabbed at her right elbow joint, holding to it as if it were in pain—or pain remembered.

Jon said, 'My lord, that's the Queen Mother. That's King Let's mother!'

'But she's supposed to be in the psycho ward of——'

'—of the General Medi——' Midway through Jon's word, realization of who these people must be, struck Alter. And a fist of nail-bitten fingers struck the side of Jon's head so hard that he slumped unconscious into the arms of the runny with runny eyes who had begun to coo.

The woman in the tin crown rushed towards Jon, then stopped, her sheet swaying from her extended arms. 'He must have it! He has stolen it!' She squatted before Jon. 'All right, what did you do with it! Where did you take it! Answer me, I say! Don't you know who I am?' She jumped up and seized the fireblade from the youth——

'Your Majesty!' Alter cried, her words broke terrified through the recalled agony of her arm. 'Your Majesty, *please*—— ' She was still holding her elbow, and the words were a frightened, raucous whisper.

The blade stayed in the air. The old head turned, damp hair stringing her cheeks. 'You . . . you called me Your Majesty,' the old woman said in the queer voice. 'You called me Your Majesty? Do you really know who I am?'

'You are . . . the Queen Mother, mother of the King, Your Majesty. Don't hurt him.'

The sword fell to her side. She straightened herself. 'Yes,' she mused. 'Yes. That's right. But he has—has stolen it from me, I'm sure.' Her eyes focused on Alter again. 'I am the Queen. Yes. But none of them believe me.' She motioned to the people about her. 'I have told them all, again and again. But *they* don't think I'm really the Queen. Oh, they follow me, because I say so. Sometimes they do what I say, because I get angry when they disobey. But—but they don't . . . don't really believe me.' She removed the circle of tin from her head. 'See, they took my crown. I had to make this tin one for the one they took away. How will anyone know I am really the Queen with a tin crown?'

Alter closed her mouth, opened it again, then said: 'I know it, Your Majesty. As for your crown, it is the idea, not the object that is important.'

A smile broke in the old woman's face. 'Yes. That's right. You do know who I am?' She set the crown back on her head, then reached towards Alter's neck. Alter cringed into the arms of the man and two women who held her. But the finger lifted the leather necklace with its shells. 'This is a beautiful piece of jewellery,' said the woman. 'I almost seem to . . . to remember it. Do I have one like it myself? Perhaps I . . . accidentally broke one like it, a long time ago?'

'Perhaps,' whispered Alter.

'You must be a countess. Or a princess of the royal family to wear such jewellery.'

'No, Your Majesty.'

'But it is of the sea. At least a Duchess or—— But one gentlewoman never inquires after the rank of another. I am forgetting myself.' She let the necklace fall. 'To know you are of my family is enough.' She turned again to Jon. 'But him! He has stolen it, I know. I will kill him if he does not give it back to me!'

'Your Majesty,' cried Alter, 'he is my friend, as noble a man as I am a woman.'

'He is?'

'Oh, yes, Your Majesty. He's taken nothing from you.'

'You're sure?'

'I'm very sure.'

'Then where could it have got to? Someone must have it!'

'What . . . what are you looking for?' ventured Alter.

'I can't . . . oh, I can't remember,' wailed the Queen.

'But you must—keep looking. It isn't here,' Alter whispered.

Immediately the old woman began to search through the creased sheet that served her for robe. 'I know I had it just a while ago. They took my crown, my sceptre, even took away my—— Oh, I can't find it anywhere. . . .'

'Even taken away your pockets,' Alter said softly, tilting her head in sudden wonder.

'Even my pockets,' repeated the Queen, still picking over the sheet. 'Everything aristocratic is gone. They have taken it away. No one believes me. I must wear a silly tin crown. It's all gone. They've taken——' Then a tendon in her neck quivered beneath the folded skin. Her eyes moistened. She raised the flashing blade and turned to Jon. 'He stole it! I know he did! If he doesn't give it back I'll——'

The hands that held her had loosened, and Alter suddenly lunged forwards and wrested Jon from the grip of the cooing girl. On her knees she turned to face the sword. 'Won't you do one decent thing in your life? Leave him alone!' The blade halted, and in the silence, Alter heard the quick splashing of feet as someone fled down the street, someone else who must have wandered upon the scene, observed from just around the corner, at last to flee terrified at this point, some mali this time who would have fought with fists and weapons, but even himself is defeated by this insanity. 'Your Majesty,' she said again, pushing the other thought away, 'don't hurt this man. You are the Queen. I should not have to tell you how . . . how little it behooves the Queen to show such anger when no offence was given. If you are the Queen be merciful.'

'I—I am the Queen?' The inflection suddenly rose to interrogative in the middle of the last word. It kept rising into a wail. Tears squeezed between the wrinkled tissue of her lids. 'I remember,' she cried. The blade dropped in the water and shorted out in a hiss of steam. 'I remember now. It was the picture.' She backed away. 'The picture of my son.'

Slowly she turned away, her voice still coming aimlessly back to them. 'I had two sons, you know.' As she walked off the others began to follow her. 'They stole my youngest from me, then they murdered my eldest. But I had a picture, a miniature picture with a metal frame, about the size of my palm, a picture of my son. It was the kind vendors used to sell for half a unit down by the wharves. But they stole it from me. They wouldn't even let me keep that. Everything, everything is gone. . . .'

Now the hemp-haired brute lumbered behind her chuckling. Almost in slow motion the boy from WARD 739 picked up the shorted fireblade and raised the dull prong into the air. Once more the girl began her cooing and followed them down the street. After them the others disappeared into the alley, each unsteady footstep shattering their inverted images on the reflecting water.

Jon was moving. As he sat up, Alter pressed her face against his damp shirt, her breath coming in staccato gasps. 'Jon—You didn't see—you didn't see her . . .'

His arm locked around her shoulder. 'I wasn't that far gone,' he said. 'I heard the last couple of minutes.'

'Talking to them,' Alter said, as last capturing the breath that fled her lungs and would not stay, 'without screaming was the hardest thing I've ever done.'

Jon pushed himself to his feet. 'Well I'm glad you did it. Let's get to that damn boat, and hurry. Hey, relax,' he added. 'You can let go of your arm now. You're safe.'

Alter took another deep breath and looked down where her left hand had again fastened around her right elbow. 'I guess I can, now,' she said, and after a moment dropped her hand to her side.

They reached the cobbled waterfront as the moon cleared the sea, scattering flaked silver. They made their way to the docks of the tetron tramps.

They came on board, registered, and minutes later the dirty boat lugged away from the docks into the flickering swell. They leaned on the rail, looking at the hollow shadows of each other's eyes, then to the diminishing spires of the city, then back to the shaking, moonlit sea.

'How many times have you made this trip to the mainland?' Jon asked.

'A couple of times with the circus when it was on tour,' she said. 'Then that spurt back and forth through the transit ribbon right at the beginning of this whole business. But that's all.' She waited while the smile she could feel him smiling but could not see became sound and floated away under the noise of the wash on the hull.

'For me,' Jon said, 'there was the time I was carried off to the penal mines, and then when I got out I got back via the transit ribbon. There was the time we first took Let to the forest. And, three years later when we brought him back.' He turned to her, to the shadows that were her eyes, her white hair moon silvered, blown from the curve within curve of her ear. 'Now we're here.' A wave larger than the others threw spray at their faces.

'What's being alone, or being with somebody?' she asked.

'Or more important,' he said, feeling somehow he was speaking her thought more precisely, 'why do you feel alone, even when you're with somebody one time—and at others ... well, not alone.'

The drop of her head, the release of a muscle in her cheek shifting the moon-shadow there told him it was her thought.

'When I know the answer to that one ...' Only he didn't know what he would do, and thought: perhaps what I would do is the answer.

'Remember when we were reading the poems?' she asked. 'We were all sort of mixed up in each other.'

He nodded.

'What was the poem we couldn't figure out?'

'Another one about loneliness,' he said. 'I don't remember the beginning.'

'I do.' She recited, 'Equivocal, maniacal, and free as great despair is great tranquillity ...'

Then a voice behind them continued, and they turned, '... Cry in the minions of the ravaged night, turn back, poet, and face the ancient dreams, as tears in moonlight fall by the sea.... That's all I can remember.'

'Where did you hear that?' Jon asked.

For answer the figure stepped from the shadow of the cabin into the moon. His head was fuzzy, wrinkled egg, where the nap had been worn from eyes, nose, and mouth, yet thinly covered his chin and scalp. 'That's all I remember,' he repeated. 'How did it end?'

'Solitary people,' Jon went on, 'by the sound of waves trudge the long, soft, sandy ground. Sadness or joy, equal and one, caused each ended race I have begun.'

The sailor sucked his teeth, shook his head, and scratched his stomach with his thumb. 'I like that one.' His striped singlet was loose over his boney chest.

'Where did you hear it?' Jon asked again.

The old sailor cocked his head, drawling, 'And what do you want to know for?' He stopped scratching and pushed a finger at them. 'Where did *you* hear it?'

'We read it,' Alter said. 'Please tell us, won't you?'

He shrugged and came to the railing. 'You make it sound real important.' He leaned one hand on the rail. His skinny arm gave and bent as he moved against the rocking of the boat. 'Kid with that funny couple told it to me. He said he wrote it.'

'A kid, with a couple?'

'He was maybe twenty-one, twenty-two. To me that's a kid. All three of them were going across. Kept to their rooms most of the trip. The guy wore this funny hood. But the kid was all over the place, talking with everybody, reciting these poems he'd written. That was one of the ones he told me.'

'Catham would be wearing a hood to cover that plastic face of his if he had to leave quickly without any vivafoam,' Jon said.

'No wonder there were no records of their helicopter leaving for the mainland. They must have ditched it back in the city and taken the boat over.' She stopped. 'Jon, he said Nonik was running around, talking to everyone, excited, happy. That doesn't sound like anyone whose wife was just——'

'I didn't say happy,' interrupted the sailor. 'That's your word. More sort of hysterical. He'd ask people strange questions, and then wait for an answer like a puppy whose paw you just stepped on. But sometimes he'd get up and walk away three-quarters through what you were saying.'

'That sounds more like it,' Jon said. 'How long ago was this?'

'Same day the military ministry got bombed in Toron.'

'So they went to the mainland too,' said Jon. 'Where did they get off?'

'Boat only makes one stop on the coast. They got off right where you'll be in a couple of hours.'

They pulled up nearly an hour before sunrise. The boat would receive its cargo at noon, when most of the passengers would disembark. 'Sure you don't want to wait till daylight?' asked the sailor. He was sitting on an overturned bucket, carving a mop handle into a series of leering totems. 'Lots of malis around here, and night-time is mali time.' He held the pole braced in his toes and picked carefully at distorted smiles and gaping frowns, the short knife blade *tic-tic-ticcing*.

'We want to get a good start,' said Jon.

The moon was large and low on the horizon, and when the sailor nodded to them the thin shadow of the mop handle swung across the deck.

'What is that?' Alter asked, pointing to a shadowy hulk down the docks.

The sailor looked up. 'The circus ship.'

'But what's wrong with it?' It was tilted sideways, and even in the moonlight one section of the red-and-gold hull showed black blisters over half its length.

'What does it look like,' the sailor said. 'I told you there were malis around. That happened maybe a month ago.'

'What happened?' Jon asked.

'When the circus came back to tour the mainland malis attacked, fired the ship, broke up the place. Killed a lot of people——'

'—killed?' asked Alter.

The sailor nodded.

'Oh, Jon!' She looked back to the wreck. 'I was working for them——'

'Come,' he said. At his touch she began to walk down the sloping ramp, turning her white head now and again to look at the ruined ship.

Walking up the boardwalk, Jon asked, 'Do you think Clea, Catham, and Nonik might be somewhere around here?'

'Why?'

'Clea also used to work for the circus. Maybe she came back to get something she'd left.' Across a field in the horizontal moon, tents still flapped on their guys. 'They probably won't be here now, but maybe they passed through.'

'I can show you which was her tent,' said Alter. They turned to the meadow. Breezes sped to the sea and bent the grass towards the waves, as beyond the sand the crushed ivory foam broke and spumed to the meadow. They neared a rippling wall of canvas. As they stepped towards the entrance a figure moved:

'What do you want out here?' His trousers were from a soldier's uniform, but the sleeveless vest that laced over his chest was fisherman's apparel. His blond hair was the short brush of a military cut three months gone.

'We're just looking through the tents,' Jon said.

'Who said you could look?'

'Who said we had to ask?'

'We don't like strangers too much, snoopin'. There been all sorts of mali stuff about. The town'—he motioned with his chin towards the collection of houses across the meadow—'don't want no strangers around. Malis raided them last week. Killed a couple of people. Didn't steal nothing. Just broke up the place.' He let out a short laugh. 'Isn't that something?'

Jon frowned as the tent wall rippled faster, then stilled. 'Hey, what's out there, Lyn?' came a voice from behind the canvas.

Lyn called back over his shoulder, 'I don't know, Raye.'

A second figure stepped to the first one's side. 'You think they're malis?' Raye, younger, darker, also wore a disorderly soldier's uniform.

'Could be,' Lyn shrugged.

'We're not malis,' Alter declared. 'Did the town station you out here to keep malis from moving into the tents?'

'Could be,' Lyn shrugged, then laughed again. It was a quiet, windy sound: the voice of a man who had lived by the sea's edge, with something in it of water over rock. Raye laughed too. Laughter was coming from behind them as well.

They turned and the laughter rose. Nearly twenty more were standing behind them. Now they closed ranks, circling. Many wore remnants of army uniforms; most were green-eyed and dark. Two were girls. The laughter broke in peak after liquid peak. 'They say they're not malis,' Lyn said again. Like a wave rolling back across sand, the sound ceased.

Jon was afraid. He was also thinking fast.

'Bet you can't prove it,' someone called.

'You know what we do to . . . malis.'

'Come on, let's show them what we do to malis!'

Seconds later, he and Alter, their arms held tight behind them, were marched through the tents. One man had gratuitously socked Jon's jaw, and it throbbed. But he was thinking, meticulously and quickly. The man guiding him once jerked him as they passed several mounds of earth.

'That's what *you* townies do to *us* malis,' Raye hissed, then pushed them violently past the graves.

'What makes you think we're from town,' Jon got out.

'I don't care where you're from.'

Jon heard Alter draw a quick breath at some injury he could not see, since she was behind him.

A fallen carpet of yellow canvas spread over the grass in the ivory stain of moonlight. They were approaching the line of aquarium wagons, locked end to end. There was talk behind him that Jon tried to correlate:

'Which one do you think'll try to save the other? Which one do you think'll run?'

'I say flip: heads we tie him up and let the girl try to save him, tails we tie the girl and see what he does.'

'Don't leave it to chance. I want to see a good show. Tie up the girl and throw him in with the knife.'

'Hell, he'll run. How much you want to bet he's a coward and runs.'

'Tie him up, and the girl is sure to bolt.'

'We'll still have some fun. She won't get very far.'

Now Lyn's more forceful voice settled it. 'Put your money away. We tie her and give him the knife. He won't let them at her without putting on some sort of show.'

Alter was pushed on to the canvas. Someone brought a rope and her arms were bound. Once they exchanged glances, neither imploring nor despairing, but rather looks of desperate concentration as each tried to find the flaw in the net of action and movement carrying them to unnamed doom. Now Jon was pushed forward on the collapsed tent.

They were shoved towards the row of aquariums. Moonlight through the misted water caught sailing shadows that darkened window after window. The water was green with algae. The tanks had not been cleaned for a long time. The great octopus that had been exhibited there had probably been the first to die from the impurities. The dolphins must have gone next, poisoned by the unfiltered water. The manta ray, a scavenger by nature, might well have survived the longest in the foul drink, but at last it, too, must have succumbed and floated belly upward on the scummy surface. The only large creatures left were the sharks. Great and gaunt, they would be the last to die of filth. Now they swam lazily back and forth nosing the glass and the corners of the tanks.

A platform with a wooden ladder had been built by one wagon's edge. Jon and Alter were man-handled to its foot, and then up on the platform at the tank's rim. What happened next—it happened inside Jon's mind—was a marshalling of dispersed bits of information, of learning and fragments of learning, of conjecture, action, and random chance. He was still afraid, but suddenly there was a bright line leading across the glistening sands of panic.

The tanks had once been separated by a system of locks so that individual tanks could be emptied and cleaned. But as the beasts died the six-foot walls between the wagons had been removed, and more water had been let in till the tank was full to the brim once more. Opened and connected, they formed a single trough twelve feet wide and a hundred and fifty feet long. Green rippled under the moon with the movement of shapes beneath. Each shark—Tritin had collected them for size—was a good four hundred, four hundred and fifty pounds. Jon held each fact in his mind as, below him, water lapped the end of the tank.

The sides were raked to prevent anything in the tank from getting out. Raye shoved Alter, still bound, into the water. Jon took a breath and dived as she went off the edge. Water hit him, of indifferent temperature. He curled up, sinking from momentum, and tore off one sandal. The pressure on his ears was lessening, which meant he was rising towards the surface again. He tore off the other sandal, broke surface, and threw his head back, to shake the water from his face. He took a last look at what was happening on the surface: to balance and separate the relevant from the irrelevant. Alter near the end of the tank was bobbing rhythmically. With a controlled scissor kick, a good swimmer can tread water a fair amount of time, even with hands tied: Alter was a good swimmer (relevant).

'Hey there!' one of the malis called from the platform—it was a girl (irrelevant)—she jammed something into the air, a knife (relevant), then flung it into the water. He dived for it, following its glittering spiral to the depths of the tank as a shadow passed over him, thinking, Should I cut the ropes that bind Alter's hands so—— The thought became an irrelevancy as he grabbed the blade from the gravel flooring: the edge of his hand nicked! The knife was so sharp that with himself moving and Alter moving, there would be no way to avoid a few cuts and scratches. Blood in the water meant death.

Was that how the others thrown bound and free here had perished (irrelevant)? He started swimming underwater, and broke surface forty feet down the tank, took another breath and drove forward again. How long would it take for the beasts to become curious. Seconds, minutes? The farther apart he and Alter were, the greater the shark's indecision. He put the blade between his teeth to free his hands for swimming. Moving beneath the surface attracted less attention than splashing over the top. He shot forward, through water like rutilant glass.

A shark nosed so close his glaucous flesh gleamed. To the surface for three breaths; he dived again, muscles electric and alert, and silently thanked Alter for her patient training (pushing down the thought of banked teeth raking those muscles; and Alter was bound).

Another dive brought him to the far end of the aquarium (which of the beasts had turned and turned in the central flood, deciding between the two figures, and chosen her, legs scissoring in green fog, white hair awash about her face). He grabbed the knife from his teeth and would have used his own flesh, his own blood to bait his plan; but something moved at the edge of his blurred, submarine vision, and he whirled and plunged the blade into it, catching it against the glass. It was a fair-sized fish, over a foot long, but grown sluggish in the diseased water. Now it flipped and squirmed in veils of blood. Jon seized the fish and ripped the knife upward towards the blood-rich gills and pressed the bleeding carcase against the glass. He reversed himself in the water (remembering her words, 'Put your head back. Now bring your knees up and roll backwards,' realizing this was the same motion) and swiped the blood meat down the side of the glass, leaving a dissolving track of red.

One instant he felt himself in blind subjection to all the factors he could not control, all that was desperate and jagged in both inner and outer environment; as he perceived it, it turned over in his mind, like a spinning coin dropping with him through the water. The other side was a sense of total control that came with the extent of his perception. He shot to the bottom of the tank, leaving a column of blood. The coin spun.

Sound travels faster in water than in air. He heard them coming, flung the fish away, then jammed himself from the glass wall, pushing with his feet. His palms scraped over the gravel and the water darkened with thunderous shapes.

Crash!

He rolled over, away from the pain in his scarred hands.

Crash! Crash!

Two more struck the wall separately. Then——

—*Cruuuummm!*——

—two struck at once, and tide jerked him upwards. His head jammed through the surface at the same time he heard the three-inch glass plates crack. He was flung into foaming air. It had worked!

With the locks removed and the extra water the pressure in the aquariums was almost five times what it was intended to be, and well over what theoretically it could be. Some chance structuring had kept the walls together. But a few blows from a couple of four-hundred-and-fifty-pound, hungry sharks barolling down a hundred-and-fifty-foot run had done it.

He struck the ground on wet grass. Remembering his falls, he flipped over and sprung open to a standing position. He staggered in the streaming weeds, panting for the agonizing breath he had held. The knife was still in his hand. Droplets became pearls as they ran down the blade in the gibbous moon.

Three of the grounded sharks twisted and flopped on the grass. He turned to the shattered wall of the aquarium. Raye, for whatever random reason, had run to this end of the tanks to watch. When the wall exploded he had been nearly severed by a shard of glass that gleamed in his ruined belly.

Jon ran to the wagon, vaulted up the waterfall, and splashed down the gravel flooring of the tanks. Alter lay face down twenty feet from the end, washed there before the level became too low to carry her farther. It couldn't have been more than thirty seconds since the wall first broke! But he was aware how accelerated his time sense was. Even so, she couldn't have——
He was already beside her. He pulled her from the water.

Alter opened her eyes and her mouth at the same time and sucked in air. Then her eyes closed again, but she kept on gasping. Jon sawed the ropes from her arms. He scratched her a couple of times, but the ropes fell away, and she hunched her shoulders and spread her elbows (and he remembered the exercise she had taught him to get the blood back into your arms) and staggered to her feet.

He pulled her to the jagged rim, jumped out, and helped her down.

Malis were running along the side of the wagons: recovered from their shock at the explosion (an aquarium is not *supposed* to explode; but it *did*—the paralysis had lasted nearly three-quarters of a minute), they were coming to recover their prey.

Jon and Alter ran through the wet meadow, strewn with glass, avoiding the long, frantic shapes flopping about them.

Alter was exhausted. Jon felt it as her wrist shivered in his hand. He himself was moving on energy left in the glowing ends of burned-out nerves. Their running became a fast walk. When they were halfway to the forest someone screamed behind them; panting, they turned to look.

One of the malis had passed too close to a shark. The animal had flipped and caught her by the leg. The others were trying to help. Jon filled his raw lungs with one more breath, and stumbled forward. He kept stumbling until leaves were striking him in the face, and the screaming had stopped.

They reached a clearing five minutes into the wood where the rocks sloped up for twenty feet. Halfway across the granite rise, Jon turned.

A quarter of the sky had gone grey with dawn. Each tree about him cast a double shadow with the glow of the old moon and the new rouge of the sun. Alter sank to the rock and ran her hands back over her forehead, smoothing her wet white hair into a helmet. Suddenly she hunched over, as if to hold what little strength was left in the cave of her body.

At the same time Jon felt the emergency catches that had tautened his body into a survival machine start to release, one after the other: his shoulders, the back of his hips, his calves; his bruised palms began to sting. He lowered himself beside her, each muscle like a metal weight dropping into the acid of fatigue. She raised her head and said, softly and wonderingly, 'We're safe!'

Jon pressed his head against her shoulder, as she had done at a similar moment in the City, relaxing in the reality of wet skin against wet skin. She put her hand on the back of his neck, and after a moment he raised his head and looked at her.

The breeze hesitated in the branches, quivering among the leaves before it rolled on.

'I can see your eyes,' Jon whispered. 'There's enough light now so that I can see your eyes.'

CHAPTER VIII

EACH person moves towards whatever maturity he is seeking in a definite direction. He approaches each observed incident from that direction, sees it from that one side; but it may not be the same side someone else sees. In Toron, when Alter cried to the Queen, 'Won't you do one decent thing in your life!' a young mali who had come upon them minutes before, at that point, turned and splashed off through the night. It was Kino.

We cannot trace here the experiences that brought the gutter youth to the point where this sentence, out of the whole exchange, struck him, tripped something in his mind that brought him up short, stayed with him when the rest of the incident had joined the many inexplicable things he had seen on the streets. He did not recognize Jon. He made no connection between the maundering speech and the hospital clothing. But for his own reasons, this hysterical imperative was what he contemplated as he fled from the blocked-off section, slipped past the guards, and came to the waterfront.

Pondering, he took a piece of chalk from his pocket and wrote over a peeling war poster: *You Are Trapped in That——*

'Kino?'

'Jeof?'

Kino turned.

'You the one writing that stuff all over the walls?'

'Some of it,' Kino said, frowning into the shadows.

The neo-neanderthal emerged into the livid moonglow. On the wharf cobbles a breeze tugged at a piece of paper stuck there by the damp.

Kino wondered if he should stay or go. 'What are you doin' out here, Jeof?' he asked to avoid the decision.

'My territory,' Jeof grunted. 'You gonna say I can't walk around in it?'

'No, Jeof. I didn't mean nothin' like that.'

'Fall out, Kino,' Jeof said. 'I'm in deep water.'

'I'm going,' Kino said. He put the chalk in his pocket. Then he stopped. 'Jeof, have you ever done one decent thing in your

. . . well, done something you could be proud of?'

'I'm proud,' Jeof said, his voice lowering. Both hands rose, open palmed, then snapped to fists in the foggy light. 'I'm proud.'

Kino drew back, but went on: 'Proud of what, Jeof?'

'You better fall out.'

'In a minute, in a minute. No, really Jeof, what the hell are you proud of?' Features readjusted themselves on the neanderthal face: brows flattened, cheeks sunk, the bar of muscle at the back of his jaw contracted. 'Nobody else is proud of you. After that business with Nonik's wife, you think fish around here think you're big? Naw. You're a very small ape. And maybe you're so small, they think you shouldn't even be around. Maybe there's a group of them right now sitting down somewhere trying to figure out how they can get you and tear you in little pieces, like you did her. And maybe they're gonna start looking for you at about ten o'clock tonight. And maybe they'll be coming over from the Inn, where they're planning it now, to hunt you out of your little hole in the ground so they can stomp on you, ape.' The last paragraph was total fabrication. Kino, having started talking, had seen the chance to revenge his friend.

'Why are you telling me, then?'

Kino shrugged. 'I just like to warn people. I do it all the time.' He felt his ability to keep up the bluff begin to fail. 'See you around—I hope,' he added, and turned away. The same fear that had caused him to fabricate the vendetta had crushed the delicate concern for Alter's sentence. Now he hurried down the street thinking, Well, I scared him some! Bet he walks around a little more carefully now!

We cannot trace the experiences that bring a man to observe a given phenomenon from a given side. Relative to our limited perception, much of his reaction is random.

Jeof stood alone on the cobbles. The paper, stuck to the ground, ripped in the breeze and flapped up the alley. Once more he clenched his fists and let Kino's words pick their way through his mind. 'I'm proud,' he mumbled, and then, 'At least I'm proud.' He looked up, and suddenly his frown twisted all out of shape into an expression with no name. 'They'll never find me,' he whispered, and lurched forward.

What routes rage followed in his brain, what directions and

misdirections it took, what caused him to judge and misjudge, also we cannot trace here.

Two blocks later he stopped, panting, in front of a small door at the bottom of three stones steps. He dropped down all three and landed with his fist pounding.

There were several secret shops in the Devil's Pot where thieves could pick up illegal powerblades heisted from a guard transport; stolen government explosives; much of the intricate equipment, made for an unfought war, had gone astray as it moved from storehouse to storehouse. These shops disappeared often and did much of their business at night. When the door was opened a crack Jeof pushed inside.

Five minutes later he took all three steps in one motion and started back down the street. In one stubby hand he held a brass sphere with a stud on one end. It was a small, powerful grenade. He had once lobbed its twin through the window of a crematorium whose manager hadn't wanted to pay protection. The burst of flame and glass, the brightness and glory, hung in his mind divorced from the destruction, a protected instant of light.

At the cellar mouth he halted. They would look first for him there. The alleys where he often slept on lean evenings were not safe. Other malis were constantly poking around in them, and he would be found out. He turned up the waterfront street where the mercury-lights hung in shields of fog.

A gate to one of the piers had been left open by accident. He crossed the street and went through There was only one boat at the dock. Jeof hesitated. At the gangplank the chain had also been left off. The small inter-island launch was dingy and unpainted. Its captain had been careless, gone off without closing up anything. Probably nothing worth stealing on it anyway, thought Jeof as he climbed on to the deck.

The boat rose and settled in the sludge that licked the city. Jeof rubbed the grenade against his hip. Another night he might have broken the windows, or found a bucket of paint and messed up the deck; tonight he was just going to hide.

As he reached the hatch a whining sound overhead made him look up. Then, beyond the buildings of the wharf, he saw a distant explosion. Jeof sucked disgustedly at his lower lip and started down into the musty hole. Another freak bombing. Keep on and blow up the whole damn city, he thought, between statement, question, and speculation. Maybe it would distract the pack hunting him—give them something to go loot. He sat in the damp corner and put the grenade in his lap. Let them come after him here. He wondered where the explosion was. The boat's movement made the darkness about him shift and sag like a half-jelled solid.

Let ran forward into the billowing smoke. It rasped the rims of his nostrils, abraded the back of his throat. He screamed, 'Petra, where are you?'

Light flared to his right from an opening door. Coughing, someone stumbled into him. 'Let, what in the world——?'

'We've been bombed, Petra. *We've* been bombed!'

Wind nudged the smoke from between their startled faces. As she stared about, Petra cried out, jerking the back of her hand over her mouth. Part of the ceiling and far wall had torn away. As a light connection broke and the last light in the hall went out, they saw the glittering bubble of the night.

She seized him by the shoulder and fled down the hall as behind them the roar of falling stone swelled, then faded to chuckling shards. 'This way.' She started up the left-hand stairwell.

'Petra!' He caught her back. 'We'll have to go the other way.' A slab of plaster had fallen from the wall, and beyond that were piles of brick. They turned back over the fallen struts and up the other stairway.

It was only after they passed the palace guard, crumpled on the steps with his head under a block of masonry, that fear realized itself, as in a mirror where the drape has been ripped away

'Where were we hit, Petra? Are they still bombing?'

For answer thunder filled the hall and they felt the floor shake. Glass fell before them: the crystal of the ceiling chronometer had broken.

In another room down another hallway someone screamed.

'What about the council wing?' Let asked as they started down the next stairwell.

'I think that's where the first bomb struck,' she said. 'Otherwise, we'd be dead. Come this way.' They turned through a door that let them out on the upper balcony of the throne room.

As they rushed past the columned railing, Let cried out, 'Petra!' He pointed down into the hall. Only one of the lights burned at the end of the room. People moved over the floor below, fingers of shadow jutting from each. 'Petra, look!'

She joined him at the railing.

'What are they doing, Petra? Who are they?'

She put her hand on his shoulder, and he felt her press down.

'What is ...?' he began. Then, in response, he crouched. The Duchess stooped beside him.

'So soon ...' she whispered, shaking her head. 'So soon ... They're here already——'

'What *are* they?'

'Look.'

The figures moved below, glancing right and left in wonder. Now one ran to the window, grabbed a drape, and tugged till it ballooned down over him. The others laughed, but the first one wrapped the brocade hanging about his waist and trailed it behind him back to the others. Another man, stopping before the jewelled inlay on the wall, was industriously prying at the glitter with the point of a knife. A third hastily shoved something under his tunic, snatched from a pedestal which had held some historical statuette.

'Looters, marauders, vandals,' whispered Petra, '—malis.'

Suddenly three new figures burst into the throne room from the far entrance: two elderly men and a woman. Their dress was as rich as the vandals' was poor, but torn, dusty, and charred as well.

'They're from the council,' Let whispered. 'They must have just escaped from the Council Wing'

The three and the many faced each other over an electric moment. Then the man in the brocade drape stepped forward. 'What you doing here?' he demanded.

The councilmen, numbed by their escape, only moved closer to one another.

The speaker, emboldened by their silence, cried again, 'What are you trying to do to us here?' A rush of guilt came with his next words. 'You have no business here. You can't keep from the ... the people what is rightfully theirs!'

In bewilderment, rather than negation, the council members shook their heads. Councilwoman Tilla's hand went nervously to the collar of sea agates at her throat. Councilman Rillum fingered the end of his gold belt. 'We were only trying to get away from——' began Councilman Servin, collecting himself.

But a vandal cried out, 'Don't let them get away! They'll tell! They'll tell! Don't let them go!' And suddenly they surged at the cowering trio.

Then one man was waving the sea-agate collar in the air, and a woman ran towards the door trailing the gold belt behind her.

Petra's grip tightened until the King winced. Realizing how tight she held him, she dropped her hand. 'Let . . .' she whispered. 'Oh, My King . . .'

'Petra?'

'Like this? Oh, not like this!'

'Petra, perhaps what you said about the aristocracy is right. Maybe it's better that it go——'

She turned to him abruptly, eyes raging in the long shadows from the single light. 'The aristocracy,' she repeated. 'At its worst, a sargasso of every conceivable neurosis society may have; by naming itself it has agreed to its own death. But at least it has had the dignity to applaud its own order of execution in the past if the document is eloquent.' She turned back to the railing and gazed down at the floor, empty save for three twisted bodies at the throne's foot. 'But this . . . No, not like this . . .' Again she shook her head. 'Even in the people, now, all that is aristocratic is gone.'

'In the forest,' Let said after a moment, 'they would say, all that is histosentient is gone.'

The Duchess looked at him questioningly.

'All that is human is gone,' he translated.

Footsteps behind them. Then: 'There they are! There! That one must be the King!'

They ran without looking, down the balcony, and turned into the maze of hallways.

'We'll catch them! It's just a woman, and the kid's got a limp!'

But they were not caught. They knew the palace labyrinth where the looters did not. At last they stood deep in an alcove of the little park behind the castle. 'Now you follow me!' the King whispered suddenly.

'But where——'

The boy started forward, however, and she followed. Through one door, over a little bridge and under an arch; they were hurrying by the wall that ran along the Avenue of the Oyster. When they reached the hive-houses she asked again, 'My King, where are we going?' She looked back where the flames tongued between the spires of the city.

'Come!' Now it was he who held tightly to her shoulder. 'There's nothing you can do now, Petra. Come with me, please!' In a moment she turned and came with him.

The city was in panic. People rushed from their homes, then rushed back in to mount their roofs and watch the spectacle. The forces that before had been trying to staunch the broken main were split in half to fight the fires that raged in the city's centre. Random chaos moved and battered through the streets. Making use of the confusion, the two reached the waterfront almost unnoticed.

Silent for the last fifteen minutes, a third time she cried out, 'Let, where are you *going*?' She turned again to watch the towers. 'Arkor is still somewhere in the castle. Jon and Alter are trying to get to Telphar——'

'And there's nothing you can do,' he finished for her. 'Please come. Please!'

'But where?'

'To the boats, Petra. We're going to take a boat and go sailing.'

'*What?* But Let . . .'

'Because there's nothing else to do, Petra. And I want to! That's the only reason. If there's nothing that you want to do, at least share this with me.'

She was confused, and in her confusion turned to follow him along the piers. Suddenly a group of ragged individuals appeared ahead, and one cried out. 'There they are! Look at their clothes!'

They turned and ran along the cobbles. Behind them the cry metamorphosed: 'Get their clothes! They must be rich! Get their clothes!'

A quarter of the way down the street a dock gate stood ajar. 'In here!' cried the King, and the Duchess followed him. He turned halfway up the gangplank of the single boat and gave her his hand. On the deck she helped him pick up the gangplank and heave it, crashing, to the dock. As they ran to the wheel house, figures filled the gateway.

Petra lingered, staring back. A moment later, something thrilled beneath the deck. The motor's whine set a sympathetic ringing in the chain railing. 'Come on up here, Petra! It's moving! We're on our way!'

She turned from the figures crowding the edge of the pier (and did not see three of them leap for the side of the boat, did not see four hands slip from the deck's edge, nor hear two bodies smack into the froth; nor did she see the two hands that held. Then an elbow cleared the deck, a dark head, another arm. As she joined him at the wheel, her breath was hoarse.

'No, Petra, don't look back at the city. Just keep staring forward! Where shall we go? To your island? To the mainland? Or all the way to the edge of the barrier and beyond? We'll go places no one has ever been, we'll discover new islands all ourselves!'

She looked forward (and did not see the crouching figure start forward, then hesitate at the sound of their voices, glance right and left: the hatch cover was open. On bare feet he darted over the deck that flickered with light from the burning towers and lowered himself into the hole) 'Oh, Let, why are——?'

Night flung out over the water, glittering and undulent. 'Remember that boy, Petra, who told me about the sun coming up over the sea, burning away the water? Well, for him, then, we'll sail straight into the morning. Whoever he was, we'll sail for him.'

'It's night——' she whispered, thinking, *Oh, Let, it's not for him, it's just another selfish gesture, like so many we have made, of the sort that has allowed it all to topple as it has——*

'But soon——' he whispered back, thinking, *Don't you see, Petra, now there is only ourselves to save, there is only this gesture to make, because it has fallen and is no more——*

As each stood on deck, woman and boy, with half-truths straining towards one another to make a whole, below deck Jeof blinked, raised himself to his elbow and felt the motor throb beneath him. Foam hissed outside the bulkhead, and he thought in terror, *Have they come for me?* His stubby hand scooped up the grenade.

A figure descended in the flickering light that fell through the hatch. Jeof pressed himself against the studded plates, the bolts bruising his shoulder. The figure turned, and for one moment his face was fully lit:

'Kino!'

'Jeof!'

He pressed the release, and on the wharf where figures still stared after the craft they saw a momentary blister burn on the water. The brilliance of colliding random energies flung light over their faces, for one moment bright as morning.

CHAPTER IX

THE breeze rolled back through the forest as they climbed down the dawn-grey slope

'We'll have to stop in about an hour,' Jon said, 'to rest.'

'Make it a half an hour?'

Jon tried to grin. 'Sure.'

Something bright and spinning curved through the air and dropped glittering into the leaves before them. 'You want to toss that back to me?' someone said from the trees.

They looked from the shadowed leaves to the metal fallen on the ground. Jon bent and picked it up. 'Here it is,' he said, holding it out. 'Come get it.'

A hand pushed at a branch and a man stepped forward. It was difficult to tell his age. Shirtless, ragged pants roped around his middle, the figure walked with one leg slightly stiff. One shoulder was vaguely humped and the right arm dangled limply from its socket. His hairy pectorals shifted as he reached for the coin with his good hand.

Jon pulled it back, though, out of reach. It was a medal with raised figures of several buildings coming to a single peak with a sunburst behind. Along the lower curve, in san serif lettering, was inscribed:

CITY OF A THOUSAND SUNS

Jon frowned and extended it again. Broad strong fingers with wide, dirt-crested nails retrieved it.

'So, you folks want to take a rest? What about clean sheets to rest on, nine inches of mattress to rest the sheets on, and a hydro-spring under that: put the whole thing in a room painted light green where no sound can get through, just morning sun through a window and darker leaves——'

'All right,' Jon said There's a point in exhaustion where such friendly torture can create physical pain, at the back of the throat, the abdomen, behind the knees. 'All right, what are you talking about?' Jon repeated.

'Come on, if you want to rest,' he said, turned, and started back through the brush.

They fell in behind him more to make questioning easier than to follow: 'Where do you want us to go?'

'Didn't you read the signet?'

They climbed boulders, pushed through more branches. The morning mist was still thick, and as they pressed at last through dripping foliage, bright light burnished their faces. They were standing on a small cliff that looked down the mountain.

As the golden fog beneath the beating of the sun's copper hammer fell away, they saw a lake between the mountains. On the lake's edge, people were building a city. The artist who had cut the shape into the cold metal had idealized it some. On the disc Jon had not been able to tell if the buildings were wood or metal. Most of them were wood. And more structures had been added since the representation had been etched. 'What is this place?' asked Alter as they started down the cliff.

'Like it says, they call it the City of a Thousand Suns. They're still building. It's only been here a little while.'

'Who's building it?' asked Jon.

'Malis.'

He saw Alter's shoulder stiffen before him as she climbed down.

'Malis,' repeated their guide, 'malcontents. Only these malis are malcontent with most other malis as well as the rest of this chaotic world.' They reached the bottom and stepped on to grass. 'So for several years they've been here in the forest, building their city here by the lake.'

'Why is it called the City of a Thousand Suns?' Alter asked.

The guide shrugged and chuckled. 'Between matter-transmission, tetron power, hydroponics, and aquadics, Toromon has enough scientific potential to provide food, housing, rewarding and creative labour for its whole population, and as well to reach out and touch the stars. So a few—a very few people have started to organize such an effort. Anyone who wants is welcome to lend a hand. It's still pretty rough out here, but we can give you a rest. The Thousand Suns are the stars they'll some day reach.'

'And us?' Jon asked. 'Why did you come out to get us?'

'Well, if you'd kept on the line you were heading you'd have missed it by about four hundred yards. Now if you'd been going straight towards it I wouldn't have had to come and get you.

Can't leave anything to chance.'

They entered the dusty streets of the town.

Nothing registered very clearly at first. A flush-pump on one corner hawked amber water down a sewage hole. A woman in coveralls was working on it with a small acetylene torch. She pushed her goggles back and smiled at them as they passed. They went by a temporary communciations tower where a man on the ground with his hands on his hips was shouting instructions to the man on the antenna. The one in the air wore a military uniform; the tenseness that flattened Jon's stomach was a conditioned response to the dress of the malis he had met earlier. It left when both men turned and waved to Jon's guide.

In one direction Jon saw fields through the wide-spaced houses, and people working in them. In another direction was the lake, and two men, a neanderthal and a forest guard, black against the sun, from opposite ends of an elevated winch hauled a glittering net from the water.

Order, Jon thought, not as a word, but as the sub-verbal perception with which one might perceive the metre of a fine and devious poem. Alter took his hand. Looking at her wide, staring eyes, he knew she felt it too.

Across the street a cart creaked to a stop before a large building. It was pushed by a forest guard, two men, and a woman. As they stepped back, wiping their wet faces—one man went to the wall fountain and drank from the brass cup below—a group of youngsters came from the building, noisy and laughing. They wore work aprons. The instructor called a young guard, already a head taller than himself, who bent over the motor case at the cart's side. He did something wrong, and the class laughed. The boy looked up and laughed too. He did something right, and the motor began to hum. The instructor spoke appreciatively, and then half the class climbed into the cart and it began to roll. Two of the kids, boy and girl, were whistling in harmony

'Come,' said their guide, and they turned and continued up the street.

'Who is in charge of this . . . city?' asked Jon.

'You will meet them after you've rested,' said their guide. They passed a lawn now where a group of people sat on benches or ambled about.

'These are newcomers,' explained the stranger. 'You'll be here after you've slept, to talk to our leaders.'

A group of children who were obviously not new to the place exploded from one street, laughing and yelling, dashed on to the lawn and dispersed among the adults. Their game had slipped over its peak, for now they broke into smaller, quieter groups.

A young soldier on the bench had taken a handful of coins from his pocket and arranged them beside him in a square with one corner missing. As he flipped a coin into the missing corner, one of the children—a burly neanderthal boy—left his friends and came over to watch, sometimes rubbing his nose. The soldier saw him and smiled. 'You want to try?' he asked. 'It's a game we used to play in the army, randomax. You see, when I flip this coin into the corner two coins fly off the far side, and we try to guess which ones they'll be.'

The boy nodded. 'I know that game.'

'You want to try a couple of rounds for fun?'

The boy walked to the bench, set the coins in a careful square, then took something from his back pocket. It was a calibrated semicircle with a metal straight-edge that swivelled about its centre. He placed the instrument along the diagonal of the square and sighted the angle. Then he measured the distance, put the free coin there and hunkered down to flip. 'Three and five,' he said, numbering the coins he guessed would leave. He flipped, and numbers three and five shot from the far edge. He rearranged the square, made another measurement, and said, 'Two and five.' Flip. Two and five jumped away.

The soldier laughed and scratched his head. 'What are you doing with that thing?' he asked as the boy measured again. 'You're the first ape I've seen play that well—like a guard almost.'

'One and seven,' the boy said.

Flip.

One and seven left the far edge.

'I'm just checking the angle of displacement of the line of impact.'

'Huh?' asked the soldier.

'Look,' the neanderthal youth explained, 'the coin you flip has a spin of, say, omega, which is most cases in negligible, so you don't have to worry about the torque. The same goes for the acceleration, as long as it's hard enough to knock at least two coins off and not so hard it'll shatter the entire matrix: call it constant K. The only thing that really matters is the angle of displacement, theta, from the diagonal of the matrix of the line of impact. Once you perceive that accurately, the result is simple vector addition of the force taken through all the possibilities of fifteen——'

'Now wait a minute,' said the soldier.

'It shouldn't be called randomax,' the boy concluded. 'If you perceive all the factors accurately, it isn't random at all.'

'That's too deep for me,' the soldier said, laughing.

'No, it isn't,' the boy responded. 'Just think like they teach you in school. Are you going to go to school here too?'

Jon, Alter, and their guide had again stopped to listen. Now Jon stepped to the lawn and touched the boy's shoulder. The soldier looked up, the boy turned; surprise hit their faces. 'Who told you that?' Jon asked. 'Who showed you how to do that?' It took a moment for Jon to realize that their surprise was at his unshaven, wild appearance, not his question. 'Who told you that?' he demanded again.

'The woman,' the boy said. 'The woman with the man whose head was all funny.'

'She had black hair?' Jon asked. 'And the man she was with, you could see through half his face, into his head?'

'That's right,' the boy said.

Jon looked at Alter.

'Jon,' she said, 'they're here. . . .'

'Please come with me,' said their guide. 'You'll have to rest, or you'll collapse.

'They must be here!' Jon repeated, looking about them.

They were taken to a room in a small dormitory building. It was green, and comfortable, and when they woke, it was evening, and the leaves shaking outside their window with the weight of a singing bird were sunset bronze against purple.

'This place,' Alter said to the forest guard interviewing them that evening. The window was open, and a warm breeze blew from across the water. 'I never thought I would see any place like this in the world I live in. It's something to dream of on another planet.'

'It's very much of this world,' the guard assured her. 'When confusion is great enough the odds are for at least a few people moving in the same direction. Human beings being what they are, order spreads, given half a chance, almost as fast as confusion.'

'How do people get here?' asked Jon.

'They hear about it; we have people all over Toromon who come back and forth, a good number of telepathic guards. We need a lot more skilled people, but we're getting them slowly '

'What about my sister, and Catham?' asked Jon. 'When can we see them? We have to talk to them immediately. We're coming from Toron. We were sent by the Duchess of Petra, in the name of the King.'

'Oh,' the guard said, raising his head and putting his hands together.

'We know they're here,' said Alter. 'We spoke to a little boy who saw them.'

'They're not here,' said the guard simply. 'They were here some time ago. During the days of their stay Clea gave several lectures in advanced mathematics, and taught a few elementary classes. That boy was probably in one. Rolth made quite a helpful evaluation of our economic situation and suggested several ways out of some problems we were already beginning to face. But they were here really only long enough to be married. Then they left.'

'Where did they go?'

The guard shook his head. 'They said they hoped to return. They also said that they might not.'

'Jon, tell him about the enemy. . . .'

'The computer in Telphar?' asked the guard. 'We know it has run wild. They may have gone there.'

'That's our destination too,' Jon said, 'if we don't find them.'

'Why don't you stay here.' There was very little question in his voice.

'We've committed ourselves to finish this,' Jon said.

After half a minute's silence the guard said, 'Did you know that both the King and the Duchess of Petra, most of the council members, and several other members of the royal family are dead?'

They listened, even after the words had stopped, in stunned silence.

'Toron was bombed again, this time heavily. The royal palace was hit. The city's population is three-quarters destroyed. Evacuees are straggling to the mainland. The report came in late this morning when you were asleep.'

Outside they walked to the lake's edge and looked at the ragged mountains. Brass fires extinguished on the water with the ending sunset. The elevated winch dropped a template of shadows on the sand.

'What are you thinking?' she asked.

'About you, and me. That's all that's left, now.'

'I'm frightened,' she said calmly.

The last sun left the water. 'Alter?' he asked, 'the boy who gave you your necklace, who died in the war, did you love him?'

She was surprised. 'I liked him very much. We were good friends. Why do you ask again?'

Silently he moved through the maze of his thoughts. Finally, he said, 'Because I want to marry you. You are my friend. I know you like me. Will you love me too?'

She whispered, and in the variation of her voice he could hear her consider and then answer, 'Yes,' and softer, 'Yes.'

He drew her closer and she held his waist. 'Marry and stay here,' he said. 'Alter? If there's nothing left—nothing, then it's wrong. . . . And I can't see anything.'

'It's what I want to do,' she said. 'If you hadn't asked me I would have asked you.' She paused. 'Jon, if there is any meaning to anything—I don't know either. But this one thing we want.'

'Then we'll have it.'

That night they asked about the city's marriage procedure. They were married the following dawn on a stone platform by the lake's edge as fire mounted on the waves.

CHAPTER X

WHILE they were sitting on the lawn with the newcomers waiting to begin orientation, the air was scratched across by the whine of planes. As they looked at the clouds, Jon felt his neck crawl as the sound increased. Alter tensed beside him. Someone else had jumped up. Then the sound faded and they looked nervously back at one another.

The man standing shook his head. 'I get stomach cramps every time I hear those damn planes. You wonder where they're going next.' He sat back down. 'Maybe I should be glad though. I was in the bombing at the penal mines; and if it hadn't been for that I wouldn't be here now. But still——'

'The penal mines?' Jon asked. 'The mines were bombed?'

'A couple of days ago,' the man explained.

'Why were you in the mines?' Alter asked.

The man chuckled. 'From Pot to pit,' he said. 'It's a pretty hungry story. I was there 'cause I got caught doing whatever I did.' He still smiled, though it was clear he didn't want to go into any more deeply.

'I don't mean to pry,' Jon said, 'but what's it like now, I mean in the mines?'

'What's it like? If they get any liquor around here some night we'll get drunk together and I'll tell you. But I couldn't take it sober.'

Trying to name the urgency within him, Jon said, 'You see, I knew someone . . . who was in the mine once, and I . . . wanted to find out what happened to him.'

'I see,' the man said, more understandingly. 'If he was there a couple of days ago'—he shrugged—'the bomb. Who was he?'

'Koshar,' Jon said, searching for a name and only coming up with his own. 'Did you know Jon Koshar?'

The eyes narrowed, and Jon thought, We squinched our eyes like that, coming from the dark shafts into the purple evenings, the sun blazing on the ferns.

'*You* knew Jon Koshar?' Surprise raised his voice, and Jon waited for him to explain. 'The kid who escaped, oh, years ago.

You knew him?'

Jon nodded. 'What about him?'

'But he *escaped*!' The puzzled smile the man wore asked in itself, Don't you know what that means?

Jon shook his head.

'Let me tell you,' the convict said. 'I got to prison maybe six months before the Koshar kid escaped. I never knew him, but afterwards guys told me his mess-hall place was just two tables away from mine. But I don't remember him. I knew one of the guys by sight that got killed, the heavy one. But I'd never worked with him or spoken with him. Afterwards, a lot of guys said they had known something was up, but I sure didn't. And I think the guys who said they knew about it all along were just trying to make out like big fish. But I do remember when it happened. My bunk was right by the window, and every night I would go to sleep watching the searchlight glare sweep back and forth outside through the steel net across my window. I woke up once that night just long enough to see it was raining. The net glittered.

'Suddenly officers were shouting outside. A siren started somewhere, and somebody came and banged on the barrack doors with the hilt of his blade. They made first one half of the barracks and then the other come outside and stand in the rain and get yelled at for half an hour. By this time it had gone around that three guys had tried to escape. The guards wouldn't tell us anything, but we knew they must have been pretty successful to cause all the noise. Finally, they let us go back to bed, and with damp hair and bits of grass between my toes, I slipped back under the thin blankets. The next morning when we came out for inspection there were two corpses in the mud.

'As soon as we were dismissed the rumours began; but *three* of them escaped; *one* must still be out! Do you think they got him? What was his name? It was the Koshar kid? Why wasn't he face down in that puddle? Maybe he wasn't in on it and disappeared for some other reason? Naw, I heard from somebody who knew they were gonna make it that he went with them. Then he must still be free. Do you think so?

'Two weeks later there was another attempted escape. They were caught before they started. One of the officers, before he knocked the guy's jaw loose, said, "What the hell did you think you were doing, anyway?" and the guy grinned and said, "I was going out to look for Koshar." That's when it began. Suddenly everybody was talking about Koshar. All sorts of stories sprang up, like how he'd pushed a rock off a guy's foot in a mine cave-in, and one kooky story about him, and another guy who was in for poisoning, messing around a makeshift lab to cook something up for a particularly nasty officer. Almost anything anybody'd ever done there, now they said that Koshar had done it. To stop the talk, they finally told us that they knew he was dead. They said he had wandered out into the radiation barrier and been cooked; that was why his body was never brought back.

'Only the news had the reverse effect. It was as if the fact that the officers thought they could destroy what was important about Koshar by saying he was dead made them laughable. And we laughed at them. That was three years ago. And even when the mines were bombed, three days back, and we were scared to death, the few of us who got out could still laugh a little and say, "Well, maybe we'll find Koshar after all."' The man paused. 'So you see, when you said you knew him it put me through some changes.' He scratched the shoulder of his uniform. 'What did you know about Koshar?'

Jon wondered whether his amazement and confused pride showed. 'Just that he did escape, even from the radiation barrier.'

'He got back to Toron?'

'That's where I . . . met him.'

'What was he——' the man stopped, face suspended in the pleasure of anticipation. Then the smile softened. '—I wonder if I want to know. It would sort of be like the guards saying he was dead. Was he all right?'

Jon nodded.

'Good,' the man said. 'Maybe some day he'll come to the City of a Thousand Suns and I'll get a chance to meet him myself.' He looked around at the buildings. 'This is the sort of place he should end up. Does he mean anything special to you? We didn't know him. You did.' He sighed, and then laughed. 'I have to think about that for a while.'

'So do I,' Jon said and turned away.

When they had walked to the other side of the lawn Alter said, 'What are you thinking?'

He looked at the grass crushing beneath the toes of his new

sandals. 'I'm remembering prison; and something I was thinking last night.'

'What was it?' she asked.

'Last night I wondered: do I, or anything I've ever done, all my attempts to improve myself, the acrobatics and everything, mean anything? When we escaped those characters back at the circus I thought that discipline was the *only* thing that meant something. When we found that the Duchess was dead, and the whole purpose of our coming had exploded, I didn't think anything had meaning—except you. And now . . .' His voice faded.

A neanderthal was coming towards them across the lawn. 'Hey there, friends,' he greeted them. 'I guess I'll be seeing you around here when I get back.'

Jon and Alter looked up.

'First I thought I'd be staying here, but I guess I'm going on.' The neanderthal wore a soldier's outfit, and his heavy arms swung in wide arcs.

'You're not staying?' Alter asked. 'Why not?'

'Like I explained to the interviewer, I have things to do back with my own people.'

'What things?' Alter asked.

The neanderthal reached them, extended his hand, and as she shook it he said, 'My name's Lug, what's yours?'

'Alter,' she told him. 'This is my husband, Jon.'

'Glad to meet you both,' Lug said. 'What I got to do is like this: there's still many of my people not here I want to teach them things I've learned, things people taught me. Maybe I can even teach them to come back here, huh?' He jabbed at Alter with his elbow and laughed. 'Maybe I can teach them to come back here and learn more. But I have to go to them. Besides'—he glanced at the sky—'the dirty planes might even come here. This is all very nice, but it may not be safe either.' Again he started and turned to call back, 'I see you when I return.'

After a moment Alter asked, 'Do you want to stay here, Jon?'

'No,' he said. 'I wanted to marry you, but somehow I got that confused with the quiet and rest and'—he gestured about him—'and this. I'm going to go on to Telphar, and stop the computer if I can. Do you want to come with me and help?'

She nodded.

'We'll come back too,' he told her. 'This is a place to come back to when you've finished.'

'We'll tell them now,' she said.

An hour later they looked back down at the lake.

Someone said, 'Don't you want something to remember the place by?' Above them, half hidden by rocks, was the man who had first met them in the woods. With his good hand he tossed the signet towards them. 'String it on that necklace of yours, young lady. Look at it sometimes and think of us.' By the time Alter picked up the disc, he had disappeared.

Once more they looked back at the City of a Thousand Suns.

'I hope we can come back,' she said.

'Then let's go on.'

Early in the afternoon from the side of the ravine they spotted ragged, straggling figures groping by the stream. 'Who in the world are they?' she asked.

They watched till the group came closer. 'More prisoners,' Jon said softly.

'I thought maybe malis. *Uh*! they look more like what malis got through with——' She stopped. 'Jon, they're women!'

He nodded. 'Shafts twenty through twenty-seven were worked by female convicts.'

Now they could hear disjointed talk below them. One woman stumbled. The leader took a breath and brushed a grimy hand across her shorn hair. 'Come on, baby. We'll never find Koshar like that.' She helped the fallen one to her feet.

'We should go down,' Alter whispered, 'and tell them the way to the City.'

Jon stopped her by the shoulder. 'The stream they're following goes to the lake. They'll run right into it.'

The women moved off into the trees.

After they had started Alter said, 'What was it, Jon?'

'I was remembering,' he said, 'about prison. The men's and women's mines were completely separated, and we never saw anything that even looked like a girl, even though they were only two miles away. It got pretty rough in there, especially for us young guys who had to more or less put up with the older ones if we didn't want to get knocked around a little. The only people who went back and forth were the guards; that's one of the reasons we hated them. There was a standing joke that if there was one thing harder than getting out, it was getting over. Well, probably it was a guard who carried the story, but I guess got over as well as out.'

The trees thinned slowly as they approached the edges of the lave fields. Once a rumbling behind the trees stopped them. They found a vantage point behind a brush-covered rise. Then a tank crashed down the greenery and rolled past. 'This must be the final retreat from the "enemy".'

'The tanks they had stored there for the "war" they're using to retreat with now,' said Jon.

'How do you think the computer is scaring them off?'

Another tank crashed on behind the first.

'However it is,' Jon mused, 'it doesn't make it seem like we've got much chance.'

The only other thing to give them pause was the group of guards they passed about an hour later. Both the men and women sitting about the clearing bore the triple scars of the telepaths. A breeze shimmered in one black fur cape. One man absently twisted a copper bracelet on his wrist. This was the only movement as the giants engaged in silent communication. He passed through knowing his thoughts were common property to them all. None of them even looked up.

'Were you thinking about Arkor?' he asked when they were minutes away.

'Um-hm.'

'Perhaps they know if he's alive, or where he is.'

'Another thing to find out when we come back.'

At the evening horizon they could see a glow paler than sunset, deadlier than the sea, a luminous gauze behind the hills. They passed the skeletons of ancient trees, leafless, nearly petrified. The crumbly dirt looked as if it had been scattered in loose handfuls, bearing neither shrub nor footprint. By one boulder a trickle of water ran beneath a log, catching light on either side. They looked up.

On the horizon, against the lines of light, as though cut—no, torn from carbon paper, was the silhouette of a city. Tower behind tower rose against the pearly haze. A net of roads wound among the spires.

They could make out the miniscule thread of the transit-ribbon that ran from the city, veering to the right. It passed half a mile away and disappeared over the jungle behind them. Telphar: he felt the word shiver in his brain. 'It's so familiar it gives me chills,' he said.

'It's pretty creepy looking,' she nodded.

They started forward again. A road seeped from under the desert, rising towards Telphar. They mounted and followed it towards the looming city. 'It's like going back to some place you've dreamed about before, revisiting some psychotic fanta. . . .' He stopped, remembering. Before them the towers were black on rich blue.

'Do you think there's any military left here?' Alter asked.

'We'll find out soon. I'm still wondering how the computer defends itself. Apparently it's got a lot of remote-control equipment operating for it, but what does that mean as far as we're——'

Ahead of them, in the shadows, was a rumbling. It quieted, then grew louder. Suddenly from the gloom of the towers a juggernaut emerged, similar to the tanks they had seen retreating in the jungle, but a superstructure of antennae feathered its roof. A gigantic beetle, it crawled towards them.

'Over the edge of the road,' Jon hissed. 'You go left, I'll go right.'

The tank heaved from the shadow. Across its front in block white letters was stencilled: YOU ARE TRAPPED IN THAT BRIGHT MOMENT WHERE YOU LEARNED YOUR DOOM.

But as they separated, the tank stopped. The antennae ceased whirling and began to swing left and right. The front of the tank rose outward and a man's voice, oddly familiar, called, 'Jon, Alter!'

Jon turned to see his wife, half over the opposite road railing, her white hair still swinging from the whirl of her head.

The figure that climbed from the tank was the young man with only one good arm. It was not until he reached the ground that Jon recognized him as their guide to the City of a Thousand Suns.

Behind him, in the tank, were Catham and Clea.

'What are you doing here?' Jon asked, when he had recovered.

'Are you trying to stop the computer?'

Clea shook her head.

Rolth stood in the bubble dome of the tank, looking up at the dark towers about them.

'Then what are you doing?' Jon asked.

From over his shoulder, Rolth said, 'We're working.'

Jon and Alter looked puzzled, but Clea, instead of answering, turned and walked to Rolth's side. With questioning still in their eyes, they looked to Nonik.

'Clea's trying to finish up her unified-field theory, and Rolth is putting the final touches to his historical interpretation of individual action.'

'Then why did you all come here?'

'For Rolth to finish his theory he had to compare and correlate as many case histories as possible of individual mental patterns. On file in the computer's memory bank are hundreds of thousands of complete psyche-patterns, literally one for every person who had anything to do with the war.

CHAPTER XI

'WHAT are you doing here?' Alter called from across the road.

Jon followed her with a more cogent, 'Who are you?' But recognition was already in his voice.

'Nonik,' the man said. 'Vol Nonik. And you already know these two, don't you?'

Now Jon recognized his sister. Beside her, the sunset flashed over the plastic inset on Catham's face.

Slowly Jon and Alter moved back together.

'The computer,' Jon said, 'we came because of the computer. . . .'

'Come in here with us,' Rolth said 'We'll take you to the computer.'

They exchanged muted greetings as they climbed into the tank. Clea pressed Alter's hand as the door swung to. 'I'm so glad to see you.' Expectation completed its metamorphosis into achievement. 'There's an incalculable amount of atomic and astronomical data that has to be processed and reprocessed before Clea will know whether her theory is correct, and to do it right here is the biggest computer the world's ever known.'

'And you?' Alter asked. 'Why are you here?'

'The transcievicule!' This from Jon. 'The Communicators you and Catham have grafted into your throats? What about them, what were they for? They were grafted in right after you left the University.'

Nonik laughed softly. 'It saved my life, didn't it?' With his good hand he lifted his limp one and then let it flop into his lap. 'After they did this to me, after what they did to her . . .' His voice trailed, and both Rolth and Clea turned and looked back at him with worried expressions, but suddenly the voice recovered itself. 'Catham was still working on his theory even back then, but he was staying at the University, which meant he was out of touch with a good part of Toromon. It's happened before: you make a beautiful theory about society and psychology; then some guy in the street who doesn't know anything about either comes along and says, 'Hey, you forgot all about such and such,' and there goes your work. I was Catham's guy in the street.' He laughed again and called to Catham, 'I was to make sure you didn't say anything too stupid in all that abstraction, eh, Rolth?'

'More or less,' Rolth called back 'What I wanted was a view of somebody definitely outside society—such as a brilliant mali leader who was an accurate enough observer to be a poet—to check my views against. You helped a lot, Vol.'

The poet chuckled again, but once more the sound ended in a middle note, unresolved and tense.

'Did you know Clea at the University?' Alter asked.

'What? Oh. No, only her work,' Vol said. 'She published a few articles in the math journal, I think it was on the random distribution of prime numbers, wasn't it, Clea?'

'That's right, Vol.'

'Fascinating,' Nonik said. 'Beautiful. Isn't it funny, we can tell exactly what the percentage of prime numbers will be between any two given numbers, yet we still can't arrive at a formula to predict exactly where they are, other than by trial and error. Unpredictable and predictable. The product of the first *N* primes plus *one* is another prime. But between the *N*th prime and the prime we arrive at there are always others lurking, scattered throughout the real numbers. Like the irregularities in a poem, the quirks in meaning and syntax and imagery that cage the violent, and the very beautiful.' And then, whispered and fading, '... she was very beautiful ...'

Again Clea and Rolth looked back. 'I guess you could say we knew each other,' Clea said. 'He'd read my articles, I'd seen some of his poems. He had printed some of them up, and copies of them were being passed around the University. They were very lucid, very clear'—she emphasized the words *clear* and *lucid*, as though they might pull him from his reverie, but he still looked down at the floor—'and put wild and dispersed things into an order that came close to me.'

'We're almost there,' Rolth said.

One wall of the room was clotted with sets of dials, loudspeakers, tape reels. A few key-punch consoles sat around the floor. 'This is one of the control rooms for the computer,' Rolth said. 'This has been set up for my work. Clea's is down the hall. The machine itself occupies several buildings to the west. You can see them outside that window when the moon comes up.

The military has completely abandoned Telphar. We are the only ones left.'

'How does it defend itself?' Alter asked.

'Quite adequately,' Rolth said. He went to a small cabinet in the wall, took out a wrench and turned. 'This is purely for demonstration purposes,' he said, 'do you understand?'

Jon thought he was addressing him, but a voice came from one of the speakers. *'I understand.'*

There were several view screens along the wall, and suddenly Rolth hurled a wrench at the screen's face. The wrench never made it. It stopped in mid-air, glowed first red, then white, then disappeared with a *poof*. 'You see, the computer has managed to take over the whole city, webbed it with induction fields; you are under its constant observation anywhere within its limits. It's self-repairing, and it also has a growth potential wired into its circuits. The thing that they didn't count on was one of the things it managed to learn from all those mind patterns it stored: man has a survival circuit in his brain; I guess that's the best way to describe it. It's a pretty important one, and nobody ever even thought of trying to duplicate it in a machine. But this machine incorporated it into itself while it was "growing". It's programmed itself to ignore any programme it's given to cease functioning——'

'About the way you ignore somebody who tells you to drop dead,' interpolated Vol.

'But when they tried to shut it off by force it began to react accordingly.'

'Suppose the person who told you to drop dead pulled a power-blade on you when you didn't?' Vol added.

'At first it was just defensive, fouling attempts to dismantle it, occasionally with drastic results. But another thing it had learned from all those warring minds was that if you were offensive once you sometimes save yourself the trouble of being defensive again and again. It quite methodically drove them out. Now it will repel anything it interprets as an offensive action, and after three or four offensive actions from the same source it will try to destroy that source.'

'What about you?' Jon asked. 'Why are you still here, then?'

'We arrived just before the last of the military was leaving. They were desperate at this point, so they let us have free reign with it.'

'But why didn't it reject you with them?'

'This is a very imprecise way of putting it,' Clea said, 'but it's terribly lonely. We were the only people who were giving it something to "think" about, something even near its capacity to handle. It's built to work at a certain level for optimum facility, and its survival circuits want it to keep working at that level. Now it's got something to do.'

'If it likes you, couldn't you tell it to stop the bombings?'

'It's not that simple,' Rolth continued. 'All the information it has about Toromon was gathered from the mind patterns of the soldiers while it was manoeuvring them through the war. All of them were wounded by Toromon to neurosis, pushed into psychosis by the training programme. It hasn't had any need to catalogue and collate all that information, and it reacts on it as a subconscious trauma. It functions as a psychotic.'

'Keeping up the analogy,' Clea said, 'the problems Rolth and I are giving it are the closest thing to psychotherapy it could have. Collating the mental patterns, it gets to observe the psychotic inconsistancies, and it's gaining a great deal of facility through sheer exercise from my calculations. Simply by occupying it we've managed to slow down its destructive action more than the military did in the whole time it was here.'

'Is the answer, then, just finding problems for it to solve?' Jon asked.

'Again, not so simple. Both Clea and I have been working on formulating these two problems for years. Anything you would think of in a week or a month the machine would probably get through in a few minutes maximum. We should be finished today, and after that I don't know what will happen.'

Nonik laughed. 'I'll just have to go on raving to it.'

'That's the one other thing that seems to occupy it,' Clea said. 'Listening to Vol. It's taken to doing a complete sonic and syntactical analysis of everything he says and running it off against all the experiences it's got collated.'

'But I won't stay put,' Vol said. 'That's the only problem, isn't it, Clea?' He moved now to the window that opened on to one of the roadways. 'You see,' he went on. 'sometimes I have to go, perhaps just around the city, but sometimes out of it, back to the City of a Thousand Suns, or even farther, looking . . . I can't help it.' Suddenly he stepped out on the road and was gone.

'It's terrible what he's going through,' Rolth said, after a moment.

'Clea?' Alter said, 'you lost someone you loved once, just like Vol. You got over it.'

'I lost someone once,' Clea repeated, 'That's how I know how terrible it is. It took me three years before I was fit for anything halfway human again. In his way, he's doing much better than I did. He's still making his poems. But he's caught in a confused, chaotic, meaningless, totally,' she paused, 'random world.'

'You said something once,' Jon told her, 'to a little neanderthal boy, that if you could perceive all the factors, then the random element disappears.'

'Don't you think we've tried to tell him that?' Rolth said.

'He tells us to predict the next prime number, and laughs,' said Clea.

'And his poems?' Alter asked. 'Are they better or worse than before?'

They were silent again. 'I can't tell,' Rolth said at last. 'I suppose I'm just too close to him to be able to judge at all.'

'They're much more difficult to understand,' Clea said. 'And in some ways much simpler. They contain far more objective observation, but the significance of the juxtaposition of imagery, of emotional tone has got so involved that I don't know whether its magnificently controlled or . . .'

'. . . or insane,' Rolth finished; she had turned away from the thought.

After practising tumbling for an hour together that evening Jon and Alter wandered up the darkening roadway. They took a stairway that mounted from one road to a higher spiral. As they came out they saw they were above all the buildings save for the central palace. This roadway curved about the dark tower through the night, and from the railing they could look down across the smaller buildings of Telphar.

Below them the City stretched towards the plains and the plains towards the mountains, which still glowed purple with the faintly flickering radiation barrier along their snaggled edges. Mercury lights along the roadway flicked on and wiped away their shadows. Looking up, they saw a figure twenty yards ahead, leaning against the railing and looking across the city.

'Were you looking for me?' Nonik asked.

Jon shook his head.

'Sometimes the "enemy" looks for me,' Nonik said. 'I go for a walk, thinking I've escaped, when suddenly I hear a voice, out of nowhere, talking to me, telling me it needs me. . . .' The sharp laugh broke from his mouth. 'That sounds crazy to you, doesn't it? But I'm talking about something real.' He turned away and said loudly, 'How are you feeling today, old child of metal insects and silenium crystals!'

A resonant voice came out of the night; 'I feel fine, Vol Nonik. But it is night, not day. Is that significant?'

Nonik turned back to them. 'Catches you up every time,' he said. 'Maddening, huh? Whole damned city's rigged. It uses an induction field somewhere about a mile down to shake the metal railing into the vibrations of speech so that this whole guard rail becomes a loudspeaker.'

'And it calls you?' Alter asked.

'It?' repeated Nonik. 'A thousand, thousand dead men, squeezed in a million transistors, polished and planed to a single voice—calls me. It's hard not to answer. But sometimes'—he looked at his fists about the railing—'I want to get away, where I don't have to speak.'

'And someone else,' Jon said, 'someone else is calling you too?'

Nonik looked up puzzled, and through the mask of puzzlement the laugh broke, but slow and quiet this time. He shook his head. 'No, you see I'm a step ahead of Clea and Rolth, just on one point. Prime numbers, or Formats last theorem, or the four-colour map problem, or Goedal's law, it doesn't matter: yes, when we know everything the random disappears, but while we're finding out we still have to deal with it somehow. So the idea of the *random* is a philosophical tool, like *God,* or *The Absurd,* or *Das Umbermench, Existence, Death, Masculine, Feminine, or Morality*: they aren't things, they are the names we arbitrarily give to whole areas of things; sharpening tools for the blade of perception we strike reality with.'

'What about your poetry?' Jon asked. 'Clea and Rolth say they can't tell whether it's good or bad any more.'

'I can,' Nonik said. 'It's better than I've ever written, than I ever could have written before. And that's the most . . . terrible thing yet I've had to think about.' His eyes had dropped, but again they raised to Jon's and Alter's. 'Poetry, or anything man makes, even to this city, is set against death. But have you ever watched an animal die slowly? Somewhere, within the process of dying, when it realizes both that its destruction is inevitable and that it is still alive, its cry soars into another, different range, octaves higher, sharp with an unimagined energy. That's where my poems are now. If Rolth and Clea don't understand them it's because they have heard very little music played in this range. . . .' Again he stopped, and the smile returned. '. . . Or it could be because, after all, I am mad. It would be easier to be mad, I think, only to have to call out for help, like my friend here'—he indicated the dead city—'easier than having to answer. Then, maybe to think madness is easier is itself mad.' He shook his head. 'You don't know about my wife, do you? I mean, other than that she was killed. You don't know who she was, what sort of a person she was, what she might have been.'

They shook their heads.

'She was an artist,' Vol said. 'She drew, and she painted, and we went hunting for clay deposits together on Carsin Island, and she brought back red clay and made shapes with it that hardened, and grew pale, and were beautiful. For what it meant, there were enough people that thought her pictures were better than my poems, and vice versa, so that we could both laugh and use the blades of jealousy that shot back and forth to pry open even further our love. She taught school, I ran a mali gang. We fell in love, and I came to read to her class, and she fled with me through screeching night raids, and we both saw quickly that, under the crumbling lies and hypocrisy, she was forced to be as destructive in her classroom—a prison to exclude ideas that would "hurt their little minds" and make her lose her job—as I was in the vicious streets; that purely through the upset in the proper places I caused, I was as constructive in my violence as she was allowed to be "creating" in school. We both had clear visions of ourselves, at least in our art. Our parents refused to admit it existed, and so we had to create our own values for it, by single word and brush-stroke. Our parents saw each of us marrying, settling down, but certainly not with one another. The Toron Museum had bought a portfolio of her drawings—seven had to be excluded for obscenity—and a Royal Fellowship had just come through for my first book—provided I would remove five poems which "brought undue emphasis to certain regrettable aspects of society, implying governmental laxity"—

and we heard of a new City on the mainland; we decided to leave. We had to leave by noon, because a friend who worked as a clerk in the governmental office had held up as long as he could a warrant for my arrest that would have confined me to hard labour in the penal mines for an indefinite period; these "regrettable aspects of society implying governmental laxity" that I had criticized had caught up on me.

'Only by noon, she was ...' the word died under the breeze that stroked their hair. 'And I was ... then I *was* insane. But I came back to sanity, carrying voices centuries dumb. I knew the heights I could reach because I had surveyed the nadirs of their foundations. I knew how shallow everything I had written till then was; I knew that till then I had not even written poetry, had not known enough to write poetry. I also saw that her pictures were as shallow as my poems.'

Alter frowned. Jon put his arm around her shoulder.

'You see, a poet is wounded into speech, and he examines these wounds, meticulously, to discover how to heal them. The bad poet harangues at the pain and yowls at the weapons that lacerate him; the great poet explores the inflamed lips of ruined flesh with ice-caked fingers, glittering and precise; but ultimately his poem is the echoing, dual voice reporting the damage. Neither of us had been wounded enough, certainly not a wound as deep as the other's destruction. Her sculptures and paintings were as trifling as my former metred utterances. Only if *I* had been the one killed might her work have contained all that mine may contain now.' He took a breath, a gulping one. 'That's why I hope I'm mad. That's why I hope what I'm doing now is drivel from the lunatic brain. I say I think my poems now are finer than anything I've ever done; I only hope that is the judgement of a ruined mind, with critical faculties shocked and fragmented on grief; because if they are great'—he whispered here, and looked away over the buildings—'they cost too much! To feed on destruction, bloating to greatness ... they're not worth it!' The last words hissed.

Something snapped in Jon. He felt it go, and saw that Alter felt it as his fingers tightened on her arm. He dropped his hand, bewildered at the thing surging in his mind, like a memory coming to the surface of turbid froth. He stepped backwards, not sure whether to fight it down, not sure how to accept it. He started to run back down the roadway. Something had already begun to form in the cool vaults of his brain, flashing like a power-blade thrust up from the dark.

Alter cried after him, then turned to Vol. 'Nonik, please . . .' They followed.

When he burst into the control room Clea and Rolth looked up in surprise. 'I . . .' Jon started.

Alter and Nonik reached the room seconds later. 'Are you all right, Jon?' Alter cried, but he whirled and caught her by the shoulders, and turned her slowly around him. Nonik, bewildered, stepped back with Clea and Rolth.

'I want you to tell'—each word came with its own breath, as the thought wrestled with articulation—'tell me something. You see, there was a plan, to stop a war. Only . . . only the people who made both the war and the plan are dead now! Alter, you and I, we were part of the plan. And when they died, you and I, we tried to stop, but we couldn't, we had to go on with it, all the way here to Telphar, even though they were dead . . . like we were *slaves*!'—he took another breath—'like *prisoners*! We were part of the plan to stop the war, but you, Clea and Rolth, you were part of the war: no, I know you were tricked into it, but you were still part of it. Clea, you *did* help build the computer, and Rolth, you *knew* what state the empire was in. You could have spoken out about it, given the same sort of help you gave to the city of a Thousand Suns when you passed through. No, don't say anything. It doesn't matter now.' He released Alter's shoulders 'I don't know what you were, Vol; the gratuitous, still point in the random world, or the random observer in a world whose order is self-destructive; that doesn't matter either. But me? To me, that matters, who I am; a clumsy kid, a prisoner, who is free now, and a man, and not so clumsy. Well, I have to ask you'—he turned to Alter, and touched her shoulders again—'you, because you've taught me, and I love you'—he turned to Clea, Catham, and Nonik—'you, because you've taught me, and I respect you. . . .' Suddenly he whirled and screamed at the wall of dials, '. . . And you too, enemy, if you can answer me, because you've taught me too, and I hate you!' He paused, shaking and angry, waiting for the machine to destroy him, as it had destroyed the "aggressive" wrench Catham had hurled at it: three blue lights merely turned red. Jon looked back again. 'In this random, chaotic world, filled with apes and demigods and all in between, where mass-murder and assassination is the pastime of the hour, where any structure you cling to may topple in a moment, where a City of a Thousand Suns may be destroyed by a machine commanded by the psychosis of an empire and beauty doubts itself as insanity gorged on death—and I am free'—again he drew in his breath—'*what* am I free to do? *You tell me what I am free to do!*'

And a universe away a city on a desert under a double sun was in confusion:

'The agents from Earth, will they arrive? . . .'

'But one of them's dead. The Duchess has already been killed. . . .'

'The other three, two of them are together at one end of the transit-ribbon, the other is hiding in rubble of the palace at the other end. . . .'

'This war, will we win it, or lose it. . .'

'The *Lord of the Flames*, where is he? You said that of the four of them he would constantly be in one. . . .'

'The *Lord of the Flames*, you said he would betray them to one another. How has he hurt them, which one is he in? . . .'

'The *Lord of the Flames*, will he come to us, will we be able to fight him, will we be able to win? . . .'

The Triple-Being made a calming gesture. They quieted. *We still have time before the agents from earth arrive. True, one has been killed, and the telepath, Arkor, is still in Toron. . . .*

'You said,' interrupted one voice, 'that the *Lord of the Flames* would be moving from one to another of them, sabotaging each one in turn. Which one is it in now, how has it done this?'

'Is it in Jon?' asked another. 'Is this why he asks this preposterous question?'

The Triple-Being laughed. *It attacked Jon first, then it was in Alter; it inhabited the Duchess just before her death; now it is crouching with Arkor in the ruins of the palace.*

'But why?'

'What did it make them do?'

'How did they betray?'

As the Lord of the Flames *has been observing this war,* answered the Triple-Being, *so we have been observing him, and we have discovered a great deal about him. You remember we said that he was a completely alien form of life, such that ideas like murder, compassion, intelligence were foreign to him. Well, now we are close enough to understand why this is and what exactly the basic difference between him and all of us here is. The essential factor in all our make-ups is that we are individuals, and as individuals, we are alone. Even those of us with telepathy are alone, for they are still working only with images. Even beings so closely linked as the three lobes of our intelligence, are basically individual and alone. It is both our salvation and our damnation, and opposed to it is the desire inherent in our aloneness to move closer to another individual, or individuals, to perceive with them, through them, to unite somehow. Many of you dual or multisexual species have this internalized into your procreative rituals. Even the monosexual creatures preserve it in syzygy. The ultimate in aloneness in each of your cultures is death. Many of you have symbiotic relationships where when one individual is completely separated from all others he will physically die.*

In the Lord of the Flames, *however, this polarity between the isolation of the individual and his desire to be united with other individuals is reversed. It goes back to the very nature of his physical make-up, and its ramifications are as subtle as they are throughout the species of this universe. First of all, he is composed of the energies created by plasmas of matter and anti-matter held in stasis. He is a collective consciousness in which the individuals are not alone, even physically, for their energies are constantly shifting and interchanging. Anti-matter and matter, as those of you whose cultures have reached atomic physics know, annihilate one another if brought into contact. As we equate aloneness and isolation with death, so it equates bringing individuals—individuals who are already in energetic unison—together as death, for when this happens their actual physical beings explode. Conversely, reproduction takes place not by bringing individuals together but by separating them, so that they re-create themselves on the basis through which matter and anti-matter are propagated when energy travels through a gravitational field. The ramifications of this reverse polarity in its attitudes towards life and behaviour are infinite.*

'And this being is preparing to make war on us?' asked one delegate to the City.

Apparently. But we are still a good deal ahead of it. It has not discovered that our life process has nothing to do with the stasis of matter and anti-matter; anti-matter is so rare in this universe that the chances of life hinging on it are impossibly low. One of the reasons the Lord of the Flames *is concentrating on Toromon so heavily is that the basic source of power is tetron, a radioactive crystal of uranium in conjunction with radioactive iodine. The fusion can only occur under atomic temperatures, as a great deal of Toromon was exposed to back in what they call the Great Fire. The balance of the two elements creates a much more controllably radioactive material, and the amount of fugitive anti-matter in the process is tremendous compared to the occasional positron or anti-proton that result from cosmic-ray bombardment. The* Lord of the Flames *is sure he will find the secret of our life form in the civilization using the greatest amount of anti-matter. That's the chemistry of it. On the higher level he is also trying to discover how our behaviour under attack differs from his: in other words, what is a war to us.*

'Does this polarity you tell us about affect the way we fight?'

It certainly does.

'More important, how does this polarity affect the way the *Lord of the Flames* will behave in battle?'

Ultimately, the social traumas that cause war are those which promote the greatest isolation of the greatest number of individuals that still keep them in physical proximity. Disaster, famine, insupportable distribution of goods, exploitation, increased population till enough individuals are denied the opportunity of being together, fulfilling their yearning towards oneness with all other individuals. In most of your cultures, even the most egalitarian, the sexes are separated during battle.

'Compensated for by a huge rise in copulation/population right afterwards,' commented one delegate.

Precautionary, stated the Triple-Being. *But the whole strategy of war as we know it takes advantage of the aloneness of man: hit your enemy in his most dispersed forces; isolate a troop and you can destroy it. Well, all of these factors are entirely reversed in fighting the* Lord of the Flames. *If you can drive as many of its elements as possible together they will annihilate themselves, whereas actual isolation makes them physically reproduce; to separate one individual component of the* Lord of the Flames *from the rest would mean you were pitted against a force that was multiplying as you attacked, would overwhelm you before you could harm it. Just as we are alone, yearning to come together, so all its components are part of one another, yearning to be alone. Just as the trauma that cause us to fight are the trauma that cause us to be alone, so its idea of a destructive act is one——*

'—that brings individuals together!' One of the delegates was ecstatic 'I see it now, now I see what it's been doing on Earth, with Toromon!'

Please allow me to continue——

'But I understand now——'

Please. The first attempt on the Lord of the Flames *to press individuals together was when it increased the radiation barrier, driving the original inhabitants of Telphar back to the coast and to Toron. But the elements of war were already fermenting in the culture. Its second attempt was, when the war broke out, instead of letting Toromon discover an external enemy to fight it fostered the idea of the computer, that would physically hold the inhabitants together while they were under the illusion that they were fighting far-flung battles. When our agents on earth managed to expose this to the people the result was that moment of telepathic contact that blanketed the empire. During this moment every individual in Toromon learned something, and so did the* Lord of the Flames. *What they learned was exactly how alone they were. A few minds were able to deal with it, profit from it, learn from it how they might come together. But for most the result was terror, and chaos. And the* Lord of the Flames *began to get some inkling of how humanity, and ultimately how life in our universe, works. By this time, to give our agents all over a fair chance to learn also, we had several times put you all in as close empathetic contact as we could simulate. Then we brought each one of you individually to the City and even gave you a five dimensional view of what-you-would-have-been-if. We hoped that this contact might help you all in rallying your forces when and if the final conflict came.*

But now the Lord of the Flames *is examining Earth, and particularly Toromon, under a microscope. It has entered its observations directly on our four agents, and instead of acts that would shove the entire society in on itself, it concentrated on urging individuals together, and observed the results. First it attacked Jon, urged him to go back to his father.*

'Then it made Alter meet her aunt?' suggested one of the delegates who had been meticulously following the discussion.

No, answered the Triple-Being. *In a world where individuals are alone no two approach the same experience from the same direction. Alter's reconciliation with her aunt was not at all the same thing to her that Jon's was to his father. The* Lord of the Flames *forced her to speak with the mad queen, who was about to kill them: that's what it did to her. Then it went on to the Duchess of Petra. It made her not only go with the young king but for a moment accept his ideas, which were so at odds with her own: even though they died moments later, perhaps it learned the most from her. Now it has moved into Arkor's mind, though he doesn't know it, and waits with him in the palace ruins. He has still to be urged to his encounter.*

'What has the *Lord of the Flames* learned from each of them?'

So far it has learned that coming together makes them more able to bear the aloneness, more able to come together with others. It still, however, does not fully understand why this aloneness is objectionable in the first place, when for it, it is the one thing desired.

'But the poems... ?'

'The unified field-theory... ?'

'The history... ?'

'You said if they can get these to us before the *Lord of the Flames* gets them, then we will know the outcome of this greater war?'

Well, answered the Triple-Being, *Jon and Alter are only minutes away from the possession of all three, and the* Lord of the Flames *is at the other end of the empire from them.*

'They still must get here,' reminded one cynical delegate, 'and an empire is not a very long distance to a creature that can step galaxies in microseconds.'

That is very true, said the Triple Being, echoing itself in its triad voice. The sand shifted across the desert as night came slowly over the white world and the double shadows lengthened. *Let us watch.*

A universe away, Rolth Catham frowned and said, 'Well, Jon, I suppose'—he paused—'I suppose each person has to answer that question for himself.'

'No!' This was from Alter. 'You have to tell him ... us ... me, something. You have to! Otherwise, what are you good for? Don't you see, you have to be able to tell us something!'

Rolth shook his head. 'I can't.'

'Well, try,' this from Vol, followed by tense, quiet laughter that hung his words ambiguously between urgent imperative and insane command.

'Clea?' Alter said 'Don't you remember, you told me once, back when we both worked at the circus together, you once told me that to be able to justify yourself to others was the most important thing in the world when you were too sick to justify yourself to yourself. Well, I don't know, but if that's true, but ... well, can't you say something now?'

Clea looked confused, her dark brows contracting. 'All I can think of is ... you're free to be anything you want, a mathematician, a historian, a poet'—Vol laughed again—'anything we're free to be.'

Jon shook his head. 'That's not good enough. I'm not a stupid man, I've got a certain amount of physical strength, I've got a certain amount of mental and physical discipline, but I'm not an artist or an economist, or a scientist, and to talk about my being free to be one is like talking about my hitching up a moth-drawn chariot and flying into the sun.'

Something behind the wall of dials began to click and several lights changed colour.

'Well, you transistorized baby with electronic tape-worm, you have an answer for him?' Vol asked.

The reply was laconic: 'No.' But the clicking continued. A panel opened in the wall, and three piles of paper were revealed.

'Rolth,' said Clea in surprise, 'it must be finished with the collation processing.'

Rolth picked up one of the piles of paper: '*Looms of the Sea,*' he read, '*The Final Revision of the History of Toromon,* I think that's an awfully good title. I just hope the theory holds up.' He picked up the second sheaf. 'Here's you unified field theory, Clea.'

She took the pages. 'What's the third pile?' she asked.

'I asked the computer would it make up a copy of all of Vol's poems it had access too. I wanted a copy.' He picked up the sheaf of poems. His naked brain gleamed grey behind the plastic. He frowned and turned back to Jon. 'If you were an artist, or a scientist, then maybe I could help you decide what you were free to do.'

'That's a start,' Vol said. 'I'm listening.'

'Basically, it would just be free to commit yourself to your work, or not to; and then, to commit your work to man, or not to ... no, not to man, but to a concept of what man might be.'

'All right,' Vol said, 'you're talking to me and Clea now. You've got to explain that.'

'I mean this. When you write a poem, Vol, you write it to an ideal reader, one who will hear all the rhythmical subtleties, will respond to all the images, will reverberate to all the references, will even be able to catch you when you do something wrong; this reader is the one you labour for when you spend hours to make sure each line is perfect. Now you can be sure that in this world there are not very many of those around, but you have to believe that he could exist: even more, that any man of the street with the proper training could be educated to be that ideal reader. If you didn't believe in him you wouldn't try to write perfect poems. When Clea propounds a theory she tries to make it as clear and as rigorous as she can. She knows that a good many people won't be able to read through it and make anything at all out of it, but she checks and rechecks it for the one person who will be able to contain the whole concept of it. The same way I check and recheck my historical theory for cultural, sexual, emotional bias, for that ideal man, who is ideally unbiased. To commit yourself to this concept doesn't mean that with your work you try to teach people how to be ideal. That's propaganda, and since most of the artists and scientists are pretty far from ideal themselves, they are more or less defeated at the start if they take that tack. It's rather to acknowledge that man, with all this chaos, even so, can be ideal, and to make your work worthy of him.'

Now Vol turned to Jon. 'Where does that leave you?'

'Free to try and achieve that ideal, or not to try.' Jon said. 'But we get our blueprints more or less from you three.'

Vol laughed once more.

'Will the machine make copies of those things for you?'

'Of course,' Clea said. 'Why?'

'I'd like copies of all of them,' Jon said, 'just to see how close I come to the ideal reader.'

Puzzled, Clea pressed a button on the console, and the cabinet began to fill again with pages. 'Is the transit-ribbon from this end open, Clea?' he asked.

'It was closed at the palace,' Alter reminded him.

'Can it be opened from this end?'

'As a matter of fact it can,' Clea said.

'I want to do some reading, and maybe get on the way to becoming that ideal reader of yours.' He turned to Alter. 'And I want to find Arkor.'

'The telepath?' Catham asked.

'That's right,' Jon said.

'What for?'

'Something about perception,' Jon said. He hefted the papers in his hand. 'I want to take these to him—give him a chance to try his hand at the ideal readership—and see if maybe he can't figure out a . . . problem.'

'Problem?' asked Catham.

Jon nodded. 'What the next problem after these will have to be. And when I—we—get it we'll be back with it, for the computer.'

While Clea was checking out the transit-ribbon, Jon and Alter told Nonik of their journey. Now he leaned on the railing and shook his head. 'But is any of it real?' he said. 'Don't you stop to wonder that?'

Jon and Alter looked puzzled.

'We all exist only in the mind of God, so some ancient thought. We are the psychotic quips of a deranged cosmic mind, perhaps? Maybe a highly neurotic mind, a bit suicidal, tending towards a manic-depressive cycle; isn't that the one which defines my existence?' he laughed. 'Shafts of divine insight!' Now he spat over the railing. 'Or maybe just in each other's minds, that's where we exist. Are you really anything at all worth considering, Jon Koshar? Or are you only the story a bunch of prisoners recall of a boy they never knew. Does your white hair, your dark skin, your dawn-grey eyes encompass the real you, Alter Koshar? Or are you the projection of children gasping before a circus poster where someone has sketched you sequined and distorted in midflight on a trampoline?'

'I think it's about time to go back,' Jon said, a little uncomfortably.

'Time to go,' Nonik echoed. 'Oh, yes, time to go.'

In the laboratory, Clea said: 'It's still functioning; somehow, with all those bombs the ribbon is still connected. I don't know what you'll find at the other end, but get on the stage.' They climbed up the metal stairway and stood below the crystal. Jon had the papers under his arm, and Alter's hand rested in his.

Clea stepped to a tetron-unit, pushed a switch; somewhere a solenoid hummed, and the first row of scarlet-knobbed switches in a bank of forty-nine swung from 'off' to 'on'.

'I want to go too!' Vol Nonik suddenly said.

'You can't go now,' Clea said. 'It isn't set up to carry that much.'

The next row of switches swung to 'on'.

'I've got to get out of this stainless-steel asylum!' Nonik said, shaking his head. Then his eyes caught fixedly on the forms that had begun to shimmer on the stage.

'We'll send you as soon as we finish sending them, if you want.' Catham said. 'With over a certain weight you can't predict the molecular destination taken through the——'

Without warning, Nonik let out a howl and leapt forward. He vaulted with his one good hand to the lip of the stage and staggered beneath the crystal.

'Vol... !'

And then something flared white beneath the bulb. A small bulb snapped with a loud pop and a fall of sparks.

'What happened!' demanded Rolth.

'The stupid...' Clea began. 'Now I don't know what happened. It's just set built to carry that much weight at once. I don't know whether they'll get there, or even where they'll end up. Or if they'll even all get there at once!'

The platform was empty.

CHAPTER XII

ARKOR lay on a pile of cloth in the corner of the laboratory-tower, looking at the sunlight falling through the broken ceiling.

The huge crystal at the end of the transit-ribbon began to glow: then Vol Nonik stumbled to the rail, screaming.

The bruised body Arkor took in at a glance. The pattern of the mind leaped through the room and quivered hungrily before him, Arkor pulled back. Hurt, injury, the long cords of pain shaking and disonant. A circuit of careful parts and patterning, precise and tremendous, yet here and there welded open or shorted out from its own heat; a painting so vivid in detail and colour that its own intensity had charred the canvas. Arkor tried to turn away mentally. 'What do you want?' he asked, sitting up.

The figure shook his head. 'I don't . . . want to talk any more, I just don't want to . . . speak.'

'You don't have to talk,' Arkor said. 'What do you want?' Nonik stared with gleaming eyes. 'All right,' Arkor said. 'Come on, then.' Vol followed him across the floor and to the door of the chamber: he couldn't shut all of the mind's crying out. Practised in rhythms, it turned wailing against itself as they climbed down the stairs to the yard.

. . . the motion of my body through smoke trickling from the broken wall recalls a clumsy behemoth in cool tides; the sun falls through the ceiling in a wide band across the steps, and at my glance the wounded giant broke off from my gaze, the shimmering points jutting in the haze, violence of sill and portal as we pass the wrecked street's agony, corded lips still before smashed masonry, the stumps of ruined dreams; O, these caverns that I cannot crawl, anguished at evening, empty of ruined dreams, machines sprung under evening's hammers, backward bounding mind mounting to tongue fire against a ribbon on the sky. . . .

Arkor watched Vol stumble ahead of him along the blasted pavement of the Avenue of the Oyster, thinking, what's one good reason why I should bother to follow either his broken mind or his broken body? But he followed, and two blocks later Nonik turned, his eyes risen to the charred sky-line, and Arkor tried to block out what pounded at him from Nonik's mind.

... the fall of the towers, O ancient Christ, the fall of the towers, and the bared knife belly-buried and streaming, the fall of the towers, I can hear her screaming, I can see her hands twisting to get free, her body arched backward, skin split, bladder loose with blood, dust and crumbled masonry, a flood of refuse in the street, screaming, her small hands coming out to meet my larger hand, brick and iron twisting to get free, the fall of the towers, my standard and support shattered, my heart jarred loose, her violence looped in a thick noose of struts, electric cable, mortar, brick....

'What do you want?' Arkor whispered again, and Nonik, his cheeks wet, looked back. 'Tell me,' Arkor said 'It would be easier for me to give it to you than to listen to this.' Fear burned in Nonik's eyes; he turned and fled. It was easy to follow him, however. The thoughts chattered like static through the ruined streets.

... a flaming woman sits in the throne of my eye; a bronze gigantic bird thrown wingward on the ruptured field crashed the iron fence that shields the chewed-up asphalt of the aircraft field; the hard knot of desire loosens, sprawls open by the long, bleak hive-house walls, male and female, embattled and become epicane, magnificent, and one: rage, and now three, five, seven, terror rips apart the wild iambic madness of the fleeing child, chaotic shards form patterings, eleven, thirteen, infinite and prime, ordered, unpredictable as rhyme: a young boy flings a rock down from the roof, vicious it cuts my thigh; what greater proof of innocence or compassion, as suddenly my eye holds for a shocked breath his startled eye; night walkers stalk the wharfs at sunset, scavengers hiding in the shadow of the slant launch siding, they see me, run over the cobbles, pause, gaze, turn, hurry off, I am alone, walking the piers, as my eyes chase a grey deflated hunger to consume the sea-waves' sepulchred wind-weaving loom....

'Wake up,' Arkor said, Nonik uncurled beside the wall like a sick cat. Arkor wanted to say *wake up and shut up*. How do you tell someone to stop thinking. 'I've got a boat for you, like you wanted.' He waited for the emotions which roared at him to resolve themselves in Nonik's face. They walked to the pier where Arkor had found the boat, deserted and fuelled. From the wheelhouse he watched Nonik look up at the transit-ribbon under the new moon.

... a whip of metal, beautiful and free, from crumpled struts leaps the crushed-foil sea, while here we stare the dark troughs lashing back along the ocean's churning nightward track, violated in depth, runnelled by keel, droplets suspended on a wire wheel, time crushed by the pressure of light and muscle, ground to discrete fragments between the sky and sand, while distant bulkhead shadows block the stars: fools and their floating gardens in the moon, raised high on aluminium pontoons, precipitate above a wave, trapped below genesis, spilled in the fall to silt fonds, a jewel-heavy skull through whose wet sockets the tetras flush, whose bone-holes acknowledge completion and redemption, polar action and evil, meridial death and love....

'Where do you think you're going to go like this, Vol?'

'I . . . I don't. . . .'

... picture my hand palm-stripped, the red harp of sinew caught on no music vulnerable, vaulted in no engine. . . .

'Where are you running, Vol Nonik? Don't say you don't know, I won't take it.'

'I . . . I . . .'

... don't want to talk, and the picture of my face—red chalk on brown paper—burned and charred till the beautiful is released and the responsible furies rage. . . .

When they docked on the mainland, after a few minutes, Nonik left the rail, glanced once at the transit-ribbon, then walked up the beach. The wind scoured sand from dune tops and threw it over the weathered walls of a deserted fisherman's cottage. The door lay on the ground, and through the window an abandoned loom set half strung. They walked farther through the empty village. *You are trapped in that bright moment where you learned your doom* was scribbled across the sagging wall of an ice-house.

... echo and re-echo, caught, held, and released, the cry of wild pigeons, and some stranger beast, crystalline and timorous, treads leaves and dried vines to the metal bottom of my mind, and the first words come back, a cupric gleam, the walls of perception shaken, this vile voice not art, but madness trapped by ritual patternings of sound, lying because the ritual is bound by the limp nerves' response, the total matrix trying to contain realities of heart and gut and brain, knowing this working realness is only a machine constructed to apprehend the real; and the existence of leaf, sand, light, and good flicker out as they are named by the beast before me, followed and fleeing, stumbling by trees, beach, beneath sun and morning, flung with the mind against the veined rock, the mirror breaks, again the beast awakes, stepping lazily from the splinters, stretching claws, preening glass-black feathers, whispering of weights world-age old, lisping death-deeds that cringle, garsh, shock new speech from the struck tongue; I will walk down the muscular anger of my voice, I will trample silence under the leaves; my hands before me fill with rushing sun spots shaken through the forest as I run: I will find new barriers, I will brush them back with burning hands....

'Eat,' Arkor said.

Nonik leaned his head on the tree, shook it twice, and turned away.

Arkor waited a moment. When he was certain, flung the food back into the fire. 'Look, the City of a Thousand Suns is that way. Over there are the penal mines.' He paused long enough to see Nonik look up to where the transit-ribbon gleamed above the trees. 'You want to go back to Telphar?'

But Nonik shook his head and lurched forward.

... these turreted Cities at noon are the mind's ruined images, perfection, death, and transition—skewered on fishbones to the streets' stone siding, where gated trees shake thunderous fleaces at the sky and children cry and change—we are leaving the long chancels of the forest for the broken rocks, the ossific trunks, rutts in the shaling ground, we are driving for a landscape more profound, yet in the livid runnels memories of green are precious as her mouth brushing the back of my neck, these plains scattered with yesterday's death, where I seek yesterday's dying, crushed trunks of petrified trees; I can see heat lightning, over the dead city sinestral as charred bone, circling the stone like a myth, and as I round the webbed towers of the cancerous dream, left-bent and gravid with her death, I am leaving also the illusion that I am alone, the giant, the beast in the mirror, the metallic wind clanging the rocks, or silent as slain rats bowled belly-upward on the ground; I will not look at the concupiscent City, I will not walk in the violent streets, nor even in the ruins where the dextral ghosts of this race gamble near leather windows and crouch before flightless stairs or watch a stubborn orchard or gnarled kahrba; these, land-locked, atavistic, have none of the sea's austerity, only the wrecked sands of an idea without voice, a world without vision; know then this journey seeks to define ends, seeks shores where farther oceans start; caged by the over-muscled heart, we are trapped in that bright moment where we learned our doom, but still we struggle, knowing, too, that freedom is imposed the very moment when the trap springs. . . .

'Stop it,' Arkor said

Evening burnished the crusted plain. Tephar was behind them.

'Stop it,' Arkor said. 'You're going to die.'

Nonik shook his head hard once; then he began to laugh, till the laugh faded into a whisper: '. . . die?' He shook his head again '. . . the trap springs closed. The barrier . . .'

'We've already passed the edge of the barrier,' Arkor said.

Bronze light gouged and pried among the naked stones around them.

'You'll die too!'

Arkor shook his head. 'I can take much more radiation than you can.'

For the first time a definite emotion seated itself in Nonik's features. He frowned: 'Have I gone too far already?'

'Turn around and come back to me, Vol?'

Nonik began to laugh again. 'But you can't even see it. I mean the limit, the place past which I can't come back. Is it here? Am I standing on it?'

Suddenly he sprinted ahead thirty feet. 'Don't you see,' he called back, 'perhaps I've just passed it.' He began to walk slowly back to Arkor over the empty, desolate rock. 'That means

I'm dead already. Every cell in my body is already dead, but maybe for an hour I'll be able to stagger around, pretending to be alive. I'm dead. This is how it feels to be dead. I'll go blind first, and then I'll stagger as though I'm very drunk.' He brushed his good hand over his face. 'Is it starting? I . . . I thought it was going dim.' Suddenly he grabbed Arkor's shoulder and cried out, 'No!'

Arkor seized the small, shaking human in his great hands. The quivering, glittering mind turned under his own mind. 'Vol, come back,' he said 'I see so much more than you. You know so much, and so little. You can't be free if . . . if you're dead.'

Nonik pulled back abruptly; fear filled his face, the face of a girl filled his mind. He turned, scrambled up the slope, and ran forward again. Slowly the chaos quieted as Vol ran farther into the rocks.

Arkor turned in the ocean of stone and began to walk back. Alone again, the telepathic giant cried.

EPILOGUE

BEETLES . . . carbuncle . . . silver fire. Jon sucked the sharpness of ozone. Alter caught his hand as she gazed down the white sand. With the sudden change in gravity, Jon nearly dropped the papers, but Alter helped him catch them up. They looked again towards the City where:

Smoke fell like silver scales through the shell of the royal palace of Toron. The stumps of the city's towers jammed at the sky. People still huddled in the streets, but many had already started to make their way to the shore. Some helped one another over the girders and fallen masonry that choked the street. Some moved by themselves. But they were moving.

Alter pressed back against him; but Jon put his free hand around her shoulder and started down the dunes.

'Have they brought the history——'

'—the unified field theory——'

'—the poems?' the delegates in the City demanded with a flood of questioning:

'Have they come?'

'Will we win the war?'

'Where is the *Lord of the Flames*?'

And the triple answer: *There is no war!*

Jon and Alter, hand in hand, paused, listening, at the edge of the City.

The Lord of the Flames, continued the Triple-Being, *has observed enough to know that war would be useless, and that if it came to war both sides would be wiped out.*

'We would destroy each other?' Jon asked.

We would each destroy ourselves first, corrected the Triple-Being.

'Destroy ourselves?' Alter asked, 'But how?' Wonder grew in them like deserts flowering suddenly beneath longed-for and familiar rain.

Beyond a certain amount of injury, life cannot exist. To desire as much destruction as a war would be such an injury. And if the injury is too great self-destruction may be necessary. Suicide is the safety valve for the sickness to dispose of itself.'

QUESTIONING, Jon and Alter approached the City, and before them they saw—

A rocky plain where Vol Nonik staggered, went on his knees, then fell forward and lay still, eyes sunken and black, neck puffy, face distended. Behind him was the silhouette of Telphar on the horizon, and as they watched, it suddenly flared, flamed, and billows of smoke rose from its falling towers.

And the triple being said, *That was earth. The same thing has happened all over the universe.*

'But what?' asked Jon.

The same thing that drove Nonik to suicide, caused the computer to bomb itself out of existence. The wound has at least been cauterized, and you may go home now, and attempt to heal.

'And the *Lord of the Flames*?'

The last random factor has been observed and put in place. And there was triple laughter. *You might say it realizes now that as different as it is from us, it is still akin to us, in that it, too, has this death outlet, and recognizes its kinship. Now it will go on searching, and there will be no war.*

'Then we can go back?' from all the delegates to the City.

And Jon whispered, 'To reach the stars,' and her hair brushed his face as she bent smiling to him.

Before them was the City of a Thousand Suns, beautiful on the lake's edge, and as they watch, Lug's neanderthal family might arrive, and Catham and Clea trudge tiredly along the edge of the lake to the City, and from the other side an elderly couple, tattered and exhausted, might also gain the City: perhaps Rara, and Old Koshar; and the tall figure of Arkor might move towards the low buildings from one side, while the figure of a forest woman, also with the triple scars of the telepath, may approach from the other, their minds having already joined and touched, experience and perception weighed against experience and perception, the music their minds made free in the double sound of their names, Arkor, Larta, that they sung to one another, all, some, or none, the choice random, and left not to chance but to you.

Free to build or destroy they, too, approached the City of a Thousand Suns, to be struck by blue smoke, dispersed by sudden lightning, dropped from a web of silver fire . . . the red of polished carbuncle . . . the green of beetles' wings . . .

New York
February 28th, 1964